Repeat After Me

Repeat After Me

RACHEL DEWOSKIN

THE OVERLOOK PRESS
NEW YORK, NY

This edition first published in the United States in 2011 by
The Overlook Press, Peter Mayer Publishers, Inc.

141 Wooster Street
New York, NY 10012
www.overlookpress.com

For bulk and special sales, please contact sales@overlookny.com

Cataloging-in-Publication Data is available from the Library of Congress

Book design and type formatting by Bernard Schleifer
Printed in the United States of America

10 9 8 7 6 5 4 3 2 1

ISBN 978-1-59020-330-9

For Zayd, for Dalin, for Light.

Perhaps the hardest thing about losing a lover is
To watch the year repeat its days.
It is as if I could dip my hand down

Into time and scoop up
Blue and green lozenges of April heat
A year ago in another country.

I can feel that other day running underneath this one
Like an old video tape—here we go fast around the last corner
Up the hill to his house, shadows

—ANNE CARSON, *Glass, Irony and God*

September 1989, New York, NY

Dear Teacher,

In 1966 I am born in cement four garden courtyard house in Beijing PRC. That house belong to the father and mother of my father. They are handsome old couple. My Grandmother is kind of lady with tall hair and wearing a jacket and winter underwears until summer. When I am small she force me to wear it too, so I have to hide in the alleyway and shed that underwears so the other boys will not curse and mock me. Her dumplings are tasty, filled with pork and garlic greens when we have some or grass when we have nothing. My Grandfather is quiet, maybe too "henpeck" by my Grandmother. Or maybe because he do not like my father. He only love books and birds. And me. I like that grandfather very much. He never speak, just read that old books and keep birds and carry those cages every day to Ritan Park. He swing the cages so the birds will feel exciting, not bored. This kind of birds love that swing activity. It trick them to think they will fly away. My Grandmother smoke a lot of tobacco but she is kindly lady. From the moment I am born, she can see my macho natural. For her it's ok. But even though later it attract many girl, it scare my mother that I am this machismo son (thank you for teach me this word. I think it express my feeling in English very well).

Da Ge

CHAPTER ONE

Septembers

✻

I MET DA GE ON A TUESDAY AFTERNOON IN THE FALL OF 1989. New York was orange and confident then, leaves breezing the curbs and towers poking above the skyline. I was teaching English as a second language at a school called Embassy when he arrived two weeks and fifteen minutes late. He stood in the doorway watching the class with an expression it was hard to identify—some combination of grin, smirk, and sneer. I thought he might be shy.

"Hi," I said, "come on in."

He didn't move. "I'm Da Ge," he said, hacking the *G* out of his throat. *Dah Guh*. I thought maybe people mispronounced his name all the time. Or that he was a chain smoker and couldn't speak without choking. When he looked up, it was from the tops of his eyes, with the sullen affect of a teenager.

"The *G* is hard," he added. "Dah. Guh." I smiled, delighted that he knew the difference between a hard and a soft consonant. Maybe he'd be my teacher's pet.

Although I must say he didn't look the part. My students and I stared at him, curious. He was wiry, wearing ill-fitting jeans held up by a metal belt. He had a double-breasted navy blue wool coat, which although clearly expensive, gave him a bird-scaring affect. A scar extended from his left cheekbone to his jaw, raw and raised enough to seem recent. His hair flopped over his eyes, and he pushed it out of the way several times. He had the cumulative undereye shadows that mark a real insomniac, and surprisingly shiny shoes. He carried a blue backpack.

When he turned to take a seat, I noticed that the backpack had a cartoon duck and rabbit on it, both wearing spacesuits. Planets floated by. Under the duck were the letters "Ur," followed by a hyphen. Under the rabbit it said, "anus." It took me a minute. Uranus! It was a teachable moment; I should have explained why it's safest not to hyphenate certain words. But I was too chicken.

"Hi, Da Ge," I said. "I'm Aysha Silvermintz. You can call me Aysha."

He didn't respond. I turned to the class.

"Run," I said.

"Ran," they said back to me.

"Tomorrow?"

Someone said, "Will ran," someone else, "Running!"

"Ingyum," I coaxed. "Tomorrow I . . ." She looked away.

"Someone help her," I said. No one responded.

"Da Ge?"

"What?"

"Do you know the future tense of run?"

He stared at me lazily, moving his eyes from my shoulders down to my waist and then back up. I felt something like irritation rise hot to the roots of my hair in a blush.

"Run," he said. I tried to mask my annoyance.

"What does it require in front of it?"

"Something to chase."

So his English was too good for my class. I decided to let him carry the backpack for the rest of his life.

"Who can help Ingyum out?" I asked.

"It's 'will run,'" said Chase.

"Thank you, Chase. Ingyum, can you use 'will run' in a sentence?"

"Um. I will run. You will run."

"When?"

"I will run tomorrow," she said. "And you will run tomorrow."

"Great!" I said. Now I felt like the teacher again.

Then Da Ge rolled his eyes and murmured, "I give big fuck," under his breath. If he'd gotten the syntax right, maybe I would have felt attacked. But I looked straight at him and tried not to laugh.

"Say it louder," I encouraged. He glared.

"The only way to make progress is to let everyone hear what you say."

"I give big fuck," he said.

"*A* big fuck," I corrected him, my mouth twitching. "I give *a* big fuck. Or, to punctuate the sarcasm, you could also say, 'Like I give a fuck.' The 'big' is weird." I waited for what I thought was a polite interval before turning to my other students.

"Let's ask Da Ge some questions," I suggested. He was staring at me with an openness I found brazen.

There were four students in the course that semester, all adults. Ingyum was from Seoul; her husband had been invited by Columbia's political science department, and their kids already spoke fast, fluent slang. Chase and Russ were cousins from the Dominican Republic who worked as security guards on the Upper East Side. They said the doorman had helped them pick their American names. When I asked what they'd been called originally, they looked at each other, confirmed the existence of some private contract, and said they preferred to be called by their new names.

Then there was Xiao Wang, a Chinese woman who never spoke unless I demanded it and had only smiled once so far—a wide, accidental beam—when Ingyum had sung a song in English.

And now there was Da Ge.

"Where are you from, Mister?" Ingyum asked.

Da Ge glowered. "New York," he said, in a tough voice. But it was difficult to be surly in someone else's native language, and he made for a skinny, inconsistent rebel. I smiled.

"Chase, please ask Da Ge some questions."

"Where is your hometown?"

"Good one!" I said.

"New York," Da Ge said again.

Chase was unfazed. "Where is the hometown of your mother?" he asked politely.

Da Ge yawned. "My mother is from Tangshan," he admitted.

Xiao Wang lit up. I called on her immediately. She fumbled for words, her cheeks flaming. "I'm sorry."

"It's okay," I reminded her. "You don't have to be sorry. Ask your question."

"I'm sorry, are your parents okay for the, um, how do you say *dizhen*?"

"Earthquake," Da Ge said.

"I'm sorry," she said. Everyone waited. Ingyum fingered a strand of pink freshwater pearls around her neck.

"Are your parents okay for the earth-cake of Tangshan?"

"They were in Beijing then," he said.

"Oh."

Again, there was silence. Russ and Chase looked at each other. Xiao Wang raised her hand.

"Yes?" I said.

"I'm sorry. I have other question. It's okay for me to ask?"

"Of course," I said. "Go ahead."

She glanced at Da Ge. "Do you miss the China?" she asked.

As he looked her over, I gritted my teeth. Maybe she won't get whatever he says, I thought, in case it was mean.

"Yes, I miss it," he said. "Do you?"

She flushed with pleasure. "For me, it's okay."

His face softened until the scar was like the line of an expression. "I'm glad," he said to her. And then he looked at me. I looked away.

When I dismissed them, Da Ge lingered near my desk. I tried to measure the distance between us without looking up, failed, met his eyes.

"Have you registered?" I asked.

He grinned. "Yeah."

"You'll need to make up the work you've missed."

"I like it very much," he said. Then he took a pack of cigarettes out of his pocket, offered me the box. It had a picture of a pagoda on it, under clear, crinkly wrapping. It looked clean. And so did Da Ge, gleaming, almost.

"Do you like a cigarette?" he asked. "It's good brand."

"I'm impressed," I said, "but you'll have to wait to smoke until you're outside." He glanced around, almost nervously, squinted at me. He had stopped smiling.

"What means this 'impressed'?" he asked.

On the way home I counted the stairs down to the subway platform, feeling like if I stood still the pavement might move under my feet anyway. The train came, and I jammed on, smelled recent cigarettes on the coat in front of me. I thought of Da Ge sliding the wrapped pack out of his pocket, looked up at an advertisement that featured a Latina girl with Chiclet teeth. Under her, the caption read: "Lose your accent now! Improve your professional life by sounding American!"

I regretted my sarcastic *impressed*, wished I had taken a cigarette just to be kind. I didn't want my students to lose their accents or "sound American." Especially, for some reason, Da Ge.

That night I woke from a dream in which I spun like a naked dreidel in front of dozens of students, and had no lesson plans. It was 3:48 A.M., and I staggered upstairs to my best friend Julia's apartment and rang the bell twice fast, once slow. She opened the door in a pink tank top and underpants, rubbing her eyes.

"You okay, Aysh?"

"Yeah. I'm sorry to—"

"Sit." She yawned and walked back in, gesturing to a stool and then lighting the burner under her teapot. I sat.

The floor in Julia's kitchenette consisted of fifteen pieces of red and white tile we had assembled ourselves after Julia peeled up some linoleum and found a festering jungle underneath. The rest of the studio floor was covered with wood planks; we could only imagine what rat and roach amusement park might be thriving beneath those.

Julia hummed quietly, poured boiling water into mugs, and dunked Sleepytime tea bags in. The cups steamed. I looked out the window, imagined manholes smoking too, waiting for men to lower themselves down ladders under the city. The urge to count something came over me like a craving for food. I took a sip of tea and scalded the roof of my mouth. I hate tea and Julia knew that, but she would never have agreed to serve me coffee in the middle of the night.

"Let's go to sleep," she said.

"But I just burnt my mouth, and it feels all hairy."

"Sleep will cure it."

I trailed her with my tea. We sat on her gigantic bed, a gift from Greg, the most recent investment banker to have dumped her. Greg, who looked like he was wearing television makeup on his rubbery mask of a face and said the word 'aggressive' constantly. Every time his mouth opened, euphemisms poured out. Needless to say, he had hoped they could be best friends forever.

But they couldn't of course, so I slept over whenever I couldn't sleep, approximately five nights a week. It was symbiotic, since Greg's bed was a lonely ocean. Once I gently suggested getting rid of it, but the delivery service had included "free removal" of her old bed, and Julia didn't want to buy a new one.

She turned off a standing paper lantern, climbed under the covers, and set to snoring the sleep of the non-neurotic. I sat up, looking out at the night. The skyline was a puzzle of metal, starless but for red light shot out every several seconds by antennae. If I blinked my eyes in time to the flashes, I could keep the city lit red. I did this for a bit; it was a kind of counting sheep, and eventually I fell asleep.

When I awoke the next morning, Julia had left for rehearsal. Giant rectangles of light made a puzzle across her floor. There was a pot of coffee on the counter. I poured a cup, scrawled a thank-you love note, and headed downstairs to my place, carrying the coffee. As I approached my apartment, I heard the phone ringing. I ran into my bedroom and grabbed it, out of breath, expecting my mother.

"Hello?"

"Hi, teacher." My skin prickled.

"Hi."

"It is Da Ge. Maybe we can have a lunch now." It was ten in the morning.

"Oh. Um. I teach at one," I said.

"I'm study in that class."

"Right."

"So we have a lunch, okay?" A smile came into his

voice. "At Tom's Restaurant? I think it's not far for you. Maybe we meet at eleven. Then I give you drive."

He hung up. I sat down on my bed. He knew about Tom's Diner. He had my phone number, knew where I lived, wanted to drive me to school. Was he a stalker? And if so, how did he manage opposite-side parking? Could he both move the car twenty times a week and take my class? I stumbled into the shower, and the phone rang again. Ready to leap out of the shower if it was Da Ge, I poked my head out, listened. My mother's chipper morning voice.

"Good morning, darling! I can't imagine where you are! Up at Julia's?" She paused, waiting for me to pick up. I stayed in the shower. "Hmmm," she said, filling half the space on my machine. "Is Adam back in the picture?"

At 10:50 I collected a set of essays my students had written about their hometowns, and some pages torn from ESL workbooks, and left. On 115th, cars were double-parked so tightly it infuriated drivers trying to get through. Some, including the street-cleaning vehicle responsible for the chaos, held their horns down in a blaring, endless honk. That, coupled with a construction team jack-hammering the pavement into kitty litter, created a deafening soundtrack. Now those New York mornings are choreographed into my memory: yuppies sipping coffee from paper cups with fake Greek font, toddlers waddling about Bank Street Nursery School, backpacked undergraduates at Columbia's gates, and me, small, dark, all eyes and bangs, easing into a diner booth on the corner of 113th. We were all extras, but considered ourselves protagonists.

I sat at Tom's, spelling words on my fingers. This is a game I liked to play then; if sentences "fit" on multiples of five fingers, they were true. The letters had to land on my pinky to be perfect. "H-e'-l-l b-e l-a-t-e." Ten clean letters, landing on my pinky. So he would be late.

And he was, by one minute. He walked in as "Batdance" came on the radio, glanced around, took off black sunglasses, his agitated movements like a music video. *Vicky Vale, Vicky Vale. I want to bust that body right, oh yeah.* His eyes were bloodshot, one of them with a bruise seeping underneath it so that the eye itself appeared to be leaking makeup. The rest of his skin was unblemished, stretched over the bones of his face. He had seen me, was making his way over.

"Hi, teacher."

When he smiled, a broken tooth punctuated the space it had left in his mouth. I knew suddenly that he had irony, although I couldn't say how I knew. And even though he was using it against me, it was still a prerequisite for my liking anyone. I liked him.

"Hi, Dah. Guh." I said, putting too much emphasis on the "guh," because I wanted to show off my ability to get it right. He slid into the seat across from me.

"Are you okay?" I asked.

"Yes, I am well, thank you."

I wasn't sure whether he was making fun of my class. I thought so, but weighed the options: make fun of him back, find out he wasn't mocking me and hurt him forever, or say nothing and look earnest and stupid. I chose the earnest and stupid route.

"I'm glad," I said. "Are you hungry?"

He nodded and called the waitress over.

"What can I get you?" she asked.

"Egg," said Da Ge. She smiled.

"Only one?"

He looked directly at her. "Maybe give me menu," he said. I felt for him, wanted to say something to make it okay that she had joked about his single egg, but couldn't think of what that would be. I fumbled with my napkin, folded and unfolded its edges.

She handed him a greasy menu. "You want coffee?" she asked.

"Tea," he said, gruff.

"I'd like coffee, please," I told her. She left.

"Did you look at the workbook?" I asked Da Ge, hopefully.

"I think I need a favor," he said.

"From me?"

But now he was distracted, staring at the menu. I wondered how good his reading comprehension was, and what he was doing here. In New York. In my diner, in my life. Crowding my space in some specific but unidentifiable way.

"Excuse me!" he shouted at the waitress's back. She returned, upset, sloshed my coffee down.

"I like tea and this," said Da Ge, jabbing a finger at the "hearty man" breakfast. Three eggs, bacon, coffee, juice, and a cheese Danish.

"Fine," the waitress said.

"Do Chinese people like cheese?" I asked Da Ge. Xiao Wang had told the class she thought cheese was a kind of dirt.

"How do I know?"

"You are Chinese, right?"

"But I'm not represent the idea of every peasant. Anyway, what are you?"

"What am I?"

"What are you?"

"I don't know. American? An English teacher?"

"I mean what *are* you, Not what *do* you."

I didn't correct his English. Just like lying about him, a habit I began as soon as Julia asked for details, the practice of never correcting Da Ge's English snowballed. As a result, I failed to teach him a single thing about language. Or anything else.

"I don't know," I started to qualify, but he interrupted me.

"This, I already can tell."

"You can tell what?"

"I can tell about you."

His food arrived, lively and yellow on the porcelain plate. I thought of Sesame Street. Big Bird. I wondered whether Big Bird lays eggs. Whether he hatched from one.

"You don't eat?"

"I eat plenty," I said, criticized.

"But now?"

"Oh." I realized he was offering me some of his sweaty food. I swallowed, gagging slightly. "No, no," I said. "I already ate." He seemed to soften at this.

"In China," he said, "We say, 'Did you eat?' instead of 'How are you?'"

"Really?" I thought of Xiao Wang, flushing when he spoke to her. His jaw was moving on the food.

"Why really?" he asked. "It's weird to you?"

"No, just interesting. I'm interested in languages."

"You are very American, I think."

"Yes, I'm American. And?"

"Everything is the thing you know. Americans talk all the time—straight to the point of what. It's never polite talk."

He was one to talk, but I said nothing. Da Ge finished his food in several bites. His scar stretched when he opened his mouth; the black eye shined under the diner lights.

"What happened to your eye?"

"Just like this," he said.

"Like what?"

"Like American talk."

He made a fist and smashed it upward, just missing my face. He blew air out in the sound of a cartoon punch. When I flinched, he laughed, a low and angry laugh that sounded like it came from somewhere underneath him, not even his stomach but a hollowed-out section of ground. I saw him with a mining hat on, moving through a dark tunnel from which his own laughter emerged. The one bright light, hot in the middle of his forehead, would lead him out behind the echo of his laugh. He was watching me.

My heart rattled in a roller-coaster, Disney-movie-dark-part way. I thought he was the exciting kind of scary, that either doesn't get realized or returns to safe and happy fast enough to have been worth it.

"What is your thought?" he asked.

I couldn't have articulated it if I'd wanted to. "What was the favor you mentioned?" I asked, feeling brave.

He shook his head a little, as if reconsidering. "Do you know about Tiananmen?"

I scrambled in my mind for what he might mean and managed, "The protests in June? Of course." I felt pretty good about having come up with at least that.

He looked skeptical. "Yeah, that 'protests.'"

"I know only what I saw in the news. Why? What should I know?"

His scar crawled up the side of his face. "Most Americans only know a guy in front of tank," he said. "But I was at that massacre. I watched that story."

"Where'd you learn the word 'massacre'?"

"In America."

"Oh."

"Your newspaper."

I didn't want to be responsible for America's newspaper. "Does *my* newspaper have to do with the favor you want?"

He looked bored. "Let's talk that later," he suggested. "No time now."

I wondered if that were true, or whether he'd judged something about me that made him want to retract the offer. I didn't question why I thought of his request as an offer.

"So," I fumbled. "What do you do in New York?"

"Now I will study English with you," he said, smiling. "My speaking not so good because I don't have chance to speak so much before, only write. I have excellent English teacher at Beijing University. He is Chinese but live abroad many years, so maybe my writing English is excellent and diligent."

"I'm sure your essays will be great," I agreed. We both waited.

"So, do you work, too? Or just study?" I asked.

"My visa do not allow this."

"Oh."

I considered asking how he supported himself, but thought he might be offended. As if he had heard my thought, he took a fist-sized roll of money from the pocket of his jeans and left twenty dollars on the table.

"For you, too," he said. "I invite."

"No, no, it's fine—I'll get my . . ."

"We do not split with me." He leaned into my face, and I took a step back.

"Fine." I put my wallet back in my bag, crushing my students' essays, and followed Da Ge out. He pointed at a ratty moped with two helmets locked to the back.

"It's okay. I drive you."

I wondered whether he always carried two helmets or had been presumptuous enough to think I'd actually ride with him. And been right. I put one on, even though I thought we'd probably die in a wreck. I didn't want to argue with him, didn't want to insult him, didn't want— what didn't I want, exactly? I pulled the helmet on and shut its plastic shield, which steamed up. When I tried to close the strap I missed the latch, and Da Ge reached under my chin to fasten it. His fingers brushed my neck, and I looked down at the pavement. Da Ge started the engine, which growled feebly, and then craned around and gestured for me to sit.

"Hold to me," he said, pointing at his waist. I climbed on and wrapped my hands around him, impassively, I thought. Then I peered forward over his shoulder as he took off into traffic. The curbs were like punctuation, rolling down into the street on either side. Parentheses. He picked up speed. The lanes shot ahead of themselves, and inside my helmet, I began laughing. Da Ge cut across to Riverside Drive and up to 180th. Sunlight bounced off the water underneath the George Washington Bridge. My scarf flew behind me like a fighter pilot's. I thought of Isadora Duncan, the dancer who died when her scarf got caught in the wheel of a convertible she was riding in. The silk yanked her out of the car by her throat and dragged her along a street in Nice, right after she had waved good-bye and called out to her friend, "I'm off to love!" My mother, also a modern dancer, had told me this story several times. When Da Ge pulled up in front of the school at 186th, I let go of his waist and stood, retied my scarf. He lifted his hand to wave.

"I can't go to class," he said, "I have business. Tomorrow I will be back to class."

I couldn't think of what to say. Attendance is mandatory? I was still wearing my helmet. "Oh!" I said, reaching to unclasp it. Da Ge put his hand on my arm to stop me.

"It's okay," he said. "You can keep this safety hat for next time."

Before I could argue, he jammed his heel down and disappeared. I turned, walked up the stone steps counting on my fingers the letters in "I-m o-f-f t-o l-o-v-e." But there are eleven letters in that so it landed on my thumb, felt wrong, didn't fit.

That motorcycle ride happened thirteen years ago this month. And now it's September again in Beijing. September always reminds me of New York during those first Embassy classes, of Da Ge walking in straight out of the square, off the plane, looking like another city. This month has been no exception; I remember that one in my bones, the way you know how to swim or sing, so viscerally it isn't even real remembering. It's just a smell or song, bringing someone back until he's standing staring at you again, even if he's been gone twelve years.

This kind of remembering is similar to the way I sometimes sense the crazy me standing behind the grown-up one in the mirror, the two of us brushing my teeth. Or walking down the street, thinking how many letters are there in that sentence, but stopping short of counting. Not spelling words out. Sometimes being an adult is about pretending to be one. The girl behind the façade doesn't matter, as long as you don't let her stand in front, because the harder you work to fake something, the more it can become true. I went from pretending to be a teacher to being a real one, from acting okay to being okay.

It's only in September that Beijing reminds me of New York. Usually the two places don't overlap. This is partly because Beijing is a frenzy of frying ginger, exhaust, tires, and sweet potatoes, and in my memory, America is mostly unscented. Yet, there's something sharp in Chinese Septembers that suggests the ride uptown to Embassy, makes me feel like I'm about to meet Da Ge. There's always some New York autumn underneath the Beijing one. Maybe it's just school supplies: binders, folders, pencils, untouched grade books, or the promise of a list of students I'll know by summer. Back to school has always been a kind of back in time.

Global Beijing, the international private high school

where I now teach, is full throttle under way, even though we started only two weeks ago. My "Introduction to American Literature" class is packed with twenty kids who range from giant marfans to wispy preteens. I always start with my favorite unit, poetry, assign Shel Silverstein, and make them write their own rhyming poems.

Today, a fourteen-year-old boy named Martin read his original piece, "The Stupid Jeff," about another kid in class: "The stupid Jeff are having cough. / He cutting medicine into half. / The stupid Jeff are playing golf. / He hitting ball onto roof. / The stupid Jeff are playing in fall. / He eat the leaf and then he barf."

I applauded vigorously before reminding Martin that it's polite in fictional accounts to change the names of your subjects and protect their privacy. And then I told everyone about poetic license, that the grammar of poems can be more flexible than that of analytical papers. This was a big relief to all of us, including me. I have empathy for my non-native speakers, since I now suffer from the nuance paralysis common to expatriates and foreigners everywhere. In fact, I've become like one of my own students. Learning a language makes you vulnerable. Your thoughts become as simple as your expression of them, making you lobotomized in Chinese even if you're brainy in English. After years here, I still wobble in search of nouns for daily objects. I am the kind of person who calls doorknobs "balls you turn on doors to open or shut." I can get things done, but there's nothing poetic or compact about not knowing the word for "knob."

Da Ge and I were forgiving of each other's misunderstandings; neither of us cared for facts or accuracy. In fact, we took a kind of delight in each other's mistakes. I still keep the Uranus backpack in my closet, for example. I've made all of his assignments, his hometown, and even what's left of his family—my own. I've been to the neighborhood where he grew up, seen the sushi bars and skyrises grow above it like a gorgeous urban forest. I watched the barefoot workers from the countryside tear down Da Ge's family's courtyard house in 1996. And I watched them build a modern apartment complex in its place. I tried on the culture shock he had in America, by moving to China so disoriented that I felt for years as if I might slip off the edge of the world.

Maybe Da Ge knew more than I did about what would happen to us. Maybe he even hoped I'd write something back then, that it would be immediate, epic, or sexy. If so, then the joke's on him. He couldn't have predicted that it would take me more than having known him and having been crazy to want to record what happened. He didn't know there would be a person worth telling.

But there is. My small girl Julia II Chen-Silvermintz, who calls herself Julia Too and said recently as I kissed and tucked her in, "There's a Chinese girl with no daddy in my class. Maybe we're sisters."

Her voice pitched up half hopefully, half sarcastically, at the end of the sentence. She resisted the full-on question mark, because she didn't want to give me license to confirm that they're not sisters. Or embarrass herself with earnestness. She meant Phoebe Taylor, a Chinese girl whose American parents adopted her from Hubei and lived in the United States until three years ago when they moved to Beijing so her dad could work for Whirlpool here. Then he left her mother, married his twenty-four-year-old Chinese secretary, and moved back to southern Michigan. He probably also bought a convertible; he had a love of cliché. Phoebe's mom, Anne, surprised everyone by deciding to stay and raise her daughter alone in Beijing.

I told Julia Too the good news: she can be sisters with anyone she wants, that girls stay friends for decades so they'll be as legit as "real" siblings someday. I want her to share my idea that girls need and love each other, that it's only in the Hollywood movie view that we're all shrews, competing for glory and boys. I said of course Phoebe could come over on Friday night, could even stay again on Saturday like a real sister. We'd have to ask her mom about school nights.

Julia Too looked up at me gratefully with Da Ge's eyes and my own mother's eyelashes curling out like flames around them. I kissed her tiny, sweet beak twice and then sat down guiltily to write this story. For her.

October 1989, New York, NY

Dear Teacher,

The courtyard house of my Grandmother and Grandfather, where I am born—used to be only eight people—my grandfather, grandmother, father, mother, and the brother of my father, his wife and son and me. But then when it is problem time the house have more than eight-teen people live there. You do not know this time, the Cultural Revolution. Some of those people are not even the family member but they need place to live. My grandfather, the father of my father must dig the tomb because he have many book he loves very much. During that time no one can have book, so before he go to the country to do work, he dig this tomb and then his book stay there for twenty years until later, after it is already in the 1980 decade now, he took those book out.

My mother feel bad during those year when I am first arrive to the world. Maybe she do not want a shouting, crying baby. My mother sleeps on stone stove with some blanket. When I am born on that stove, crying with a lustily cry, my mother hear this voice and she know I can be trouble to her. Maybe she do want a baby but I am the kind of son my mother do not want. Even though maybe it's better to have son, my mother would rather to have daughter. Maybe someone quiet and unusual with freckles like you.

Because later although I am successful student and leader, especially as you can demonstrate in English class, I am also feel angry. I beat people and have lot of trouble. My mother and grandmother always call me little hooligan. Maybe my grandmother mean it kindly like calling me little *baober* or treasure. My mother mean it like you will probably go to prison. Maybe she is right.

Da Ge

CHAPTER TWO

Octobers

THE FIRST TIME DA GE SHOWED·UP AT MY APARTMENT IN NEW York, Nixon was in China, dining with the premier, alternating between "Don't let China sink into a backwater of oppression and stagnation," and "Please pass the shark fin soup." Da Ge was sitting on my stoop 6,847 miles away, reading newspaper reports of the visit. He had a giant cardboard tube on his lap.

I had come home from a Halloween party with my neighbor and best friend, Julia, when I saw him, his moped, the crumpled *Times*, and the cardboard tube. I wondered what the tube was—some sort of piping? Julia was dressed as a wizard, and I as a witch. I deliberately avoided looking at Da Ge, and he appeared not to see me either. I didn't know how I'd manage to introduce Julia, especially since she was wearing a beard and carrying a stick. Julia, who would not have cared whether Da Ge found her manly, was nevertheless not likely to approve of my students stopping by in the middle of the night. But maybe he guessed I wouldn't like to introduce them, since he didn't approach me. Julia and I rode the elevator up together.

"Call me if you're unhappy or can't sleep," she said.

I spelled out "Da Ge is here," on my right hand. D-a G-e i-s h-e-r-e. Perfect. He had barely been to class in the weeks since he'd joined, and the few times he'd shown up, he had remained quiet. He hadn't mentioned our lunch once; I had almost come to think I'd imagined the entire interaction.

I unlocked my door and turned the lights on. The downstairs intercom rang and I said hello into the grid.

"I am Da Ge." His voice rose up through the walls of the building.

"I'm in 8-A," I said. "Come on up."

I buzzed him in, knowing I had roughly one minute if he noticed the elevator, and four if he took the stairs. I frantically threw my witch hat off as I raced to the bathroom, smoothing my straight bangs down with my hand. In the bathroom mirror, I saw that I had returned from looking witchedy to looking like Popeye's Olive Oyl, zero to sixty. Why was I, even out of costume, so absurd?

I flicked off the bathroom light and went to get Da Ge's helmet from my closet, where it had shifted the impossibly tight balance of objects only realizable in New York apartments. A roller skate fell from the top shelf, and I dodged it and then stuffed it back in on the floor with two suitcases, an air conditioner, and blankets and pillows. I threw the witch hat on top. My mom had rented the place for me when I dropped out of college during my senior year. Her only criteria were that I be close to her place on 97th and even closer to Julia and Columbia. She hoped Julia's sanity might inspire me to develop some of my own and that having Columbia in my line of sight no matter where I turned would remind me that I needed to finish school there.

Da Ge knocked, and I opened the door; he was wearing a black jacket and his shiny shoes. He reminded me of my older brother Benj as a teenager, stuffed into dress clothes, buttoned up and miserable at choral cavalcades or bar mitzvahs. The tube in Da Ge's hands was almost three feet long, extending past his shoulder and down to his knee. His hands looked knotted on the sides of it. He glanced at the helmet and then at me.

"What are you doing here?" I asked.

"To see you," he said.

I contemplated what a professional response would be, and settled on, "Uh, you can see me in class."

"That's not you," he said.

This was weird enough to make me a little nervous. He was still standing in the hallway. I didn't know whether to invite him in. His voice sped up.

"Anyway, it's just to bring you this and say sorry for I miss so many class." He handed me the tube gingerly. I set the helmet down, but he didn't take it.

"What is this?"

"It's a language. You're interested in this."

"A language?"

He darkened. "A thing of language. Here," he said.

He reached into the hallway and took the tube back. It occurred to me that he would hit me with it, but once he didn't, I couldn't believe I'd thought it. Inevitability is like that. Once things happen the way they happen, there's no chance anymore that they could have happened any other way. And once there's no chance anymore, there was never any chance. His feet were outside the door. Setting the bottom of the tube on the floor in front of him, he pried the top off and laid the thing down, forcing me to take a step back. Then he crouched down and his shoulder blades spread out over his knees. He slid a scroll out slowly and stood up as he unraveled it. H-e-s i-n l-o-v-e w-i-t-h m-e spelled itself out on my right hand, fitting neatly.

The scroll was longer than Da Ge was tall; it stretched out past his feet on the floor between us. It was made of rough cream-colored fabric and had a huge Chinese character at its center. Circling that character were dozens of little ones.

"It's dragons," he said. "Ninety-nine of that word and one other."

I was quiet.

"It's for you," he said.

"Um," I said, "it's amazing. I mean, thank you. Maybe we should, um—"

I bent down to lift the bottom half of the scroll from the floor and felt his eyes on my back as I did it. I rose again, and he was holding his two corners and looking at me. When our eyes met, I imagined we were folding sheets together. We would move into the center, fold over each other, pull back out, and fold again. Then one of us would take the remaining square of a sheet and finish the project. I'd probably be the one, I thought. He would watch. We lifted the dragon scroll onto the table, and I spread it like a cloth.

"It's okay for you," he said when I finished, and then he turned to go. "It's a thing belonged to my mother. That old kind of writing . . ." He shrugged.

I waited.

"Well," he said, noncommittal now, perhaps embarrassed. "It's old. Then, China have hope."

"And now?"

"Today they take the army out of the city. Now your old president Nixon are there. Used to be he visit happily in the 1970. Maybe because he is there, so there are no more soldier on the corners. Maybe he will talk to the leaders. But Chinese people do not get to talk this story. Only leaders."

"I'm not sure I understand," I said.

"The time of thing getting better, moving up, moving forward—that hope time is over," he clarified. "For me, New York is the final place. But here I am stranger."

He turned to the scroll. "Those characters—it's different way to write 'dragon.'"

"You said there was one other one. What is it?" I hoped for something, but couldn't have put my finger on what it was.

"Long life," he said. His voice didn't move over the words; they came out flat, painted on. I spelled them out. L-o-n-g l-i-f-e, two extra fingers. N-o l-o-n-g l-i-f-e, I tried. Or "Yes, very," and it fit, too. Y-e-s, v-e-r-y l-o-n-g l-i-f-e.

He walked to the door, which I now regretted having left open.

"Wait, Da Ge?"

"Yeah?"

I wanted to know what he meant, for him to come back in and tell me something, to say or do something. I wanted to ask where he'd gotten the scar on his face, why he was in the city with his mother's dragon scroll in my apartment. I wanted him to stay.

"Um. Thanks again for the—"

"It's nothing," he said, walking to the elevator.

"Wait, Da Ge?"

He turned again, patient. "Yeah?"

I felt the blood rushing into my limbs. "I read your assignment."

"What?"

"The essay about your birth."

He smiled. "It's great event for China," he said.

"What was Beijing like then? I mean, when it was still hopeful."

He moved back toward my doorway for a minute, looking me over as if to determine whether I could be serious. Then he shrugged. The elevator arrived.

"1966?" he asked.

"Is that when you were born?"

"It's the Cultural Revolution begin," he said. "People are suffer then." He thought for a moment, perhaps imagining my perspective, remembering he was talking to an American girl. "Maybe for you China is like photograph with no color. Mao is leader before your McDonalds makes the promise to arrive. When I am born in Beijing, it is totally different place. I think you cannot imagine." The elevator left.

"*My* McDonalds?"

"This McDonalds of your country. Very tasty."

"Is there a McDonald's in China?"

"Next year it will arrive like VIP Amcrican guest who come to China."

"An American VIP guest?"

"All American who come to China are VIP. Like Nixon. They come like world police and tell China—okay do this, not okay do that." He moved back toward the elevator, pushed the button again.

"Does China listen?"

"Of course China like to *pai* the *ma pi* of America, your beautiful country."

"Pay the what?"

"Pat the ass of a horse."

"China likes to pat the ass of an American horse?"

When he laughed, his missing tooth looked like a Halloween costume. I wanted to put my fingers in his mouth. But he left. He was still laughing when he turned back to look at me, then slid into the elevator out of sight. The doors closed, and he was gone, swallowed and digested by my building. I hung the dragons in my hallway. Now, as I write this, they're in my Beijing bedroom, where Da Ge has never been and will never be. Where I'm more of an American than I ever was in New York, but less of a VIP guest than a Chinese horse-ass patter.

The day after Da Ge brought me the dragon scroll, Xiao Wang arrived at school early and stood next to my desk.

"Do you have a question for me?" I asked her.

"I'm sorry," she said, "Do you like to come to my grand-mother's house for dinner with me one night?"

"I would love that," I told her, honestly. "When?"

"Maybe tonight," she said.

"Really? Tonight? Of course. Perfect."

"We can go together after class."

"At three-thirty? Isn't that early?"

"Maybe my grandmother like to eat quite early."

After class, Xiao Wang took my arm and held it the entire way to her grandmother's, as if I had never left Embassy alone. Or taken the subway. She hosted me from the moment she invited me until I left her grandmother's apartment five hours later, in a string of polite gestures I found both bizarre and endearing. On the train that afternoon, Xiao Wang gave me a nervous look.

"Maybe I should tell you about my grandmother."

"I would like that," I said.

"My grandmother is very old lady. How do you say, ancient?"

"You can say 'ancient,' but probably not in front of her," I suggested.

"She come from China many years ago. She is seventy-eight now, but she still don't, you know, used to America."

"I can understand that."

"So sometime she say the rude thing about American. I hope it's okay for you."

"It's definitely okay for me."

"Also, maybe the food she make is too hot."

"It should be fine. I'm sure it will be delicious."

"Maybe she believe American are rich and lazy. Sometimes fat, too."

"She's not wrong."

"Well, you're not so fat."

"Thank you."

Chinatown was all Chinese signs, garlic, electronics, suitcases, pajamas, "I Love New York" souvenirs, and people rushing up and down, horizontal on sidewalks, vertical in building elevators and stairwells. Xiao Wang led me through the crowds to her Grandmother's apartment, a sixth-floor walk-up next to a flophouse called the Eternity Hotel. The building was cramped and dingy; hot noise from the hotel spilled into the windows. Each of the six flights we climbed had twelve stairs. At the top, Xiao Wang unlocked a door marked 6-C. Xiao Wang's grandmother padded over to greet us. She was wearing a cotton jacket and cloth shoes. Her features were soft with age but suggested a former bird-like clarity. She smiled and said something in Chinese.

"Welcome you warmly to our house," said Xiao Wang.

"Thank you." I looked around. Pipes hung low across the ceiling, which had intricate maps of water damage and looked like it might sag and fall through its own cracks. There was a gray-and-blue-flecked fold-out couch, a wicker rocking chair, a twelve-inch television, and several folding chairs around a plastic table. To the right was a kitchen that couldn't have held more than one person at a time. A metal hood fanned out over the stove. To the left was a bedroom with a dresser and double bed visible through the open door. The bed appeared to have been made to military standards. I imagined bouncing coins on its quilt.

Xiao Wang's grandmother gestured toward the couch and said something else. I nodded as she spoke, unsure of whether to look at her or Xiao Wang, when Xiao Wang began translating.

"Please sit," Xiao Wang said, so I perched myself awkwardly on a folding chair. "My Nai Nai say we are grateful for the teaching English. She say I often talk about the class and that I like it. She do not say that when I come home, I often give her the lesson of that day, so she can feel like to be a part of this class I take."

"I'm so glad," I said. I wondered if I should offer to come by and tutor the old woman, and I thought that I would like to. But maybe she and Xiao Wang cherished the recycled lessons. "I would be happy to help in any way I can."

"Thank you," said Xiao Wang. She translated for her grandmother and then told me, "You can call her Nai Nai, which mean grandmother in Chinese."

"Great," I said, "Thank you."

Then, to my astonishment, Nai Nai sprang up from the rocking chair like an action hero and set about putting nine plastic plates on the round table. Xiao Wang and I stood and tried to help, but she swatted us away. I thought of my mother's mother, my Grandma Leah, setting her table until she died at eighty-seven, fifteen years after losing my grandfather. Her heavy silver forks curled up at the ends like flowers. She left those and three strands of pearls to me, treasures boxed up in my mother's apartment.

"We should sit at the table," Xiao Wang instructed.

I examined the dishes: dumplings, squares of tofu in a reddish-brown sauce, wilted green vegetables, bean sprouts, scrambled eggs and tomatoes, a drizzled stack of chicken strips, spareribs, cellophane noodles tossed with cucumber and carrot, cabbage in hot red oil, fried peanuts, a whole fish, and a bowl of soup with eggs floating in it, so thin they looked like tissue or leaves. Nai Nai handed Xiao Wang and me each a bowl of rice and a set of chopsticks. I imagined stabbing each individual piece of food with my chopsticks, revealing myself as the savage I was. Xiao Wang, always a hawk for social nuance and the smallest hint of anyone else's discomfort, quietly got me a fork.

"No, no, it's okay. I'll use these," I said. I had used chopsticks many times, of course, but never under what I thought might be the scrutiny of Chinese chefs. "When in Rome," I said, stupidly. And then, "We have this saying—When in Rome, do as the Romans do.'"

Xiao Wang broke into a polite smile, pretending she had understood.

"This food looks amazing," I said. She told her grandmother.

"No, no, it's nothing," Nai Nai said, via Xiao Wang's translation. "Eat more! Eat more!" She went to get tea and then stood over us, refilling our teacups every time we took single sips, and heaping more meat onto our plates. It was only when we had stuffed ourselves to the point of sickness that she took a modest helping of the tofu dish and picked at it delicately.

I've noticed that old people in China are more vibrant than in the West. Every street corner in Beijing has a gym for babies and their grandparents, and everywhere you go, old people are hugging trees, stretching their legs, ballroom dancing, and skiing on stationary cross-country machines. Now that I live in Nai Nai's country, I often wonder what her old age would have looked like here. She would have exercised with friends in the parks and been surrounded by people she knew, who spoke her language, vendors selling the ingredients she wanted to buy. Was she breathless with loneliness in America? My grandma was faint with it after my grandfather died; she stayed above water by coming to my mother's four nights a week, by continuing to host Passover until it was physically impossible (at which point my mother and her sister did the Seder according to my grandmother's instructions at my grandmother's apartment). What would my grandmother have done in China? Or anywhere without us?

Xiao Wang says no matter what Nai Nai felt about her own life in the United States, she would have done anything to secure citizenship for Xiao Wang's future children. She believed it was worth it, *it* being the diminished state of immigrants' lives—in honor of the expanded possibilities their sacrifice created for future generations. It's everywhere in New York, this sacrifice: in every biologist delivering fast food, teacher giving manicures, artist working as a busboy.

"I miss the river," was all Nai Nai would allow when I asked that first night if she felt homesick. "We swam in the river, naked to our feet."

"What river?" I asked Xiao Wang, who was translating.

"The Mekong," Xiao Wang said. "Maybe she miss the nature life. Maybe for her, New York too commercial. In New York River, no children can swim." She turned to Nai Nai and repeated this in Chinese. Nai Nai nodded vigorously.

I thought the Mekong must be pure, unlike the Hudson, and didn't want to tell Xiao Wang and Nai Nai that the Columbia rowing team had recently spotted a floating corpse in the Hudson. I said nothing.

The China they described sounded inviting, perhaps complicated with the problems and secret histories of other people, but free of mine. I wanted to go. I could leave New York forever, I thought, and swim in the Mekong, naked to my feet, whatever that meant. Now of course I realize that there's nothing pure about the Mekong; kids just swim in the pollution there.

"You are from New York?" Nai Nai asked me, via Xiao Wang. "It's your home?"

"I am from here, yes." My mother lived in a penthouse apartment on 93rd and Riverside, a place my grandparents had bought her and my father in 1966. She had jade plants on the roof deck and a blue velvet couch in the living room, where I used to sit reading for so many hours straight they'd come to check if I was breathing. I remembered the energy

of the house before my father left. How it went from chaos
to silence. My mom, brittle on the blue couch.

"Nai Nai want to know do you live—how do you say—
with your family at home?" Xiao Wang asked. I wondered
if I emitted a kind of unhappiness siren.

"I have my own apartment now," I said, "but I go to my
mom's a lot."

"Isn't that lonely? Don't you wish you live at home with
your mother?" Nai Nai asked. Xiao Wang translated and
then waited for my response.

"It's not so much wanting to go home," I said, "but
wanting to go back in time." Then, embarrassed at having
said so much and concerned that they hadn't understood, I
chattered on, "Back in time, you know, back to an earlier
time, backwards."

Xiao Wang nodded. "Your family is okay?" she asked.

I told her no, not really, and when she waited, I said my
father had left my mother. She stopped translating, and Nai
Nai watched us, rocking slower and slower. I couldn't tell if
she was increasingly attentive or drowsy.

"When?"

"When I was seventeen," I said.

"Oh! It's quite recent."

"Well, five years ago."

"What is problem?" Xiao Wang asked.

I shrugged and blushed. Xiao Wang turned to Nai Nai
to fill her in.

"Nai Nai say maybe Americans feel—how do you say—
casual—about end of the marriage," Xiao Wang said.

"Divorce," I said. "But I'm not sure about that. I think
maybe one of them was having an affair."

I stopped short of the truth, which is that my father fell
in love with a colleague when I was sixteen. I actually saw
them together on 111th and Amsterdam, as if in a tacky

movie. I was on my way to meet Julia at the Hungarian Pastry Shop. When I had walked half a block past 110th, I spotted my father across the street in front of the cathedral where three peacocks live. My hand moved to wave, but I stopped it and my voice. My father? He had his hands on the hips of a woman in a straight skirt and brown leather boots. I stared, thought those high boots do not belong to my mother, moved my eyes to the woman's neck and face, which was turned up laughing toward my dad. And I ran. It took me a year to get the words out of my throat to tell my mother. And as soon as I did, my dad left us and married the laughing woman instead.

"What means *affair*?" Xiao Wang asked. She was translating for Nai Nai, who I feared would be horrified by the tale of my father's infidelity. But when I looked over again, she was asleep. Apparently for a seventy-eight-year-old woman, there was nothing new about this story. Who could blame her for sleeping through it? Xiao Wang stopped translating and covered Nai Nai with a blanket.

"You know," I said, "having an affair—being unfaithful, having another lover—someone other than your wife or husband."

Xiao Wang nodded, as if she knew a lot about such matters. "I'm married," she said, perhaps sensing my doubt that she could understand.

I looked around the room, and she laughed.

"My husband is in China. He start a tourism business in Jinhong. Now he is travel often in Beijing. Anyway, maybe we do not consider marriage how you do in America."

"How do you consider it in China?"

"It's not simple like here," she said, marking the beginning of more than a decade of responding to every question I ever asked with some variation on "It's not simple like you think."

"Maybe we have to get married for various reasons of the family or the society," she said. "But those are also involving love, I think. Not the television love of America, but a kind of marriage love."

"People in the West get married for all sorts of complicated reasons, too," I suggested. "Not just TV love." I smiled, thinking of the kind of love Xiao Wang might mean. *Roseanne* was America's most popular TV show, along with *The Cosby Show* and *Cheers*. I can see why, if Xiao Wang got her information from American TV (which even now she admits she did), she would find our ideas of romance simple. Of course, as I often tell Xiao Wang, if I defined Chinese love by Chinese television, it would be a drab, state-run affair.

"And maybe it is," she says, laughing.

Back then, I just said that people left each other for complicated reasons, that nothing like that was ever simple.

She said, "Why do your father leave?"

I told her the story. It was the first time I had ever told anyone other than Julia. I didn't know why I felt safe with Xiao Wang. Maybe it was Nai Nai's soft snoring in the corner. Or the comfortable, if incorrect, notion that someone who didn't speak fluent English wasn't a real listener in the same way as someone who did. Or wasn't a critic, anyway.

I said my father's name, John Mitchell, disliking the taste of it in my mouth. Then I said he had grown up on a farm in Iowa, the fourth son in a family of Roberts, Jameses, Williams, and Johns, that two of his brothers had died in a car accident as teenagers, and the other took over the farm. My father, in a surprise move unlike any other the family had ever imagined, broke away to go to college and then graduate school, where he wrote a dissertation on Gatsby that was apparently shimmering with brilliance and promise. So he and one of his best chapters got to fly to a conference in New York, where he yapped away without irony or experience about Daisy and the predicament of the modern American marriage. And met my mother, Naomi Silvermintz. It was his first trip to the East Coast, and she was in a dance recital some professor took my father to see. I imagine my mother was all of New York to him, sharp-tongued and mysteriously sleek. Even her name sounded like jewelry: shining and minty music to a farm boy. My father, to hear the pre-divorce version, loved my mother the instant he saw her barefoot in that black leotard. "It wasn't ballet bullshit where the women are weightless and floating," he used to tell my older brother Benj and me before he abandoned my mother and me. "It was the stomping, barefoot, modern dance that suited your mother." He relished this story, loved casting himself as the lover of a strong girl more than he actually loved her, I think.

Xiao Wang said, "He must love her sometime though."

"Of course," I said. "I think he even loved her later, after—I mean, I don't think it was so much about her. He was just disappointed in his life."

"Why? It must be he has an okay life, right?"

I had a hard time explaining without making him sound luxuriously self-indulgent. I mean, all that happened was that his stardom never materialized. The Gatsby dissertation was published as a book six years after he finished it, but he never wrote anything else. He married my mother, and they had Benj and me, and she danced and taught dance while he cobbled together a collage of adjunct positions until he eventually got a job teaching history at a private high school. If my mother found this as disappointing or unsexy as he did, she hid it. She came from enough money to be unconcerned with whether he made any, and found my dad unorthodox and bohemian hot. So she watched for years as he threw himself into projects and hobbies, to the compulsive exclusion of sleeping or eating. He made shelves, beds, paintings, pottery, business plans. She complimented his intensity, loved whatever he built, tried, dreamt up. She said he was unusual, a genius, and at their dinner parties, she helped him hide or glorify his Iowa farm past, depending on his mood.

Then the laughing woman became his new project. And my mother had nothing to say about his genius anymore. The woman was of course like my mother, just significantly younger, less wealthy, and more freshly impressed. I felt awkward telling Xiao Wang this, as if the cliché were my fault. But I held on to the naïve hope that she wouldn't recognize the hackneyed trope of it all.

That didn't pan out.

"It's so common story," she said when I'd finished. I couldn't help laughing.

"It feels personal nonetheless," I joked.

"Of course it's difficult. I didn't mean it's not difficult!" She apologized. "Why you don't have family name?" I was surprised she had noticed this.

"I changed my name when I turned eighteen," I said. "I wanted my mom's."

"Maybe your parents' bad decision will make you good to choose more true thing for yourself," she said. "They don't keep in unhappy love. It can make you—liberation."

"Free," I said. I looked over at her sleeping Nai Nai.

"My grandfather die many years ago," Xiao Wang said. "She come to America many years after he do, when he is sick, to help him. Then I come to help her because maybe now she will be too old."

"I'm sorry," I said.

"It's nothing for sorry. He was more than eighty."

"Still," I said.

"I'm sorry about your bad family story," she said.

"Thank you."

Then Xiao Wang walked me all to the subway, and right before I descended into the tunnel, I hugged her impulsively, and she leapt backwards like I had pulled a knife.

"I'm sorry!" I said, horrified.

"No, no, of course," she said. "It's fine, this embrace. Maybe I am not so casual to embrace, but no problem. It's the American habit. I will, how do you say—used to this."

She patted me on the arm.

I love studying Chinese. There's something satisfying for an obsessive-compulsive in the compressed logic of it, the ability of each sound to have dozens of meanings, often including conflicting ones. There are the stroke marks coming together to form characters that look like the nouns they describe. Da Ge was proud that Chinese was both more sensible than English and more expressive. I like a language somewhere in between, a Chinglish hybrid that allows for importing the most expressive components of each language into the other.

Julia Too, who has grown up in Beijing and is stunningly bilingual, shares my love of Chinglish, especially of the effortful translation variety. When she and I rode down from our apartment on the twenty-seventh floor of Luscious Gardens this morning, our building management had posted the following notice on a bulletin board facing the elevators: *"Comply with Public Morality; Strictly prohibit casting articles from high. On October 15, a flaming dog-end was flung from upstairs and burned a fabric chair. It happened that the resident of the chair did not sit in the chair when the dog-end fell so a more hated outcome was avoided. But that heinous activity reminds the danger of casting fireous dog-ends from high. Really, we have warned this many times already. Kindly hope those individuals take others' safety into account. Stop bad bombarding behavior.*"

Bad bombarding behavior! Someone had thrown a cigarette butt out the window. Julia Too immediately tore down the notice and tucked it into her Chinglish notebook. I have helped her be balanced by providing terrible Chinese for the collection, including Julia Too's most beloved of my gaffes, when I said, *Wo ye yao*, or "My leaves are shaking," instead of "I'd also like one," in reference to a bottle of mineral water. My personal favorite was thanking a Chinese colleague for inviting me to *ta ma de* birthday, his "mother fucking birthday party" instead of his "mother's birthday party." Who knew that pairing up a possessive with a mother equals "mother fucking"?

I recently heard Julia Too say innocently to the mother of one of her Chinese friends, "My mom speaks a little Chinese." Julia Too is so fluent that to her, I am the kind of person who uses expressions like "casting fireous dog-ends from high" in Chinese.

Da Ge tried teaching me to speak the year we knew each other, but I didn't actually learn anything until I arrived in Beijing in 1994 and hired Teacher Hao, a gray-plumed, retired professor who tutors me. Gray hair is unusual here, and Teacher Hao wears his shiny mop like a peacock's tail. He's shy about everything except his fabulous do and my unacceptable pronunciation. In these two areas, he's on fire.

We talk almost exclusively about Tang poetry and Julia Too, conversations that require me to use the word "daughter," which, after eight years of trying, I apparently still can't pronounce properly.

"My daughter has a—" I said yesterday.

"*Nu'er*," he said. "Daughter."

"*Nu'er.*"

"No! *Nu'er.*" He peered into my mouth, as if he'd find some kind of mechanical problem in there, which I hoped he would. Finding nothing in the physiology of a foreigner that should excuse such pronunciation, he sighed. "*Xing,*" he said, okay, go on.

"My daughter has a new friend, whose main interests are boys and U.S. culture."

"Is your *nu'er* also interested in such things?"

"Well, she's at a disadvantage."

"Why?"

"Phoebe lived in the U.S. more recently."

As I explained to Teacher Hao, Phoebe has a superior grasp of hip and all-important American cultural touchstones, and for some reason, knowing about American culture and knowing about boys are related. She who knows the most about one is guaranteed to know the most about the other.

"Maybe your daughter should spend more of her time with the daughter of Xiao Wang, your Chinese friend?" I thought of Teacher Hao's daughter, a sixteen-year-old who has been forbidden to do anything but study since the moment she was born. The one time I met her, at a dinner so socially awkward I had to sneak beta blockers in the bathroom, she was practically wearing a burlap sack. I don't like designer jeans or pointy shoes on little girls—too much fashion screams creepy pageant, but there's a delicate balance somewhere. Teacher Hao's daughter wants to study abroad and will have to compete with hundreds of thousands of other applicants. What time does that leave for lip gloss, or for dating?

"Julia Too and Lili do spend a lot of time together," I said, defensively. "But she needs to have more than one friend." I was annoyed by the implication, even though I had provoked it and agreed that it was probably true, that a Chinese friend would be a better influence than an American one. "Kids need spare time, hobbies, leisure. Or it stunts their creative growth."

"Maybe American friends are just heavier influences than Chinese ones," he said.

"Not in my life," I said. I laughed, but Teacher Hao gave me a stern look.

"Maybe she should go to a Chinese school."

I rolled my eyes, and he cracked a smile. "Then, as you like to say about my daughter, she'll have no time for friends," he said. I took the joke as a gesture of camaraderie, since Teacher Hao does not find my sense of humor funny. Perhaps embarrassed, he promptly changed the subject to a poem about sailing a river of yellow flowers and retreated into the details of its lines.

After my lesson, Julia Too and I rode up Changan Jie, the Avenue of Eternal Peace, its sidewalk tiles clattering beneath our wheels, light rising up from Tiananmen Square and the Forbidden City. The city smelled like urban autumn, its usual curtain of coal and restaurant smoke hanging above us, garlic and meat cooking, always the faint scent of fresh-poured pavement underneath. At night, I can't imagine ever leaving Beijing. But sometimes during the day I wonder whether Julia Too will grow up lost.

She seems to be doing okay. Phoebe came over last night, and they made spy notebooks, which they mysteriously call "goggies." They're fourteen pages each, with pouches for erasers, pencils, and extra note cards. Julia Too has been fascinated with spying since 9/11 happened last year, deciding that she could make herself useful by collecting information. When I asked, "Useful to whom?" she rolled her eyes. I don't think her intentions are patriotic, but I'm not certain. She's going to New York to stay with my mother and her husband, Jack, over Christmas. Maybe this is her way of preparing.

By this morning, she and Phoebe complained to me that I was too boring a subject for their spying, so we rode to the China World Hotel to ice-skate. Phoebe sat on the back of Julia Too's bike, and they giggled while I wondered if this was something Phoebe's mother, Anne, would allow. There was more giggling in the locker room, while they tried to figure out how they would glide around the rink, overhear juicy conversations, and then record them in their "goggies" without falling or drawing attention to themselves. Right before they went out on the ice, they put on lipstick (which Phoebe had brought). Lipstick. I don't even know what to think of this development for Julia Too. I sat on a bench and graded *Grapes of Wrath* papers while they twirled and slipped across the rink. I was more than halfway through the set when Anne arrived. "How are they?" she asked.

"Not a good batch," I said. "But some had thesis statements, so that was encouraging."

"I meant the girls." She glanced nervously at the rink.

"Oh, of course."

"Was Phoebe well behaved?" I followed her gaze to Phoebe and Julia Too, who were holding hands and skating in a straight, white line. Ice shaved into curls around the sides of their blades.

"Phoebe's always lovely, Anne. She's welcome anytime."

"Thank you. GB is such a good environment for them, don't you think?"

I sighed. Anne and I have had this conversation before. Whenever we talk, I'm re-disappointed that Americans are not effortlessly accessible to one another. "Especially your math program," she was saying. "Phoebe wasn't learning anything like algebra at her school in Michigan, and that was a private school too!"

"Yeah. International private school math programs are good compared to their domestic counterparts," I said. I considered gnawing my leg off to escape the rest of the conversation. "Julia, sweetie!" I shouted across the rink. "Put your shoes on—we have to meet Old Chen!" She nodded, gliding toward the exit.

Xiao Wang loves to remind me that the Chinese government recognizes Jews as an official Chinese ethnic group. So maybe I'm more Jewish or Chinese than American, because American strangers now seem especially strange. Although I was never much of a friend maker, even in New York. Julia Too takes after my mother in this regard, thankfully. She and Phoebe came dancing out of the locker room, their faces flushed from the cold rink and an interaction they'd had with some hockey-playing boys. Fodder for the goggies, I hoped. We waved Anne and Phoebe into their car-with-driver, and they headed for a gated neighborhood out in the suburb of Tong Xian, probably in a villa with at least one of the words "Jade," "Legend," or "Dragon" in its name. Anne and Phoebe are bona fide expatriates. Phoebe has seen recent movie releases that were not taped in the theater and full of people leaping up to get more popcorn in the middle of the show. She does not ride her bike everywhere in Beijing or snack on chicken feet at the beach, like Julia Too and I do.

Julia Too and I are fake expats, somewhere between imports and locals. We eat two-dollar bowls of noodles from street stands, have no maid, and wear knockoff clothes from the silk market. At the same time, we live in a temperate apartment with HBO, so I don't know how much authenticity we can actually claim; these things are all relative.

Old Chen was waiting in the Luscious Garden parking lot for our Saturday afternoon dumpling date. We knew him even through the tinted windows of his black sedan. As soon as Julia Too pedaled into sight, the old man burst out of his car, and she leapt off her bike, tossed it into the rack, and ran to greet him. I watched her, my lovely, gangly string bean of a girl, throw her arms around his formal neck. They greeted each other in Chinese, and he scooped her up and then nodded in a shy way in my direction. I blew him a kiss. The driver opened the trunk, and Old Chen and Julia Too went digging in there together. He had brought a kite for her, a string of red butterflies they spent the rest of the day teaching to fly.

November 1989, New York, NY

Dear Teacher,

   You say we should write about our "family history." Mine
are like this. My father is man who prefer to be the head of
chicken than tail of ox. But maybe that because he know if
you are first head of chicken then you can become head of ox.
My father speak precision English. He study himself every
morning maybe for hours. He say China will open some day.
We will need to speak it. He try to teach me and even I try
not to learn I can't help learn some of his perfect English.

   My father became rich. He have big black car with black
window and big hands and big house and big plan I will be the
management of a company. My mother will hate this if she
know. She already hate my father before, even hate the way
the world became. So she self-kills in 1982. Mao is dead. She
know my father will never do the thing they promise each
other to do. Because my father is cynic but my mother not.
And he is right. The revolution fail. And many people regret
later, especially my mother who believe in it so much.
Because even she would realize what she do is not good,
that it don't work out so the country sinking. This become
impossible situation for her. My mother is kind of person
who care about the truth. She want to find the truth no
matter it's good news for her or not. But she cannot even do
that. She is pretty and extravagant when she swallow many
medication. When I find her, she was already dead in the
bedroom. Before that happen, she cleaned up and made some
food for me.

         Da Ge

CHAPTER THREE

Novembers

*

I BOUGHT MY ENGLISH-TO-CHINESE DICTIONARY THE DAY I read about Da Ge's mother's suicide. I still have the plastic book, with its dirty red cover and shredded pages. Xiao Wang calls it the Aysha primer, because it's red and I carry it with me like a believer.

The first words I ever looked up in Chinese were "Da" and "Ge." I was sitting in my thimble-sized living room on 115th with his desperate essay. The Chinese section was alphabetized easily. I found *da*, which had dozens of meanings, including "big, great, and beat (as in hit, with a stick or fist)." *Ge* meant "cut off, lyric, spear, place, knot." I could not tell then what they mean when put together: big brother.

I flipped to the English section and found suicide. *Zi sha*. *Zi* meant self, and *sha*, kill. The English word "kill" seemed suddenly flimsy and pale yellow. The Chinese characters were purple with metal edges. I closed the book and stood up, poured myself a glass of wine.

Then I called Adam. Adam was my ex-boyfriend and former poetry instructor at Columbia, an advanced-degree fetishist for skinny undergraduates. He was a guy who liked bruisable skin. He wouldn't have hurt anybody, he just appreciated the potential violence in paleness. If, for example, I died of insanity or consumption, he would have wanted to carry me away and then write a tragic narrative in which my face had wobbled on a string-bean body, and my kewpie-doll mouth had breathed its last breath. Maybe that's too mean; even Adam probably wouldn't have used "breathed its last breath." He was a pretty good teacher and crossed out clichés in our poems.

When he arrived, we stood in the doorway together. He was just as I had left him. It had been four months since we'd broken up, and two since we'd slept together. He had glasses on, as he had the first day of the class he taught, as he always did. The metal rims looked cold against his face. His hair flopped down over the tops of the glasses. He was nerdy and earnest, in brown corduroy pants and a wool jacket. I wanted to unwrap him, undo the buttons of his coat, and peel it off his shoulders, press my mouth to his neck.

"Come in," I said, turning.

He followed me into the living room, where I poured him a glass of wine.

"Thanks." He sat on the futon, and I turned the stereo on, hoping whatever was in there wasn't too embarrassing. Tom Waits's "Blue Valentines" came on. Adam was looking at me.

"Are you okay?" he asked.

"Why does everyone ask me that all the time?"

"Because you're delicate," he said.

"Spare me, Adam."

He grunted. "Don't be hostile."

I gulped my wine.

"Jesus," Adam said. "Are you drinking a lot lately?"

"No," I said. "I'm okay."

"Is teaching going okay?"

"It's interesting," I said. "I have a student I think is a dissident from China."

"No shit. Did she say she was kicked out?"

"It's a guy. He implied it. And he's the kind of guy you can imagine standing in front of a tank."

"Is he seeking asylum here?

"I have no idea—I just met him, and he's quiet and surly."

Adam looked me over. "Surly, huh? Do you have a crush?"

I grinned. "Dating you hardly constitutes a history of liking surly guys."

"It's a bad cliché to sleep with your students, Aysh."

"I'm glad you came over nevertheless," I said.

He looked at the floor. "I meant him."

"I know," I said.

"I'm seeing someone."

"I know." The girl who was now there whenever I called. I never asked about her, didn't want to know. And I didn't think Adam would have shown up at my house if he didn't want to have nostalgic sex. I waited, quietly, and Adam suddenly laughed, flaunting rows of straight white teeth, the skin on his jaw stretching to accommodate them. When he swallowed, his Adam's apple rode down his neck. We both knew we were going to keep sleeping in our post-breakup bed, even though that's almost always an unhappy backwards crab walk. Adam, finished laughing, stood up bravely, and faced me. It was a clumsy moment, and I loved him for his awkwardness. I laughed until he put a hand over my open mouth.

The gesture reminded me of Xiao Wang, covering her mouth whenever she giggled in class. Adam pulled me close; he smelled like soap and his suede jacket. What I liked about him was precisely the opposite of what he liked about me. He was vaguely blond and sleepy looking; even his coloring suggested a carefree inner state.

"Stop laughing," he said. "This is a romantic moment."

"You're right. I'm sorry," I said, reminding myself again of Xiao Wang.

I reached my hand down the collar of his T-shirt and stretched the cotton from his neck. Feeling the groove of his collarbone, I closed my eyes. He unbuttoned my shirt, pushed me onto the couch and deftly took off the rest of my clothes. I undressed him, listening for the varied rhythm of his breathing, counting his breaths as they came close together. Counting A-d-a-m i-s h-o-m-e. When his hips were pressed against mine, I rested my hands in the small of his back. When he rose, I slid my hands up to his shoulder blades, sharp and expansive as wings. I thought of the dragon scroll, realized Da Ge's words—*pretty* and *extravagant*— were fluttering around in my mind. As was the phrase *when I find her*. There were occasional sirens in the street.

I kept seeing Adam that November, even as my interest in Da Ge intensified. Adam made me feel safe. Maybe like a dad. Whenever I was with Adam, the Da Ge business seemed like an innocent and contained crush. Da Ge skipped class more than he showed up, and we hadn't spoken since he turned in the suicide essay. So I was free to call Adam while I cultivated my fantasy of Da Ge: one that involved my lifting him out of his dangerous, difficult life into mine, being his Adam, keeping him safe.

Da Ge finally came back to class one day in mid-November when I had assigned my students to do "chat skits." It was almost Thanksgiving; people were in a holiday mood. I put them in unlikely pairs and situations: Xiao Wang and Chase, whose native language was Spanish, were strangers in a bar, having a "casual conversation."

"Hello, lady!" Chase said, as soon as Xiao Wang had settled in a chair. I bent to take notes, stifled a laugh. I didn't want to interrupt and prevent them from feeling casual.

"Hello, Chase," said Xiao Wang. "Oh! I'm sorry. I forget! Hello, mister."

"How are you doing?" Chase asked. It's amazing what a difference the word "doing" can make at the end of "how are you."

"I am doing okay," said Xiao Wang. I had told them that "okay" sounds better than "well" in conversation, even though it's grammatically less accurate. She smiled out at me from the skit stage, to see if I'd noticed her apt use. I smiled back.

"I would like to treat you to a drink," said Chase. "It will be my treat. Is it okay?"

I scribbled a note to tell him about "Can I buy you a drink?"

"It's okay for me to have the drink from you," said Xiao Wang.

"What will you like?" Chase asked.

"I cannot drink beer," said Xiao Wang.

"You do not enjoy beer. What will you like?" Chase repeated.

I turned a little bit to find Da Ge in my peripheral vision. He was watching Xiao Wang, perhaps with concern, but when he felt my eyes on him, he turned toward me and smiled, holding my gaze until I looked away.

"I would like the water with gas," Xiao Wang said. I wasn't sure what this meant, but Chase was, since apparently in Spanish water comes with and without gas, too. He nodded and beckoned an imaginary waiter.

Da Ge had turned his attention back to the performance, and now he said something to Xiao Wang in Chinese, in which the English word "bubble" made a cameo, and Xiao Wang covered her face with her hands.

"It's okay," I said. "Don't stop."

"Excuse me," she said to Chase. "I would like bubble water," she said.

"I will go to the bar to get bubble water," Chase said. He stood.

"Thank you," said Xiao Wang. She dipped her head in a kind of bow.

I clapped with the rest of the class.

"I'm sorry! This mistake of the bubbles!" Xiao Wang said. "I think you know that this in Chinese is like to carry gas." She said two Chinese syllables. "I don't know what this is in English."

"You can call it mineral water, seltzer, or sparkling water."

"Seltzer," Xiao Wang said, without the *l* or the *t*.

"Yes," I said, "seltzer." I pushed the *t* out, tongue to the roof of my mouth.

"Seltzer," she said again, this time with the *t*, but an *r* instead of an *l* in the middle, and an *l* instead of an *r* at the end.

"Good." I called Da Ge and Russ up to the front. They were supposed to be in a library.

"Hi, Da Ge," said Russ.

"Hi, Russ."

"What are you doing at the library today?"

"Just hanging out."

"Really? I am here to check out books."

"What books?"

"English books," said Russ.

"I am here to check out girls," said Da Ge. Chase and Russ and I laughed, but Xiao Wang scrunched her eyebrows. Ingyum looked up from her notes. I felt the room lift with Da Ge's unusually good mood, felt a surge of something for him, affection maybe, or desire. When he looked at me again, I thought I saw that we had agreed to be in love. I smiled back this time.

"Do you have homework to do at the library?" Chase asked Da Ge.

"Fuck homework," said Da Ge, "let's go to the bar and have some beer." I waited to see how Russ would respond to this "real life" situation.

"That sounds good," said Russ. "I prefer beer to book."

I applauded enthusiastically, keeping Da Ge in my line of sight. He was wearing a cream sweater, jeans, and work boots, and looked somehow more American than he had before. Eager to talk to him, I dismissed everyone and stood in the doorway waiting. As soon as he approached, my pulse sped.

"Hi, Aysha," he said. There was something calm but suggestive about his voice, my name he'd never said before, how close he was standing to me.

We walked outside together. His skin was flushed across the cheekbones and bluish under his eyes. He lit a cigarette with one hand cupped over the flame. He was wearing a jade ring.

"Did something happen?" I asked.

He looked confused.

"You haven't been to class in two weeks."

"I'm sorry for that," he said. "Sometimes I am not—how do you say—feeling so good to come to class."

"Have you been sick?"

He looked side to side, as if trapped and searching for an escape. I did not want him to leave. He dropped the cigarette and crushed it with his right boot heel.

"Your essay was terrific," I said quickly, "the one about your mother."

"My writing English is better, right?"

The combination of this response and my having said the word "mother" made me feel callous. "I hope it's not, you know, none of my business," I corrected, "but I wanted to say I'm sorry about your mother. I was surprised when I read your—"

"Well," he said. "I'm—how do you always say—use to it."

"Right."

We stood awkwardly, and my vision panned out. I saw us there in the slush over fall leaves, Da Ge motherless and me fatherless, and I thought again that I could love him. I felt myself spin a bit, brought my eyes back to his, stayed put looking at him.

"What about your father?" I asked. Maybe he found this odd. He squinted, lit another cigarette. I felt relief that we had at least enough time left for him to smoke it. I wanted to slow time down when he was around. This, I now know, is a kind of love.

Da Ge said, "My father work for Ha Ha bottle water. He is fat cat."

I laughed, in spite of my feeling that he might not like it. Two teachers, Emmanuel Stern and Ben Rosenbaum, walked by, and I took a small step back away from Da Ge, cleared my throat.

"Hi Aysha," Ben called.

"Hi," I said. Ben's eyes were on me, and I looked off into the distance, watched two squirrels chasing each other up a tree as if they were a fascinating documentary. Da Ge grinned as if he had seen something, knew me. He lit a third cigarette off the one he was still smoking.

"My English teacher in China teach me how to say that, 'fat cat.' It's funny to say that?"

"You used it very well," I said. "Was your teacher American?"

"No, he's Chinese guy. But he know a lot about America. And my father can speak English," he said.

"Right, you said that in your essay." I thought of his father, speaking into an empty house, his wife dead and his son in America. I wondered what he was like; maybe he had a mistress-wife like my father. "He must miss you, now that you're here."

"I don't think so," Da Ge said. He dropped the cigarette, didn't light a fourth. "Anyway, I don't have choice to stay in China. I am dissident." He gave the word an extra hiss, either proud to call himself one or to pronounce the word properly.

"A dissident. Really?" I asked this with interest, which he mistook for doubt.

His voice sped up, turned white like heat. "You don't think I am? You think it was only bookworm like Wang Dan?"

"Who?"

He looked at me, and his face softened as if he had remembered something.

"It's nothing," he said. "Don't worry that." I hoped it was me that he had remembered, that had made his face sweet like that. But then he said he had business, and left.

At nine that night Da Ge rang my doorbell, unannounced, carrying groceries. "I can cook some food for you," he said, when I buzzed him in. He set down the University Food Market bags hanging from his arms.

"Wow," I said. "Okay. Come in." I did not ask what he had been planning to do if I wasn't home. I thought maybe this kind of pop-in was culturally acceptable in China.

In my kitchen, he chopped chicken and bell peppers into quarter-inch pieces as perfect as jewels, and expressed such shock over my lack of a wok it was as if I had killed a person he loved. I watched his arms move over the food. He saw me looking and pushed the sleeves of his cream sweater up. Then he mixed thick condiments he'd brought and coated the cubes of chicken. He threw roots into a frying pan, put the chicken in, took the chicken out, and braised pepper gems until they turned neon green and red. As a finale, he fried everything together in a splash and sizzle that turned my entire kitchen into a stir-fry. I had never seen a bigger mess.

I was rapt, spelling out I'-m i-n l-o-v-e w-i-t-h h-i-m on my fingers as he presented his glistening chicken exhibition and apologized that it was inauthentic.

"It's perfect," I said, "I don't cook." I was thinking should I be nervous? That he's in my house, that I don't know him, didn't ask him over? That he's my student?

But it was cold outside, and I wasn't nervous. I was happier to have him in my apartment than I can express, even now. He made me feel dangerous and interesting even as I dreamed that I might make him feel safe. Da Ge was like having a working fireplace; every room he entered heated up with him in it, and just out the windows was instant winter wherever he wasn't.

He was rummaging through my silverware drawer, and I was relieved to have a few pairs of disposable chopsticks left over from takeout. We stood across the table from each other, and I poured water from a Brita into mugs while he spooned rice into my bowl and put chicken and peppers on top.

I sat down. He sat, too, waited for something. I took a bite of chicken, and the sesame oil and ginger and sugar bloomed in my mouth.

"It's fantastic," I said. "Thank you for making dinner."

"It's nothing," he said, delighted. "Many Chinese men are excellent cook. Next time I make a fish." Then he served himself, picked his chopsticks up, and mysteriously rubbed them together before taking a bite. The food seemed to cheer him up. He smiled at me. It was very quiet in my living room.

"So." I thought I should probably ask what he was doing coming over uninvited to make dinner at my apartment, but couldn't think of a polite way to frame it. He took another bite, chewed.

"What's your scar from?" I asked, surprising myself.

He reached up as if remembering it was there, and ran his fingers over the rise of flesh. "It's from accident. Long time before," he said in a cold orange voice. Wanting to avoid the trapped glance I had seen at school, I changed the subject fast.

"How's New York? You adjusting okay?" My inner critic berated me for being tedious, but Da Ge was looking straight at me like a laser. I would have liked to know what he saw.

"In America I think I am good guy. Not like Beijing where I am hooligan."

I laughed. "*Hooligan?* Did your English teacher in China teach you that word?"

He ignored this. "One time I was smoking with my artist friend Hong Yue, and I put the cigarette down on some paper. Maybe I am drunk, too. It's accident. But the room, in my father's house, burn quickly. A kind of surprise this burning. Exciting."

"You burned your father's house down?"

"It's accident. Actually, we think it's kind of funny, me and Hong Yue. But later my father make me work for many months to pay him the money to repair that room."

Da Ge poured us both more water and chewed quietly. I didn't know why he had told me that story or what to say. Was he going to burn my house down?

"China is not like New York," he said. "Maybe for some people, like Xiao Wang, it's difficult to live here. In China are many rules for face. There are rules for eating and drinking and talking."

"I think that might be true here, too," I tried. "And Xiao Wang—"

"Not the same rules."

"What do you mean by rules?"

"It's hard to say that in English."

"So teach me some Chinese."

"*Ni hao*," he said, "hello."

"Knee how," I repeated.

"Good," he said, "your pronunciation is good."

"Maybe you can take me to visit China, in that case," I joked.

"I can't go to China now," he said, not amused.

"Oh. Because of Tiananmen?"

"A lot of reason. I come to America right when China need me, so maybe it's my—how do you say—fate—I stay here. Anyway, maybe you would have to live in China for many years to understand the logistic." He smiled.

"The logistic?"

"That way of thinking. The Chinese thinking. Like the government."

"Is there a way of thinking common to all Chinese?"

"Common?"

"Chinese thinking? What does that even mean?"

"Now you know," he said, "the Chinese government will rather kill its young generation than lose face."

"But that's not a Chinese way of thinking," I said. "I mean, you don't think that way, and you're Chinese. Xiao Wang doesn't think that way, and she's Chinese."

"I believe in democracy, so I am different to Xiao Wang and that government."

I wondered how well he and Xiao Wang knew each other.

"Used to be I really believe that democracy can come," he was saying. "Because I am like my mother; we think if you want something so much it's enough that that thing maybe can happen. But now I know it's impossible, and this make me more Chinese."

"I doubt cynicism is particular to the Chinese way of thinking," I said. "There's very little hope for social justice or change in America, either."

"Well," he said, "even though I hate the government, I will rather die than lose face, like that government. So maybe it is Chinese way of thinking."

"You would rather die than lose face? Then you can understand what the government did," I proposed. I took another serving of his chicken, even though I wasn't hungry. He watched me chew.

"China just want to be stability, not to boss and control the rest of the world like America. Maybe the government did that because it feel weak. I can understand, but I can't be that. Do you know what I mean?"

"Maybe," I said.

"Anyway, now I am foreigner. And every country have a kind of box for foreigner. In New York I live like in that dark box."

"But isn't that just because you don't feel at home here yet?"

I considered what it might like to live in a dark box in his hometown. Sadly, it sounded good to me. I imagined going to China with Da Ge, tucking myself into a safe, dark box. It would be like making a fort out of blankets in my parents' living room, hearing them talking in the dining room, knowing night meant a bath, my dad reading *Charlotte's Web* to me again and *Narnia* to Benj, click of the pink lamp going out.

"You'll get used to New York," I told Da Ge, collecting myself. "Maybe I can help—by teaching you some things?" I put a red pepper in my mouth.

"It's not just language," he said. "If your English is okay, okay, so maybe the box have window." He laughed a short hard laugh. "But even then you are cleaning clothes or deliver food on a bicycle for twenty years, you still cannot belong."

"There must be lots of Chinese students and artists and businesspeople here, too. And lawyers and doctors, I mean—"

"Sometimes I see clearly," he interrupted, setting his chopsticks down, "about America. Or maybe my life in America. When my life in China, I am part of that place. I cannot see where China stop—" He chopped his hand down on the table and then lifted it and gestured to himself. "Where China stop and I start."

I nodded.

"But in America," he continued, "I am not part of it. I can see my life, but maybe I also can't see anything, don't know who I am. Who I could be here. If I am American. Do you know my meaning?"

"I think so," I said. "I think it might be culture shock. Have you heard of—"

"In Chinese we have this saying—the players of the game of—how do you say, with king and queen or horse?"

"Chess?"

"Right. That players cannot see clearly. Only who stand to the side—the *pangguanzhe*, watcher of the whole game, can see clearly. Understand?"

"Of course I do. Your English is beautiful."

"Thank you," he said, but he was humoring me, worried I had missed his point. "But beautiful English not enough. That maybe keep me from being totally Chinese anymore, but it does not make me American. I am in the—how do you say—no place."

I thought, *me too*, let's keep each other company, let's run away. His way of talking, interrupting, gave me a jolt of being alive. Somewhere in between what he said and what I understood was a place I wished to inhabit. I thought I wanted to understand him. But in fact, what I wanted was to feel whatever it was he felt. Instead of what I felt.

When he excused himself to go outside and smoke, I worried that he might leave without warning me, as he had arrived. But after a few minutes, he came back in and helped with the dishes in my small kitchen. We didn't speak; he cleared the table and I washed, both of us working quickly. The sounds reminded me of my parents' apartment, and I closed my eyes, clink of dishes in the sink, slip of Ivory soap on my fingers.

Da Ge was standing so close to me that I could hear him breathe. He began humming something softly, a song I had never heard, but liked. I thought we knew each other well, after our dinner together, even that we were alike in some way I couldn't define. I wanted him to stay, to watch a movie, keep talking, sing whatever song it was out loud, take off our clothes, have sex, make breakfast in the morning. I was hunting for words or a way to be brave when he straightened up and said, "Thank you for dinner."

"No," I said, "thank you. It was really nice to—I was— do you—"

"I see you soon in class," he said. "I have some business. I should go."

Then he was gone. I stood in the hallway, wondering what "business" he meant, whether he had heard my invitation and turned it down, or whether I hadn't made it, before turning back to the dragons and longevity on my wall. I touched the soft paper edge of his scroll, felt the two hours we'd just spent underneath me like something to sleep on. My apartment smelled better than it ever had before, alive, beloved, as if a family lived there.

During my wretched, failed senior year in college, Adam made me see a shrink. I thought I was happy, but Adam suspected otherwise. He was a good reader. And he spent more time with me than anyone else did, so he realized I was in trouble before it became undeniable all around. As much as my particular weirdnesses charmed Adam, he worried, too. He expressed surprise, for example, that I'd never been to a therapist, what with the divorce being my fault and the barely speaking ever again to my dad or the brother I adored.

My brother, Benj Mitchell, with his long eyelashes and huge capacity for empathy, was away at Berkeley when our father left. Benj was so instantly forgiving that my mother and I had trouble forgiving him, although she would never put it that way. Maybe it was easier for Benj because he didn't have to live at home when it happened. He would have been reading in People's Park in sandals, his hair a little bit too long and curling down around his ears while my mom and I were watching movers take half our family's books and tools and pottery to a brick box house next to a fake lake in New Jersey. He didn't see our mom on the blue couch for six months, thinking. He didn't see her drift around the kitchen like a wisp of dust. He wasn't up at night with the two of us, each in her own room, each pretending not to know the other was awake. Benj got to pack his sweet mind with useful facts, apply to law school, and get accepted. That's why he could stand to stay with our father and his new mistress-wife in their Jersey colonial during vacations from Berkeley. That's why he told me that parents are worth forgiving, no matter what they do, because they're yours and you must love them anyway. What if they don't forgive you, I asked Benj. He said they always do.

I used to stalk my father and his wife drive-by style, watching her tulips and daffodils bloom in spring and wither in the summers when they were away. I didn't know where they went. The first winter after my dad left us, a snowman appeared on their lawn, and I cried in my car, wondering what kid had built it, whether they would have kids. That snowman demonstrated to me that she had a family, people she loved and who loved her. Children who rolled around her yard, making angels. Sometimes I dragged my friend Julia on those drives, and we'd see my father's windows lit up, and I would speculate about what he must be reading, sitting in a big soft chair. Hawthorne. Melville. Northrop Frye? Now, thousands of safe miles away, I Google him and his wife occasionally—find conferences they natter at, articles they publish on education. I try not to care anymore.

Back then Adam nagged me enough that I agreed to call a doctor he knew, a guy named Mark Holderstein. Dr. Holderstein was a bit like a fastidious lit critic, in his sweater vest and argyle socks that showed some spindly leg when he crossed his ankle over his knee. He was a carrion man, circling for specifics in whatever he read, the type to descend upon a person and devour dead flesh. After diagnosing it, of course.

"Do you read books?" I asked.

"Yes. Why?"

I didn't answer. "When you read them," I said, "do you have lots of preconceived notions before you start about what you'll find and analyze in them?"

He smiled. "Is this a metaphor?"

I tried another line of questioning, equally immature and unproductive. "Before I delve into the deep recesses of my mind, I'm curious how you feel about your patients."

"Well," he said, "my patients are regular people with individual needs and issues. I have specific relationships with each of them."

"Do you think they're stupid and pathetic and weak?"

He was nonplussed by this. "No."

"Do you ever fall in love with your patients?"

"No," he said. "But therapy is, in large part, about the relationship between the therapist and the client, so sometimes I spend time with patients discussing the ways they feel about me or our sessions." He paused. "Why are you here?" he asked gently.

I looked around the office, noticing it for the first time. A photograph hid the spines of five books, probably self-help, on the shelf. In the picture, his wife had a sporty body and sailboating ponytail. Her smile was sly and squinty in the sun; tan kids grinned from under her rippling arms. I

imagined objects not pictured: play equipment in the back-
yard, the plaid or paisley beds they maybe slept in, shafts of
light on plush rugs, lotion, likely Clinique, on her bathroom
counter. Somewhere a yacht bobbed, waiting for weekends
when he, finally away from the despair of others, was
allowed to be happy with his family. I felt a jolt of resent-
ment, as if injected into my arm.

"My bossy boyfriend thought I needed therapy," I said.

Dr. Holderstein nodded. "Did you think so, too?"

"I don't know. Relative to what?"

"Why did you agree to come and see me?"

"Mainly to get Adam off my back, but I also thought it
might be interesting."

"I hope it will be. Do you want to tell me about what's
going on in your life?"

Pouring out your dark secrets to a professional has some
of the same allure as having an emotional or online affair.
The space between you and the doctor fills with information, and in the flash of your first confession (if it's true),
you're cheating on the people you're talking about, back-
spacing your lovers into ghosts as soon as your bond with
the shrink exceeds your intimacy with them. The doctor
becomes your confidant and boyfriend, the new one with
whom you analyze and thus disparage the old.

Maybe that's why I was so worried about what Dr.
Holderstein thought of me. I was consumed by the possibility that he would find me pathetic. Or insane. Anxious
to demonstrate a normalcy I couldn't even have identified,
let alone embodied, I talked about Columbia, my classes,
Adam. I thought Dr. Holderstein would be dazzled by how
normal and together and smart these anecdotes made me.
But I chose the wrong details: the pigeon nesting behind
the chalkboard instead of my coursework, the blinding
white of certain Mondays, Adam's candle-scented way of

speaking. Dr. Holderstein told me he hoped I'd come
weekly.

And I did, for the first semester of my senior year. I
enjoyed the habit of our meetings, even when I despised their
content. I told him about my Eliot, Joyce, and Pound seminar, about the course called "Riot and Rebellion." I
described counting my letters, which Dr. Holderstein called
obsessive-compulsive behavior, a term I liked. He said if it
wasn't getting in the way of my living a productive life, it
wasn't a problem.

"It makes me feel happy," I said. Even as I said it, I
added "really," so it would fit: i-t m-a-k-e-s m-e r-e-a-l-l-y
h-a-p-p-y. Somewhere deep, a small alarm sounded, suggest-
ing this was not true, even if it fit on twenty fingers.

I told Dr. Holderstein that Mondays were white,
Tuesdays were blue, Wednesdays were yellow, Thursdays
brown, and Fridays red. He said people with colors for days
have "synesthesia," and I was less surprised to know he had
a word for everything than I was to learn that not everyone
had colors for the days. I could not imagine there were those
who did have colors, but that theirs differed from mine. I
longed to set the record straight.

In fact, the life in my mind was itself increasingly colorful, cluttered, difficult. When I admitted that I had stopped
sleeping, Dr. Holderstein was concerned. I said I didn't need
sleep, and for the first time, he objected forcefully. He threw
the word "mania," onto the desk between us, where it
writhed and struggled for air. I said nothing, watched the
blue, slippery word, hoped it would suffocate. He said there
was the possibility, in someone who was "racing" the way I
was, of an "episode." I was unhappy when he suggested I
take some lithium.

"Why?" I asked. It was, I thought, confirmation that he
was judging me after all.

"It will even you out a bit; you seem hypomanic."

"Hippo what?"

He smiled. "Hypomania is mania without psychosis, but it can sometimes turn into more serious mania, and I just want to make sure you don't spiral."

"You do know that my father cheated on my mother and I saw him and told her about it, and then he never spoke to me again, right?"

"I know only what you've told me."

"My brother Benj forgave him. They're still in touch."

"But you and he are not?"

"You have very good grammar," I said.

Dr. Holderstein smiled kindly. "Have you tried to contact him?"

I nodded.

"And how has he responded?"

"He hasn't." Every year after my father left, I wrote him a letter. He never wrote back, even though he and my mother continued to speak sometimes about Benj and maybe me and certainly other administrative matters. When I was finishing high school, stunned under the cloud of my parents' breakup, I predictably considered the whole thing to be my fault. Of course my father didn't want to have anything to do with me ever again—I had ratted him out, after all. But maybe he just wasn't an adult, still isn't. Maybe my mere presence was such a breathtaking reminder of what a villain he'd been that he couldn't endure it. So he chose ways to blame me, shedding his guilty skin and suffocating me under it. I stopped writing the letters when I moved to China.

Dr. Holderstein, to his credit, cut right to the question at the center of things: "Do you and your mom ever talk about what happened with your father?"

"Not really."

"Why not?"

I considered this. "That's a good question."

The minute my father left us, my mother and I became colleagues in the office of our house. We protected each other by not talking about him, and as a result, she stopped being my parent and started being a person, a disturbing development. I shrugged.

"I don't want to hurt my mother's feelings. And anyway, now it's been years. Bringing it up would be weird. I turned out fine. She did a good job—it's not like she was insufficient after he left."

Even as I said this, I knew what an overcompensation it was.

"Isn't any single parent insufficient in some ways?" Dr. Holderstein asked.

I didn't respond at all to this, although now that I've been a single parent for a decade, I have a few thousand answers. I know what he meant, anyway. Maybe Dr. Holderstein was just eerily prescient, since his question turned out to be the primary focus of my adult life.

I told Dr. Holderstein what I knew then and could bear to hear myself say: I wanted to escape. If I'd had one wish, I said, it would be to go somewhere safe, where nothing excruciating had ever happened to my family. Where no one knew who I was.

He thought I meant denial, but it turns out I meant China. I got my wish, even if Dr. Holderstein never got his, which was to help me avoid a manic episode. He tried valiantly. Before we were out of time, he gave me a detailed rundown of the potential side effects of lithium and said repeatedly that while he wasn't a big prescriber of either antidepressants or mood stabilizers, he thought this might prevent worse medications for me down the line. And maybe it would have, but I threw the prescription out on my way to the subway and never went to another appointment.

On the train home that day, I peered out at everyone, furious. I must have looked like Da Ge, a defiant teenager glaring up from under my eyelids. A woman walked into the subway car yanking at her tangled hair and kicking something invisible in front of her, turning me into a portrait of stability and balance. Insanity is relative, that's the funny thing. Who was I to be spending thousands of dollars on therapy when there were people with actual problems? Rows of the less insane ran their eyes along the lines of newspapers and magazines while the kicking woman growled out, "So fuck that, just fuck that. You think that, fuck that. You die alone. You die alone! Fuck that." She pushed sideways through the door to the next car.

A couple of teenagers giggled. We were all, of course, both connected to, and implicated, by the woman. Everyone has at least one nutcase in the family, and in most families, no one can even agree on who it is.

If I saw Dr. Holderstein now, I wouldn't know whether to apologize, thank him, or gloat. He warned me, and if I had listened, it might have spared me (and my mom) some genuine suffering. On the other hand, I survived, am maybe a better person for having gone under water that deep. I won the silver lining of a lifetime in Julia Too. So I guess I could tell Dr. Holderstein that he was right and so was I: it's all relative. I didn't need a shrink after all, because all it took was loving Da Ge, and I was never the crazy one again. He stole that thunder, turned me sane.

Julia Too and I spent Thanksgiving of 2002 in the suburb of Shunyi at my friend Shannon's house. Shannon is my closest American friend in Beijing and the mother of one of Julia Too's classmates, a firecracker of a kid named Sophie. Sophie broke a window at the school last year, painted a naked man for her final art project, and filled condoms with water on "water balloon" day. As a teacher and role model at Global Beijing, I'm supposed to find her behavior abhorrent, but she's a twinkly, charming girl, and I rather like her troublemaking. Of course, it wasn't my window or my condoms. And she's not my kid.

Shannon is something of a rebel herself; when she arrived in Beijing at age twenty-two, she was a radical leftist. She dressed in Communist Party kitsch, wore her hair in Mao-girl peasant pigtails, and dated Chinese intellectuals. She still has a CPC star tattooed on her right hip. But to hear her tell it, she got so tired of soapboxing and being soapboxed that she has cast herself, mostly for entertainment's sake, as America's advocate. So now she runs a media consulting company and fights flirtily with her husband Zhang Sun, pretending to be more patriotic than she is. Partially, this is because living in China for decades at a time will make you feel an occasional stab of patriotism and nostalgia no matter how critical of the United States you may be, but mainly it's a staple of her and Zhang Sun's romance. He likes the idea that she's an untamable, wild American girl, even if it's basically untrue.

I love Zhang Sun because he's charming and unflappable, looks like a young Mao, and loves to tell dirty jokes. He likes me because I'm the only one who laughs. The funny thing is, I barely even get what he's saying, but I find Zhang Sun's delivery hilarious. He has an unusually expressive face. My favorite of his jokes is the one I'm sure I do get, about a peasant named "Old Wang," who is famous for his huge "second brother." When Old Wang dies, a doctor cuts off the "second brother" and is studying it by the light of a desk lamp when his wife intrudes. Surprised, the doctor drops the specimen, and his wife, upon seeing it "roll across the floor," cries out, "Oh no! Old Wang is dead?!" Zhang Sun always looks devastated when he gets to that line. Sometimes he even tears up. I love it.

Shannon hates the Old Wang joke, but she enjoys setting me up on dates. No one who is happily married can tolerate a single friend in her thirties. Shannon doesn't mean for the dates to be monotonous and mortifying. But I hate them. I say awkward and inappropriate things, and then I can't stop the sarcastic parentheticals from running through my mind like ticker tape about whatever the guy says to try to rescue or amuse us both. It always feels like bad TV.

On occasion, Shannon's candidates have ended up being my boyfriends, but even those liaisons have usually ended in embarrassment so profound it only narrowly escapes classification as tragedy. She sets me up with any new Westerner who comes to town, creating and replicating a dynamic so predictable and tedious I almost fall over in the first five minutes of conversation: "You've lived here how long!? Wow! Your Chinese must be great! Where can I get (fill in the blank: a lava lamp, a SIM card, a Chinese tutor, a bike helmet)?"

The embarrassing, fetishist truth is that I prefer Chinese guys. Maybe they just remind me of Da Ge, a racist and tacky possibility. But more likely, it's because Chinese men ask fewer questions than Westerners do, and I'm grateful for the privacy. Clichés about girls have always surprised me—that we love relationship maintenance, would rather cuddle than have sex, want to talk about our feelings and "work things out." Maybe I'm a guy, but I prefer sex and breaking up.

Whenever Shannon has sent me out with Zhang Sun's Chinese friends, the relationships have blown up, plateaued, or led to marriage proposals over fire liquor and hot pot, when my eyes are watering from garlic smoke and I've mumbled incoherently *I can't but it's not you, it's me.*

All this to say I had low hopes when I met Yang Tao at dinner. I could tell Shannon had invited him with me in mind because he was well cast, hanging on the periphery like an uncomfortable teenager. I always like men like that. It's a relief to find someone who is at least as awkward as I am, because then he's likely to be thinking about his own social anxiety instead of mine. Plus, I like shy guys; they have secrets. Yang Tao looked like he was in his late thirties, which meant he had to be a divorcee. It's tough to stay unmarried past thirty-five in China—the pressure to produce a grandson is too great. Yang Tao was wearing the kind of glasses that inspire mockery at school. I was glad he wasn't a little kid anymore, and wondered if his childhood had been torturous. The thought that it might have been filled me with confidence and resolve, and I walked over to him and introduced myself in Chinese. He smiled and said hello in English, his pronunciation so crisp I thought maybe he was Asian American and that I had committed a small faux pas. But then he said he taught linguistics at Bei Da. Linguistics! Good work, Shannon.

"Are you from Beijing?"

He nodded. "My parents are still here in the city."

I laughed. "Do you live with them?" I asked in Chinese.

He shook his head no, but I suspected they had family dinners together five times a week. Chinese men are filial. And they can cook.

"And you?" he asked.

I gestured over to Julia Too. She, Lili, Sophie, and Phoebe had gone from reading magazines to leapfrogging first over one another's backs and then up onto the couch. Pre-teenage girls strike me increasingly as hybrids of teenagers and toddlers. I was worried that they might break their necks or the couch, but decided not to intervene.

"I live in Beijing with my daughter, Julia, and teach at Global Beijing."

Yang Tao looked interested. You can gauge a lot about people in the first five sentences of a conversation with them. At the word *daughter*, for example, eyes may rise up and away in search of an escape. Yang Tao's gaze settled momentarily on Julia Too and then came back to me. "She looks like you," he said, and I smiled. To Chinese people, Julia Too looks utterly American, with her light, wispy hair and green eyes. To me, she's a striking replica of Da Ge.

"Do you teach English literature?" Yang Tao asked.

Shannon must have told him. "How'd you guess?"

He looked at me patiently. "You don't look like a math teacher," he said.

Then we sawed at hunks of turkey and had meaningful eye contact during dinner. Xiao Wang and Anne talked politely about the difference between the Chinese school Lili was enrolled in, which required nine hours of school and six hours of homework every day, and Global Beijing, which fostered creativity and "individual time." I could hear Xiao Wang tsk'ing disapprovingly when Anne said that Phoebe, Sophie, and Julia Too were auditioning to be shabop girls in GB's "Little Shop of Horrors."

"Kids should have a little fun," I interjected, grinning.

"Maybe it's okay to do free-time activity on the weekends," Xiao Wang said.

"You're a slave driver," I teased her. "You don't even let them play on weekends, which is why they always sleep at my place."

Xiao Wang sighed. "Someone has to be guidance for them," she said. Whenever Julia Too sleeps at Lili's, Xiao Wang wakes them pre-sunrise to pursue culturally enriching activities. At my house, we stagger out of bed at ten and make waffles.

"Waffles," I said, and Xiao Wang rolled her eyes. Anne looked bewildered.

"I love waffles," Yang Tao said, and I knew I'd sleep with him. I was impressed that he knew what waffles were, and certain that he did not, could not, like them. Which meant he was scrambling for shared interests. Shannon raised her eyebrows up and down, and I ignored her.

"Zhang Sun," she said, "go get the potatoes—I forgot them in the oven."

He left agreeably and came back carrying a tray of shredded, stir-fried potatoes.

"Sorry whities," Shannon joked. "I had to make something with *wenr*," flavor. Zhang Sun and Yang Tao and Xiao Wang were all pushing turkey around on their plates. Chinese people hate turkey, and they're right—it's a dry, hideous bird that tastes like beak and bones. Everyone devoured the potatoes right away, and Shannon sighed. "We should've just had Chinese food," she said.

"There's still time!" Zhang Sun said, and ran back to the kitchen. We could instantly hear sizzling oil and smell garlic smoke from whatever he had begun stir-frying.

I excused myself to peek in at the kids' table in the living room; the girls were chatting at the table, and I stood there, my own childhood Thanksgivings on a gritty film strip in my mind: my father attaching leaves to the grown-ups' table and carving wings, my scrawny cousins in floral dresses, my mother and her sister Ruth interrupting each other and laughing with my grandmother, whose earrings had so many dangling parts they looked like the skeletons of thousand-limbed beasts.

"Mom! What are you doing?" The girls had all turned and were looking at me. I wondered how many minutes I had been standing there, silent.

"I'm, um, taking a picture of you guys." I looked around.

"I forgot the camera!" I said, "Silly me," and went to get a camera. I overheard Phoebe say, "Your mom is weird."

In order to demonstrate my normalcy, I came back and took pictures of the girls, who promptly forgot my weirdness once they were grinning and posing.

But on the way home, Julia Too was anxious. She's been preoccupied lately with what she calls "the way different people see the same things," a philosophical question about consciousness. For her, it expresses itself as: "Okay. I look at blue and Lili looks at blue and we both call it blue, but how do I know what she sees is actually blue? I mean, how do I know my blue isn't her red, but we both just call it blue?"

"I don't know what my friends mean sometimes," she said in the taxi home. "I don't know if words mean the same things to all of us."

"What happened?"

"Do you think I'm weird, Mom?"

I thought about this. "I don't think being weird is a bad thing."

She sighed, annoyed. "That's not what I asked."

"I think you're interesting."

"So you do think I'm weird."

"I don't really like that word for it—I think you're unique, special, imaginative."

"Weird," she said. Her stubbornness reminded me of Da Ge, scared me. But maybe her weirdness reminded her of me, scared her.

"You're the best person I've ever met," I said, "fascinating, hilarious, brave."

"You're my mother."

"I consider myself lucky."

"I don't think the kids at GB think I'm the best person."

"But what do *you* think of them?"

It's not that I don't want other kids to like her; I'd just

prefer it if she cared less whether they do. Most of my girl-friends, including the original Julia, are so preoccupied with whether people like them that they forget to consider their own preferences. This seems especially true in their relation-ships with guys. I may have been certifiable, but I always cared whether I liked a guy more than whether he liked me. I'd like to pass this trait on to Julia Too. But she didn't answer, and I didn't press it, which makes me think I can't stop the slipping toward becoming my mother. Even knowing we're becoming our moms doesn't make it possible to change course. My mother had a policy of "sparing me pain," which included not telling me anything that might hurt me and not asking anything that might embarrass either of us. Her inten-tions were loving and protective, but the results, not so good, are obvious. Fatherless girl raises fatherless girl, and in trying to spare her pain, pains her. I'm repeating history in such a lit-eral way it's like a monkey exhibit. See, do.

So here's a new family tack, disclosure. I will tell this story whole, including the unsavory parts about my insanity, complicity, failure. Naturally, neither Teacher Hao nor Xiao Wang approves of my telling Julia Too about Da Ge; they're scandalized that I'm writing any of this down at all. Xiao Wang can't believe I even keep a diary. "Why write those pri-vate businesses down?" she asked me recently. "What if somebody reads them?"

"That's the idea," I said. "I want Julia Too to have an account when she's older."

"It's very American," Xiao Wang said, "you want to make the private thing public. Like reality TV."

"Except nobody wins any money," I said, laughing.

So here, a free tidbit for the sake of truth: tonight, Julia Too was asleep, our apartment sweet and peaceful, and I happily alphabetized every condiment in the kitchen.

December 1989, New York, NY

Dear Teacher,

Before she die, I learn important thing from my mother. She say do not become famous. Famous is like pig becoming fat to cook and eat. She say stay in back. But I can not enjoy life this way so I am always a trouble to her, always the loudest speaker, biggest hooligan, one who have the most ideas about what he hear and read. This make my mother afraid and my father proud, because he is famous and fat like delicious pig. Now I see the poor people in New York, with no home, sometime the crazy people. I hear both the idea of my father and mother. She say I should give money and clothes—because I have something they have nothing. My father think this begging is a job and I should not support this big boss who tell the beggar what to do. Even he is also big boss, with unhappy peasant to work for him.

I always give money. Maybe I am more the son of my mother than of my father. And I can not be successful career. My father would never be proud. The money I give really his money, but this thought do not make me guilty. Because people should share. The problem with China maybe not with Mao idea. In this way, China is like America. The idea is good, just the real thing do not work out. In Tiananmen last summer we think democracy is the highest goal and America is the amazing free life. Now I know America and New York are terrible mess with people in the street and on the train and sometime they have been released from hospital but they need hospital. I know some of them, maybe, and so do you. Maybe we all know those people. Now I think even the idea of America is not good. At least in China, we believe to help other people,

and not let them live on the street like here, people are
dying of AIDS must live in cardboard box. Chinese idea is
everyone should be equal. Everyone do the work, and share
the problem of the country and the good part. In your
America, everyone must be alone. But because of the money,
everyone who is not American and do not realized this
want to come here anyway. Million of people line up every
day to the American embassy in China and other country.
Now I live here and I feel surprising. When I come to
America, everyone say it would be heaven. But when I
arrive or begin to live here, I know that America is like the
idea of China—just an idea. Not a real revolution. Not a real
dream place. Not even democracy. Don't you agree?

Da Ge

CHAPTER FOUR

Decembers

DA GE HAD SKIPPED ENTIRE WEEKS OF CLASSES WHEN AN Embassy administrator stopped by my classroom the week before Christmas. Bonita Verna might as well have had a "Hello! My name is Bonnie!" name tag on her forehead. The first time we met, at a training seminar, she told me during the lunch break that she could type 118 words a minute. I was stacking salami on rye bread. I wondered if I could count 118 words a minute. I looked up from my sandwich and said, "That's fantastic!" and she liked me tremendously for it. I wondered what other faculty at Embassy had said.

I was writing my daily maxim on the board when Bonita bounded in. My plan was to write a maxim every day until the last day of class, when I would write, "There is nothing so useless as a general maxim." My dad always liked that sort of nerd humor.

"The devil makes work for idle hands!" Bonita read out.

"Very good, Bonita!" I said. "You're coming along."

She laughed. "Two quick things," she said, "One, this Chinese kid, Dodger."

"Guh," I said. "The G is hard."

She looked at me. I looked down at my shoes, black with silver buckles.

"He's sensitive about that," I said.

She seemed to like that. "Oh," she said. "Dah Guh."

I watched his name jag out of her mouth, all sharp and silver like cutlery. Chopped proverbs came at me: *easy come, a bird in the hand, curiosity killed, don't bite the hand, birds of a feather, a man is known, too many cooks, if you can't beat them, don't count, easy go, is worth two in the bush, the cat, that feeds you, flock together, the company he keeps, join them, your chickens*—Stop! I thought.

"Are you okay?" Bonita asked.

"Yeah!" I said, loud and unnaturally, "I'm fine. I just, uh, haven't had coffee."

"Oh, no wonder!" she said. "Well, I just stopped by because we are implementing mandatory staff meetings on Wednesday evenings from four to six on business English, TOEFL, and Cambridge exams prep. We have to certify you all and renew our ACCET accreditation. And we want people to sign up and begin preparing now."

"No problem."

"And about your new student," she paused, ready to say his name right, "Da Ge."

"Yes?" I asked.

"I need you to sign his registration form." She shuffled some papers around, and I felt relieved. She hadn't noticed anything off; this was a bureaucratic house call.

"Here." She pushed the form toward me, and I took out a pen. Then she lowered her voice for a moment. "So, what's he like?" she asked.

"Who?"

"Dah. Guh."

I shrugged. "He seems nice enough. Why do you ask?"

"No reason," she said. She took the form and slipped it into a manila folder. "How's his attendance?"

"Pretty much perfect." It was out of my mouth before I

had time to wonder why I would lie. This wasn't high school. He couldn't get in trouble for skipping; we were all adults and he paid to take my classes. But I didn't want him to attract attention.

"Oh," she said, "I just heard he was kind of—I don't know, trouble."

I swallowed. "Hmmm," I said. My students were filing in, and I was relieved to see him come in and slump into a chair at the back of the room. I glanced at Bonita as if to say, see? He's here. She nodded and left.

Then I asked the class to read from their "personal essays," on which I had given them all A's—to encourage confidence and participation. I liked for them to read out loud in class; it helped bond us together in the struggle for pronunciation. Ingyum finally raised her hand. She felt sorry for me, I was pretty sure.

"I write about cooking dinner in American for my husband's friends," she said to the class. They smiled, encouraging her. She cleared her throat and looked down at the paper in front of her. I could see my red A at the top, and felt a flush of pride.

"I am living now in America," read Ingyum. "Here, it is difficult for me to have big dinners with many people because the grocery store with ingredients is far away and different from what I want. It is not easy. It is difficult. Sometimes I think I will never be able to tell the difference, but then I cook and the difference I can tell."

She read on, covering half the food vocabulary, adjectives, and maxims we had learned so far. I clapped when she was finished. There was a knock on the door. Bonita slid in, nodded apologetically, and handed me a cup of coffee.

"Thank you," I said, "that's really sweet." She smiled and ducked out of the room.

"Anyone else want to read from an essay?" I asked. I took a sip of coffee.

No one else took pity on me so we turned to the text-book story about American protagonist Freddy's extended family at Christmas. I was impressed by how many Americanisms the textbook was able to fit into each of its absurdly simple chapters, although it would have been nice to include some holiday other than the birth of the baby Jesus. I tried to make up for it by asking my students to write about the holidays they celebrated in their countries. After class, Da Ge walked out with me.

"Where have you been?" I asked. It came out angrier than I'd meant it to, and he looked so flustered that I regretted my tone.

"Sometimes I have other business," he said sadly. "I like your class very much."

"Oh, okay."

"So where will you go now?" he asked.

I shrugged. "I don't have plans. You?"

"I don't have plan either. Do you want to go somewhere?"

"Sure," I said. "Where?"

"I don't know. Maybe some New York place."

I took him to Rockefeller Center. Unimaginative, I guess, but it was December in New York and I had a whole sparkling afternoon with Da Ge in front of me, stretching out luxuriously. It was snowing, and metallic holiday music piped through the city's speakers. Sugar smoke funneled off carts of roasting chestnuts. The Christmas tree's blue and silver jewelry was so decadent I was embarrassed for America, even though I love Christmas and used to decorate Julia One's trees until they practically toppled under the weight of my desperation for holiday cheer. Let's be honest: Hanukkah is no compensation for not getting to celebrate Christmas. My mom was religious enough that she didn't allow even a

Hanukkah twig in her house, although most of my Jewish friends got to have "Hanukkah Bushes" that looked suspiciously like Christmas trees. My dad, a lapsed Lutheran, didn't care one way or the other about holidays, so I grew up deprived of the central fun of being American.

I was chattering incoherently about this to Da Ge as we approached the plaza, pointing out plastic Santas, women in fur coats, store windows, beggars, horse-drawn carriages. The Salvation Army. I couldn't stop talking. He was either bored to numbness or overwhelmed by vocabulary. I rushed him through the ticket window and into the locker room and stuffed him into a pair of rental skates.

"It's my first time to do this, you know," he said. He looked shy, adorable, hobbling on the rubbery ground. He was such a cardiac arrest of tough and vulnerable; I had never met anyone like him. I was giddy, didn't even know what I liked so much about him exactly; he was young and sexy and—exotic? Yikes.

"It's mostly tourists," I said. "No one you'll ever see again."

"What about you?"

I took this to be flirtation. "What about me?"

"You'll see me again, so I can't—how do you say—skate ice." So he *was* flirting.

"I'm not going to judge you on your ice skating," I said, delighted.

"What you will judge?"

"That depends," I said, batting my eyes.

He looked bewildered. Maybe he hadn't been flirting. I turned my powerful hope to a new possibility: that as soon as we got onto the ice, I would twirl and leap and win his love and admiration. Then I would thank my mom for the ice-skating lessons I had hated. We stepped onto the ice, and I immediately flailed about, slipped, and grabbed first onto Da Ge, who was clutching the wall, and then, when he fell beneath me, to the wall itself. He pulled himself up and, in a macho effort to save me, tripped again, this time falling at the feet of some overdressed New Yorkers.

"Maybe we get off the ice," he suggested. So we scrambled around the rink once, holding the wall the entire way, made it to the exit, and rushed off. After we put our shoes on, we drank instant cocoa with those plastic marshmallows bobbing in it. He said his favorite holiday was for "sweeping graves." He wasn't sure of its name in English.

"*Qingming* day," he kept saying. "Relative Day? Do you have this one?"

"I don't think so," I said.

"When do you care for the tomb of your relative?"

"Um. We visit my grandparents' graves on their birthdays," I said.

"Like *qinggming* day."

"I guess so. That's kind of a weird holiday to be your favorite though, no?"

"I don't like the—how do you say—light holiday, with no meaning. *Qingming* day already that will be about my mother. The other holidays I feel not so okay to celebrate anyway. I would rather it be ordinary day so I don't have to think about that."

As if to punctuate his sorrow, Christmas break followed our date. I didn't see him for two weeks, and it's mild to say I counted the days, hours, letters. Maybe he didn't want to be intrusive, because he neither called nor showed up, and I kept a log in my wild mind of the minutes it might be until I found him again, at school, on 115th, in a diner booth, wherever—my handsome dissident ice-skater, falling all over the place.

I didn't mention Da Ge once during the holidays in 1989. My mother was ecstatic because I had "finished an entire semester of teaching at Embassy without falling off the edge of the world and because she was in sudden love with a man named Jack Benson, the CEO of a company that made soda-can-shaped vending machines. He invited us for dinner at his house in Westchester one night during Christmas break. At four o'clock. I've often wondered why non-Jews like to have dinner at four o'clock. But I didn't think my mom would like my asking. Jack Benson was a large, round guy with large, round glasses. I wanted to recite Wallace Stevens's "Le Monocle de Mon Oncle," when we met. How do people know what to filter out and what to leave in? Maybe we're permeable, and insanity is the loss of that membrane; everything floods in and out, uncontrolled.

Jack's daughter Emily was twenty-nine and pretty, with straight blonde hair jutting halfway down her back. I wondered if she looked like her mother. There were, of course, no pictures of Emily's mother in Jack's house. Just like there were no pictures of my dad anymore in our house. Emily had long legs and big, brown eyes. Describing her in my mind, I thought maybe she was horsey. But she wasn't, because she had delicate teeth.

"Wow," she said, beaming. "It's really great to meet you." I was afraid she would say, "I've heard so much about you," but she somehow knew better. Jack's son was outside pushing a snowblower, but then he came in to meet us. "Mighty brisk out there!" he said, bringing a shock of cold in with him. He had red streaks across his cheeks and was cute in a Frosty-the-Snowman way, as if had stepped from a children's book or song.

Jack Sr. had ordered food from a Jewish deli. I found it funny that we were going to eat pastrami and dill pickles with Jack and his blond angel children. Had my mom told them about me? Maybe she had told Jack late at night.

We sat to eat, my mother hovering over me, stacking food onto my plate, her arms moving like the branches of some thin, flexible tree. Her sweater had little fur cuffs at the wrists.

"So, Aysha, how's teaching going?" Jack asked. She had definitely told him.

"It's great, actually," I said. I was overwhelmed for a moment with the desire to tell the four of them everything: about Russ, Chase, Xiao Wang, Ingyum, and Da Ge. About their skits, Da Ge on ice skates, his desire for democracy, the way Xiao Wang had stopped apologizing before she spoke in my class. That I was in love with a dissident.

"My students are smart and interesting." I picked one. "One is married to a distinguished Korean political scientist. He's at Columbia for the year, and she can hardly speak English but tries valiantly to host dinner parties for him."

Jack and my mother smiled at each other. Maybe she had only told him good things, worried that if he knew the truth, he would leave her. Maybe she'd spring it on him years from now, when it was too late for him to go.

Jack Jr. said, "I led a computer-training seminar once and was such a terrible teacher that the students knew less when they left than they had when they arrived."

I laughed politely. He waited for something, and I thought maybe it was a self-deprecating response from me, but I couldn't manage one. The Embassy School made me a real person; my students had to learn from me or I would spin out of focus and be a useless being. I couldn't joke about it, even if Jack Jr. would never like me.

"Aysha is a natural-born teacher," my mother said. I worked not to roll my eyes.

"My mother got me the job," I reported, "through a friend of hers."

"Emily is working in publishing," my mother said, out

of the blue. Then everyone looked at me, waited for a response.

"Great," I said.

"Call me when you write your first novel," she said, smiling.

I liked her. I detected a light hum of sarcasm behind the things she said. She was acknowledging both the awkwardness of my situation and the dual reality: that I am someone who might write a novel and someone who recognizes that everyone thinks she might write a novel. I smiled back.

"So, Nicholas has taken up photography lately," she was saying to Jack. She turned to me, "Nicholas is my husband." I saw her in a new light and wondered why she wasn't wearing a wedding ring. She saw me looking at her hand. "I get serious rashes from rings," she said. I felt stupid and caught.

"Me, too," I said. "That's why I'm not married."

My mom looked up from her food, worried that this wouldn't go over well, but Jack Jr. was laughing big choking laughs, with his mouth open. I saw pieces of bread and some of his fillings, but was grateful for the laugh. Emily laughed too. And my mom, seeing that it was possible for things to go well, glowed with relief and happiness. It was already hard to say why, but Da Ge was the best secret I'd ever kept.

Before I reveal the details of the secret I've always liked less, I should say I know the shocking truth: lunacy is boring. Hollywood loves the nut trope, features the split-personality girl writing violent and fascinating lines on an ancient typewriter, skinny cigarettes and white-walled asylums as glamorous as she is. The bipolar father amuses his family by jumping naked on a trampoline. But anyone who's actually seen or experienced a breakdown up close (and recovered) knows that actual insanity is a slow, narcissistic slog of redundant monologues. I'll try to avoid those here.

It's best put like this: things went dark quick. The spring before I met Da Ge, I was halfway through the second semester of my senior year in college. I had stopped seeing Dr. Holderstein, rejected the drugs he suggested, and begun painting my dorm room with teeny, evenly spaced, silver acrylic bubbles. Then I failed some midterms, and within weeks of that, I was staying awake for four, five, sometimes six nights straight, outrageously happy. I had powers that no one else had or could possibly understand. I waited until it was totally irresistible and then broke the news to Adam.

"You have what?" he asked, looking at the silver bubbles.

"I know it sounds weird," I said, "wings."

"Wings," he repeated. He shook his head.

"It's not obvious from the outside," I said, "but I could fly if I wanted to. I mean, so far I haven't wanted to and that's okay—it's okay not to want to, but if I did want to, I could. I can go anywhere!" I said. "I can do anything I want to! I know everyone's mom tells her that when she's young, but for me, it's actually the case— I can—"

He stared at me. I gathered he didn't have the surge I did, and couldn't really understand. I was writing twenty-page papers when I had been assigned to write ten. I had started a novel about a teenaged dwarf who gets involved in a sex scandal and written 280 pages. I was busy all night every night; I was emaciated and in love with my hunger.

"It feels fantastic to be hungry," I explained to Adam. "I'm like a polished poem, revised down to the most essential version of myself! I mean, when you're like me, your body doesn't need as much food as other people's. My mind feeds me."

"That's terrifying," he said, pushing sandwiches at me.

But I trampled him on a race through days, powered by a force that can only be described as chemical. My mind filled the whole page in a chorus of horrible non sequiturs. There was no punctuation anywhere. My body was deprived and exhausted, but I thought I was a superhero. There were white lights everywhere, the city orbited me.

I was baking but not eating complicated cookies that involved coconut, running eight miles a day, reading the dwarf novel out loud to Adam, and handwriting letters to long-lost high school friends when I went blank. Maybe the cumulative exhaustion caught up, because everything stopped; my world blacked out.

My roommates didn't know how to rescue me. Julia had known me since our Bank Street primary school days, so for her the changes were gradual enough to seem subtle. She never believed I was sick the way Adam did. He was the one who called University Health Services, after respectfully warning me first.

"I'm calling someone, Aysha. I think you need some help, and as long as you're enrolled in school here, the university is responsible for you," he said.

I was furious. "I'm responsible for myself," I said.

"It's okay to need some help. Why deny yourself even that?"

I remember thinking—*even*? What else did Adam believe I was denying myself? He, in the final moments of a Ph.D., was older and wiser; I was a patronized, babyish undergrad. So he called the school. And they called my mom.

I woke up and spring was gone. It was sometime in June, and I was in a tall white room at St. Luke's–Roosevelt. I thought I could hear the ocean, but it was an echo of medical equipment. Adam was a sad shadow in the corner. My mother perched on the edge of my bed, so small and hurt she looked like she might snap in half.

"Where are we?" I asked her.

"You're in the hospital, sweetie," she said.

I never forgot that she said "you're" instead of "we're."

"In a city?" I asked.

"Of course, darling. We're at Fifty-Ninth and Tenth. In New York. Home."

Her voice had a fragile edge—lace doily, paper-cut snowflake.

"Are you okay? Is everything okay?" I asked. Adam was looking at the floor. People often look at the floor when they can't find answers in their minds.

"Yes," my mother finally said, "I'm here to take care of you." She looked over at Adam. "*We're* here to take care of you," she added, politely. She was not originally in favor of my dating my poetry instructor. But when Adam called health services on my behalf, my mother came to appreciate him. In both cases, she was sensible, actually. He was a wreck of a boyfriend, and yet it was right of him to intervene when he did.

The hospital lights were especially bright, spectacular over the bed. I looked down at my red-and-white-striped flannel pajamas.

"Who put these on me?" I asked my mom.

"I did," she said. "I brought them."

It all made sense. She had seen my room, read the novel, picked up my pajamas.

"What did you think of it? Did you like that she was under four feet tall? Did you see my silver collage? Did Adam tell you about the wings? Is that what this is about?" My mother stared. I knew right then that she knew nothing about me.

"You're on the outside, Mom," I told her.

I could hardly hear her voice, "The outside of what, Aysh?"

"Of me," I said. I noticed how powerful my own words were, spearing out of me. "See how my words are sharp? I own the language. I'm like a language ballerina, spinning on a linguistic dime. See? The weather!" I stood on the bed, bouncing my mother as if we were on a seesaw. I pranced to the window. "Look!" I said to her.

"At what, Aysha?"

"It's perfect outside," I said, meaningfully. She was quiet.

"It's a sign!" I told her.

"Of what, baby?"

"Of this contract I have—not with God, really, I mean it's not a religious thing. But it's a contract I have—where, if I guess things in advance, then I'll be right."

"About what?" she asked me. I was annoyed. How could I expect someone as unendowed as my mother to understand this epiphany? Adam had vanished.

"When you see my performance you'll understand!" I told my mother. Tony, who came to be my favorite nurse at St. Luke's, walked in. She wore a white skirt, white shirt, white shoes, held in her right hand a glass of water and in her left a pill. It was the "worse" medicine Dr. Holderstein had been trying to save me from, Haldol. It made me dull, made my hair fall out, and cured psychosis and delusions of grandeur. On occasion, I tried to cheek and spit it out, but there was no tricking Tony so when she said *here, honey*, I opened my mouth, put the pill on my tongue, and swallowed. Now they make those drugs dissolve in your mouth. My mother thanked Tony and watched me take the meds before turning away toward the window, but I could see parts of her face fighting one another for control. She never lets herself cry.

In the first years that followed it, my breakdown seemed blended up. Time was thick, ground with geography and relationships into a granular paste. Sometimes I could identify in it grains of what my life had been, but I couldn't hold on to anything.

Now that memory is itself only a memory. It's counter-intuitive, but the more years between it and me, the clearer my breakdown looks. So that now, even though I'm as far away as I've ever been from that time, it's easy to see the shape of it. It was just a season and a half: spring and part of the summer of 1989. My mother was a fixture in the corner, on the bed, on the phone, carrying food trays, organizing lilies on the windowsill. She brought lasagnas, baked brownies and wrapped them individually, even showed up one day with framed pictures from my high-school bedroom and hung them on the walls.

In my memory, she is all-powerful, rewiring the hospital with less fluorescent, more hopeful lights, painting, renovating, running the staff, and controlling the weather. In fact, she combed my hair every morning, brought fresh flannel pajamas, jeans, and panties printed with hearts and cherries. She fed everyone, including the other patients, and never showed up without something bright and good-smelling. The nurses kept a cot for her in my closet against the rules. Tony used to change the sheets, so there was always clean linen clinging to my mother's propped-up cot. Once my mom made a cake with Tony's name embossed in frosting.

Adam and Julia were there too, usually together. Prior to that, they hadn't really gotten along, and since I believed there was a deep connection between all people, I was glad Julia and Adam could enjoy it, too, even if only in their mundane way. Julia brought Pixie Stix and Twizzlers, which I hid under the pillow and gave away to other patients.

"You like these, right?" she asked once, holding a half-sweet Charms lollipop.

"What does it mean?" I asked her.

"What do you mean, what does it mean?"

"The half-sweet, half-sour thing. Is there something to that?"

"It means I love you," she said, but she never brought another one. Instead, she brought magazines and a battery-operated Scrabble game I should have loved but never played. Each time she came after she'd bought the game, she carried new batteries.

"The world is bigger than this game or its screen!" I told her. "I can't focus on something that small." I stood on the bed to illustrate my point.

Sometimes Adam came there at night, after visiting hours, and climbed in the bed with me, held on to me until I fell asleep. The drugs made me too dull for sex, and I wondered whether he was taking care of me or whether he was just terrified himself, and seeking comfort.

Then I got out one morning that June and left the hospital with my mom, Adam, Julia, a new shrink named Dr. Meyers, and a list of pills and strict instructions. My mother talked endlessly about stabilizing, normalizing, and "getting better," an idea she measured in milligram reductions of this or that drug. She rented the apartment on 115th, in case moving back in with her might make me feel like I had failed at life. She set up the Embassy interview with the director, Pete Batwan, an acquaintance of hers. I wanted to appear normal, so I kept the conversation on books. When he asked the surreal, "What do you see yourself doing in five years?" I said, "Reading," and he gave me the job. I was so unqualified that I had to wonder if he and my mother had ever had been lovers.

As soon as my mom went back to her life a little, I was

first overwhelmed with relief by her loosened grip, and then grief-stricken. I wondered how my father could have left without missing her. Because when my mother leaves a room, lightbulbs and heaters flash, pop, go black and cold.

"I'm like a fat old lady," I told Adam one night, "sitting in this dark room without my mom."

"You're certainly not fat," he said. Even he could hear that this had come out wrong, so he backpedaled, "It's going to be okay. You're already so much better."

I flinched. The room looked numb and creamy. "I'm lobotomized," I said. "I can't even remember where or who I am, and I'm about to start a job I'm totally unqualified for. What if I never even finish school myself? How is that better? Better than what?"

Adam swallowed. When he looked up, his eyes were red around the edges.

"Oh my God," I said. "Are you crying?"

"No." He looked down. I had seen Adam cry before. Each time, his eyes turned red around the edges five minutes before he actually cried. I always said *oh my God, are you crying*, and he always said *no*. There was comfort for both of us in this pattern.

"We need to talk," he said.

Adam had a literary interest in my breakdown. He thought he was being empathetic, but when he wanted to discuss the minutiae with me—what I had felt and thought while I was "having my breakdown"—I found it voyeuristic and annoying. Did I remember the person I'd been then? Who was I now? He was lonely, looking for a me he knew. Who could blame him? But I couldn't answer his questions and chose instead to talk about whatever bizarre tangent was most attractive to me. During this particular conversation, it was a list of "ph" words, clicking like Scrabble cubes in my mind: pheasant, phenomenon, phylum, phoenix.

"Do you want to hear the 'ph' words I'm thinking of?" I asked.

"Why can't we have a conversation, Aysha? Please?" he asked.

"I'm sorry. Please don't cry."

"Sometimes I feel like the biggest asshole ever," he said, and pushed his floppy hair out of his eyes. His glasses seemed to me to be sliding down his nose, but he made no move to fix them. Something like fear moved into my back and arms.

"The fact is, you're much younger than I am," and the feeling was up to my neck. "I don't know if I had it to do over again, whether I'd be able to change anything, but I think we need to rethink this," he said.

I spelled it out on my fingers. H-e-'s l-e-a-v-i-n-g. The "me" did not fit. But he was leaving. He was leaving me. I thought. Phenol. Pharaoh. Farah Fawcett. I thought of those plastic makeup heads, wanted to comb the straw hair on one I'd had as a kid.

"Had it to do over," I repeated. "Are we breaking up?"

"You know I love you, right?"

"It depends," I said.

"On what?" he asked.

"Are you leaving for a new freshman?"

"We didn't date until you were almost a sophomore."

"Adam, have a shred of perspective, okay?"

"No," he said, "I'm not leaving you for anyone else."

"But you will eventually date another one of your writing students."

As I spoke, his Columbia apartment zoomed into focus in my mind, tall bed in a blue room. Flannel sheets hung over the mattress edges, and Adam's foot stuck out of the right corner. He had sturdy feet. His room was visible from the street outside, on the corner of 121st and Amsterdam. His was a mini-window I had headed for hundreds of nights in a row, sundress breezing my knees in summers, scarves against my collarbone in winters. The same homeless guy sat outside the building the whole time Adam and I were together. The guy sang "Pop My Neck" whenever anyone walked by. I gave him three dollars each time I went to Adam's. I wondered whether the new girl at Adam's would know the words to "Pop My Neck." The rims around his eyes were red. My God, I said again, you *are* crying. He left. It was 8:06 P.M., warm, breezy summerish. I opened the windows and floated through the new apartment alone. Unopened boxes lined my walls. Dust had collected next to them. For the first time in as long as I could remember, I was alone. N-o-w I-'m a-l-o-n-e. I ripped a piece of tape off the top of one of the boxes, looked lovingly at the spines of my books inside. I began to take them out, place them on shelves. I wasn't despondent, I have to admit. In fact, now that there was no one left, I was thinking I could get off my meds and soar back up to the heights of mania.

Da Ge didn't call after our ice-skating date. I waited until the last day of vacation and then called Xiao Wang, asked if she'd come shopping. I was hoping she would tell me something important about Da Ge, although I wasn't sure what it might be. We met at 8th Street and 5th Avenue, where every store sold identical, badly made, and overpriced shoes.

"How's Nai Nai?" I asked, pushing open the door of my favorite place.

"Now maybe it's too cold for her, but she have a new bird—I don't know how to say. Maybe you don't have English word for this bird," Xiao Wang said.

"We probably do. Most languages have names for everything. What's it like?"

"It can talk! Maybe you can teach English to this bird!"

Xiao Wang laughed, covering her mouth. "In Chinese," she added, "We call this bird *ba ga*."

"I bet it's a mynah bird," I said.

"Mine bird?"

"M-y-n-a-h," I said, feeling the delicious fit on the five fingers of my right hand.

Xiao Wang handed me a plaid, rubber boot. "I think maybe this is okay for you?" I felt obligated to try it on and was relieved to find that the store didn't have my size.

"Maybe they have *your* size, though," I suggested.

"It's okay for me," she said, and I didn't know whether this meant that she, too, disliked the boots but thought I would like them, or that she already had boots, or that she wasn't interested in general, or that she couldn't afford new boots. I felt awkward in any case. I took a pair of red platform shoes off the display shelf and asked a salesperson for them in a 7. A stunned look appeared in Xiao Wang's eyes. Maybe they were hideous.

"Do you think these are ugly?" I asked.

"Maybe it's quite ugly," she said.

I laughed. Then I bought some black boots fast to put the trip out of its pain, and we walked all the way to City Bakery in the cold, small-talking. Once there, we sat with a tray of pretzels and hot chocolate between us. Into the silence, Xiao Wang asked, "Sometimes you are friend with Da Ge from class?" It was as if it was clear that this was the reason we were there, and she had been the one to admit it.

"He asks for some extra help sometimes," I said. I picked some salt off a pretzel.

"I think he is trouble person," she said, sipping her cocoa.

So they knew each other well, I thought. "A difficult person himself, you mean? Or trouble for others?" I asked.

"I think he will be hard friend for you to understand."

"Why ?"

"Da Ge is very Chinese."

"What do you mean?" I finished picking salt off and took a soft bite of pretzel.

"I think he have a lot of anger for China being so—closed for long time."

"Repressed," I said.

Xiao Wang took a dictionary out of her purse. "Can you show this word to me?" At the time, I thought it was funny that she had a dictionary with her all the time; now I don't know anyone who doesn't carry one. I pointed to the characters for "repressed."

"Yes," she agreed, "China repressed Da Ge. He feel he need to be free. But China is also—how do you say—also maybe inside of Da Ge. He is also repress himself too. Maybe he's not so *zhishuai*, straight to the point, like Americans."

"Straight to the point?" Da Ge said that too," I said. "I know my experience is limited, but I think you two might be the most straight-to-the-point people I've ever met."

"Oh," said Xiao Wang, looking surprised. "I think Chinese people are quiet what they think. Maybe Americans talk more because they don't feel repress."

"I don't know about that. Americans have our own angers and repressions. And we create our stories, too—it's not like being direct and being honest are necessarily the same thing. And Da Ge interrupts a lot, don't you think?" I stopped for a moment, deciding to ask and then asking, "Are you two close?" I gulped some chocolate.

Her face betrayed nothing. She bit into her pretzel, chewed, swallowed, and dabbed her lips. "We live near to each other," she said. "You know, I meet him in your class, but he and I are different. I do not feel the same anger of Da Ge about China. And I am—how do you say—balance in the mind."

"Do you think he's imbalanced?"

"He has some problem of the mind, maybe."

I wasn't sure where to go from there. She was warning me, but the words "problem of the mind," made my own problematic mind seize up.

"What kind of problem?"

"I don't know how you say that. Maybe it will be difficult for Chinese and American to understand each other."

I intentionally misunderstood this. "But we can try, right? You and I can be friends?"

"Of course. For our friendship it's very nice. Anyway, how are your meetings with Da Ge?" She smiled and her face relaxed.

"They're okay. I find him—interesting. I like his company, I guess."

She nodded. I wondered what she either knew or thought she knew. "Maybe you are lonely sometime," she said. "I am too, when I feel scary that my grandmother would die. But then I say, okay, you can always back to China." She paused. "I am happy I have already married. Even though Jin have to stay home in China, I do not feel I am alone."

"You must have gotten married quite young."

"I marry to Jin when I am twenty-one, in agreement of our parents. Now I am twenty-five."

I didn't know what to make of this. "An arranged marriage?"

"Not so official, you know. He is son of my father's friend, and they think it will be suitable for us to marry."

"Was that okay for you?"

"It's okay for me," she said. "He is very lovely boy. He will visit this summer, because I like to have a baby now. So maybe we will try that."

"A baby? Already?"

"Twenty-five years are not so young," she laughed. "If

I am thirty in China without baby, I should be dead like of old age."

I couldn't imagine even meeting a baby, let alone having one.

I laughed. "Thirty's not too old to have a baby."

"I don't mean too old to have one," she corrected. "I mean to not have one."

"Does your husband want a baby?"

"Of course! All Chinese man will want that." I noticed how neatly Xiao Wang's bangs were cut, straight across her forehead. Her eyes, lively with mischief, seemed to contradict her hair.

"Do you think your husband is the person you would have married if your parents hadn't known him?" I asked.

"But my parents do know him. They like him very much."

"No, but I mean—what if there was someone you would have loved more—I mean, if you had picked for yourself?"

"Oh. You mean is that—how do you say—romantic love. But maybe romantic love isn't the only important things."

"But were you upset that someone else chose your husband for you?"

"It's not simple. My family make this choice together, because that will affect everybody. It is too selfish if I marry someone my family do not approve, or unsuitable to our family. I am one person. I do not think my own idea is the only one."

I wanted to ask Xiao Wang what would happen if she fell in love with someone in the United States, but thought it might be too abrasive. Plus, I was worried that she was in love with Da Ge, and I didn't want to be responsible for knowing it.

That evening I told my post-hospital shrink, Dr. Meyers,

that I had a new friend who was changing some of the ways I thought about the world and myself. I liked Dr. Meyers because she wasn't Dr. Holderstein and didn't annoy me. I tried to tell her the truth. But I did not mention Da Ge.

Outside Dr. Meyers's windows, fists of snow were pounding down. By nighttime, there were thirteen inches, and I put a parka over my moon pajamas, slipped on red rain boots, and walked across Riverside, shivering into the park. Then I sat on a bench facing the street, watched headlights streak by in a blur of bright beads. Two kids stomped across the snow to a nearby playground, craning back to see their footprints under the streetlights. When one of them tipped her head back and opened her mouth, I wondered if she thought each flake she ate could never exist again. That she was gobbling up the sky. If so, she was wrong. Even snowflakes repeat. Maybe they vary on an atomic level, but it's a myth that no two look the same, just like the wrongheaded truism everyone loves about the Great Wall being visible from outer space. You can't actually see it at all.

It's December in China, and 2002, a lovely, round blue year for Julia Too and me, is almost gone. Beijing is preparing to celebrate American Christmas with Chinese characteristics: giant trees are buckling under ceramic pagodas and pandas, LED screens flicker with scenes of reindeer intercut by children eating congee and pork, and all the life-size gingerbread houses in hotel lobbies seem oddly reminiscent of courtyard-style Chinese mansions. I get to be a welcome and guiltless participant in Christmas, since almost no one here believes in Santa or Jesus either. We might as well all be Jews together.

Last week, the Saturday before Christmas, Yang Tao took me to a restaurant called Bitterness and Happiness, a place with two menus. One is meant to represent excess, and features meats, soups, and stir-fries. The other is a list of weeds and roots, reminders of scarcity. Portraits of Mao adorn the walls, and the furniture is a mix of kitsch and antique nuanced enough to suggest the owners have both irony and genuine nostalgia. Our first date was given an additional surreal kick by waitresses decked out in Santa hats, red with flashing lights and white braids.

"Happy Christmas!" said our waitress.

"You too, Santa!" I said.

Yang Tao ordered from both menus, slabs of meat from one and bark and leaves from the other. I like dichotomies, liked him.

"What do you think?" Yang Tao asked, gesturing around to the room.

"I like it. Very hip."

He sipped some tea. "I'm glad," he said.

"So, where were you during the Cultural Revolution?" I asked, picking a little Red Guard chopstick rest off the table and turning it over in my hand.

"Wow. Well, I was here. In Beijing."

"Your parents?"

"They were here, too."

"Were they party members?"

"Yes. My parents were very private. And they had good records, came from farm families. They mostly hid in our house until it was over. Why do you ask?"

There was a clipped quality to his English, a kind of accent unlike any I had heard. If I had met him on the telephone, I wouldn't have been able to tell he was Chinese. But I might have thought he was reading out loud from a book, rather than talking. His speaking, so crisp and studied, contrasted his soft, expressive face.

"I was thinking of Julia Too's dad—of something he once told me."

"Do you want to tell me about him?"

I was struck by the shrink-wording of this question, wondered what he thought of my directness. Bringing up Da Ge on a date was a rare gesture for me, so I must have wanted to tell Yang Tao about him. But I didn't really like being called out on it.

"Yeah, I guess so. Do you want to know anything about it?"

"It's up to you," he said.

"He died."

"I'm sorry."

I smiled, perhaps meanly. "I'm a widow."

"So you are," he said, in Chinese. It was the first thing he'd said in Chinese.

I switched to Chinese, too, said, "He was my student in New York right after the Tiananmen Square massacre in 1989. He was extremely, uh, disturbed. But I loved him."

I braced myself, but Yang Tao just nodded as if he had been expecting this news, and in the context of where we were and what we were doing, it made perfect sense.

"Of course you did," he said, in English. "That was a disastrous time."

A waiter brought a plate of weeds to the table. "This is from the bitterness menu," Yang Tao grinned, putting some on my plate. I picked at them with my chopsticks, trying for delicacy and failing.

"How is it?" Yang Tao asked, taking a bite of weeds for himself.

"Good. Did they have access to sesame oil and sugar and what else is in here—plums—during the bitterness era?"

"No. That's—how should I say it—the tasty sauce of modernization."

Tasty sauce of modernization! I decided right then that I would show him off to Xiao Wang. They hadn't had a chance to speak at Thanksgiving, and I wanted to know what she thought. She would no doubt tell me he was "very Chinese."

As Xiao Wang once put it when she was still my student at Embassy in New York, "When a Chinese man falls in love, instead of judging her, he would become the fan and love whatever the girlfriend is. Though, after marriage it could be another story."

January 1990, New York, NY

Dear Teacher,

When my parents are gone for the Cultural Revolution I live
with my fat grandmother and my grandfather. My grandmother
smoke cigarettes and die because of this. Or maybe because she
is fat. Sometimes the heart stops for all that fat. My grandfather
very thin, almost like a tree. Before she die, my grandmother
tell me a story of my mother, of what she say when I'm arrive
to the world—at least it's a son. My Grandmother tell me other
thing, too, like go get her tobacco because she roll cigarette
herself. And even though her finger are also fat, she can roll it
perfectly. Maybe because she roll so many dumpling. She say do
not marry a person like your Grandfather who only read all day
because they don't help with the practical life. But she is proud
that my Grandfather is intellectual. I never saw them fight even
one time. During those years I asked my grandfather what he
was doing sitting in his chair, eyes close, but not asleep. He
whisper to me I am reading in my mind. And I said what? And
he tell me he read his books so many times before that he have
pages already in his memory. All he have to do to read them
forever, is close his eyes to look inside his head.

My only friend then are some children, and I spent all the time
to play games with them. Once, we are so hungry that we thief a
bag of sugar from our house and eat sugar sugar sugar from our
hands. That was the sugar for everyone to use for more than two
months and we eat all of it. I am the leader and the other kid call
me big brother. I am strong and handsome and popular, even with
my sugar teeth and hooligan habit. Maybe to American girl like
you, this seem like the bad time for China, but to me it is also the
charming time, before my own bad time come.

　　　Da Ge

CHAPTER FIVE

Januarys

✳

BY JANUARY OF 1990, THE WORD "CHINA" HAD BEGUN TO LEAP from the page at me, the way misspellings and mistakes would later turn red after Microsoft took over parts of my mind. In 1990, I learned to read the papers carefully.

The world can shift quickly. I had never considered China; it had always been a faraway place with its own literature and way of folding the world into compartments. Anything outside of the English alphabet had always existed only outside of me.

But once Da Ge and Xiao Wang were in a conversation with me about China, everyone else seemed to be, too, from random Chinese people on the subway to the *New York Times*: China rejected criticism of its human rights record. Ten thousand students had been executed or imprisoned following Da Ge's protest, all of them, I imagined, his best friends. Chinese officials called the uprising "counterrevolutionary," but the *Times* implied that the students were revolutionary heroes, and for me, they were embodied in Da Ge and, later, in Xiao Wang. Even though he was crazy and she claimed not to be interested in politics. The government believed that the students had tried to overthrow a legitimate government, one that was itself "revolutionary." The students believed they were leading a revolution and were true patriots. I believed Da Ge had been delivered to me fresh from the battlefield. One Chinese official said that there was "no such thing as political prosecution in China," and that "therefore there is no such thing as political prisoners." This seemed to me to be a clean, linguistic kind of logic. I wondered if Da Ge resisted such clauses or fell prey to them himself. Of course the answer was both, and that's true of me as well.

Old Chen likes to take Julia Too to the neighborhood where Da Ge grew up. He's proud of the staggering progress that has transformed Beijing from historic to space age in a single decade. Their old courtyard house is gone; in its place is a towering skyscraper. Our favorite sushi bar is less than a mile from the old-school alley where Da Ge was born. His street has been expanded into a wide boulevard down which privately owned Mercedes, including Old Chen's, speed remorselessly. Gone are the donkey carts piled with pig innards, as well as houses without heat or running water. Even Beijing's poorest citizens, migrant workers who crack their spines under the weight of modernization's worst work shifts—constructing, sewing, cleaning, massaging—say they're better off than they were in the 1980s or '90s.

I know better than to wish for a return to Da Ge's China. But I can't help being nostalgic for what I'll never get to see or know: what his neighborhood and house looked and smelled like then. Where he walked, played, carried his book bag to school. Who his mother was. Who he was.

Shannon complains good-naturedly about her Chinese mother-in-law, says the old woman snatched Sophie from the hospital and has spent every second of Sophie's life hovering over them since the instant Sophie was conceived. I would love a Chinese mom-in-law, bossing me about not bathing Julia Too until she's old enough to tolerate the water, feeding her the right balance of hot- and cold-inducing foods, and advising about nursing, weaning, even bringing up a twelve-year-old. I'd love Zhang Sun's mom. Or Da Ge's mom. She might have been another Naomi. A lasagna-making, Zabar's-shopping, teaching, interrupting, bowling-you-over grandma like my mom. Of the dumpling, noodle, drunken chicken, Sunday morning tai-chi-chuan variety instead. Maybe she'd have taught Julia Too to fan-dance in Ritan Park. Julia Too would have had a name for her, like Nomi.

At least she has Old Chen to draw out the zodiac, fly kites, teach her *cheng yu*, four-character Chinese maxims. Last time we visited the place where Da Ge grew up, Old Chen said proudly to Julia Too, "*Yi ri qian qiu*," or "One day, a thousand autumns," meaning look how fast and brilliantly China is changing. It's among his favorite sayings, and usually Julia Too just repeats it back obediently. But that day she responded, "*Yi ri san qiu*," or "One day, three autumns," and Old Chen's mouth opened but no more words came out. His hands, which had been gesturing enthusiastically, fell to his sides. Julia Too took one of them and held it in hers, walked that way for a while. I asked her later what "One day, three autumns" means, and she said, "It's like when you love someone but they're gone from your life, so you miss them a lot. Then one day feels like three years. Or something."

"Where did you learn that?" I asked.

Julia Too shrugged. "At school."

"What made you say it today?"

"I thought Old Chen would be proud I knew it."

It seems ironic now, from this glistening city, that just as China began its lift and fix after Tiananmen, Da Ge started spiraling. By January of 1990, intellectuals were on their way back to Beijing, less concerned with getting arrested than they were with getting jobs. Nixon visited. Kissinger

visited. China stamped out "six evils," including prostitu-
tion, pornography, the sale of women and children, drugs,
gambling, and "profiteering from superstition." I wondered
what the last one meant.

I pored over articles that winter in New York, searching
for clues into his inner landscape. I needed a project, found
him fascinating, couldn't wait to see him back at Embassy
the first week of class in January. I hoped to joke about my
discovery that China had identified five "great loves" for its
citizens: "the motherland, the Communist Party, the socialist system, the capital city, and work." I loved that China
counted, was reminded of myself. I even wrote a card for Da
Ge in which I proposed a sixth love, but I never sent it.

"Welcome," I said our first day back in class. Everyone
was seated; he was there. I forced myself not to stare.

"Welcome," my students said.

"Vacation," I said. "Last week I was on vacation."

"Vacation," they said. "Last week I was on vacation."

"Let's warm up before we talk about our vacations—
with a quick dictation," I said. "Everyone take out a piece
of paper." Some of them took out paper. The others watched
and realized that they were supposed to take out paper.
Eventually, everyone had a sheet. When they were all looking down, poised like track stars to write fast once I spoke,
I had my first chance to look at Da Ge. He was wearing
jeans and a blue zip-up sweatshirt with his usual shiny black
shoes. He wasn't exactly how I had pictured the love of my
life, a furious beanstalk of a Chinese student with whom I
shared a vocabulary of five hundred words. Yet in spite of
the distance between him and a dream boyfriend, seeing him
again did not make me want him less.

"One. How was your vacation?" I said. The scratching
of pencils filled the room.

"One," I repeated, "How was your vacation?"

"Two," I said, "Was your vacation relaxing or stressful?" Everybody wrote.

I was calm and in control. I walked toward the back of the classroom, making my way to Da Ge, checking their papers without being disruptive. Some of them finished early, looked up and smiled. "Two. Was your vacation relaxing or stressful?"

Da Ge had written nothing on his paper. There was a drawing in the center of the page of a long rope. A stick figure hung from it.

"Three." I said, "My vacation was exciting and fun, thank you."

"Three," I repeated. "My vacation was exciting and fun, thank you."

Da Ge looked up at me, unsmiling. His eyes were so hard and red they looked like marbles. I cleared my throat. "Four," I said, "I'm glad to be back at school."

They turned in their papers, and we talked about whom we had visited and what holidays we had celebrated. "Naomi is my mother, and I spent the Jewish holidays with her and her boyfriend Jack. We celebrated Hanukkah, a Jewish holiday." Then I said, "Who can make up a sentence that involves both family and holidays?"

"He is my uncle," said Russ. "At Christmas, I do not love him."

"Excellent," I said. "Why don't you love your uncle, Russ?"

"Because I do not have uncle," he said. His eyes were wide and earnest.

Once I started laughing, I couldn't stop. Maybe it was the tension over Da Ge, or my feeling that something bad was about to happen, a feeling I got the moment I met Da Ge and never lost until something terrible did happen. But I was uncomfortable laughing in my classroom, and didn't want

Russ to think I was making fun of him, so I pretended to be coughing and excused myself. In the hallway, I bent over the drinking fountain and heard my mother's voice say, "Don't touch your lips to the drinking fountain," which made me laugh more. I wondered what Dr. Holderstein would have thought of my mother's obsession with not putting her lips on a drinking fountain. I was still laughing when Bonita, the ever-cheerful Embassy administrator walked up.

"What's wrong?" She asked, whacking me on the back.

"Nothing," I said, "Nothing. I just had a coughing fit. I'm perfectly fine now."

She hit me on the back again, this time lightly. "Well, take care of yourself," she said, and walked away.

Back in the classroom, the atmosphere had changed.

"Sorry about that," I said. Everyone was silent. "What's wrong?" I asked them, but nobody said anything. I stared at them, bewildered. Xiao Wang had her hands over her eyes. I walked to her desk. "What is it?"

No one spoke. "Can someone please tell me what's going on?" I said.

Russ said, "Xiao Wang and Da Ge fight." He was staring at his hands.

"About what?" No one said anything. At a loss for what to do, I opened my book. I'm just going to start the lesson again, I thought, I'm just going to—

"Fuck you." Da Ge said. I couldn't tell who he meant. He pushed his chair back and stood so fast that he knocked it over behind him. Xiao Wang moved her hands from over her eyes to over her ears. Chase stood up, as if to warn Da Ge that he'd protect any one of us Da Ge chose to attack. I was not afraid that he'd do anything.

"It's okay," I told Chase. "Da Ge, maybe you should go outside." My voice was absurdly high and came from somewhere other than my body.

"I am outside," he said. He swung a hand at the class, including and insulting us.

"You fuckers are inside. I am outside."

When he came to see me that night, I was already standing by the window, watching for him. He pulled up, and I went downstairs and stood on my stoop in the snow. Streetlights reflected off the wet pavement, making the night unnaturally bright. Da Ge saw me and raised his head almost imperceptibly. He did not smile or wave. Soon he was standing silently in front of me, his helmet on his right arm. His head seemed to weigh his neck down. He looked at his shoes, losing their shine in the slush.

"You okay?" I offered. I reached out a bit toward him, but he didn't seem to notice the gesture. My arms felt heavy. Would they drag when we walked inside?

"I am sorry for class today," he said.

"What happened?"

"It's a lot story."

"A long story?"

He looked up, ready to fight, but then blinked instead. I saw him give up.

"I mean long story," he said. It was the last time I ever corrected him.

Upstairs, we were less formal. But he didn't sit on the futon with me, just took a seat at the table and rested his chin on his open hands.

"I have some trouble," he said.

He feels watched, I thought, potentially ambushed, so I stood and put on an old CD of my dad's, Vivaldi cello sonatas. I wanted music with no words.

"Do you listen?" he asked me.

"To the CD, you mean?" I said.

"No," he said, "to me."

"Yes!" I said, too loud. "Of course I do. I wish you would talk more."

He swallowed, and I watched his throat move. "I wish you listen more," he said.

I was hurt by this and worked not to be defensive. Don't hurt him, my mind reminded me. He's not entirely wrong. I looked up, tried to meet his eyes.

"I do listen to you. I like to listen to you."

"But not only," he said.

I was quiet, spelling. I d-o-n'-t l-i-s-t-e-n w-e-l-l. Fifteen letters and true.

"Aysha?" He was looking down at the floor. "It's okay I stay here tonight?"

I took this to be the most overt pass that had ever happened and felt reckless and thrilled. "Sure," I said, trying for nonchalance. I shrugged. "If you like."

"I can sleep here," he said, and patted the sofa next to him. So maybe it wasn't a pass. When his hand came down on the sofa, I watched it, wanted to see the blood move through his veins. I wanted to pick his hand up off the couch and put it under my shirt. He looked disturbingly calm. He was difficult to follow, unlike most guys I knew. When Adam lied, which it turned out he did frequently, it was so obvious that his pants burst into flames. When Da Ge spoke, I had to inspect him for signals of dishonesty, and then I couldn't read them. He was like a book with whiplash plot twists. Choose your own adventure, written in a hybrid of English and Chinese.

"I have sheets and extra pillows," I said, backing into the hallway to get bedding.

"No," he called. "Please, no trouble."

"It's no trouble at all, really," I told him. I sounded like an English teacher. I opened the door to the closet and managed to collect a set of flannel sheets from behind the air conditioner. Back in the living room, Da Ge had stood up. He was looking at black and white photos on the wall above my table. I began making the futon into a bed.

"It's you?" he asked, pointing to a faded photo of my brother Benj and me in full-length sleepers with feet; I am on Benj's lap, my head thrown back, laughing. He has one arm around my waist and is tickling me with the other. Sam the doll, now Julia Too's, is lying on my lap, her plastic eyes blinked shut. Benj is six, I am three, and Sam is new—we look as if we've been stacked like blocks in order of descending size.

I nodded at Da Ge, swallowed the rise in my throat. I stopped fanning the top sheet over the futon, let it fall into a wrinkled mess. Da Ge was watching me carefully.

"Do this question make you feel unhappy?" he asked.

"It's just a long time ago," I said.

"You are fat and white," he said, smiling.

I stared at him. The CD began skipping, and I went to fix it.

"*Pang pang bai bai de,*" he said in Chinese. "It's good things for a baby."

I liked it when he spoke Chinese to me. I had written down "*pai* the *ma pi* of America," in case I ever found myself in a conversation with a Chinese person and needed to talk about horse-ass patting. Of course, I had no idea at the time how well it would serve me. As with fat fat white white, which I've used to describe every baby I've met for a decade.

"Who is this?" Da Ge asked, pointing at Benj. In the photo, Benj's hair is standing on end in a halo of static. Maybe our mother had just pulled a sweatshirt over his head. I felt my heart move up closer to throat. I sat on the messy sheets, put my hands in my lap. They looked like they were someone else's.

"That's my brother, Benj," I answered, and the grief in my voice was so revealing that I called upon my English teacher voice to hide me for a moment. "Do you have any brothers or sisters?" I asked.

Now Da Ge's eyes clouded over. He looked mean, and I remembered how he'd seemed the first time he'd come to class. But when he said, "No, it's just me," his voice was so dark blue that it reminded me who he was now. Or who I thought he was.

Maybe he wanted to hide, too, because he said, "China has a rule of this. You can only have one kid. For population." Of course this rule hadn't been in effect when he was born, but this was before I knew that.

Then he stood up straighter all of a sudden, and looked oddly formal.

"Aysha," he said. "I need to have certain history of my life, and for this I must become American."

"I don't understand."

"Maybe I like to marry with you, so I can be American. I know it's a rude favor. I am sorry for this. Maybe you cannot agree to it. Or maybe I can pay you some money?"

I stood up, reeling and dazed, felt myself catapulted into a soap opera. I sat back down. It was as if as soon as I didn't know what to do with my words, I also lost track of what to do with my body. I gathered some of the sheet in my hand and squeezed it. "We hardly know each other," I heard my voice say. I looked around the room as if a teleprompter might appear and guide me.

"I have to tell you that I take your class so I can meet you," he confessed. "Sometimes even before that, I follow you. I feel I like to know you, to marry with you."

I stood again and began pacing. I considered walking straight out the door and into Julia's apartment, telling her everything, saving myself. Because the "I follow you" was even less what I had been expecting than the proposal, and it scared me.

"I think what you need is not to be a stalker," I said.

Some light in his face went out. "I don't know this word," he said dejectedly.

What offended me most, I know now, was the offer of money. Right off, I relished, in the way only a cracked person could have, the idea that Da Ge wanted to marry me. I would be the protagonist of a bodice ripper, the wife of a Chinese dissident, his savior. We would be madly in love. If he hadn't offered me cash or called it a favor, I could have coolly omitted the awkward fact that we had met three months before. Because I found Da Ge, in all his wanna-be-thugged-out bookish splendor, fascinating. I had started to dress more sexily, to consider before teaching whether I had lipstick on. I took time in the mornings to slick my bangs with various gels. I dreamed of going to China with him, trading my broken life for a new, improved, international one. Or at least seeing *The First Emperor* together at the IMAX. Marrying him would mean the effort I had put into seducing him had paid off; it would be less sordid than simply having sex with my student, which I thought I couldn't resist in any case, should it come up. I would be like one of those teachers who seduces her student and gets pilloried by American society even though men bed their female students like unapologetic rabbits and no one seems to mind.

I went to get the red, plastic Chinese dictionary. When I came back, holding it, Da Ge's eyes widened. "Why you have this?"

"So I can understand you."

"I can go now," he said. "It's okay."

"No, no. Stay."

I sat down, thumbed through the dictionary.

"What is the word you use?" Da Ge asked me. There

was no entry for "stalker," and I couldn't think of a synonym. I found stalk and walked over to the table. I stood behind him and showed him the entry, pressing my fingernail into the soft page just beneath the word. His hair smelled like peppermint shampoo.

He looked at the entry under stalk. "This is like grass?"

"No, wrong word," I said, annoyed even though the whole stupid thing was my fault. "That's a different kind of stalk. I can't find the right one in there. Forget it. A stalker is someone who watches someone else."

"A bad word," he said.

I shrugged.

"It's okay for me to go," he said.

"Stay."

The phone rang. "I'll let the machine get it," I said, hoping it wasn't Adam.

"Where are you?" said Julia's voice. "Call me as soon as you get this." I wondered how I would both not call her until the next day and not tell her anything. I wondered why I didn't want to tell her anything about this.

"Do you want to sleep?" Da Ge asked. He said nothing else about getting married. I didn't know what he meant by sleep.

"Uh, sure."

"If I stay, it's okay I shower?" Da Ge asked.

"Yes, of course." I handed him a towel and a washcloth, and put a quilt my mother had made out of my baby clothes over the futon. Whenever she made her bed at home, I liked to jump on it immediately and lie there, flat, seeing how little damage I could do to the fresh blankets. Da Ge stood quietly, watching me. I hoped he would leap onto the bed and ruin it. But he hadn't moved at all. I considered offering to help him shower, but wasn't sure I could get the nuance right.

"Good night," he said, and started toward me.

"Good night."

He crossed by me, giving me the sense of an edge—of something straight and horizontal, a wall, maybe or a window. Da Ge had a sharp, glassy flavor about him, more a metal color than a smell. I heard him close the bathroom door, turn water on. I went into my bedroom and read the first page of *The Remains of the Day* over and over until I heard Da Ge back in the hallway. Then I turned off my light, cracked the door, and peered out. He had wrapped the towel around his waist. Now he sat on the futon, his shoulders wide and thin. He looked like a wasp ready to lift off. The skin over his stomach was stretched taut, the muscles underneath it square and even. Then he folded so that his elbows rested on his thighs and he held his face in his hands.

I should have gone in there, apologized for the awkwardness, said I would marry him or asked for a week to consider. I should have climbed into bed with him. We both had a lot of face at stake, which seems stupid now, but doesn't protecting your face always seem idiotic with hindsight? I, for one, keep doing it, even knowing. Back then, I wasn't even considering what motivated me. I guess I didn't want to risk his turning me down for sex, even though he had just proposed marriage. It's ludicrous, but I couldn't be brave. And I figured we had all the time we needed. I crept backwards into my room, took a sleeping pill from my nightstand, and swallowed it without water.

I woke the next day with an icy start. Da Ge was gone and the futon was made. There was a note on it: *Thank you to Aysha.* At the bottom were two Chinese characters, and underneath them, *Da* and *Ge.* I put it in my jewelry box and called Julia.

"I was sleeping when you called last night," I lied.

"Was someone there?" she asked.

I thought for a minute and then said yes, Adam had been here.

"No," she said.

"How do you know?"

"He called me last night to see if I wanted to have a drink. He said he wanted to talk about you. He was worried. That's why I called. I wanted to talk to you about it."

"Really?" I asked. "The truth is, he slept here the night before."

"Yeah," she said. "He said so." We both waited.

"Come over," she said. "I'll make you coffee."

I put on sweatpants and went to her apartment. She answered the door in tights.

"Why this?" I asked.

"I have an audition," she said.

"Julia!" I said. "That's great! Is that what you called to tell me last night?"

"Sort of," she said. "There's something else, too."

I sat down on a stool. I had sat in this precise position thousands of times. I wondered if this was the thousand and eighteenth or the thousand and thirtieth. Julia turned to the stove, poured boiling water into a French press. The smell of coffee filled the room. Suddenly, I hated her.

She was silent, but her shoulders were moving in a gesture I recognized instantly.

"Why are you crying?"

"It's complicated," she started, "what I have to tell you."

I decided not to help. Time dragged across the kitchen, carrying a stick with its possessions tied to the end. It was a crayon-drawn mouse, moving out. Tom and Jerry.

"I saw Adam last night," Julia said.

"Right. You said he called. So?"

"I slept with him."

In spite of myself, I felt a laugh rising up into my mouth. "You're kidding," I said.

"Aysha, I'm so sorry. I can't—I didn't mean—It was just—it was a mistake."

She threw some monosyllabic words around—drunk, we, fucked, up—I heard the consonants catching in her throat like metal hooks. Mistake words have a lot of *k*'s in them. They'd fucked? Yuck. I tipped the stool forward and walked out, took the stairs back down to my place. I swallowed, thought I might digest my heart since it had been in my mouth. Julia and Adam? Something about it reminded me of the way most people feel about their parents having sex. It was dirty, disconcerting, off. And they were my only friends. It was wretched that they had betrayed me together. Who would be on my side about it? I could hear Julia calling down the stairs after me. I closed the door behind me and stood in my hallway, thinking.

"I'm sorry," said Da Ge, and I realized that he had appeared from the living room and that I was crying. "I bring breakfast," he said, holding a paper bag. "Some bagel."

I wondered why he hadn't mentioned in his note that he was coming back. And how he'd gotten back in. I wiped my eyes.

"Why?" he asked me.

"It's nothing," I said. "I went running. The wind. You know. Thank you. For the bagels, I mean. Uh, let me take a quick shower. Maybe you can toast them? I'll make coffee when I get out. Oh, wait, you don't drink coffee, do you? I'll make tea. Just wait here a second, don't go." I heard my mania, mostly suppressed for the last six months, surface in my voice like a friend who'd been abroad. Welcome back, I thought.

In the bathroom, I reached into the shower and turned the water on, stripped my sweatpants off, and climbed in. Within five seconds, Julia was knocking on the front door. I climbed out of the shower and grabbed a hand towel to hold over myself as I collided with Da Ge in the hallway. I put a finger over my mouth, and shook my head toward the door.

"Don't open," I mouthed.

He nodded and backed away. I turned into the bathroom, wondering, in spite of my misery, whether he had taken a look at me in my small towel. I turned the shower up full blast and sat down in the tub, figuring I'd count the streams of water as they came out of the nozzle. I was at 83 when Da Ge opened the door. He pulled the curtain back and I shrieked.

"It's okay," he said, "don't feel nervous."

Then he turned the water off and bent down. He was holding a towel. He reached into the tub and picked me up, wrapped me in the towel like a child. Then he carried me to my bedroom and set me on the bed. He covered me up and then he lay down, too, on the outside of the quilt and put his arms around my mummified body. We didn't speak, and after a while, I fell asleep. By the time I woke up, he was gone.

Much later, I would ask Da Ge why he had come to get me in the bathtub that day, and he would teach me a Chinese grammatical construction I now know better than I ever knew him: *ni shangxin sile*. "You were heartbroken to death."

Julia Too spent New Year's of 2002 in New York with my mother. She'll turn twelve in February. and she and my mother propagandized me for months about this trip, finally convincing me that that means she's old enough to fly alone. In honor of her first solo flight, I taught her "Avanglavish," a secret language my aunt taught me and Julia One in third grade. We practiced until we were so fluent we could have hours of conversation about other people in front of them. It was a scrumptious tool. Avanglavish is a simple formula, really: just add an "av" before every sounded syllable of English. Julia becomes "Javulaviava," Lili becomes "Lavilavi," elbow "Avelbavow."

I told Julia Too that she and Lili (whom she decided to teach) have to be nice with the language, that they're not to use it to exclude other girls. I don't know how that will work out, really, or what the point is of having a secret language if you can't use it to keep secrets, but I thought I should remind her of the rule about being nice to other girls anyway. We were packing. I was barely stifling my panic at the impending week away from her, a prospect that sent a vacuum of blood away from my heart.

"Havair bravush," she said, putting her hair brush in the suitcase. Then she asked, "What about Chinese Avanglavish? Chavinglaivsh? Navi havao is *ni hao*!" She ran to call Lili, and I thought I'd like to tell Yang Tao about Chavinglavish. He'd appreciate it.

When Julia Too came back, I asked her why she'd chosen Lili, and she knitted her brow. "I don't know about Phoebe yet," she said.

"Don't know what?"

"Mom?" She fiddled with the ear of a ratty teddy bear. "Was my dad a criminal?"

"No," I said. "What gave you that idea?"

"Phoebe said everyone in Beijing knows that."

"I see. It's not true." I said it without pausing, and she nodded, ready to believe me.

"I'm sorry Phoebe is making up stories that hurt you," I said, trying to hide my horror. "You should try as hard as you can not to worry what other people think."

"But Phoebe isn't other people. She's Phoebe," Julia Too said. "And she was just telling me so I would know what everyone was saying."

I could hear that this was something Phoebe had said. "What about Sophie?"

"Sophie's opinion is important, too."

"What is Sophie's opinion?"

"She always agrees with everything Phoebe says."

"I see. What about Lili?"

"She doesn't even go to our school."

"But is she on your side?"

"Yes." That night, I sat up watching Julia Too sleep in a bed crowded with a stuffed lion, two monkey puppets with Velcro arms wrapped around each other's necks, and a doll named Sam. I remembered Julia Too's baby life, how many mornings my mother showed up, packed Julia Too and the diapers, wet wipes, sippy cups, Cheerios, balls, sunscreen, hats, and countless other necessities, and went to the park so I could read, bathe, or sleep. So I could get sane and finish Columbia. So I could eat, teach, manage. Even after she married Jack, my mom was always everywhere all the time. And I don't know whether it was in his nature or my mom tutored him, but Jack is loving and generous too, signs cards Grandpa Jack. So how big a favor is it to put Julia Too on a plane to see them? My mother would pick her up at JFK. Julia Too would be fine. I kept reminding myself. There are so many ways in which I do not want Julia Too to be like me. I'd like her to feel safe. Whenever she cried as a baby, I snatched her up immediately. What was in store for her seemed already so terrible; how could I let her weep over lesser tragedies?

Unlike me, Julia Too was thrilled about her first solo flight. At the airport she patted her backpack when she said good-bye to me, as if to say, "I have everything I need; I'll be fine." It was a gesture I found stunningly mature, even though I knew the bag held Sam-the-doll, a Hello Kitty wallet, lip gloss, *The Perks of Being a Wallflower*, and vanilla milk. Julia Too tapped her pink cell phone.

"I'll call you as soon as Nomi picks me up," she said, and walked away, turning around once to grin and blow me a kiss. Her bangs flopped over her eyes.

Seventeen hours later, in my Beijing evening, the phone rang. I was in Julia Too's room organizing stuffed animals by color: shelf of black and white penguins, pandas, beagles, seals, polar bear. A rainbow basket held red Elmo, an orange doll, two yellow ducks, the green monster, blue cat, hugging purple monkeys. I had done the dollhouse first; each miniature creature waited in place for Julia Too's return—at the table, in the bathtub, in bed. She was outgrowing her toys faster than I was my love of arranging them. Her young-adult books were alphabetized by author, the kid ones in order of descending size. I leapt up and ran for the phone, tripping over a stack of pink pigs and the dress-up trunk.

Julia's voice sounded close, and I could hear my mom's whole place through the wires: swirly antique rugs, blue velvet couch, the lunch I knew she had already set out, had probably been considering for weeks even though it was just for her, Jack, and Julia Too. Lox, tomatoes, bagels from Absolute on 108th, homemade quiche, rugelach. I could see my mother's hands under a stream of water from the silver faucet. Her kitchen island with its bowls of apples, avocados, olives, and lemons; my Grandma Leah's painted glass shakers full of salt and pepper. I even imagined my dad, leaning against the counter with a cup of coffee in one hand, mail in the other, laughing. I closed my eyes.

"I don't have the jet lag!" Julia Too shouted gleefully, a rare trace of Chinglish in her English. "Nomi and Jack are taking me to Rockefeller. They got me my own skates! I won't have to rent skates at the China World anymore!"

Her voice on the phone gave me a rush of hope—that she's tougher, better adjusted than I ever was or will be, in spite of Da Ge and his genes. That she's an unbroken girl.

I hung up happy, finished her room, put on tight jeans and a red sweater, and headed for a place called "Intercourse Bar," my favorite for its transliterated drinks and straight-forward ambitions. I ordered Jack Daniels wi-si-ki on the rocks, and called Yang Tao from my cell phone. The numbers lit up as I pressed each one. 137 01234 8898, round, even numbers, all dark blues and purples. Auspicious numbers in Chinese, where colors for the digits make better sense than ever.

He showed up twenty minutes later, breezing in with the street on his clothes and face. He drank Coke with no ice and smiled at me, the lines around his mouth inviting. My whiskey was smoky and tasted like flowers. I thought I would like to kiss him.

I said, "Julia Too invented a language. Chavinglavish. Your name is Yavang Tavao." I was flushed from the heat of my drink.

Yang Tao laughed. "Is yours "Avai Shava?"

Call me nerdy, but I found his immediate fluency in Chavinglavish sexy. So when he said, "Gaven wavo havui javia, bava," or *come home with me*, I did.

His apartment was clean, and his body, lovely. He said less than any boyfriend in the history of the world ever has, inspiring me to wonder even more what he might be think-ing. I did not ask, because I did not want him to think I har-bored the implied desire of that question, that the answer be "you." In fact, I actually wanted to know what he was thinking, even, and especially, if it wasn't about me. Maybe it was the shape of the morning we woke up to, the color of a certain Chinese character, or the sound of winter light singing into his windows. Maybe he was thinking about last year's taxes. Any glimpse of his private mind would have been fine.

February 1990, New York, NY

Dear Teacher,

This week we should write about food. I know it's not modest, but you already know I am excellent cook, like many Chinese men. I make delicious fish, with scallions and ginger. And succulent chicken—drunken chicken. I soak it in complex sauce.

Chinese men are help women. In class, when you talk about the right of women, that men should consider women equal, I think this is American problem. In China, in 1949, the government already say that men and women are equal. In China men like to cook for girlfriend and wife, even my father who is selfish busy person still like to cook. Chinese men are helpful. Even though sometime, in backward place in China, maybe in the peasant village, some men might feel angry to hear that the wife have sex business with other men. Then I read in American newspaper that maybe he will throw this kind of acid on her face. I never know this when I live in China. Maybe only in America they report that Chinese men do this action. I think American newspaper use this story to hide the story of American men, what American men do to American women. It must be happens everywhere, especially in violent society like this. I wonder in China do we print story about American men. America is hypocrite and bully.

Even American food is not kind. And also not tasty. Who wants his own plate of meat and several potato with no sauce?

    Da Ge

CHAPTER SIX

Februarys

✳

DA GE USED TO LEND ME BOOKS. "I WANT TO GIVE TO YOU some things," he told me one day before class at Embassy. "*Diary of a Madman*, and *The True Story of Ah Q*. It's both by Lu Xun. He will teach you about China, even though the books are maybe quite old fashioned." He handed me one of them, held on to the other.

"Thank you," I said. "I'll read them and maybe we can talk about them."

"Maybe I can read it to you now." He opened the book in his hands.

"Yeah? Of course. That would be nice."

I still remember the single passage Da Ge recited, standing in front of my desk. It was Tuesday, February 6, 1990, and he read from *The True Story of Ah Q*, in which Lu Xun's protagonist, Ah Q, "changes defeat into victory" by beating himself up. "Raising his right hand he slapped his face hard twice, so that it tingled with pain. After this slapping his heart felt lighter, for it seemed as if the one who had given the slap was himself, the one slapped some other self, and soon it was just as if he had beaten someone else—in spite of the fact that his face was still tingling. He lay down satisfied that he had gained the victory. Soon he was asleep."

The only word Da Ge mispronounced was "tingled," in which he substituted an *r* for the *l*. Other than that, it was brilliantly executed. He didn't ask or add anything, just took a seat in the back of the room and left immediately when I dismissed the class. Even so, and even though I never learned to like Lu Xun, I took that first taste of a book in Da Ge's voice to be an invitation. I wanted to follow him somewhere, maybe to China.

It was Xiao Wang who taught me to read Chinese for real. She found Teacher Hao when I moved to Beijing, and she read me everything from Mao's poems to letters posted by students on the Democracy Wall in 1957 and Wang Shuo's short stories. She showed me a folder of love poetry her father had written when he and her mother were young. Xiao Wang said they had a political undercurrent, like most Chinese poems. We watched illicit films from the time when she—and Da Ge, I guess—were teenagers, including one called *Frozen*, about a guy who fakes his death to see how people will react. Everyone mourns horribly at first, and he's satisfied, but then within a few weeks, the world's parts fall back in place. The sun still sets and rises; his friends recover, move on. Furious at having been forgotten, he revives.

I always find Da Ge in Chinese books and movies. Sometimes he's the satirist, coolly observing and narrating. Others, he's the earnest, innocent victim. Often he's an extra, a few scattered sentences or a single line. But he's always around, because for me, he's endless characters. I can't help it. Even though Da Ge once made fun of me for this, I still think of him as the dissident he wanted to be, a skinny one-student army standing in front of some tank even he couldn't quite identify. Trying to stand up to a larger power and failing. The only constant is he's always gone by the end of the story.

At an Embassy staff meeting that February, Bonita Verna introduced the director, Pete Batwan, as if we didn't all know him already. I glanced around the room, wondering first whether anyone else on the staff found it weird and then again why Pete Batwan had possibly hired me. I wasn't the newest staff member at Embassy anymore; lots of the teachers there were part-time, and the turnover rate was fairly high, which meant that no one, including Pete, really noticed me. I liked it this way.

A teacher named Ben Rosenbaum was the exception. He liked me. I think it might have been in part because he mistook my interest in him for something it wasn't. I noticed him because his name was Ben, and he noticed me notice. Ben Rosenbaum let me wonder what my brother looked like, whether he still had dark hair curling down around his ears like Ben Rosenbaum did. Ben Rosenbaum talked a lot during staff meetings because he wanted everyone to know that he was smart. His students must never have had a chance to practice their English. Maybe they learned by listening to him, but he used expressions like "MO," for modus operandi, whenever he had a chance. Or maybe he was just happy to have the chance to abbreviate since everyone spoke English so well.

"Does anyone have any questions?" Mr. Batwan was asking.

"I have a question," said Ben. "I have always availed myself of the materials in the New York City Public Library because it is my philosophy that teachers who belong to a specific community should set an example for their students."

Where was the question?

"So," he said, "maybe it would be a good idea for us to establish a requirement that all students enrolled at Embassy be formally trained in how to use the New York Public Library by a current member of our faculty."

When he said faculty, a light spray of saliva misted the air in front of him. My Benj was nothing like him, I decided, and wondered how I could get out of taking his course on Cambridge Prep. Mr. Batwan took this opportunity to demonstrate his flair for making us a part of the administrative structure of the school.

"Let's see a show of hands," he said. How could my mother have slept with him?

Bonita was taking notes so fast I wanted to warn her of carpal tunnel syndrome. What could she possibly have been writing down? A flurry of hands went up. I couldn't bring myself to raise mine.

"Aysha," Mr. Batwan said, "do you have a diverging opinion on the library?"

"Of course not," I said. Everyone was looking at me. "I'm just slow to raise my hand." I put it up in the air, slow motion.

Then a teacher named Jessica Noonan piped up about library cards, and I dissolved into the back of my chair, thinking I really had to go back to school. I couldn't stay on at Embassy forever, teaching one class, hating staff meetings, and not finishing my own education. I vowed to start reapplying, as soon as—and here I had the delusional thought I had started having frequently that spring—I had settled down with Da Ge.

I thought he'd show up that night, so on the way home I bought snapdragons and put them in an orange vase in front of the ninety-nine dragons scroll. I turned a track light on above them.

He noticed right away when he arrived. "It looks nice," he said.

I smiled. "I'm glad you think so." He touched one of the flowers.

"Do you know what they're called?" I asked.

"Flowers," he said.

"Yeah, but I mean the name of this kind."

He raised an eyebrow and looked at me.

"Snapdragons," I said.

"Snapdragons," he repeated.

"Another kind of dragon," I added, stupidly. "You know, to keep your ninety-nine dragons company." What was wrong with me? "Come in and sit," I blathered, gesturing at the futon. "How are you? Are you doing okay? How have you been?"

As soon as he was settled, I sat next to him, perhaps too close for comfort.

"My Yeye dies," he added, "the father of my father."

"I'm so sorry! When did he die?"

"I speak to him just two day ago. Then he die."

I heard the suggestion in this of a causal relationship between the two events and was considering how to create a question that would be both comforting and grammatically accessible when he asked, "Excuse me, do you have water?"

I leapt up, apoplectic that he'd been dying of thirst in my house. No one has ever been hungry or thirsty in my mother's house. I vowed at that moment to do a complete grocery shopping and to keep foods Da Ge liked in my house. In the meantime, I took chips and salsa out of the cabinet and put them in bowls while I waited for his water to make its way through the Brita filter. I set the snack in front of him.

"Thank you."

"The water will be ready in a second," I said, and then, when I brought it in, he stared at it, as if trying to determine what possible preparation it could have required.

"I cleaned it," I said, knowing he wouldn't know the word "filter." I poured some into a glass for him.

"Filter, yes?"

I folded my legs up on the couch, hating myself. "It's not cold," I said.

"I don't like cold water. Thank you." He took a sip and continued, "My Yeye, my grandfather. He was old, maybe like ninety-one years. He leave certain things he want to give me, but those are in Beijing. Maybe when he's alive he always want me to marry a nice Chinese girl and give him grandson. Maybe if he knew I would never do that, then he won't leave me his things." A great-grandson, I thought, although I resisted correcting him. Da Ge's glance shifted around the room, as if he were looking for his grandfather.

"What would be wrong with marrying a nice Chinese girl and having a baby?"

"I do not want these old-fashioned marriage idea. I want to have democratic marriage, what is my free choice, and anyway, I don't deserve to be back to China."

"What do you mean, *deserve*?"

He ignored this. "My Yeye have a lot of old books. Used to be we read these together, but now I don't want to think of it. Maybe he left it for me. He wish I will get married." He tilted his head up, a question.

"I'll marry you if you want," I said. I had considered us in love for weeks; he might as well, too. Marrying Da Ge would be sinister and safe at the same time, a sexy combination. And since I had never seen a good marriage, I had the wild notion that this might lead to one.

"Are you sure it's okay you can do that for me?" Da Ge asked. His eyes were glittering with excitement.

"Yes, I'm sure." I felt a rush of adrenaline, "It'll be like an extension of teaching English. Extra credit."

Da Ge stood up. "Thank you," he said. He walked over, and I thought he might pick up my hand or kiss me, but he did neither. "I will make it easy. So no work for you. And I can pay if you—"

"I'm not interested in your money."

What did he believe motivated me? Generosity? Stupidity? Or did he simply have better perspective than I did and choose me because he knew I'd do it?

In exchange for my vows and the bonus green card that would come with them, I asked if he would teach me Chinese. He laughed. Happily, I want to think. And then, right there, he began writing out characters, starting with numbers, because they were easiest. The number one was only a short horizontal line. "Should be okay for you, this one!" he said. "Two" was two lines. "Person" was also two lines, like a tepee.

"No," said Da Ge when told him it looked like a house. "It look like a person. Chinese language make sense, unlike your English. Each thing look like the thing it is." He drew a box with a line through it. "See?" he told me. "Sun!"

"That looks like a sun?"

He drew a box with no line in it. "Mouth," he said. "Like your big mouth."

He left that night as usual, and I continued to hide him from everyone who mattered: my mom, Julia, even Dr. Meyers, who did well with truth. Da Ge was my trump card; I would bring him out last, I thought, shoot the moon.

Yesterday was warmish for February in Beijing. Julia Too and I went shopping in Sanlitun, where we bought her fake "Miss Sixty" shirts, Diesel corduroys, and some new sneakers. My mother had sent Julia Too home from New York with red, pointy shoes of the sort that I forbid. I'm too mean to buy her such shoes myself, but not mean enough to take them away from her, so Julia Too wore them every single day of January, even though it was so cold I worried we'd have to amputate her feet.

At the market, she climbed out from behind a sheet that doubles as a dressing room, wearing a striped, hooded sweaterdress. She looked like an old-fashioned candy stick, and I wanted to gobble her up like I used to when she was a baby.

"How does it look?" she asked me.

"Delicious," I said. "You're the love of my life."

She grinned, pulled the hood over her head. "You're still mine, too," she said. We have an agreement that as soon as I'm not the love of her life anymore, we'll have a bottle of champagne in honor of the new love, even if she's only eleven.

For lunch, Julia Too chose Pure Lotus, and Yang Tao came to meet us. I had seen him a dozen times, for coffee by his office at Beijing University, for lunches during my breaks at Global Beijing, and for two sleepovers when Julia Too was sleeping at Lili's and Phoebe's. When he walked into Pure Lotus, I stood up and kissed him on each cheek. Julia Too was busily ordering for the table: sweet and sour tofu fish wrapped in a seaweed approximation of skin; fake Peking duck with pancakes, scallions, and sweet dark sauce; spareribs with bones made of bamboo shoots. Then she sipped ginger apple juice while Yang Tao asked her, in English, about school. She replied in Chinese. This was both a forgivable choice and a gesture of subtle hostility. All the bilingual children I know have the ability to divide the world up instantly and with astonishing accuracy—they know immediately who speaks native English and who speaks native Chinese. But Yang Tao also knows both that Julia Too considers herself American, and that in the teenage world of Global Beijing, English is "cooler" than Chinese. She was making the unfriendly point that Yang Tao is not in the inner circle of our family, that she and I speak an English so fluent and intimate that he's not welcome even to try to participate. I disliked this undercurrent, but hoped Yang Tao would accommodate her and speak Chinese if she preferred that.

As if reading my mind, he switched. "What are you reading in English class?" he asked in Chinese.

"Nothing," she said in English. Then she excused herself, left for the bathroom. I saw her take her cell phone out, wondered who she was calling.

"I have something for you to read," I told Yang Tao, hoping to make up for Julia Too. I handed him the treasure I'd been saving, an article I had clipped from China Air's inflight magazine, entitled "Custom of Wedding." It described a ceremony in rural Anhui province, in which, it said, "in accordance with local custom, the bride shall be screwed off the fine hair on the forehead on wedding day."

"You win," he said. Our contest was for who could provide the other with the worst translation copy. It started when I showed him Julia's "dog-end cast from high" flyer and he, perhaps in a quiet protest, brought me a photo of an American basketball player with the Chinese character for broccoli tattooed on his neck.

"So as a victory gift, maybe you can tell me what this means." I was laughing.

"You have to rescind your victory if you ask the native person for a translation."

"Wow. *Rescind*! Show off. Fine, I rescind."

"I'm going to guess it either means tweeze or braid. Probably tweeze. Is this what you've been spending your time researching? Rural wedding customs in Anhui?"

Just then, a girl roughly Julia Too's age came into the restaurant selling roses wrapped in individual plastic sleeves. She wore a man's army green coat and shoes that looked like they had belonged to someone else first. She shuffled from table to table, looking at the floor, repeating "Buy a flower for her" to the men at each table. I was justifying in my mind why not to buy flowers: her boss was a tyrant who took her money anyway, working children are part of a despicable mafia, giving money is giving in to the system, and so on. But before I had convinced myself, Yang Tao was beckoning her over.

"Buy a flower for her," the girl said.

"How many do you have to sell?" he asked. She shrugged.

"How many to be done for today?" he asked.

She looked at him. "Buy a flower for her," she said. She didn't look at me, just nodded her head in the general direction of where someone might be sitting.

Yang Tao took three one hundred Yuan notes from his wallet, almost fifty dollars. "Here," he said, "Please give them to me."

"How many, mister?"

"All of them." He handed her the bills. She paused for a moment, incredulous, then tossed the flowers onto our table and ran.

I looked up to see Julia Too standing there. She blew her bangs out of her eyes in a gesture that struck me as uniquely adolescent. She moved her eyes slowly from the roses, which now looked naked and grotesque to me, to Yang Tao.

"Show off," she said.

That night at bedtime, Julia Too climbed under her tiger blanket. "Let's tell the story," she said. I sat on the edge of her bed, tickled her back.

"Which one, Bean?" I asked, because there are two.

"The one about my birth."

"The night you were born, the moon in New York was a white sliver. I could see it from the cab on the way to St. Luke's and again from the window in my room. Naomi and Julia were there, and we sang Xiao Wang's Mekong River song, about the light over Lijiang. When you arrived, everybody said, 'She's perfect,' and you were. I said you looked like your daddy, Julia One said you looked like me, and Nomi said you looked just like yourself, and 'give her here.'"

"Did you?"

"Of course. She snuggled you half to death."

"Now the other one," Julia Too said.

"Your daddy was very sick."

"Was I there?"

"I was pregnant with you."

I sighed. We have had this conversation many times, and I don't mind—it's my retribution, I guess. But sometimes, even now, when I'm telling it, I can feel the two sections of my heart—one red and the other white, slide apart like a puzzle. Julia Too doesn't like to vary the wording or the cadence.

"He didn't know me."

"Right. He didn't know you. But he would have loved you. I am certain."

She turned away from me. "Let's stop there," she said.

"Okay, sweetie."

"It's a pity, right, Mom?"

I leaned down and kissed her. "Yes. It's a pity."

After she had closed her eyes and started breathing sleepily, I took seventeen steps from her bedroom through the living room, past the roses Yang Tao had bought, now in a tall vase on the coffee table. I poured a glass of Dragon Seal wine and sat up alone, watching my favorite TV series, *Don't Talk to Strangers*, about a doctor who flies into jealous rages over his schoolteacher wife.

I fell asleep hours later and dreamt of a wedding in Anhui. Julia Too and I rode horses side by side, our hairlines plucked, our matching taffeta dresses sounding like prom, looking whiter than an overexposed photo or a ghost. I woke glazed with fear and stumbled from the couch into Julia Too's room. She was safe in her bed, one flannel pajama'ed leg sticking out from under the covers. I tucked it back in.

✶ I used to wonder what it felt like to be as estranged as Da Ge was from the world, what it made nights like to have had a mother who couldn't bear to stay alive. I didn't have my dad anymore exactly, but I could always go home to my mom. The first time I started rereading Da Ge's early essays was that February, and I made a conscious, stricken decision not to return them. How much did I already suspect about what I'd need to keep? Or what I'd lose? I never took notes on his work; he wrote in red ink, making my teacher pen redundant. And since I never gave him any feedback anyway, I began to read his essays over and over, and keep them. As soon as I'd admitted to myself that I was going to do it, I set about organizing his assignments into my journal.

It was one of many projects I created in the weeks after Julia and Adam betrayed me together, leaving me with the feeling that my life was a shallow sitcom and I had no friends. Alone in my apartment, I kept busy. I was too proud to call Julia and too annoyed to call Adam, so I made collages, typed up comments on student papers, wrote an essay to Columbia about why they should let me back in, and reread *Anna Karenina*, *Madame Bovary*, *Angle of Repose*, and *Gatsby*. I like reading books I've read before, because they remind me who I am. That February, I read Lu Xun, too, thought he might remind me who I was about to be. Reading someone new can make you someone new, I find.

But every time I closed a book, I landed hard on the same thought: Julia. Julia in her leotard and tights, Julia in primary school, hanging from the playground bars, Julia at fifteen, smudges of Kohl eyeliner shadowing her eyes, Julia eating Koronet Pizza, laughing, a dimple creasing her right cheek, Julia making tea in her studio, painting silver stars on my toenails, Julia asleep in her investment banker bed, Julia in the moment she made the conscious decision that selling me out was worth a few minutes of guilty fun with Adam. Or worse, finding the guilt fun precisely because it was at my expense. Or worse yet, not thinking of me at all. Maybe they were in love.

Movies became a montage of the two of them, him hoisting her up in the nurses' station at St. Luke's, railing her while I languished. So I watched nothing. Music was a soundtrack for their skipping through sunny fields somewhere without me, weightless until they tackled each other in the tall weeds, ablaze with lust. So I watched nothing, just read books that didn't involve us, and told myself I had moved on anyway, was engaged.

I told Dr. Meyers that Julia and Adam had had sex. She did not say, "How does that make you feel?" Instead she said, "Shit."

I laughed. "That's how I felt, too," I said.

Then Adam called me. His "hello" came down the wire and wound my stupid heart up like a jack-in-the-box. I put a hand on my chest, kept the lid on.

"What?" I asked, pleased that it came out sounding angry rather than panicked.

"Oh, Aysha." There was pity dripping out of his voice. I remembered sponges he used to forget to squeeze out in the sink, filthy, rotting, and reeking. I threw out dozens of moldy sponges while we were together. And he never once wiped a counter or sink. I used to think maybe guys just weren't taught how to make a wiping motion. Maybe since they pee standing up.

"Yes?" I longed to wring the words out of him. Open the cabinet under the sink, let the smell of the plastic garbage bag rush out, see Adam's words stuck to its sides.

"Julia said you and she had an extremely awkward conversation." He swallowed. I couldn't help laughing. "You mean about how the two of you were fucking above my ceiling right after you fucked me? That wasn't awkward."

"Uh. It sounds worse than it is," he began, "but I just—"

I couldn't hear him out. "Nothing sounds like anything other than what it is," I said, "except when you open your mouth."

He sighed. "I don't know why I try," he said. "But here, I'll try: you and I haven't been a couple for ages, Aysh. Julia and I were worried about you. We're only close because of you. The fact is, we drank a lot, and we made a mistake. It was weird and desperate, and I'm so sorry. If you never want to be my friend again, I can accept that, but please forgive Julia."

"You repulse me," I told him. "How dare you call me on her behalf? Do you think she and I don't know each other better than you and she do? Or better than you and I know each other? She'll laugh when I tell her." This was only partially true, of course. I couldn't imagine ever speaking to Julia again, let alone laughing with her about Adam.

I could hear my voice bubbling but I didn't stop. "Let me understand this, Adam. You're calling me after you came over here and slept with everyone at this address—to tell me that you're worried about me? You're the one who walks the halls of our building, shedding your pants, asking for takers. Julia and I are worried about *you*."

I hung up and the silence around me buzzed. I allowed myself one minute to think about Julia and Adam. It was 7:06. 60, 59, 58 . . . How many times? Just that once? Unlikely. Did it start while I was sick? Did they congratulate each other on how generous and loving they were being, bringing candy to the crazy ward? 19, 18, 17 . . . Had they come in separately to fool me? I couldn't think of an instance. Had my mother suspected? I was out of time. Did Adam put his hands over Julia's mouth while she laughed? The phone rang again.

It would be Julia, I thought, confirmation of their partnership. He had called her as soon as I hung up, reinforcing their superior intimacy. I let the machine get it. Waiting for a voice, I thought how Julia's was as familiar as water, food, or paper.

"Hi Aysha," said the machine. "It's Xiao Wang."

I grabbed the phone.

"I hope it's okay for me to call," she said.

"Of course," I said. "I'm so glad you did."

"Maybe you would like to watch movie with me."

"Absolutely," I said.

"What movie?" she asked.

I laughed. "What movie do you want to watch?"

"Maybe you can decide for this."

And so began our Wednesday movie nights. I said we could watch at my place, and suggested *Casablanca*, *The Godfather*, or *Lawrence of Arabia*, classic films.

"No, no," she said. "These we already have in Chinese, or with Chinese subtitle. I want to see the movies you watch when you are young American. Not this kind of classic movie, but the movie you think are cool when you are growing up," she said.

So I rented *Pretty in Pink*, which Xiao Wang found almost as stunning as my apartment. She went through everything as though the place were a museum, commenting that my teddy bear and old doll were "cute and pretty," and that my quilt, which I explained Naomi had made out of my baby clothes, was "artist's love." She came upon the picture of me and Benj in pajamas.

"You are so pretty baby here," she said. "*Pang pang bai bai de*!"

I couldn't resist. "Fat and white?" I asked.

She raised her eyebrows. "How do you know this?" she asked.

"Aren't you impressed? Da Ge told me."

She took this in for a second before managing a complete recovery. "Maybe we can both help to teach you some Chinese."

"I would love that," I said. "I'd like to go to China someday."

"Maybe you can visit my family in Jinhong. Meet my parent and Jin. We smiled at each other, both thinking it would never happen, both wrong.

"Let's watch the movie," I said. "It will give you a sense of teenage life here."

Xiao Wang asked why Molly Ringwald was a star, why "Ducky" was in love with her when he was so clearly "same sex love," and why the rich guy was desirable. I said it was a materialistic moment for America and that for hundreds of years gay people had to pretend to be straight in Hollywood movies. And not only the actors, even gay characters had to pretend. Chinese people, when they appeared in the movies we watched that year (almost never), were bucktoothed emasculated minstrels, innocent exotic lilies, or dragon ladies. For this I had no explanation.

It was in describing those nights to Dr. Meyers that I realized I had never noticed anything about my own culture until Xiao Wang sat me down on my couch and showed me the movies I was showing her. She and Da Ge were the first people who ever forced me to pay attention, to look out and see in.

Julia Too threw a combination Valentine's and birthday party for her twelfth birthday last Saturday. With her signature little-kid bangs pulled off her forehead in a silver barrette, she looked like she had high cheekbones. She wore a denim skirt and the pointy red shoes Naomi had gotten her. Her eyes were lit with excitement, and sometimes when she turned toward me, I felt like I could project forward and see her adult self. At other moments, when she was busy, serious, or thoughtful, it was as if Da Ge had spun into the room in a gust. Then she'd catch me staring at her and grin—and he'd be gone.

Because this was the first boy-girl party Julia Too had ever hosted, I had called Naomi ninety times in the two weeks preceding the party, to beg her to come or, short of that, at least tell me how to bake cupcakes, make nonalcoholic punch, string up balloons, and not embarrass Julia Too.

"Why would you embarrass her?"

"I don't know. Standing too close, looking too parental, looking un-parental, serving the wrong things?"

"Here's what you serve: enough food for an army. Chips, salsa, cheese, crackers, vegetables and dip, cookies, nut mixes, candy, birthday cake. And have one main food station so that kids will have an excuse to congregate. And don't stand too close to it."

"Thanks, Mom."

"Did I ever embarrass you?"

"Of course." We hung up.

Two minutes later, she called back. "Is Old Chen coming?"

"I don't know. I invited him, but I sort of doubt he'll make it. I don't think it's really his kind of scene."

"I want to come!"

"Last I heard, there are direct flights on United and Air China."

"Wah!" she said, "I wish I had retired so I could go to your birthday parties."

"You can't give notice tonight?"

She laughed. We hung up.

Ten minutes later I called her back.

"Are balloons stupid? I mean she's almost a teenager."

"Ask Julia."

"I did."

"And?"

"She said she wants them."

"Okay then."

"I think she might be humoring me. Might think I want her to stay a baby."

"Put the balloons up, Aysha, and calm down."

"When you say put them up, what does that mean exactly?"

"What kind of ceiling does the venue have?"

"I don't know."

"Well, if you can't tack them into the ceiling, then tape them in bunches to the walls. Or get some helium balloons and tie them to chairs. Streamers, too. Those prevent the balloons from looking shriveled or lonely."

"Shriveled? Jesus, Mom."

"I didn't want to say *limp*."

"Well, now you've managed both."

She gave me a cupcake recipe, bossed me about the details of buttermilk and muffin tin papers, and then said she had a lunch date and told me she'd be out of reach for an hour. I didn't know if I could handle it.

When the kids arrived at Julia Too's party, they looked like little approximations of grown-ups, so nervous that they glittered under the thousand eyes of our borrowed disco ball. Julia Too hung close to Phoebe, who trailed Sophie, and Lili dragged behind them. I hoped they were all being kind to each other, and that Julia Too would not betray Lili by excluding her in favor of the ever-cooler Sophie and Phoebe. Xiao Wang and Phoebe's mother, Anne, were there. Jin was in Yunnan, tending to various businesses I can never keep straight. He and Xiao Wang have apartments in Jinhong, Beijing, and Guangzhou, but Xiao Wang and Lili stay mostly in Beijing. She does not want Lili to lead the life of a big shot's daughter, doesn't want her spoiled or shallow. Whenever I suggest she live it up a bit more, Xiao Wang piously invokes her Nai Nai, reminding me of the sacrifice her Nai Nai made, moving to America.

"But didn't she make that sacrifice precisely so that you and Lili could enjoy a more comfortable life than the one she had?"

"We already do," she says. "I don't want Lili to be—how to say—fancy."

Lili wore a simple white dress to Julia Too's birthday. Xiao Wang looked so stuffy in her pantsuit that I teased her mercilessly about dancing with other men, even though there weren't any there. Anne stood by, listening. Shannon showed up with a Baskin Robbins ice cream cake and Mylar balloons, dying to hear about Yang Tao.

"It's working out, right?" she shouted. "I knew it! That'll be fifty dollars!"

Xiao Wang had to work not to shush her. She thought talking about men in proximity to the girls inspired bad behavior in them. But I smiled at Shannon.

"You did well this time," I told her. "He never talks, so I should be curious enough to draw it out at least another day or two."

She rolled her eyes. "He's fantastic," she said. "You should give him the benefit of the doubt. He and Zhang Sun were classmates—they've known each other for like twenty years, and Zhang Sun can vouch."

"What's he doing unmarried?"

"Well, he apparently was engaged, but the woman broke it off."

"No kidding. When was that?"

She shrugged and gave me a vague look. "Quite a while ago," she said.

"Quite a while like fifteen years? Or like two years?"

"Closer to fifteen, I think. You should ask him."

"He'll never tell me."

"He is very Chinese," Xiao Wang piped up, and I couldn't help laughing. "I don't think he is likely to tell you about this earlier business," she continued.

"You've been happily married to a Chinese guy since you were a teenager," I reminded her. "I don't know why you keep trying to keep everyone else out of the club."

"I'm happily married to a Chinese guy, too," Shannon reminded us.

Xiao Wang raised her eyebrows, as if she knew more about Shannon and Zhang Sun's marriage than Shannon did. Shannon, who liked Xiao Wang, pretended not to notice.

The party was not going well. Boys were glued against the far wall, girls in a giggling amorphous mass a mile away. Nobody came near the dance floor. One of Julia Too's friends was deejaying, and he came on the mic and insisted that people come out and dance. He put on "Macarena," and a few especially brave twelve-year-olds scuttled out and waved their arms up and down for a few minutes before retreating to various corners of the room. Only the dauntless Sophie remained on the dance floor, sticking out her legs and swinging in a way that suggested a windmill. She wore a Band-Aid sized miniskirt and a blouse she had hiked up and tied at the waist. She had a hoop earring through her bellybutton, and a tattoo on the small of her back.

"Shannon—is that a real tattoo?"

"Of course not. Did you see that thing? It's a motorcycle surrounded by roses. Eventually it will fall off, thank God. But it's only a matter of time before the fight for a real one kicks in."

"Well, she's a fabulous dancer."

Shannon laughed. Sophie is adorable, and during our conversation, either in spite or because of her dancing, an invisible flip switched and the party became a rollicking success. Since there was no alcohol, it's hard to say what happened, but all of sudden a Canadian boy named Kevin asked

Phoebe to dance and then pecked her on the lips at the end of the song. I happened to see it, and then to see her and Sophie grab Julia Too and Lili (to my delight and relief) and pull them into the bathroom to begin what I guessed would be a year-long series of debriefings on the kiss.

It was right as they emerged from the bathroom, looking serious with whatever pact they had made, that Yang Tao appeared. Julia Too had tied her blouse at the waist, and taken off the tights she'd been wearing under her skirt. Yang Tao was carrying a giant box. Julia Too noticed him right away, and noticed the box, but did not walk over. She looked suspicious. I hoped the present was neither ungenerous nor too ostentatious—I didn't want her to be mean to him, and I didn't want her to feel like it was a token or an overstated effort to buy her affection. Why are small gestures so difficult to get right, and why am I so uptight? Why couldn't I just enjoy the fact that he appeared, that he was courting my angry baby, and that he brought her a gift at all?

Yang Tao and I went outside so he could smoke. I had asked him please not to smoke around Julia Too. It was bad enough that her lungs were full of coal smoke and diesel fuel. I leaned up against the wall of the building. He lit a cigarette.

"Are you having an okay time?" I asked.

"I never had a party like this when I was a kid." He blew out thin smoke.

"Of course not. You probably weren't allowed to date until you were twenty."

"Good guess," he said. "I was pretty innocent, in fact."

"Until you met me?"

He laughed.

"Shannon says your heart was broken."

"Yeah?"

"Who broke it?"

"*Mei shi*," he said. "It's a long time ago."

"I'm curious."

"You don't seem curious."

"What do you mean?"

"You never ask about this kind of thing," he said.

"Do you wish I did?"

"I don't know."

"I like to respect your privacy," I said.

He smiled and tossed the cigarette butt down, put it out with his heel. "Except about Chinese riots."

I laughed. "If you wanted to tell me about your love life, you would, right?"

"This *is* my love life. This right now," he said.

I found that quite charming. "Good enough," I said.

A black sedan pulled up to the side of the curb, and Old Chen climbed out, astonishing me. Yang Tao looked at me, curious.

"You came!" I called to Old Chen in Chinese. I approached and hugged him, and he patted me awkwardly.

"Should I wait here?" his driver asked through the window.

Old Chen shook his head no, indicating that he wanted to stay for more than a few minutes, and his driver headed toward the parking lot.

Old Chen turned his attention to Yang Tao.

"This is Yang Tao," I told him, "a good friend of mine."

"Glad to meet you, sir," Yang Tao said. Old Chen nodded and they shook hands.

I was not in the habit of introducing Old Chen to male friends, and watched for any sign of discomfort or angst on his face, but none registered. He glanced toward the party, and we walked in together. When Julia Too saw him, she held up a hand to cut off whatever conversation she was involved in, and glided over to the door to say hi.

"Happy Birthday," Old Chen said, and slid a red envelope into her hand. She grinned. I wondered how obscene an amount of money was in it, and sighed.

"*Xie xie*," she said.

Then he handed her a red belt with a gold horse buckle.

"Wow," she said, and set about fastening it around her waist. Even without the blouse tied up above her waist, it would have looked absurd. But Old Chen beamed. Julia Too was born in the year of the Horse, and since the Chinese zodiac repeats its animal every twelve years, her year is coming up.

"You should wear this every day," he said, not joking.

"I think I just might," Julia Too told him. Her dimples deepened.

Old Chen loves to remind Julia Too that if China used the inferior Western calendar, she'd be a sheep, which he considers less auspicious than a horse. This is because in 1991, the year she was born, the Chinese New Year fell on February 14, three days after Julia Too's birthday. It wasn't until the fifteenth that the sheep moved in.

"Do you want to dance?"

Julia Too was clutching Old Chen's hand. His eyes widened in horror, but she had already shoved the envelope of cash into my hand and begun dragging him out to the dance floor. Some of the twelve-year-olds tittered and whispered, but Julia Too either didn't notice or didn't care. She danced with Old Chen to Kylie Minogue's "Can't Get You Out of My Head," for the entire duration of the song. He held her formally, at arm's length, and they looked like an old Chinese couple, ballroom dancing outside in Beijing on a summer night. I didn't know whether to laugh or weep. Xiao Wang's reaction helped me clarify though.

"*Wo de tian*," she said. "My God! This is difficult situation for old Chinese man."

After their dance ended, Old Chen retreated from the floor with Julia Too, his burning face reflecting light from the disco ball. She delivered him to Xiao Wang and me, and he accepted a cup of fruit punch before shaking hands with Yang Tao again and heading to the door.

That night, in an uncharacteristic move, Old Chen called me after ten. Without any mention of who it was or why he was calling, he blurted out: "I think she has a big, natural talent for dancing. If you agree, I will start formal lessons."

"I'll talk to Julia Too about it," I told him. "Thank you for offering, and for the generous gift."

He cleared his throat.

"Other business you want to chat about?" I asked.

"Your friend," he said. I waited uncomfortably.

"Um. I think he has a kind nature."

"I'm glad you think so," I said. "Thank you for telling me."

"Maybe he can join us for dumplings sometime."

I hung up and returned to the living room, where Julia Too, Sophie, Lili, and Phoebe had opened their Valentines and Julia Too's birthday presents into a heap on the floor, including the silver charm bracelet I had given her. Yang Tao was watching from the couch as the girls organized and analyzed cards, candy, some makeup Julia Too and I were going to have to negotiate about, and finally, the only gift left, Yang Tao's big box. I wasn't sure whether she left it for last to honor or to insult him. But as she opened it, she reverted instantly to her joyful, baby self. It was a collapsible stage and curtain, made up of several dozen red boards and an enormous piece of red velvet with gold ropes. It included a hand-held mike and a portable spotlight.

She looked up at Yang Tao with an expression so utterly Naomi that I did a double take. "Holy shit!" she said, "I love it!"

I didn't say anything about her vocabulary choice. Yang Tao responded, "I know you're a good actress and dancer, so I considered it a professional investment for you." He couldn't mask his delight.

Later that night, when I tucked in Julia Too and kissed her good-night, Sophie was on the phone in the kitchen and Phoebe was in the bathroom brushing her teeth.

"Happy birthday, brilliant girl," I said to Julia.

"Thank you for my party," she said.

"You're welcome. Where'd you learn the expression 'Holy shit'?"

"Soph."

"Right."

"Mom? Do you think he would he have gotten me good birthday presents?"

"I do. You can consider whatever I get you to be from him, too, okay? And/or whatever Old Chen gets you."

"Red and gold horse belts and cash," she said, smiling. Neither of us mentioned the red stage Yang Tao had brought her. Sophie and Phoebe and Lili emerged, unrolled sleeping bags, and argued over who would sleep in the other half of Julia Too's double bed. I left them to work it out. When they were asleep, I showed Yang Tao the first pages of this story. It was a test, and he passed.

"I like the story of you," he said, setting the pages on the coffee table. He moved closer to me on the couch, put an arm around to pull me in. "You're a pretty good writer. And a great mother. I wish you were my mother."

I laughed. "Well, wouldn't that be sexy."

March 1990, New York, NY

Dear Teacher,

   You tell us we should write about a cultural convention of
our country. Marriage is a cultural convention of the world.
People marry for various reason. Sometimes because they are
in love they will marry. Other times their parents will com-
plain so much that they will finally sacrifice to marry so that
their family will be quiet about this. Some people will marry
because they want to make forceful team that work for the
government of their country. There are many reason to marry,
not easy to say right or wrong.

   My parent marry because the revolution. China like all
its people to marry so will not be chaos. But my parents
marriage become unhappy. This is bad luck because maybe
in the beginning there is chance for them to turn out love
each other. But it turn out they have stupid marriage that
end in tragedy and chaos. I am sorry we are all just like
our parents. This is something hard to avoid it. Even if
you are not old person yet, even you have no knowledge,
you can know this if you read a few books. Everybody will
become their parents. It's such, as you often like to use
this expression, obvious fact.

   Da Ge

CHAPTER SEVEN

Marches

※

In March of 1990, Da Ge brought a brochure from the New York justice of the peace to class. I read it. A couple who intends to be married in New York State must apply in person for a marriage license to any town or city clerk in the state. The application for a license must be signed by both the bride and groom in the presence of the town or city clerk. Once you have your license, you can have a ceremony and get a certificate of marriage; you just have to wait twenty-four hours.

Da Ge had highlighted half the words and written characters next to them.

"What's this?" I asked.

"*Xin niang*," he said. "Bride."

"And this?"

"*Guan*. Groom."

I felt a little chill. We walked out of the classroom together and passed Bonita in the hallway. Self-conscious about whether we might be walking too close to each other, I said, "Your work on the last one was good." Bonita smiled at us.

"The last what?" Da Ge said.

"Looking up these words, I mean."

"No, you don't."

I said nothing.

"You say this so that woman thinks we talk about home-work."

I was annoyed. "Look," I said. "It's not as if our relationship is exactly normal. You are, in fact, my student, and I don't want to lose my job."

"You will not lose job for marry me," he said. "We have friendship. That's all."

"Can I ask you something?" I asked, hurt.

"Okay."

"Why do you want to marry me?"

I don't know what I was expecting. Something either revelatory or euphemistic, I guess, because when he said, "I need to be American," I felt bitterly disappointed.

Perhaps in an effort to raise the stakes, or maybe just because I wanted him to, I asked Da Ge to hold hands with me when we got to the city clerk's office. He looked at me and smiled.

"Good idea," he said, and he took my hand right away, even though we hadn't even gotten on the train yet. His hand sent a shock up through my arm, and I moved my fingers around a little bit, sexily, I hoped, but he didn't seem to notice. His hand was bigger than mine; he was like a basketball player, palming my hand effortlessly. Maybe he would bounce it onto the table when I had to sign our marriage license application.

The office of the city clerk was in the municipal building downtown. We got out of the subway at Park and walked over, still holding hands. Da Ge only let go when we stopped to buy pretzels from a street vendor. I squeezed a perfect skeleton of mustard along the middle of mine while Da Ge brushed the salt off his onto the sidewalk. The white grains looked sad, as if they were leftover from winter, when they'd had a job protecting people from slipping. I stepped over them.

When he finished his naked pretzel, he forgot to take my hand again, and I was too embarrassed to suggest it a second time. Inside the municipal building, we rode in a mirrored elevator to the second floor. The smell of Lysol reminded me of St. Luke's. I began to spell out on my fingers: i-t w-i-l-l l-a-s-t and w-e w-i-l-l not g-e-t d-i-v-o-r-c-e-d.

A sign on one of the office doors read, "Marriage License Applications," and when we pushed it open, we immediately saw all the pregnant couples waiting in line. I wondered how those girls felt about getting married, wished for a moment that I was pregnant, too, that that's why we were there, a passionate accident rather than a calculated maneuver. At the window next to the one we finally approached, a seventy-something man wearing a bowtie sat with his hand on the thigh of a woman who was probably forty. She wore a giant diamond ring and a gold skirt two sizes too tight; she was pretty and tense. The bureaucrat behind the glass was asking the old guy about three previous divorces. "Who initiated that one?"

"*She* did!" the old man said of his ex-wife. "They all did!"

"Maybe that's because you refused to pay," suggested the bureaucrat.

The old guy laughed uproariously, but his new wife looked away. I hadn't realized that if you try to get married at City Hall, they're allowed to ask you about all the other times you accidentally married the wrong person. I hoped my dad's mistress-wife had been embarrassed when the official reminded her she'd been his second choice.

Da Ge had someone there, waiting for us, which surprised me. Would he be our witness at the actual ceremony? New York had a twenty-four-hour waiting period so that people at least had to commit to taking the subway to City Hall twice. That way, you couldn't get married while still drunk or under a delusion that lasted fewer than two days.

Da Ge's friend hardly looked at me, until Da Ge said, "Zhen Ming, this is Aysha." Zhen Ming nodded at me and finished filling out forms.

"Aysha, this is my uncle, Zhen Ming." I felt slighted that he introduced us in this order, making me known to his uncle before making his uncle known to me. Now, knowing the Chinese rules for face, I realize it couldn't have been the other way around.

I stared at Zhen Ming. He had a bowl cut, straight chopped hair that poked down his forehead in a Frankenstein way. His eyes were set wide apart, and his glasses exaggerated this quality, since they had heavy, black frames. He wore a dark business suit and carried a briefcase. I thought he couldn't be older than forty. He was handsome in a disturbing way, with a face so tight and inexpressive that it looked cast out of wax or plaster. His skin was as clear as a child's, gleaming in a thin sheen of sweat, and his jaw was set with a determination that suggested the capacity for ferocity. Yet when he spoke, he was mild-mannered. I instantly disliked him.

Our bureaucrat was a plump and pale man who reminded me of Mr. Batwan, the director at Embassy. His name was Michael Schmello. Schmello? I stared at his name tag in disbelief. He had tired rings around the bottoms of his eyes. Maybe he was thinking fifty percent of us would get divorced anyway, why should he waste his time. I wondered whether he was the same person who had to oversee couples signing their divorce licenses.

Da Ge handed me a pen. I watched it spill ink into the curves of my cursive name, got the same warm rush I've gotten since second grade when I learned to write curling, linked letters. They always look so smooth and sure of themselves, dark against the blank spaces on paper. I felt better as soon as I saw my name on the page. Da Ge took his Chinese

passport out of a leather folder. Michael Schmello was waiting, so I put my arm around Da Ge's shoulders. I hoped we
looked natural, although my heart sounded to me like a car
alarm. Could Mr. Schmello hear it? Maybe he'd think I had
prewedding jitters.

He disappeared with Da Ge's passport and returned several minutes later, said our certificate of marriage registration should arrive within four weeks, and if it did not, we
should contact the office again. Da Ge took out a roll of
money and handed Mr. Schmello two twenties. Then he
turned to leave.

"The processing fee is thirty dollars, sir," Mr. Schmello
told Da Ge. He knocked on the window and pushed Da Ge's
change through.

"No matter," said Da Ge, and turned. "You can keep that."

It was a minor miscalibration, but Mr. Schmello took
offense.

"Excuse me, sir!" Schmello said, much louder than nec-
essary. "The office of the city clerk does not accept bribes!"

I don't know what Da Ge would have been bribing him
to do: marry us faster? Marry us in a threesome with his fat,
pasty self? We had to wait twenty-four hours for our ceremony no matter what, weeks for our license. I had to complete an I-130, Da Ge an I-485 for his "conditional" green
card. We would still have to fill out a thousand foreign
national spouse forms and applications, interview and prove
our love, jump through so many flaming bureaucratic hoops
it would be Olympic. Did Mr. Schmello think we believed he
could save us from all that for ten bucks?

Da Ge, who didn't understand Mr. Schmello's reaction,
waved the extra ten-dollar bill and receipt into the window
hole and then left both there, half in and half out, before
turning and walking toward the door. I took the money and
tried to make meaningful eye contact with Mr. Schmello.

"Customs are different everywhere," I said. "My fiancé meant no harm."

Da Ge had turned around. The veins on his neck were standing out. "What are you doing?" he asked me.

"I am completing our transaction," I said. It was the weirdest thing I had ever said. Da Ge walked briskly back to the counter and pounded on the window.

"You will not talk to her anymore!" he shouted. The regular noise of the office flared out. "You accuse me of what?" Anger made Da Ge's English choppy, and he was furious that I had talked about him with Mr. Schmello in a way that excluded him. I put my hand on Da Ge's back and led him out of City Hall. His uncle Zhen Ming, who had stood watching the commotion like an absolute statue, called something in Chinese. I never found out what it was. Congratulations?

We didn't speak on the walk back to the train, and then he went wherever it was he went, and I rode home, lonely, almost married. Back in my quiet apartment, as if I were looking for a comic sequel to my day with Da Ge, I called Xiao Wang and invited her over to watch *Dirty Dancing* with me. I told her it was my favorite movie ever, even though it made fun of Jewish people.

"Chinese people love that Jewish person," she said.

"What Jewish person?" I asked.

"Jewish and Chinese are similar."

"How's that? You also have expensive summer camps where middle-aged women with nose jobs take advantage of hot-bodied workers?"

"Hot bottle?"

"Hot body. Means sexy."

"Nose what?"

"Nose job."

"What is it?"

"Surgery to make your nose smaller."

"I think for American it's a good idea. Many people here have too big, how do you say—enormous—nose. Tall, too, up on the face like a mountain."

I laughed.

"Especially Jew," she said.

"Um, it's okay to say that to me, but you should probably avoid it in public."

"No, I don't mean you. You don't need it, this job. But your nose also not small."

"Right. So why are Jews and Chinese alike?"

"I don't mean that we have this kind of, how do you say, place for play. Jews and Chinese both care most for family and education."

I shrugged. "I'm not sure," I said.

"It's true," she said. "And Chinese and Jews are also good at making money."

When Jennifer Grey got a nose job two years later, I showed Xiao Wang an article in a celebrity magazine. It featured before and after shots. Xiao Wang shook her head.

"Oh, no," she said.

"But I thought you liked nose jobs on Jewish girls."

"Not for this one," she said. "Now she is some other, boring person with plain face and nothing about her." She grinned, in a rare lighthearted moment. "I think she won't make so much money anymore. Now that she isn't Jewish."

She wasn't wrong, exactly.

✳ I look forward with an addict's love to the mundane routine of my Sunday morning lessons with Teacher Hao: the tea jar he brings, the metal sound of its cap coming off for sips, the clean lines of Tang poems, his repetitive, unsuccessful explanations of why I'm syllabically and tonally off, the sunlight shifting outside my living-room windows, first imperceptibly and then so completely until the room

and the pages of our poems appear to be on fire. We end at
noon. This week we worked on a poem about drinking
alone, one I love but that Teacher Hao insists I can't possibly understand, what with my American nature. It's a Li Bai
poem, and Teacher Hao says it has a masculine bent. I've
been ribbing him that Li Bai was in touch with his feminine
side, in love with flowers and moonlight.

"Those are not feminine things," Teacher Hao said.

"Really? The natural world isn't, by most definitions,
feminine?"

"Tang poets are men," he said.

"But that's because women weren't encouraged to write,
and their writings weren't published, right? Like in the
West."

"Let's look at this part again," he said, ignoring me. He
read in a lilting Beijing accent: "I lift my glass, invite / the bright
moon, who casts back a shadow / Making us three. / But the
moon can't drink / and my shadow studies me carefully."

He stopped there. "What do you make of it?" he asked.

Aware he might dislike it, I said, "I wish the moon could
make us three."

"That's very American," he said, meaning that if you
make a poem about your daughter and her lost father, you're
focusing on yourself, thinking from the inside out.

"This is a poem about universality. About the condition
of man, and the contradictions that provide balance in both
the natural world and poetry: loneliness and companion-
ship, dark and light, reality and shadow," Teacher Hao said.

"Mom, let's go!" Julia Too called from the hallway. I
pushed my chair back.

"Coming," I said.

"Where will you go today?" Teacher Hao asked, closing
his books.

"Rock climbing," I said.

He shook his head in disbelief, maybe at the risks we took, or maybe at the frivolous lives of Westerners here. In either case, I agreed.

"She loves it," I said, shrugging guiltily. "And it's good exercise."

I thought of his look as Julia Too and I biked past by the U.S. Embassy. The line, always long, seemed especially infinite, twisting out the back of the silk market and around the block. After 9/11, they moved the line away from the embassy itself, and created a series of ropes to control the crowd. There are also now three different layers of security, even if you just stop by to add pages to your passport. Americans have always been able to enter the U.S. Embassy without waiting in line, which both makes sense and feels miserably unfair and awkward in front of the hundreds of students and grandparents lined up for visas—most of whom will be denied. As we approached the park, I saw laborers scaling buildings, hammering and scrubbing, even as urbanites and tourists climbed the shiny rock wall in the park. No wonder Teacher Hao arched his eyebrows.

Anne and Phoebe were already there, putting on climbing shoes. I was surprised Anne wanted to climb. She and I said hello, and then, with that conversation over, looked around, as if hoping another subject would walk up to us and present itself.

Julia Too leapt onto the wall. She's a talented spider, and the young guys who run the place love her because she's fearless both about scaling the wall and pushing off in her soft purple climbing slippers. Anne and I stood together watching our girls climb, fall, and swing out over the park, a sight that always leaves me breathless with fear. I was coaching myself about not being overprotective, not shouting *hold on*, not holding my breath and passing out while I watched my daughter move through life without crippling neuroses. Let her go, I was thinking. Anne sighed.

"Maybe this is too personal a question," she said. "Feel free to tell me if you don't want to answer it."

Delight shot through me. "No, no," I said. "Go ahead." I watched her.

"Do you ever get lonely here? I mean, living alone in Beijing?"

"Of course," I said. "Everyone does. This is a weird place, especially to be—" I paused, deciding whether to ramp up the stakes and then doing it, "a single mom."

She winced. "Yeah," she said finally. "I keep thinking I'm not really a single mom." She blinked a few times so fast it looked like she had a tic. "I mean, I know it's silly, but I can't help but keep thinking it's just a matter of time before he comes back."

"I know what you mean," I said. "I used to think Da Ge, Julia's dad, would appear somehow. Reappear."

"Do you ever think it now?" Anne asked.

I shook my head no.

When Yang Tao showed up, he agreeably put on slippers and a harness right away, even though he had never been before and clearly thought climbing was a horrifying idea. And although he's somewhat spindly and might have been light, he was a dreadful rock climber. From the instant he clambered onto the wall, he clutched it like a dying person and tried to pull himself up with his arms. The key is to put the weight and burden on your legs—no one has the upper-body strength to last long pulling himself up a ninety-degree incline. But Yang Tao didn't trust his skinny legs. Watching him flail about increased my affection for him, but it had the opposite effect on Julia Too. She likes cool kids more than I do.

"God, he's like a total spaz, Mom," she said.

"It's his first time rock climbing," I reminded her. "It's brave of him to try."

"Because he's old and frail, you mean?"

Anne, hearing this, smiled at me over Julia Too's head, and I felt a surge of something I can only describe as the opposite of loneliness. Julia Too stepped onto a small rock jutting out and began propelling herself back up.

"Don't fall, sweetie," I called. I hate watching her swing off the wall. What faith can I really put in a pair of elastic underpants?

Julia Too twisted around to face me. "When you fall, it's like flying," she called. "Falling is the fun part."

"Oh," I said. "So fall, I guess." I blew her a kiss. Let go, I thought again, let go. An image of her first shoes flashed into my mind. How I bent to buckle them and she stood, waiting to run into the first school she ever attended, a festive place on the Upper West Side called Basic Trust. Julia Too cried less at "good-bye" than the other toddlers, and I used to wonder if this was because she expected less than they did, that her heartbreak was set in motion before she was born. Even on days when she felt mixed about seeing me go, her way of putting her mittens in her cubby and pulling out her mat for morning meeting seemed to me especially stoic. Julia Too blew me kisses through the windows of classrooms for years, butterflied her way through swimming, dance, and pottery lessons, made and kept friends from every corner, including Beijing. I thought the impossible circus of moving and being the international new kid might shatter her, but she's apparently made of some trauma-proof material; I'm the glass one.

Yang Tao rappelled off the wall, hanging in space for what must have been a terrifying moment—before returning to the ground. He was unable to disguise his relief.

"You hated it!" I said.

"Hate is a big word."

I smiled. "Remember when you said I could ask you anything?"

"Did I say that?"

"Who was it that Shannon meant when she said you weren't married because you'd had your heart broken?"

"You're still on that question? A girl from Hubei," he said.

"Hubei! Where is she now?"

"She married my college roommate."

I tried to see his facial expression, but he was shading his eyes from the sun, and I couldn't make much out.

"Were you crushed?"

"It was a long time ago," he said.

"Right. Was your heart really broken, though?"

"Yes."

"How long did that last?"

"Unclear," he said, in Chinese.

"Are you ready to belay me?" I asked.

He nodded, and I roped myself to him and climbed until I reached the bell at the top of the wall. Ringing it, I had the thought that rock climbing is like sex. The exertion narrows your mind to a single focus: where the limbs go next. Don't fall. Or do.

Our processed marriage license arrived, and I passed it to Da Ge in class. Now all we had to do was go to city hall for a "ceremony," and we'd get the real certificate. A marriage certificate! I wondered if I would hang it on my wall next to the fat fat white white baby picture of me and Benj. I hoped so. Maybe Da Ge would ask to move in with me. He said nothing after class but called me late that night.

"I like to see you," he said.

"Come over," I said. "Now that we're almost married, maybe you'll kiss me."

"Do you want?"

"Yes."

I went downstairs, propped the lobby open with a Bedford grammar handbook, and left my apartment door unlocked. When he arrived, I was lying in the dark, undressed, the covers up to my neck. He closed the door, bolted it, and pulled the chain across. I heard two controlled thumps as he set his shoes in the hallway: one shoe, two shoes. His socks brushed the wood floor toward my room, the door creaked open, and a little hallway light washed over the bed.

He walked to the shelf and set something down. The textbook. Then he appeared at the side of my bed. I thought he'd ask was I asleep, and that I wouldn't respond, even though I had just brushed my teeth and had a pounding cardio pulse. But he said nothing, simply lifted his shirt over his head and then undid his belt buckle. He took his jeans off and folded them. Then he stood in his boxers in front of me, touching the bed. I turned onto my side and propped myself up. His stomach tensed when I reached out to touch him, wrapped my hands around his straight hips. He put his hands on my face, and I closed my eyes. It was too dark to see when he slid into the bed and pressed himself against me until our bodies were touching entirely. I could feel his thighs against mine, and remembered wondering what it would feel like to touch him, taste him. This was what. He felt like beach glass, tasted minty and urgent. The city was dissolving out my window, lurching forward without me. I could feel the muscles in Da Ge's back, the pulse in his neck where I pressed my open mouth. A car outside came to a grinding, screeching halt, and I listened for the smash of metal, but it never came. Da Ge's arms were under my waist, lifting and arching me toward him. He smelled like shampoo and newsprint. He had brought the city inside my apartment with him; the skin on his face was still cool from the night. When his hips were moving against mine, and his breathing jagged and rough, he put his mouth over my ear. His voice was like heat, his words so clear I can still hear their edges. "I want you unbelievable bad," he said.

When Da Ge and I slept together that first time, it was March of 1990, and I had two friends: Julia One and Xiao Wang. Telling Xiao Wang was not a possibility. I had no idea how she'd react, and I didn't want to risk our friendship. But I wanted to tell someone, and it couldn't be Dr. Meyers or my mother since I was on such a lie roll with both of them. So I had to forgive Julia. There was no one else to keep me company about how weird or not-weird it was, or to help decide if he was a stalker or the love of my life. Julia might not approve, but she was my best option.

I decided to start a conversation as if she and I had just left off the day before by some accident, and not to acknowledge the Adam debacle at all. Maybe we could just pretend so hard that it hadn't happened that it wouldn't have. But I would leave out the part about marrying Da Ge, I decided. I could handle the salacious sex with a student, the no-condom aberration, the general slut narrative, but the marriage part felt like too much.

Weirdly, I put on lipstick before going to Julia's apartment. When she opened the door and saw me, her eyes watered. But she stood there, maybe scared. "Hey," I said.

"Hi."

"Um. Could I have some coffee?"

"Of course," she said, turning. "Come in." We sat in her kitchen, on the stools, the red and white floor twirling up at us.

"So," I said. "I slept with one of my students."

Her face broke open into a smile of such relief and gratitude that I laughed. This was how it was going to be. We were going to be okay.

"Which one?" she asked, collecting herself.

"He's Chinese," I said. I wasn't sure whether to say his name.

"Wow," she said. I could see her scrambling for nonchalance, for a return to our normal way of speaking. But when she asked, "Are you going to be one of those teachers who goes to jail," I felt invaded.

"He's not fourteen," I said. Even though I had invited it by coming over and telling her a secret, I resented that she felt entitled to take a tone of intimacy with me ever again. She sensed the change in my mood instantly and was cautious.

"Do you like him?" she asked politely.

I shrugged.

"Can he speak English?"

"That's enough talking about it," I said.

"That came out wrong," she said. "I didn't mean it to sound so—"

"No, it's fine." I cleared my throat, contemplated giving up the whole project, leaving, and never having another friend. I could feel Adam's presence. He had been in her bed. I willed myself not to look over at it. Try again, I thought. She's your only friend, and you need her. I inhaled.

"He was involved in the protests in China last summer," I told her.

"Really? In what way?"

"I don't know."

"Is he a dissident?"

"I guess so."

"Does he tell you about it?"

"Of course."

"So what does it mean?"

"I don't know. Just that he's intense and political. And his mother is dead; apparently she killed herself. And he and his father are estranged. I don't really know the details," I admitted.

"Oh," she said.

We both waited.

"None of that sounds good to me," she added, unable to lie, even though she owed me a lifetime of niceties. We were in a movie about ourselves.

"I know what you mean," I gave her, "but it makes him interesting. I mean, he's cared about something in his life. Something more than himself or his own neuroses. In some ways I think he's like me, but a better version."

"I think that might be a weird perception," Julia said. She had promised after my breakdown that she would tell me if she thought I was being paranoid or delusional. But predictably, I didn't want to hear it and didn't agree. And now that she had slept with Adam, she had no right to tell me anything at all, ever again. I reminded myself again that I had decided to be forgiving, that she would have forgiven me, had the situation been reversed. Of course, I would never have slept with her boyfriend, no matter who he was or what the circumstances, and we both knew it. For a reason still difficult to articulate, this was more about her weakness than anything else, and it made us both feel bad for her, not me. I may have been crazy and friendless, but somehow I was confident about boys in a way Julia wasn't. Maybe I just spent enough time in my own mind to have a certain hard-to-get allure. Julia was too good, too eager to please, too organized, too kind. So she got dumped a lot. Guys like a bitchy girl. This has been a bonus for me.

"Thank you for being honest," I said, meaning to mean it. But it came out so hostile that we both recoiled.

"I'm sorry," I said, "that came out wrong, too. I didn't mean to—"

"No, no—it's fine," she said. We waited, as if some third person might speak and save the day. It didn't happen.

"All I meant was that I'm not sure what makes you two alike," Julia said. I could never remember her ending a pause before, and I was grateful.

"We're both different from everyone else."

"He because he's Chinese, you mean? But there are a billion Chinese people in the world. How does that make him different from everyone else?"

"That's not why. He's just—unusual."

"I see. And you?"

"Because I'm, I don't know—a peripheral person somehow. You know what I mean, on the edges of things. You're my only friend, and, well, Da Ge makes me comfortable. We understand each other."

"Okay, then I guess that's good," Julia said, but she didn't sound convinced or convincing. "As long as he's nice to you, I guess."

We both thought about how Adam hadn't been nice to me, and it was Julia's fault.

"I should go," I said.

"Do you have plans tonight?" Her voice broke over the words.

"Um, yeah."

"Aysh," she said, "Thank you for stopping by—I just wanted to say again how—"

Before she reached "sorry," I held a hand up to stop her, started to say it was okay, that we didn't need to talk about it now, that I loved her enough that we could pretend it had never happened, but I wasn't sure it was true. So I left without saying anything.

All these years later, I still miss the Julia One who existed before the Adam slip. She and I are long-distance friends now, and of course I've forgiven her and long since let Adam go, but something was broken in those moments. What a stupid, lonely waste.

On the phone that night, without knowing why, my mother was worried.

"Can I come over?" she asked. I was tempted to tell her about Julia and Adam, but my mom has an impossibly long memory, and I knew she'd never forgive either of them. Even though that's what I wanted short-term, her anger on my side, I also knew I should preserve the possibility of getting back together with at least one of them without my mother disapproving for life.

"How about tomorrow, Mom? I'll come for dinner. I'm about to go to bed now."

"Yes! Tomorrow. I'll make lasagna and bake a cake. Do you want cake? How about applesauce chocolate? You sound skinny," my mom said.

"Mom, you can't *sound* skinny."

"*You* can."

"I'm not skinny." I walked to the kitchen and crunched down on a chip, half expecting her to tell me that it's rude to eat when you're on the phone.

"I can hear how stale that is, Aysha."

"Mom! Try to be reasonable."

"Promise me you'll eat my applesauce chocolate cake, and I'll be reasonable."

"I'll eat cake," I said, "and can I bring a friend?"

"Really?" she asked, ecstatic. "Of course! What's his name?"

"*Her* name," I said. "Xiao Wang."

Today for our weekly date, Old Chen's driver came to get Julia Too and me early because Old Chen wanted to take us to the Summer Palace.

"It's best in cold weather," he told me on the phone. "Fewer people."

"Good strategy," I said. Julia Too, listening from the kitchen table, giggled.

We've been to the Summer Palace three years in a row, always on the coldest day in March; Old Chen just likes to remind me of his logic. And he wants to keep us here.

So he tows us everywhere, even after all these years, maybe ticking off his own personal cultural checklist. When the ice festival happened outside of Beijing last winter, we went to look at the life-sized model-worker Popsicles. Julia Too and Lili raced about, posing, skating, sliding their mittened hands along ice walls and animals and public works. When an art gallery opened next to the Forbidden City, Old Chen insisted we go as his dates. Julia Too looked like a traffic light in the red velvet dress Old Chen's assistant had been sent to get her, and I wore something similar. Old Chen likes to see us dressed in red. Maybe it reminds him of his roots. Or the Ha Ha Water corporate offices. Or maybe he just doesn't like women in understated, Maoist colors.

I like the Summer Palace best in winter, too, especially at sundown when light slinks across the lake and sets over Empress Cixi's marble boat. I knew Old Chen would soapbox Julia Too and me about what happens to countries when women are put in charge of them—and she would roll her eyes but secretly love the lecture, the attention and seriousness Old Chen pays her, the whole Saturday stretching out in front of the three of us. She loves everything about Old Chen. He lets her draw on the whiteboards in the Ha Ha conference rooms and gobble up their executive buffets. He's given her every corporate gift he's ever received; her room is full of engraved pen sets, globes, and paperweights. He has repeated the same Chinese zodiac lessons thousands of times. They never tire of each other.

In the car on the way to the Summer Palace, Old Chen handed us surgical masks. "Put these on," he said. "There are more cases of this flu than they think."

Julia Too put the mask on. "Yeah. They told us about it at school," she reported, her voice muffled.

"About the flu?" Old Chen asked. "What did they say?"

"That we should stay home," she said.

"From school?" he asked, scandalized.

"Nope, just everywhere else."

"Oh, good," he said. "Is your classical Chinese improving?"

Julia Too nodded diligently, grinning. Her cheeks creased up above the top of the mask. "We're learning the *xuzi*," she said, referring to the particles, or "empty words," around which Classical Chinese is organized. She lifted her mask up onto her head like sunglasses and smiled gleefully in my direction, knowing how much Old Chen would love this invitation to tell her about *xuzi*.

He turned around gravely from the front passenger seat and spoke in Chinese.

"Oh," he said. "*Xuzi*. Don't be confused by this term," he advised. "Even though the empty words don't mean anything themselves, they change the meaning of what's around them."

She nodded lovingly. "What else?" she asked in Chinese. In the rearview mirror I saw Old Chen's driver smile.

"They can mark an utterance as strongly imperative, link two phrases in a causal relationship, express uncertainty about the content, or identify something as 'commonly said.' So in this way, they are like a certain Chinese ideal, the Dao, where nonaction, nonassertiveness, or being like water, accomplishes all things," Old Chen said.

Julia Too scrunched her nose. "Do you actually believe that, though?" she asked. Old Chen and I were both surprised by this. The driver kept his eyes on the road now.

"Believe what?" Old Chen asked.

"That thing about 'being like water' accomplishing the most. I mean, you're not really a go-with-the-flow person yourself, are you?"

"Sometimes *xuzi* can be tied to a thought about quiet actors amidst the chaos," Old Chen said. "You don't have to be loud, fat and famous to be the one who shapes events and influences people. Sometimes it's the quiet people in the back who are having the most effect." He smiled, but the corners of his mouth twisted as if they wished to frown. "Not so much like me, really. More like your mama."

"*Xie xie*," I said. Thank you.

"I should have been quieter," Old Chen said, letting the smile disappear. "Maybe I would have heard more." He reached into the glove compartment and handed me a China Post envelope.

"Open when you get home," he said. Then he turned to Julia Too. "Put your mask back on, Little Treasure," he said in Chinese. "It only works if it's covering your nose and mouth."

At the Summer Palace, Old Chen and I sat on Empress Dowager Cixi's stone boat and took off our masks to chat and eat sausages wrapped in plastic. Knowing I would like it, he decided to stay all day, watch the sun set. We drank tea from a kiosk to stay warm, while Julia Too danced on the deck in her surgical mask, like a sci-fi ballerina.

April 1990, New York, NY

Dear Teacher,

   Lately I try to have hobby, as you suggest to be New York
life. I watch old American movie and go to see baseball game.
Those movie were big and dramatical, with explosions and
violence. I must remark that the women were frequently
naked. I watch *Scarface* and *Dog Day Afternoon*. Albert
Pacino is a talent. And I like this new public enemy music
about power. Maybe you know? Everybody in the U.S. like to
listen to music or watch movies, and wish their life will be
movie. In New York even when there is no violence you can
feel that there will be soon. America gives movies to other
countries like China, and the people in other country become
more American. They wish for movie life, for democracy or
violence. And when they fight for this they are killed. Like
my friends.

   I move to America and sit in theater to watch *Glory*
and *Goodfellas* and *Total Recall* and even this stupid joking
movie *Home Alone*. This American child left alone and
become independent and violent. That make me want to see
my Grandmother. But she is gone. I go to Yankees game with
the brother of my father. He bring his colleague from New
York so now I know many fact including Yankees win three
"world series" or Mariano Rivera is the great pitcher ever. I
know American women like to watch sport only with the
personal information about the players. Actually Chase and
Russ say this. I think its valuable knowledge for me to have to
approach American habits.

   Maybe the strategy of a government or country is not different from baseball. This could be why people enjoy so much

to watch baseball. Here is funny thing, I think. The baseball players must be are the best ones in the world. But that is not true for those government leaders. This situation is stupid. Why do you have to be big talent to be athlete or Albert Pacino in America but you can be cruel or stupid and still can be leader? Like Reagan. My father say that commoners in America have better life than commoners in China. But leaders in America have bad life compared to leaders in China. Leaders in America are mocked by American commoners and newspapers. Maybe my parents believe this is not suitable. But I think the leaders deserve it. Maybe Chinese leaders behave better if they became mocked by Chinese commoners and newspapers. But I guess it hasn't made America's leaders smart. So maybe the tryout for leaders should be like that one for baseball or your American Hollywood.

Da Ge

CHAPTER EIGHT

Aprils

ON APRIL 9, 1990, I FOUND OUT THE FIRST HORRIFYING TRUTH about Da Ge. I was by then planning our city hall wedding and lying and omitting with tremendous flair to my mother, the only person at this point in a position to ask me probing questions.

That night she walked into Cucina de Pesce where she'd arranged to meet me and Julia One for dinner, and threw her arms around me as if we lived thousands of miles apart. In fact, I had been at her apartment every day for two weeks, had introduced her to Xiao Wang, and Xiao Wang to matzo ball soup.

"Look at you," she said to me, hugging and then gazing at me.

"Just me," I said, pleased.

"How are you, honey? Everything okay?"

"Everything's fine."

"Julia, you're spectacular as always," she trilled, hugging Julia. A surge of unhappiness moved through me like a current.

My mother ordered a Bombay Sapphire martini and calamari. When the squid arrived, she used her fork to pick up a single fried ring and dip its edge into the marinara sauce. I picked a lemon wedge from the side of her plate and squirted it all over the food.

"Maybe Julia doesn't like lemon on hers," my mother said.

"I like everything," Julia said.

I tried to wash down the sarcastic feeling with a swig of my mother's martini.

She and Julia glanced at me nervously. You're not supposed to drink on mania drugs, and mostly I didn't. Sometimes I had red wine, but I was never much of a drinker, am still not, which surprises me. I strike myself as the drinking type, but maybe Jews tend not to be alcoholics because we're in touch with our neuroses, and therapy and interrupting your relatives and shouting about politics reduce the need to self-medicate.

The waiter brought my Diet Coke with lemon. I was tempted to squeeze more juice onto the calamari too, but I resisted, ate my mother's olives. She and Julia asked me repeatedly how I was. It started raining, and having established that I was fine, we talked about whether we'd be able to get a cab uptown, and the mystery of why as soon as a drop of water falls from the sky, every cab in New York City turns on its "off duty" light. We moved from there to a spate of kidnappings in New Jersey.

Then my mother inhaled. "Um. Jack asked me to marry him, and I said yes."

"You're kidding!" I said, stunned. Now ravishing Emily and I would be stepsisters. My mother was peering into my eyes, almost shyly.

"Congratulations, Naomi!" Julia said.

"Yes! Congratulations, Mom."

My mother blushed. Julia grinned at me, and I felt bad for having despised her a moment ago for "liking everything," since now she had reminded me in this important moment to congratulate my mom.

"How did he ask you?" I asked.

"What do you mean, how did he ask?"

"I mean, what words did he use?"

"We went out to dinner and he said, 'Will you marry me?'"

"On one knee?"

"No, not on one knee."

"Did you leap into his arms?"

"Only figuratively."

"When are you getting married?"

"Next spring."

"With a huge, real wedding?"

"No. Something understated. I hope you'll read a poem or make a toast."

"Of course." I looked out the window, saw rain bouncing off the streets, tuned out. When we left the restaurant, my mother took a compact umbrella from her handbag and tried to hold it over all three of us. The cab we had fought to get swam up the West Side Highway. I watched the wet city glitter and rain pound the river. At 96th Street my mother asked if she could come over. I disliked the idea, since I thought Da Ge might stop by. But she was so excited about having told us her news; I didn't want to hurt her feelings. I suggested we all go to her apartment instead, but she said she didn't want to inconvenience Julia and me. In fact she wanted to check my fridge and make sure the place looked sane and clean. My mother liked to sneak visits in, and pretend to be peeing while she scrubbed the bathroom—or to be having a glass of water while she mopped my kitchen. I couldn't say no. So we arrived at my place, dried off, and turned on *Casablanca*. I paced back and forth, agitating Naomi. This is precisely why pacing is calming—it makes everyone else nervous, they share the burden, and you relax.

"Sit down, honey," she said. I did not. "How about we turn the movie off and I give you guys manicures, then?" she suggested.

I went to the closet for my manicure kit, a present from her.

Then I heard the buzzer. I tried to think of an excuse to run outside for a minute and come back alone, but there was no way I'd be able to trick my mom or Julia. So I stood frozen in the hallway.

"Aysha!" My mom called. "Someone's at the door! What are you doing in there?"

"I'm looking for a nail file!"

"I have one with me. Just bring a color, darling."

I was holding the whole plastic kit, full of files. The buzzer rang again.

"Now who can that be?" my mother said.

I was surprised that she sounded like such an old person. "Who says, 'Now who can that be,' Mom?" I asked her.

"Apparently I do!"

"Keep practicing saying *I do*," I told her, as the buzzer rang a third time.

"Why aren't you getting the door, Aysh?"

"I am," I said. "I am." My mother walked into the hallway to see what was stopping me, and then stood there watching. I didn't listen for Da Ge's voice over the intercom, just pressed the open-door button. I planned to let him come up, assess the situation for himself, and then leave.

That's not how it worked out.

When I opened the door for him, my mother was still standing behind me in the hallway. I wondered which of us saw Da Ge first, since I had turned to look at her behind me. I think I saw him register in her face before I saw him myself.

"Da Ge!" she said to him. Her pronunciation was gorgeous.

He had rain in his hair and eyelashes. All of a sudden, he swooned against the door frame, moved in toward me two steps, and slumped down against the hallway wall. He was so drunk that he hadn't even said hello back to my mother.

Julia craned her neck into the hallway to see. "Who is it?" she asked.

My mother said, "He's one of the kids from the hospital."

I spun around to look at her. She looked back at me, innocently.

"He's my student," I said. My voice came from far away. I didn't look at my mother, just bent and tried to help Da Ge up. My mother closed her home manicure shop. She and Julia and I half-carried and half-dragged Da Ge into the living room. He glanced around at us, blearily.

"Who's Aysha?" he asked. The words ran together like rain. I remembered the storm and looked up at the window, streaming.

"He means where am I," I told Julia and my mom. Even I was surprised at how pathetic it sounded.

"Of course he does," my mother said. Julia was staring at him. I wondered if she'd met him, too, how I'd convince her he wasn't the Chinese student I'd mentioned sleeping with. She quietly slipped out, returned to her apartment.

My mother poured a glass of water and set it on the windowsill. Then she busied herself putting clean sheets on the futon for Da Ge. The shock began to crystallize.

"How did you know his name? How did you know how to pronounce his name?" I asked, trying to keep my voice on a calm blue line. I had heard my mother say hospital. Had I heard her say hospital? I wasn't ready to understand what that meant.

"Hang on, sweetie. Let's tuck Da Ge in, and then we'll chat in your room."

She pulled the covers up over him lovingly, and then we sat on my bed.

"He was in the hospital when you were," she said.

I said nothing.

"Did he not tell you we had met?" she asked me.

Anger burned my mind blank, whited out the panic. "He mentioned it," I lied.

Now we were quiet. My mother, knowing this couldn't be true, was at a loss. She and I were not in the habit of calling each other out on little lies. In this respect, we were quite Chinese. Americans love to confront and pin each other to the wall. Chinese people don't do this so much; they move sideways in conversations and negotiations, leaving you room to escape even your own fabrications, exaggerations, and euphemisms.

"Is he really in your class?"

"Yes."

"Oh. Is he okay? Does he behave normally toward you?"

"How do you mean normally?"

"I mean, what kind of relationship do you guys have?"

Even though it wasn't my mother I was angry at, I couldn't help taking it out on her. "What kind of relationship do *you guys* have?"

"Come on, Aysha. He was at St. Luke's when you were there. He was recovering from some kind of trauma," she said evenly. "When I met him, he told me he had just been through the democracy protests in China. Apparently he was upset. All I know for sure is that he was in the psychiatric ward. He had a lot of bruises, and some stitches in his face. I only asked him once what happened, and he said he'd fallen."

"But—?"

"But nothing. I thought he had probably tried to hurt himself."

My mother has never used the words "commit suicide" or "kill himself" in my presence. I think my single episode terrified her so much that she imagines if she planted either of those phrases in my mind, even now, they might inspire me to take action. But the truth is, I've never felt particularly suicidal. I was astonished to hear that Da Ge had.

"You didn't ask him why falling landed him in a mental hospital?"

"I didn't want to challenge him, honey. We didn't know each other that well, of course, and I wasn't interrogating him. Plus, you know, his English wasn't perfect, and I wasn't sure I'd be able to communicate sensitive stuff like that." She stopped herself. "How close are you two?"

"We hardly know each other," I said, and as I heard the words, I realized they were true. A visceral dread seized me, one that started in my bones and rose out until my hair prickled with it. I wanted to unzip my skin and run from my life. But I caught my breath and started lying. "He sometimes stops by to pick up homework assignments."

My mother was tickling my back in a lullaby gesture. "Late at night?" she asked.

I moved my back away, and she put her sad hand in her lap. "Obviously this was an exception to the normal visiting-hours rule," I told her.

"Don't snap at me. Do you have social relationships with any other students?"

"Of course. They need extra help all the time. You've met Xiao Wang."

In all the years I've taught, Xiao Wang and Da Ge are the only students I ever developed social relationships with (if you can call them that.). Mania allows for such connections. Later, when I was sane, I knew more people, but in less intense ways.

That night Da Ge slept on the futon, and my mother stayed over and slept in my bed with me. When we woke, he was gone. The futon was folded up. My mom took me to the Museum of Natural History, where we sat under the blue whale. She put both of her arms around me. On the way out, she bought freeze-dried Neapolitan ice cream from the gift shop, and I ate it on the walk back to her place like an astronaut, ready to lie my way through the next few months, marry him anyway, take a trip to the moon.

The flu Old Chen was worried about has twisted Beijing into a horrible tornado of public relations scandals, apologies, travel warnings, and rushes on hospitals. There's been a mass exodus of diplomats and expatriates. Events are being canceled daily and there's no one on the streets. I've never seen anything like it. Half of Global Beijing is absent; parents are too freaked out to send their kids to school. Maybe I'm reckless, but when I look at the numbers of people infected, it doesn't seem as threatening as hepatitis. But I guess if you can catch whatever it is by being in the same country as someone who has it, then it makes sense for the UN to issue a travel advisory.

Shannon and Zhang Sun agree with each other for once. They think the flu is a conspiracy to bring China down. We had a picnic on Saturday in an empty Ritan Park.

"Where are the people? Everyone believes this? It's just bullshit propaganda!" Shannon kept saying. "Twenty people have flu and the world boycotts Beijing? Are people insane? More people die of diarrhea every day than have died of this ever."

"Not rich people," Zhang Sun pointed out. "Hey!" he shouted, standing up. He hopped off the blanket and raced toward the entrance of the park, where his mother was buying her twenty-cent entrance ticket from a woman in a surgical mask and hairnet. Zhang Sun took his mom's arm and led her over to us.

"Xu Nai Nai is here, stand up," he told Sophie, and I felt a twinge of envy. Sophie got up from the blanket where she and Julia Too were stretched out looking at last year's GB yearbook and whispering secrets. Their surgical masks were up on their heads like headbands, a cute look. Zhang Sun's mom ran over and swatted Sophie on the butt.

"Xu Nai Nai!" Sophie said. She kissed the old woman, leaving a big lip-gloss print on Xu Nai Nai's face. The old woman began immediately to frisk Sophie in what I recognized as a pathological long-underwear check.

"So few clothes!" she said in Chinese. "You don't fear cold?"

"I fear heat," Sophie responded, and collapsed again onto the blanket. Julia Too craned her thin neck around and smiled at Xu Nai Nai, gave a little wave.

"Have a seat," Shannon said, "I brought tea eggs and sausage for you."

"You eat first," said Xu Nai Nai, "you eat first."

"We've eaten," Shannon said.

"Why aren't you wearing masks?" Xu Nai Nai asked. She reached into her bag and pulled out an unopened box of surgical masks. "Here," she said, "extras!"

"Eat some lunch first," said Zhang Sun, handing her a paper plate with a tea egg and red-plastic-wrapped sausage. "Then we'll talk."

"Why aren't *you* wearing a mask, mom?" Zhang Sun asked.

"I'm too old for such bullshit," she said. "I'd probably choke to death on the mask. I'd rather get the flu."

Shannon laughed with her mouth open at this. "But you should wear one, Shannon," Xu Nai Nai said in Chinese. "You don't want to pass anything to Sophie!"

Xu Nai Nai is hardly the only old woman to be worried. I've promised my mother that things will have calmed down by summer when she's supposed to visit. But right now it's hard to say. Julia Too wears a surgical mask all day; I've forgotten what her mouth looks like. And since no one goes out anymore, she works full-time on a project she has yet to show me.

I know vaguely what it is. Old Chen's envelope was filled with frayed pictures, dozens of a fat baby in buttless pants, crawling, sitting on his mama's lap, and lying immobilized by enormous padded winter costumes. Then there were four shots of a scrappy kid in the streets of a *hutong*, and two of the same boy in underpants on the Beidaihe shore. There were two of him climbing Fragrant Hills, three sleeping, and two riding a bike. There was only one teenage photo, in which he sits alone on a bed, surly, out of focus. And that was it. Not a single adult photo.

Julia Too bought fourteen pieces of handmade paper, maroon and textured, and some photo corners. Then she retreated to her room for three weeks of evenings. She's illustrating a book, that much I know. I haven't asked her anything but how it's going. She nods seriously, says *fine*. I figure she'll show me when she's ready, but some nights, when I see her bent over in her room, cutting out pieces of paper or drawing on those pages, I think my heart might claw its way out of my chest.

The Monday after he stopped by drunk and ran into my mother, I cornered Da Ge before class, not caring what my other students thought.

"You told my mother that you fell?" I asked him. "You were in the lunatic ward because you fell? You knew my mother from the hospital? Why didn't you tell me that?"

"We can meet after school to have some chat, okay, Aysha?"

Xiao Wang was staring at us, unblinking, as if she had always known it would come to this. I took an eight-second breath and walked to the front of the room to read Langston Hughes's "I, Too, Sing America." Its perfect fifteen-letter title fit on my fingers. No one noticed I was counting them over and over in my mind. Or that every sentence I uttered fit in multiples of five. My right hand moved like a running spider on the side of my leg. I was spelling everything. I was in control. Then Ingyum was standing, describing how to knit a scarf for "hobby show and tell." It felt interminable, even though I normally loved this sort of lesson. Xiao Wang had done a stir-fry demonstration, holding an imaginary wok and saying, "then you put the meat in, then you take the meat out," and I thought I would teach her the hokey-pokey when she next came over to watch movies. Chase and Russ had done baseball, complete with bat and ball, although I asked them just to "mime" hitting the ball. They were brilliant, throwing around baseball words like pitch, strike, and slide, and ending with a rousing description of home runs. Everyone cheered. I wanted to be happy, to focus on the words and celebrate, correct, and clap, but I felt like a fly, buzzing above the room, my dozens of insect eyes all looking in different directions. When Ingyum finished, I dismissed the class, dying to clear them out and hear whatever lies Da Ge was going to use to comfort me.

On a payphone close to Embassy, I called Dr. Meyers to cancel my appointment with her—for the first time. I said I had a fever. Could she hear the traffic whipping by?

"Take care of yourself," she said, the way Bonita had. The way Adam always did.

Da Ge was waiting outside the phone booth, his backpack slung over one shoulder, the muscles in his jaw moving. Maybe he was grinding his teeth. His eyes had sunk further into his head since I'd met him. I closed my eyes and told myself that when I opened them, if the first number on the phone I saw was even, everything would be okay. I didn't even know what that meant. When I opened my eyes, I saw all the numbers at once. He hadn't brought an extra helmet, but I rode on the back of his moped anyway, half-hoping we'd crash and never have to have the conversation. But we

survived and arrived at Tom's Diner. Safe in our booth, I sat
with my stomach grinding.

"I had a accident," said Da Ge, eating fries with a fork.
"I meet your mother in the hospital when you are there. I'm
sorry I don't tell you. I don't want you to think I am—"

"What, insane?"

He raised an eyebrow, then tucked a paper napkin
around his burger before picking it up and biting so tidily it
reminded me of my mother.

"What kind of accident was it?" My words came out
thick with dread, a dark mess of mixed paint. Da Ge spun a
forkful of the spaghetti he had also ordered. I had never seen
anyone order both a burger and spaghetti. He put the noodles in his mouth.

"Oh my motorbike," he lied, chewing.

"Oh," I said. "You crashed it?"

He finished chewing, swallowed. "Your mother is very
worried for you then."

"She told you that?"

"I can tell."

"But what about you? Tell me about the accident."

"I fell the bike."

"You were thrown, you mean?" I couldn't stop supply-
ing him with excuses.

"Right."

He looked so young and skinny, eating his two entrees. I
wondered if he had envied me in the hospital. For the first
time, I thought how grateful I should have been for my mother's care. "Who took care of you at St. Luke's?" I asked.

"The doctor."

"No one else? Did anyone visit you?"

"I take care of myself around that time. Maybe my
father's brother, Zhen Ming."

"What about your father? He didn't come?"

"No. He doesn't know this."

"You didn't tell him about the accident."

"This will be too much trouble for him."

"Maybe he would have come." I said.

He said nothing, shook his head no.

"All right, maybe not. But why were you on the floor for mental patients?"

"I suffer mind thing," he said.

I heard the echo of Xiao Wang's words in his. Had she known about this all along? Or somehow guessed it?

"You mean, the accident was because of the mind thing? Or the mind thing was because of the accident?"

He was wrapping more noodles around his fork. I wanted to throw his plate at the wall, hear the porcelain shatter, spray the place with pasta sauce.

"The other thing you said," he said calmly.

"What?"

"Because the accident, my mind become weak."

I wanted to believe him so badly that I offered up the word. "Shock," I said.

He nodded.

"You were in shock because of the accident?"

"Maybe," he said.

"But did you plan the accident?"

"What does this mean, plan?"

"Did you want to crash the bike? Did you want to hurt yourself?"

"Who says I crash the motorbike? I just have an accident and fall. That's all."

We looked at each other, and the right side of his mouth edged up into a smile. I smiled back, agreed to let it go. Da Ge gulped some Coke, reached into his backpack.

"Maybe you can help me," he said, pushing a fat folder across the table.

I opened it, found American citizenship application forms full of bizarre vocabulary. I recognized some from our marriage registration process: Petition For Alien Relative, Registering Permanent Residence, Supplement A to Form I-485, Application to Register Permanent Residence, USCIS Form G-325A— Biographic Information U.S. Citizen, Affidavit of Support Contract Between Sponsor and Household Member. He pointed to a practice booklet for a test about U.S. history. "You will help me with some study? It's okay for you?"

"Of course," I told him. "And I'll fill out all the forms for you."

"Thank you, Aysha," he said. Hearing my name in his voice gave me the feeling of falling. Like in a dream. I jolted, caught myself, studied the tabletop: metallic patterns winding inside Formica.

"Can I ask you something, please?"

"Zhen Ming have a doctor to do the medical thing," he said.

"That wasn't the question. It's not about your citizenship."

"Oh," he said. "More that accident?"

"No. What happened on June fourth?"

He stared at me. "There was a student uprising in Tiananmen Square," he said. "The People's Liberation Army came into the square to kill the students."

I wasn't going for it.

"I mean what happened to you."

His eyes had the red marble look. He waited a minute before he said, as if it were an attack on me, "I wasn't there."

"You weren't there," I repeated, hot parrot, confused.

"I am already in America because my father send me here earlier. He offer me a ticket to America and I take it."

"When?"

"May twenty-eighth," he said, looking down. Eight days

after the Chinese government declared martial law, a week before June 4. Two weeks after my own breakdown.

"Oh," I said, the weight of it coming at me. "Oh." I tried to remember when exactly I'd been hospitalized, to grasp the coincidence.

Da Ge's head snapped back up. "So I am not your guy in front of the tank."

I ignored this. "You had the 'accident,' and went to St. Luke's in June? When?"

"I don't know," he said, "maybe sometime. June. I am far away and rich and safe, just like my father."

"Did your father send you here because you were depressed? Or did he do it because he guessed what was going to happen?"

"He bought me," Da Ge said, and dropped his voice an octave. "Here, Da Ge! Take this—money and ticket to *Mei Guo*, pretty country—there you will see your democracy! And you have to do nothing for it! Here, here!" He took his wallet out, grabbed a wad of cash, and threw it up so that the bills scattered. Other people looked over at us. I made no move to retrieve the money. Bills floated to the floor.

"I took it," he said. "I took that ticket, those moneys. All those meetings, who was I? I was nothing! I put folding chairs. I print leaflet. I call myself strong fighter? Even my mother would be disappoint. Maybe if she's alive she don't want democracy. But of course she will want me to be hero. But I fly away safe to America because I am weak—"

"You're not weak," I said, "It's not your fault—you didn't know . . ."

"In America what do I do? I watch sport and meet pretty girl. Everything is for money in this nothing life. I will never be my mother, who believe in something. And I will never be my father, who don't believe but live well and feel happy."

"But you'll be you. And you're—" I don't know if I could have put the words together to say what I meant even if he hadn't interrupted. That I found him soulful and brave, that he was my favorite person. Or just that I loved him. That would have sufficed.

"Used to be I think I want China to be free," he said, "but really I just want I myself am free. I realize that selfish thing but then it is too late. I am already here. I have what everyone in the world dream of—to come to America. But I don't want to live here, once I know. America is too easy. You fight for nothing. You never have like June fourth."

"That's not true, actually. Have you ever heard of Kent State?"

"What state?"

"It's a university where the American government killed protestors."

"Students?"

"Yes."

"Short time ago?"

"Unacceptably recently, yes."

"How many students?"

"Four."

"What was that protest?"

"The students were against the Vietnam War."

"American government killed those students?"

"Yes."

He took this in. "What happened from it?"

"Nothing."

"What means nothing?"

"I mean nothing happened. The government didn't learn its lesson."

"How do you know?"

"Because ten days later they did it again at another school—two more students during a protest against racism."

"Do you think they will do that now?"

"That American police would shoot at students, you mean?"

"Yes."

"Given the right context."

He finished his last bite of spaghetti and pushed the plate into the dollar bills, still lying on the table like awkward, dead things.

I planned to tell the immigration officers that his favorite food was spaghetti, in case they asked during the test to see if we were in love.

"Students have hope," he said, collecting the bills into a pile. "Governments crush hope so students can graduate and join the hopeless governments and run the countries."

"That's a bleak view."

"Do you know anyone from that schools?"

"I was a baby when they happened."

"I know the ones at Tiananmen. If I am not so weak and selfish, could be it's me there with my friends."

"Are your friends okay?"

"I don't know. I'm not contact with them."

"Couldn't your father find out for you?"

"I don't want to talk to him."

I should have told Da Ge what my brother, Benj, had tried to tell me, that parents are too important, that it's worth trying forever to forgive them, that making up and loving your mom and dad are worth any sacrifice. But I didn't know it myself yet.

"Maybe things will get better," I said. I hoped for both of us that this was a possibility.

"I remember I first meet your mother walking around the hall in the hospital," Da Ge said. "And then I see you. You are so pretty, I think. Sad and so pretty. But you never see me. I don't know why. I always watch you when you walk on the hall with your mother, you with dark hair and big eyes and the light face and this—" he reached across the table and touched my mouth "—this small mouth."

"Why didn't you talk to me?" I asked.

He kept his fingers on my face. "I don't know how," he said.

"Did you talk to my mom?"

"Yes."

"Did you ask her what was wrong with me?"

"Yes."

"What did she say?"

"She say you were terrible hurt by her and your father."

When we stood up, Da Ge put his arm around me. Outside, he kept holding on, and I shut my eyes. We walked the three blocks to my apartment this way, slowly. I don't know if he knew I had my eyes closed, but I didn't hit anything or get run over. I heard traffic lights turning, cars blowing by, the bookseller closing his van stuffed with paperbacks. The clouds shifted into patterns I would never see. Walking this way, blindly, made me feel like there was all the time in the world.

After lying to me about his "accident," Da Ge came to every class for the rest of the semester and participated as if he were my teaching assistant. Maybe he was atoning. That April, everyone had to read either an article or an entire book in English and write a summary of the piece they'd read. I brought in some books from my childhood.

Chase and Russ did book reports on *Ramona Quimby*, which Chase described as "the moving tale" of a young girl who makes many mistakes, "like forgetting to wear underclothes to school." Russ said he had not enjoyed the book because it was too silly.

I assigned Xiao Wang to read *Forever*, knowing she'd be shocked. Her report read like a book-banning pamphlet, and

I couldn't stifle my laughter in class when she read it out loud. "This book is inappropriate for any children under the college age," was her first sentence. She went on to say that it was full of "details of the act of sexual relations," and that it was no wonder America has so much violence and the children here have sexual relations instead of studying. According to her book report, that was why test scores were lower in the United States than in China.

"Do you think Chinese teenagers don't have sex?" I asked her in class.

Everyone else was surprised and delighted that the conversation had taken this turn, except perhaps Da Ge, who made a point of looking away.

"Chinese teenagers are quite innocent," Xiao Wang said.

"Don't you think it depends on who the teenager is?" I asked. "I mean, isn't it possible that *some* Chinese teenagers have sex?"

"Maybe possible," she said, "but we do not have books like this that tell them they should think all day about sexual relations."

"I'm not sure that's the point of the book, but good job on the report," I said.

Ingyum had read *Tales of a Fourth Grade Nothing*, and wrote that it helped her understand her own fourth-grader, a self-proclaimed Yankees fan who preferred painting pictures of dogs and building intricate Lego spaceships to playing baseball.

Da Ge alone opted not to borrow a book from me. He came to class carrying a shriveled copy of Kafka stories, its pages covered with Chinese characters. He had translated almost every word. When he stood in front of the class in his gray cargo pants, my pulse galloped. We're getting married, I thought. Married! I had a surge of his body in my bed, his arms around my waist, his face against my neck. My stomach somersaulted. *He belongs to me in some way*, I thought, *even if it's a small way*. My adrenaline was mixed with wrongheaded relief, a feeling that nothing could ever be off again. Because I was in love with him, the teenage kind of love that's both so idiotic and naive that it's not the real thing, and so idiotic and naïve that it's the only real thing.

"In the story," Da Ge was saying, "the prisoner is killed by needles that spell out what he do. He bleed until he die. He live in police society, where whatever you do you are killed by authority." He put his paper down. "I learn a new word from this book," he said. "That is transfiguration.'"

He was looking at me. "It mean change. After the man die, Kafka say his dead body show no sign of that 'transfiguration.' So maybe the point is that it's waste. Or maybe the point is there is not difference from being alive and being dead. For me, the point is it doesn't matter what the point is. Because we are punishing ourselves."

I only heard the lilting grammar, the surface. I wish I'd been ten years older then, that I could have been the person I am now, without having sacrificed Da Ge to become her. I would have said no, that he was wrong, that there were countless other points and ways to read that story and the world, possibilities for how a live plot could work out. I might have loved him out of it. But maybe it took that failure to grow me up. And now the best I can do is try to save Julia Too from her genes, her father's genes, her grandmother's genes. And to be perfectly fair, from my genes, too.

At dumplings this Saturday, Julia Too gave the book she's been working on to Old Chen. He had just finished eating, and his maid, wearing not only a surgical mask but also a hospital-issue gown and hairnet, was clearing his chopsticks and vinegar dish.

Julia Too grabbed her bag, carried it around the table to Old Chen, and unzipped it. She looked so much like Da Ge that I stared. She's growing out her bangs, and her dark hair flopped over her eyes and she smoothed it behind her ears before it immediately fell onto her face again. I walked over, stood behind her, twisted her hair into a little bun and secured it by poking a chopstick through.

"Thanks, Mom," she said. She pulled her project out and placed it on the table.

"*Gei ni zuo de,*" she said to Old Chen. "I made this for you." She stayed behind him, peering over his shoulder. He held the book for a moment as if steeling himself. Then he opened it up and took a full minute per page. When he had finished, he passed it to me. Each page had a single photo of Da Ge in its center, secured by four silver corners. They were surrounded by Julia Too's designs: black ink flowers, twirling vines, fish, butterflies. Against the maroon pages and around the old photos, her doodles looked avant-garde and foreign. On the final page, underneath Da Ge as a teenager, she had written out two lines from a Wang Wei poem Da Ge once read me and that I now sometimes read to her: "I'll ask you nothing else. White clouds forever."

Old Chen hadn't said anything, and I felt nervous for Julia Too.

"The book is beautiful," I said. "How'd you choose those two lines?"

"It's all I could fit," she said. She rested her hand on Old Chen's shoulder.

"*Xihuan ma*?" she asked Old Chen. Do you like it? "I made it for you."

"It's a thoughtful thing you made, Zhu-Lia," he said, "the calligraphy is especially good. It must have taken you a long time." He reached around and pulled her in. "Thank you, *baober,* Little Treasure. But I meant for you and your mama to keep the pictures."

"I know," said Julia Too, "but we can share if we keep them here. I thought you might want them. They look nice with the drawings, don't you think?"

"*Zhen shi de*," he said. They really do. Then he stood up and wandered past the couch, a modern yellow leather thing with metal feet and a plastic cover still on, to a dresser sitting atop an oppressively patterned silk rug. Old Chen insists on staying in a renovated courtyard house, either his way of staying true to tradition or close to the memory of the house he lived in with his wife and son.

He looked old and fragile, walking across the room. His wrinkles seemed singed into his face suddenly as he hunched to pull out the Go table. I was too paralyzed with sorrow to offer help, just watched him bend and set the game up on his overstated antique coffee table. It was more than just his age. The grief became visible, physical in that moment, as if a rock a day had been stacked on his back for three decades. I hated Da Ge. Old Chen leaned down and began organizing shiny black and white half marbles, looking like he might collapse. I looked away.

"Zhu-Lia," he said in Chinese. "Come and play Go with me." He straightened up.

"*Lai le*," she said. I'm here.

She sat on the couch across from him, tucked her feet up under her, and lost game after game of Go. He instructed her patiently, and I sat on a Ming-inspired chair, flipping through a *China Daily* full of flu news, a "10-point battle plan" to contain cases, China's soaring aquatic product exports, the unearthing of ancient bronze workshops by archaeologists, and a piece I tore out for Yang Tao about ethnic minority women discovering cameras, called "Hill Dwellers Climb Cultural Mountain." I put the remainder of the paper down and sat watching as Old Chen and Julia Too clicked black and white glass drops along the marble-inlaid table and laughed at each other's strategies.

When Julia Too is around, Old Chen stops organizing his life until it gleams with precision—and plays. I remember when he taught Julia Too to ride a bike. She was four, and he held her up like human training wheels—for a year. Then she was five. The day she let him let go and sped away, I watched him watch her pedal into the distance laughing, her hair flying back. She moved so fast she was instantly a dot in the distance. At first he and I were clapping, but suddenly he ran as if she had fallen although she hadn't, bolted across the park to bring her back—make her life-sized again.

During the Go game, Old Chen's maid and cook, both dressed in flu scrubs, peeked over and over into the living room to glimpse their boss made grandfatherly by my little girl. Then each time they receded into the kitchen, disbelieving and gleeful, giggling behind their masks.

Da Ge's and my wedding ceremony was an understated affair. We got married on a rainy day in the spring of 1990. We had known each other for less than a year. I meant to tell Julia One that we were going to have a city hall ceremony, to ask her to be our witness. But I wanted no part of reason, and I couldn't risk giving her a chance to talk me out of Da Ge. So no one knew, and Julia wasn't our witness. I regretted this that day at the municipal building, and still regret it a bit now. Da Ge's uncle Zhen Ming was working, and I didn't like him anyway. So no one was present except the slightly pregnant girl we asked to be our witness because she was standing there, and the justice of the peace.

Da Ge wore a trench coat over cargo pants on an elastic drawstring and a gray hooded sweatshirt. His scar looked blistering, and his eyes twitched. He looked more than three-dimensional to me, he was so agitated. I wanted to calm him down. He didn't mention my dress, even though I rarely taught in one and had bought a trim cream frock with buttons for the occasion. We sat on a bench, and I put my hands in my lap.

"My uncle Zhen Ming says we need to have it," he said.

I looked around. "Have what?"

He took a box out of his pocket. In it was a plain set of gold bands.

I smiled. "I like them," I said.

He looked surprised by this.

"Oh," he said, "good."

He handed me the little one.

"No," I said, "You take this one and give it to me during the ceremony. I take the big one and give it to you. We can put them on each other's fingers."

"Okay," he said, holding the smaller ring.

The justice called our names, and we went into a corner room. I wished we had invited Xiao Wang and Russ and Chase and Ingyum, that we were having a real wedding, with our whole ESL class. We could recite vows together. "In sickness and health," we would say. No one would get the "th" sound right. "Health," I would say again, "heal*th*."

"Do you take this man," the justice asked, "to be your lawfully wedded husband?"

I realized we were actually getting married. "Excuse me," I said. "I'm sorry to do this, but can you wait one minute?" Da Ge looked at me, terror stripping across his face. "It's okay, darling," I said to him, tasting the fake word like grape-flavored candy. "I just need one second to catch my breath."

"I will come?" he asked.

"No, no," I said, "It's okay." I handed him my purse, as if I might come back for such pitiful collateral.

The hallway was cool and full of oxygen. I breathed wildly, drinking it up, found a payphone, called my mother.

"Are you okay?" She asked.

"I love you," I said.

She paused. "I love you too, Aysh."

"That's all," I said. "I just wanted you to know it."

She shifted her weight; I felt it. "You sure you're okay?" she asked.

"Never better."

"Where are you? Are you taking your meds?"

I was annoyed. "I'm downtown. And yes, I'm taking my meds. Can't I call you without seeming like a psychopath?"

"Of course," she said, and blew me a kiss through the phone. We hung up, and I walked back into the room where Da Ge was waiting.

"Sorry about that," I said. I looked at the justice of the peace. "I do," I said. She nodded, annoyed that we had taken extra time. We put the rings on. Then we were lawful and wedded. She said nothing about *you may now kiss the bride*, but I stood on my tiptoes anyway and kissed Da Ge with so much force I hoped it would make the whole thing real. Exactly the way I wanted to. He stumbled back.

"*Tian!*" he said. *My God.* One of the few expressions I had already learned.

"Congratulations," said our knocked-up witness.

Da Ge and I had to create a photo album of the life we'd need to prove we had together. I made him keys to my apartment, and we spent a few days sightseeing, making memories, taking pictures. We went to the Central Park Zoo, where sea lions darted under water like fat, slippery spears and polar bears slept, their toys floating pointlessly in a bright blue pool. Monkeys leapt and swung, stuck their tongues out at us. Da Ge stuck his tongue out back. I took a picture. One monkey picked nits out of his friend's fur.

"You would do it for me?" Da Ge asked me, tugging on my hair.

"Do you have nits?" I asked him.

"What is this nit?"

"This nit's the egg of a bug in your hair," I said, laughing. It was shocking how bad my own English was getting.

"Egg of a bug?" he asked.

"Insect," I said, and made a buzzing noise, waved my fingers around like flies.

"Oh, that," he said. "Bug have eggs?"

"I think so," I said, no longer sure.

"Do you have?"

"Do I have what?"

"This nit!" Da Ge grabbed me by the waist and pulled my stomach toward his. He peered into my hair and then picked at it with his fingers.

Our one spring. We walked to the Central Park duck pond, where cherry blossoms were falling on the grass and families pushed strollers by. We sat on the library steps while Columbia students inflated a thousand blue and white balloons. We ate Thai food, bought socks at a street fair, watched the cannibal horror *The Cook, The Thief, His Wife and Her Lover*, which I found dizzying. Maybe Da Ge wanted a reality check, too, because he put his hand under my skirt, played with the elastic edge of my underpants.

"Did you like that?" I asked afterwards. We were in Young, New Seafood on Amsterdam, buying dinner. I was worried he'd hold me and/or Americans responsible for the movie.

"Like what?" He grinned. I probably giggled at this.

"I meant the movie."

"That was too crazy," he said. "I think it's meant to be joke."

The fishmonger handed him a whole red snapper.

"What are you going to do with the eyes?" I asked, unable to resist.

"What eyes?" he asked. He glanced at the paper-wrapped fish. "Those? Nothing."

We went to University Food Market so Da Ge could buy bean sprouts, ginger, and scallions. I bought some rice cakes and Popsicles.

"Do you have the soy sauce and sesame oil?"

When I said I had soy sauce, he looked as if he had been expecting this answer. Here we are, I thought, a regular married couple, shopping in the supermarket.

"Next time we go to Chinatown," Da Ge said. "Here, there is nothing."

At home there were streaks of rain on the windows. I turned on all the lamps, lit candles. Da Ge took over my kitchen again, chopping and frying and pouring things onto the stove. I tried to help, but he shooed me away. It was just as well, since I was put off by the slack-bellied fish. I used to like my meat filleted and clean, its animal life kept secret. Now I've changed. I prefer my flavored potato chips have pictures of twitching shrimp on the package, and I've eaten things I never knew existed: sea slugs, "horse whip," mosquito eyes. Apparently bats devour mosquitoes but can't digest their eyes, so chefs roast whole bats, slice them open like melons, and scoop out the seedy, googly clumps. What makes that tasty is that somebody thought it up in the first place. But since Da Ge's life was what made me adventurous, he never saw the fruits of his effort. I tasted his dishes, but I doubt he thought I'd ever devour turtles, eels, tripe, or feet the way I do now.

He showed me a plate. "Tiger food," he said. Cucumber, cilantro, pepper, and scallion in sesame oil, hot chili, and sugar. I tasted it. "Crispy and sharp," I said. "It's delicious." The fish stared at me.

Da Ge took his disposable chopsticks, rubbed them together, and tore off a hunk of cheek flesh. I thought he was joking, but he leaned across the table and set it on my plate.

"Really?" I asked. He rolled his eyes, a gesture that struck me as imported. Maybe eye rolling is an American habit, since it contrasted oddly with his slapping a fish cheek on my plate.

". . . the best part," he was saying.

I ate the cheek. "It's great," I said. Now Da Ge was eyeing me, giving me the sense that I had passed some kind of test, even if I was an ingrate, faking it.

"My mother always like this dish," he said, gesturing to some shriveled green beans under a blanket of sauce and ground pork. "My father like to make that."

"Yum," I said. I put a green bean between my teeth, hoping to look like my mom.

"My father have a lot of girlfriends. Thin, fat, tall, every kind."

"Your father had mistresses while your mom was alive?"

"I mean after, but maybe before, too. Every Chinese businessman has it."

"You're hard on China," I said. "Men have mistresses everywhere."

"In your family?" he asked.

I stared at him. "Yeah," I said finally. "My dad, too, I guess."

"You don't know?"

"I do know. He cheated on my mom, and I saw him with the woman." It came back to me in a surge almost as sickening as the one I'd had when I saw them: her curly dark head tilted back so she could look up at him, my father laughing in a way I'd never seen. Her lips were red and wet, waiting for my dad to press his mouth against them.

I inhaled. "I decided to tell my mom," I said to Da Ge.

"Of course you do," Da Ge said. He set his chopsticks down, reached across the table, and put his hand over mine. "That was right. Of course you tell your mom this."

"I don't know if it counts as a mistress anyway, since my dad married her."

Now Da Ge nodded. "Maybe now he married her he will also have a new one. Usually men who are like this—are like this."

"I know what you mean, but I don't think my—"

"My mother hate the men like this. Maybe even my father and me."

I gulped some wine. What did he mean? Was he "like this," too?

"She couldn't have hated you," I said.

"My mother had honor," he said. "I am the product made by my father, maybe she hate this product."

"You were her baby," I said, "not a product. She definitely loved you, and she must have loved your father at some point, enough to have had you, right?"

He sighed. "I think she do love him. He can be kind. He like to talk the zodiac with me. Or fly kites. When I'm a kid. Maybe my mother believe he is—how do you say—mouth of a dagger, heart of tofu."

"Do you believe that, too?"

"Believe what?"

"That you father has a heart of tofu?"

"I used to think it's right."

"And now?"

"He sent her away and now he also sent me away. I believe nothing, like she finally believe nothing, even after she believe so many thing in her life."

I considered this, arranged tiger food into a spicy doily on my plate. "Did she leave you a note?"

"No. She say nothing. My mother is, how do you say,

internal person." He took a sip of water. "Maybe her heart break because my father and me, even she doesn't know yet how bad we will both be. Or maybe she do know."

He leaned back in his chair, and I gasped, thought he might fall. But he caught himself, hooked a foot around the leg of the table. "My mother see from history more bad thing will happen," he said. "She will be too much sorrow. She won't be able to live."

I placed my chopsticks in parallel lines next to my plate. "But that's not your father's fault," I said, groping. "Or yours." I didn't know whether I believed this or just wanted to. In fact, I just wanted to believe it so much that I did. And I still do. "People kill themselves because they're ill," I said, thinking it was precisely what my mother would have said in that conversation, especially if she'd been having it with me. "Not because they don't love their families. I'm certain she loved you."

"You're easy person to be certain," Da Ge said. He stood up and started clearing the dishes. I stood up too, and stopped him, put the plates back on the table and my right hand on his face. I felt him slow down. Encouraged, I added my other hand, held his chin.

"I am not an easy person to be certain," I corrected. "But maybe your mother thought that if she said good-bye, she wouldn't be able to do what she felt she had to do."

How many times I would replay that stupid speech in my mind.

"What she had to do?" he repeated. I heard my voice in his. "Do you mean leave me forever?" He twisted his face away from my hands.

That dinner was our honeymoon.

May 1990, New York, NY

Dear Aysha,
   Now you are not my teacher anymore, but I think
I will still write you letters. Is that OK for you?

      Your,
      Da Ge

CHAPTER NINE
Mays
＊

THREE YEARS AFTER JULIA TOO AND I MOVED TO BEIJING, I HAD collected enough courage to call the one Chinese friend Da Ge had ever mentioned by name. He's a painter who calls himself Red Moon. I had followed him online, thinking he might be able to give me some history, a kind of ghost fix. But it took me three years to call information and get his number, which I dialed from school. When he picked up, I sat down on the floor of my classroom.

"*Wei*?" Hello?

"*Nihao*," I said, hi. "I'm, um, is this Hong Yue?"

"*Shi de*." Yes.

I contemplated hanging up.

"*Wei*?" he said again, "*ni shi shei*?" Who is this?

"I'm a friend of your old friend Chen Da Ge," I said in Chinese.

At this, he switched to choppy English. "You are her wife?"

"Yes," I said. My heart banged in its cage.

"I heard you are Beijing."

"I am in Beijing," I said. "I'd like to meet you. Would that be okay?"

"*Dangran*," he said, of course.

So I took Julia Too, who was six at the time, out past

Tong Xian to the countryside. Hong Yue's house and studio are part of a forbidden-city-like compound built by a wealthy friend, patron, and probably lover of his. The buildings are concrete, kilns in the summer and freezers in the winter. They surround an enormous square, grassy courtyard with four stone statues in its corners. The first two are a set of lions, the male rolling a ball under his paw and the female a cub under hers. Their presence makes the second two statues seem out of place: a ballerina in a dress that fans out around her, and a brawny socialist realist worker wiping sweat off his brow.

Our first time there, Julia Too ran from statue to statue, touching them. I looked at Hong Yue, to make sure that was okay, and he nodded. Then he led us into a soaring room with paintings everywhere: hanging on the white walls, stacked against each other, in progress on easels, part-framed. They were red, black, yellow, and green. I walked over to a row of birds, some dressed in People's Liberation Army uniforms, others hot mynahs in bikinis. Two of the birds were depicted as old cadres, clapping their wings at a performance. On the wall opposite the birds were self-portraits: a baby, naked except for a CPC cap, floated on an ocean of blue so bright it hurt to look at. A toddler-sized Hong Yue sat atop a mushroom cloud that tossed him like a rag doll, rode a rocking horse on which he transformed into Chairman Mao, and struggled inside a box that contained other boxes. On close inspection, I saw that those boxes were full of smaller and smaller Hong Yues, also struggling.

"These are my new ones," he said, pointing to a row of panty-clad poultry. A less sexy, actual live bird stood on a twig in a wicker cage near the door of the room. It reminded me of the mynah Xiao Wang's Nai Nai had kept in Chinatown. I wondered what had happened to that bird.

"How long do they live?" I asked Hong Yue.

"What, birds?"

"Ba Ge birds."

"They can live twenty-five years," he said, tilting his head at me. Maybe Nai Nai's mynah was flying around New York City somewhere still. Julia Too walked over and began squawking *nihao*'s back and forth. "*Ba Ge* loves girls," Hong Yue told her in Chinese. "But *nihao* is his only word, so he can't make good conversation."

Then he pulled out a basket of shadow puppets for Julia Too to play with, and poured me some tea.

"I love your paintings," I told him.

"Thanks."

We looked at the walls.

"I spend five years experimenting," Hong Yue said. "When I come to the kind of paintings I want to do, I spend the next five years doing them. But it takes me half a decade every decade to figure out what to do for the second half."

We wandered back out to the courtyard, where sunlight was blasting the grass so hard I wondered how they kept it alive. I shielded my eyes. Hong Yue and I sat at a low stone table and sipped our tea. Julia Too propped the shadow puppets in a parade at the foot of the female stone lion.

"Now I am mostly painting my bird, because I'm an old man and old men love birds," Hong Yue said.

I laughed. He was thirty-five, the age I am now, and I often tease him for having made it seem like the edge of death.

"But you don't want to hear about this, do you?" he asked, squinting up into a flash of sudden sun that had burned through cloud sheer. "Let's talk about Da Ge."

"I would love to," I said. "I didn't know if—"

"I'm as *zhishuai* as an American," Hong Yue said, as *straight to the point of what*, as Da Ge had put it. "You can ask me anything."

"What was he like?"

I looked over at Julia Too, who had abandoned her puppet parade in favor of a snail she'd found on the ground. She was turning it over in her open palm, listening to us.

"*Tian,*" Hong Yue said, my God. He continued in Chinese: "Da Ge was difficult. We burned his father's house down once, smoking. He refused to apologize, and his father was furious, made him pay. Da Ge used to beat the shit out of people when we were young, including me. Maybe because of, you know, the business with his mother. But he was quiet, too, I guess. He read. He was always giving me books I hated."

"He beat you up?"

Now Hong Yue looked at Julia Too. She was absorbed, studying the snail.

"Da Ge could be a son of a bitch."

"Why did he beat you up?"

"Over a girl."

"Oh. Why do you say it was because of his mother?"

Hong Yue looked me over, perhaps trying to determine how I could possibly know so little about a person I had once married.

"Maybe the way she died was—well, in China, it was embarrassing," he said.

"Oh."

"So if people brought it up. You know. He was angry."

"Right."

"Sometimes he was angry at me, too, because my life seemed easier, maybe."

"Was it?"

He smiled kindly. "No one's life feels easy to the one living it. But my mother was okay, and that was enough."

"Enough to make him feel bad, you mean?"

"Enough to make my life seem easy. Then again, I was poor, really poor, and he used to steal money from his father to 'buy my paintings.' Then he'd leave them here 'accidentally' so I could sell them to other people. Except for one. He had a favorite, one I painted right before the Tiananmen business, right before he left for America. I don't know what happened to it. He paid me ten times what it was worth."

He stopped and looked over at me as if he were trying to remember who I was, where we had met, why we were having this conversation. I weathered the pause, spelled p-l-e-a-s-e t-e-l-l m-e s-o-m-e m-o-r-e. It worked.

"Da Ge used to steal food when we were kids," Hong Yue said. "Everyone was poor as hell then, even his big-shot old man. But Da Ge gave shit away, down to the final grain. He could be sweet, even though that's not how people thought of him."

Julia Too had put the snail down and was turning somersaults in the grass.

"How *did* people think of him?"

Hong Yue shrugged. "Once I got busted for drawing on the wall outside the gym at school. Da Ge told the officials he'd done it. I would have had to do self-criticisms, which were a nightmare and would have conflicted with the only art class I had in those days. So he did them for me. For eleven fucking months. Every day." Hong Yue grinned.

"What was it you drew by the gym?"

At this, he laughed like a trumpet. "My name," he said, "in big, red characters."

"Your name? How did—"

"Da Ge said he'd framed me—as a practical joke. He practiced imitating my writing so he could prove his own guilt. But he didn't even need to. I mean, he was always in deep shit at school, so they were happy to believe him. Eleven months of my self-criticism and humiliation."

He poured more tea. Julia Too stopped somersaulting, retrieved her snail, and trotted over with it. She handed it to me, and I looked at the brown whorls on its shell.

"Very nice one, sweetie. But maybe he likes to live in the grass, and we should put him back."

"It's a girl."

"I see. Maybe we should put her back."

"I can make a fort for her in the grass."

"Good idea!"

"But I need a shovel."

"Do you have a shovel?" I asked Hong Yue.

"A what?"

Julia Too asked him in Chinese, and he went to get her a shovel. When he came back, he said, "Maybe you can tell me about Da Ge's New York life. Because when he left, he was out of his fucking mind. I was glad his old man sent him off. I thought if he went somewhere else, he might get over what had happened. I mean, I thought if he stayed here, he would do wild shit and we would lose him. Of course—well," he cut himself off, started over. "Were there good things about his time in New York? Happy moments?" He smiled at me warmly. "There must have been, married to you."

"Thank you," I said. "I hope there were. I took him ice skating once. And we went to Central Park, to the zoo. He cooked, showed me movies. He wrote brilliant, funny things about American culture."

Hong Yue leaned back, stretched his arms behind his head as if it made sense that it had taken me three years to come find him, as if we had forever to remember Da Ge together while Julia Too dug up the courtyard, burying snails. I was so grateful.

"I have that painting, the one you mentioned," I said finally. "I don't know why I waited to say that—sorry. I guess I was scared you would ask for it back. Anyway, it was in his apartment in New York, and I took it. It's here, at our place."

"No shit!" Hong Yue said, "That painting came back to China! That is crazy, beautiful news."

It's funny he should have used those words. The painting is the craziest, most beautiful thing I own, even now, even though I've bought one of Hong Yue's paintings every year since I met him. I plan to continue that pattern, even if I live to be a hundred and they keep getting more expensive. I'll be one of those batty New Yorkers whose belongings topple over and kill her, just transplanted so that instead of junk mail and decades' worth of *National Geographics*, the clutter that crushes me will be dead letters from the love of my life, and modern Chinese art.

Da Ge and I took the train from New York to Garden City the night before our citizenship interview and stayed in a shack of a hotel, watching porn, each expressing polite surprise that the other liked it. This is one of several ways porn works, I think. Everyone likes porn. But part of the appeal for guys is the false truism that girls dislike it, which allows for the titillating revelation that we're dirty enough to watch it, too. Part of the appeal for girls is getting to scandalize guys with that discovery. Fun all around.

The next morning was less sexy. In a nondescript, government-issue building, we went through security, handed our "invitation" to an exhausted bureaucrat behind a bulletproof window, and then waited for three hours on round-backed plastic chairs. There were thirty other couples in the room. Eventually, a blonde woman appeared from behind a door, and asked ten of the couples to form a line. Da Ge and I got in place with the nine other couples and followed her like obedient ducklings down a long hallway, up a staircase of ten stairs, to another waiting room. Six of the couples had lawyers with them, and I wondered if we were in trouble. Various "officers" began to appear from the doorway and call people in. I studied each one, hoped the young black guy would do our interview. But we got a middle-aged white woman named Ms. Tritzen.

Right away she asked me: "Have you been to visit China?"

I lit up with a smile and pinched Da Ge's leg. "We're going this summer," I lied.

He nodded. We had agreed that I would say nothing about myself, and he was to say nothing about himself. We would each talk only about the other, and that way we wouldn't contradict or appear not to know each other. Maybe we'd even seem smitten. I tried to think of shallow, chatty subjects.

"I'm already used to Chinese food because Da Ge is such a good cook," I tried.

"What does he make?" Ms. Tritzen asked me, unsmiling.

"Tiger food!"

We both said this at the same time. Da Ge couldn't resist smiling. Even Ms. Tritzen seemed to soften a bit. "What's that?"

"It's cucumber, cilantro, and peppers mixed with sesame and hot oil," I told her.

"And scallion," Da Ge said. I shot him a look, so he put his hand on my leg.

"What does Da Ge like?" she asked me.

I considered possible responses.

"Spaghetti."

"Do you two have any photos?"

I took the album out of my bag. We had cobbled it together, pasting in ticket stubs from plays, movies, and concerts I'd been to with Adam or Julia, menus from cafes where I ate with my mother, and blank postcards with pictures of China on them. Our scanty zoo and picnic photos were scattered throughout. The "Thank you to Aysha" note with Da Ge's characters at the bottom was featured on the last page.

Ms. Tritzen asked, "What does that note say in Chinese?"

"It's the characters for Da Ge's name."

"What were you thanking her for?" She turned to him bodily, punctuating the fact that she didn't want me to interrupt. I was nervous that he might fuck this up.

He collected words.

"She took me out," he said. "I think it's polite to thank her for this."

I stared at him, thinking I adored him, unsure whether it was an act or not.

"Where did he leave the note?" she asked me. Before I could answer, she said, "Write it down," and passed me a sheet of paper. Who divides and conquers married couples? I hated her.

I wrote "sofa," on my note, worried he wouldn't know the word "futon."

He wrote "futon" on his.

Ms. Tritzen pushed her chair back slightly. "Da Ge," she said, "I'm going to ask you to leave the room for a few minutes." He got up. I tried to catch his eye as he left, hoping to impart something, although I didn't know what. I wondered if Ms. Tritzen would be less formal now that he was gone. She wasn't.

"Draw a map of your bedroom," she instructed me.

"A what?"

A diagram of where things are placed in your bedroom."

"What things?"

She glared at me and slid a piece of paper across the desk. On it, I drew a two-dimensional bed with stick figures spooning across on it. I wanted to ask "Do you like it?" but thought better of it. I thought we needed her not to fail us on this test.

"Is there any furniture in your bedroom?" she asked me.

I drew in the dressing table and saw it, wooden in the corner with its mirror backed up to the wall. I drew a jewelry box on top. A tube of lipstick.

"You need to mark obvious things," said Ms. Tritzen, annoyed. "Please put an X where the closet and door are."

When I had finished my art project, she asked me to let Da Ge back in the room and to wait out in the hall. I stood up dizzily and walked to the door. I knocked before opening it, thinking he might have his ear pressed to the outside. But there was no response, so I pushed it open and peered out into the fluorescent hallway. Da Ge was leaning forward on a plastic chair, and I thought of him the first night he'd been in my house, sitting on the edge of the futon backlit by streetlight. He jolted when he saw me, as if he associated me with Ms. Tritzen now that she and I had been alone in that room.

"You can go back in," I said.

"But for you?"

I smiled. "I have to wait out here now."

"What will she do?"

"Hello?" Ms. Tritzen called out from the room. I thought of recesses and hall passes. Did she think we were making out? Cheating? Da Ge dragged back in, and Ms. Tritzen told him to close the door.

The hall seemed to me to be liquid, blurring in and out. I felt nauseated by the lights and the bumpy walls, had a dizzy sense that a cement truck had turned sideways and poured them vertically.

Ms. Tritzen's door opened, and Da Ge gestured to me to come back in. We both sat. I looked at the desk and saw Da Ge's drawing of my room.

"When did you know you loved Aysha?" Ms. Tritzen asked him.

How dare she.

"In the beginning," said Da Ge.

She wasn't buying this.

"The beginning of what?"

"She buy a Chinese dictionary," he said. "And I see her with her mother."

"What does this mean?" she asked me. In spite of my feeling that she was racist to exclude him by asking me what he meant, I was aware that it was something I might have done, too.

"I bought a Chinese dictionary after we met so that I could look up his name." These words felt hard and sharp. I wondered what he would think. I looked over, but his expression hadn't changed.

"And that's when you fell in love with her?" Ms. Tritzen asked him. I wondered if she was married and going by Ms. Tritzen anyway.

"When I see her with her mother," he said, "I can tell about her love."

A knot formed in my throat.

"My mother and I are close," I told Ms. Tritzen.

"Have you met his mother?" she asked me.

"His mother is dead," I said, with none of the it's-going-to-be-okay-when-you-apologize-inflection she expected.

"I'm sorry," she said.

"Yes," I said, as coldly as possible "So are we."

And that was the end of the meeting.

We traveled back to New York together shyly, not knowing if we'd passed, each unsure how much the other had actually meant. We were, of course, faking it, meaning to convince only Ms. Tritzen that we were in love. But it was tricky to keep that straight, at least for me. Da Ge said he had business in Chinatown, that we'd see each other later in the week. Bereft of him, I rode home and called Xiao Wang.

"I haven't rented anything," I told her, "but I have *The Graduate*. Could you please come watch it with me?"

"I will love to come," she said. "I never saw that movie."

I said nothing about Da Ge, just ordered Chinese food from Hunan Balcony and put the movie on. As soon as Dustin Hoffman got into bed with Anne Bancroft, Xiao Wang asked, "Why does this young guy love to be in bed with so old lady?

"She's a sexy woman though, don't you think?" I asked.

"It's not common situation. Usually, old women never get this kind of romance, and just live the practical part of life, caring for children and husband.

"What about the husbands?"

"It's easy for them to have younger love."

"Don't you think that's outrageous?"

"Out races?"

"Outrageous—something that's like, grossly unfair or offensive."

"Maybe sometimes you're not practical person."

There was no denying that.

Ben Rosenbaum was standing at my classroom door when I arrived to teach the final week of class at Embassy in 1990.

"I hope your weekend was productive and fun," he said.

I thought about how "How was your weekend?" would have opened up the conversation and given me a chance to speak, and how he never took those routes.

"I saw an impeccable performance of *Hamlet*," he said. I nodded and walked to the front of the room, set down my books, and begin to write the Golden Rule on the board.

Ben surveyed it. "My philosophy is not to teach religion

or the trappings of its language as part of an ESL course," he said.

"Religion or the trappings of its language?" I asked.

Unsure whether this was critical of him, Ben spent a rare moment reflecting. I headed back to the far end of the chalkboard and began listing phrasal verbs and their idioms: *bring the subject up, bring the house down, bring home the bacon, bring about change, bring out a new album, bring up your baby, bring it on.* I was wearing my wedding ring, watching it as my hand made chalk words. Ben walked back toward the door, and I turned to see Da Ge lingering there, the veins in his neck standing out again like the Incredible Hulk's. When Ben went by, Da Ge said something so quietly under his breath that I couldn't make it out. I couldn't tell whether Ben had. I thought I didn't care.

"Good morning, guys," I said to the class, twisting the ring on my finger.

"And girl," said Xiao Wang. I was happy she had stopped apologizing before she spoke, that we were friends, had a history, even if it mainly involved fictional characters.

"Yes," I said, "good morning guys and girls. But it's okay to call everyone 'guys,' too. It's better for gender equality that way."

"What is this?" she asked. Da Ge mumbled a word to her in Chinese. She lifted her chin, did not look at him. "What is this thing you say?" she asked me again.

"Gender equality. Justice for women—equal rights."

She nodded vigorously. "In China, we say, 'Women hold up half the sky.'"

Da Ge was watching her. I wondered, in a moment of fleeting panic, whether he'd told her we were married. If he had, I wished I had told her first.

Xiao Wang glanced at Da Ge, who looked away. "This guy," she said to me, "the other teacher who come to class—"

"Who, Ben?" I asked. I immediately regretted saying his name, as if knowing it at all were an admission of some mutual interest between us.

She nodded. I wondered where she was going with this. Xiao Wang kept Da Ge in her peripheral vision. "I think he loves you," she said, meaning Ben. Her voice was as crisp and unapologetic as I had ever heard it.

Now that I know Xiao Wang as well as I do, I'm certain that punishing Da Ge wasn't her only reason for saying this, although that must have been part of it. She also said it because she thought it was true and that I would be flattered. She had to sacrifice a certain measure of personal restraint to blurt out what she thought was a compliment.

"You think so?" I asked, pitching my voice up to sound hopeful.

She pumped her head up and down.

"Yes, he loves you. And he's—how do you say, *shuai*, handsome!"

Maybe that *handsome* flipped the switch, because the veins bulged back out in Da Ge's neck, and he spoke Chinese to her, something curt, short, mean. Before she could react, I turned to him. "Da Ge," I said, "Can you speak English, please?"

"Xiao Wang can translate," he said. Her face was burning.

"Xiao Wang?" I asked, "Are you okay?"

"It's too bad word," she said. "I do not know that in English."

Da Ge stood, turned on the heel of his shiny shoe, and walked out.

"What an asshole," Chase said. Everyone waited.

"Good usage," I said.

When school ended the last week of May, I wrote, "There is nothing so useless as a general maxim," on the chalkboard, without joy. We had a good-bye party, everyone except Da Ge, everyone proud of the dishes we'd brought, everyone speaking in English about how much we would miss each other. Then I never saw Russ or Chase again. I ran into Ingyum once grocery shopping at University Food Market on 115th, and another time on Broadway, and I built an entire life around Da Ge and Xiao Wang. As a sane person who contains her former crazy self, I can see both how bizarre that is and how, if I had a do-over, I might do it again. So there it is.

Summer came down that May in New York just as it has in Beijing this year, a hot towel over the city. The streets reeked of spoiled fruit. Buses blasted by, scorching everyone with exhaust. When Embassy classes ended, Da Ge and I languished in my apartment, taking baths and eating Popsicles. He was urgently unhappy. I did not ask about his last fight with Xiao Wang or where he went when he wasn't with me. I kept the shades drawn, let him sleep for hours a day, and read in the dim light from a textbook he had discovered called *David and Helen Go to China*. The American protagonists travel to Beijing to study and experience culture shock. They can't adjust to spicy Chinese food. They go running and are exhausted by the vast city. Finally, they meet Chinese friends in the dormitory, only to bestow upon them inappropriate gifts like green hats and clocks, which suggest cuckoldry and imminent death.

While Da Ge slept, I studied the vocabulary in *David and Helen Go to China* with a ferocity matched only by that of my Embassy students. When he was awake, Da Ge helped me, wrinkling his brow if I worked sloppily or added extra parts to a character.

"Don't be American barbarian," he teased. His mood would improve in those moments, and I'd feel hopeful as he closed his hand over mine on the pen, or rewrote the lines of each character with a patience I never saw him demonstrate in any other situation. When it was light, he slept and slept. I woke him sometimes to ask if he wanted a meal, others to seduce him. He always said yes, but was somewhere else at my table, someone else in bed. I liked even the stranger version of him, quiet, agitated, with his eyes perpetually open. He watched me like a mirror, as if searching for a secret about himself. I hoped he'd find it, thought if I just waited, fed him, met his eyes, he'd be back.

I tried to learn Chinese so he'd feel at home. I wrote *ni hao* seven hundred times. I wrote *ni* and *wo*, you and I. *Wo men.* We, us. I wrote *Da* and *Ge*, filled pages with his name.

When I missed my period in late May, I did not tell anyone.

I was as giddy with this new secret as I had been with his proposal. I stopped taking my meds right away and waited to see what would happen in June. I stepped up the counting. "I-'m p-r-e-g-n-a-n-t" fits perfectly on ten fingers. I always spelled it that way, with "I'm" as a conjunction rather than "I am," since that doesn't fit. Maybe because I wanted to be pregnant. There are ways to spell whatever truth you want. Just add a "very" or a "really," to even out the number of letters. I sometimes let myself believe Da Ge wanted a baby, too, since he never once asked whether we were avoiding one. Maybe he assumed I was on the pill. Or had a cultural aversion to condoms. At the time I spelled it out the way I wanted it: h-e w-a-n-t-s a b-a-b-y, t-o-o. It fit.

Dr. Meyers was not as easy to convince as I was. She did not believe me when I omitted, euphemized, said my life was fantastic. "You're distant," she said. "Are you racing? Doing okay with your meds?"

"I'm fabulous," I said. "I think maybe I'm stabilizing." This was a word I had learned from shrink books. She nodded politely, disbelieving. I told her I was learning Chinese, how satisfying the characters were. I could count strokes endlessly.

She zeroed in. "Who's teaching you?"

I could have said Xiao Wang, but didn't. "I have a houseguest."

"Have I heard of him before?"

"Not really."

"He's Chinese?"

"Yes."

"How did you meet him?"

I ruled out telling her he was a student. "Um, through Xiao Wang," I said.

"I hope you'll tell me more about him at some point. I'd like to know who he is."

"I hope you like him," I told her, "but I have my doubts."

"Do you like him?" She smiled kindly.

I swallowed. "A lot." I looked away, signaling that I didn't want to discuss it.

"Have you told your mom?" Dr. Meyers asked.

"No. I told Julia."

Dr. Meyers was relieved to hear this, because we both knew that my appointments with her were suddenly filled with lies. Of course so were my dates with Julia.

She took me one night to a Paul Taylor concert, wanting to show off a dancer she'd been vaguely dating. We sat so close the beads of sweat stood out on his body and sprayed in a rainbow as he leapt and bent and twisted across the stage. His muscles looked especially animal, as if he might have been twitching and flicking flies off his haunches and calves. My right foot fell asleep and I stamped the needles out as we clapped for the dancers. "He's great," I said.

Afterwards Julia wanted to get coffee. We sat at a café, but coffee sounded oddly unappetizing. I wanted something white, ordered steamed milk.

"Steamed milk?" Julia said. She stared at me. "Are you sick?"

She waited, and I shrugged. "Milk? Are you pregnant?"

"Ha ha."

She paused again, this time to see if I was actually joking. I won the stare-down.

"Is there a chance that you're pregnant?" she asked.

I grinned. "Isn't there always that chance?"

"Have you not used anything?"

"I had to get off the pill, remember?"

"Of course there are other possibilities."

"But they suck," I said.

"Are you using nothing?"

I shrugged.

"I don't mean to judge, but maybe—"

I cut her off. "Let's not talk about it right now."

She took a sip of coffee. "Okay. How's Dr. Meyers?"

I felt tired suddenly, deeply, terribly tired, as if my bone marrow were giving up on me. I couldn't remember ever having felt this tired before. "Dr. Meyers is fine," I said.

"Do you tell her more about the Chinese guy than you tell me?"

"She asked the same thing about you."

"You don't tell me much of anything anymore, Aysh. Should I be worried?"

"I've been spending a lot of time with Da Ge," I admitted. She must have been worried. She had seen him drunk in my hallway, knew he'd been in the hospital and that I was potentially pregnant with his baby. It all sounded worse than it was, I thought. But that's always how it feels when you're the one on the inside of some very wrong thing.

"Where?" she asked.

"Where what?"

"Where do you guys spend time together?"

"Mostly at my apartment, but sometimes out in the city."

"What about his place?" she asked.

I felt attacked. "Not yet," I said. "Maybe it's not as nice as mine and he's embarrassed or something."

"Maybe," she said.

"Is your point that he's a squatter and needs a place to stay? It's not true," I told her. "He has plenty of money, and he doesn't stay with me every night."

She shrugged. "I don't care if he has money, Aysha. I just want him to be nice to you—past that, I don't care."

"What about you, Julia?"

"What about me?"

This was the first time I'd asked her anything since Adam. I was half-scared that she'd tell me they were in love, married, pregnant. "How's your love life?"

"I've been out with that dancer a few times," she said, "but he's too vain for me. And I don't think he's ever read a book."

Unlike Adam, we both thought, and the conversation collapsed.

When I got home that night, Da Ge was in my living room, his American history textbook open on his lap. I love to come home to someone reading, the lamp, the quiet, the eyes on pages, the way men's hands look holding books. I was breathless to see him, spinning with the feeling of his waiting for me in my house. My apartment was charged, red and orange like hot blown glass. And sparkling. I cleaned around him like a tornado, bought flowers, hung prints, baked cookies. I checked on him, kissed him, tucked his feet back in, pulled the blankets up over his shoulders. I had never taken care of anyone else before, believed I could revive Da Ge. He slept and slept, and I hardly slept at all.

Now I walked over. He put the book down, and I sat on his lap, facing him.

"Where were you?" he asked, monotone.

"I went to a concert with Julia. Are you okay?"

"What concert?"

Was he testing me? "A dance concert. Why?"

"What about after?"

"What do you mean? We went for coffee—"

"I woke up," he said. "I was looking for you."

"I'm sorry," I said. "I would have left you a note, but I thought you'd still be sleeping when I got back."

I thought for a moment. "Did you live alone before you started coming here?" I asked. I put both hands on his shoulders.

"Yes," he said. "Zhen Ming rent apartment for me."

"Do you still have it?"

"Have what?"

"The apartment."

"Yes."

"Does Zhen Ming stay there too?"

"It's in his building."

"Where?"

"Chinatown. I told you."

"Do you ever hang out with Xiao Wang?"

He put his hands on my hips. "I don't have so many friends in New York, actually," he said. "Mostly, I am alone."

His inflection didn't accuse me. He just sounded like a little kid who's been excluded at recess.

"I don't have so many friends, either," I said, hoping he would find it comforting. "Just Julia, really."

He moved his hands up my sides until they were under my arms, as if he might lift me up or off his lap. "And sometimes you hang out with Xiao Wang, right?"

"Right."

We ended it there, wondering what we had told each other. Da Ge moved his hands back down and put them inside my shirt.

"Why are your hands cold?" I asked.

"Please warm them," he said. I leaned down, put my mouth on his.

Since Da Ge never left my apartment anymore, that Wednesday Xiao Wang and I saw *Pretty Woman* in a theater. I told Da Ge I was going out with Julia. Xiao Wang and I were nervous; it felt like a date. We stayed quiet about everything except the movie and Xiao Wang's bizarre preference for sugar on popcorn. As we walked out, she held my hand. So apparently hugging a Chinese friend was totally unacceptable, but she was cool with being my girlfriend in public.

"Americans are casual about love and sex," she said, swinging my hand.

I laughed. "Aren't we just holding hands?"

"What!? I mean that movie!" She let go of my hand.

"I was just kidding. And I think the point of the movie might be the opposite. Americans can't even have professional sex without falling in love and getting married."

"She's, how do you say, *jinu*, prostitute! All she need is money to be happy!"

"Love, too. And how is that evidence that Americans are *casual*?"

"Because who will know if it's real love with that guy or if she just marry him so she doesn't have to, you know, sex with other men for money."

"The movie means to imply that it's true love."

"I think it's just like *Pretty in Pink*. All she need is a man for her life, and America think that will solve all her problem."

I smiled, delighted. "That's a good feminist analysis," I said.

"And the man have to have money, too," she said.

"Hey, you wanted to watch teenage pop movies. We could have watched American classics—those do exist, too."

"Do you ever have romance like this?" she asked me.

The street got hot, as if we had veered close to something smoldering and unpleasant.

"Like what?"

"With person you don't know, for the difficult reason of personal life?"

"Of course not," I said. I descended into the subway tunnel and rode home to Da Ge, who was asleep on top of my bed, dressed in Columbia sweat pants and a white wife beater I'd gotten him. I shook his shoulder gently, woke him.

"Hi, teacher," he said drowsily. Then he spread his arms open so I could climb in.

The last day of May, two weeks after the Paul Taylor dance concert, I called Julia. "Remember how you asked if I was pregnant?"

"Yes. Why?"

"Time for the test," I said.

"My treat!" she said.

Julia and I had a long-standing arrangement. Whichever one of us thought she was pregnant did not have to suffer the dual indignity of buying and taking the pregnancy test. The nonpregnant witness supplied the test and kept the potential mother-to-be company. This was no exception. Julia arrived twenty-seven minutes later. "You went to Love Drug?" I asked.

"You know it," she said.

"Did the cute Hispanic guy sell you this?"

"Of course," she said. "I don't mind taking the slut rap for you."

"The slut wrap," I said. I peeled the plastic cover from the test and took the cap off the pee-stick. "Not for children or swallowing."

"Don't say children," Julia said.

In the bathroom, I peed onto the stick and then set the cap back on the stick and waited for the lines to appear or not appear. I had a moment of dizzy revulsion, mixed with anticipation.

"So," Julia called in from the hallway, "did you pee on your hand?"

"Don't ask."

"Is the thing blue?"

I was staring at it. "It's not that kind," I said, my voice low. "It's the double-lines kind."

"Oh my God," Julia opened the door and came in. "What are we going to do?"

"I can't speak for you, but I'm going to wash my hands," I said. I passed her the stick with two enormous parallel pink slashes in its display window. I felt oddly calm.

Maybe it's further evidence that I was unstable or impractical, or maybe it means I had learned from Da Ge that having someone to take care of would cure my own woes, but I didn't consider an abortion.

"It's not necessarily right!" she cried out. "Stay put. I'll go get another one."

"Don't bother," I told her. "They're like ninety-nine percent accurate, and I can feel it kicking."

She looked at me. "A ninja?" she asked.

"That's Japan, you racist bitch. He's Chinese." I started laughing, and once I had, coughing, too. It felt unbelievable, that choke-laughing, and as weird as it is, I remember it now as my first experience of a new kind of joy: the shrieking, doubled-over brand that Julia Too introduced to my world.

"Don't laugh so hard," Julia One said, "you're scaring the baby."

June 1990, New York, NY

Dear Teacher,

Thank you for letting me to stay so often and so long at your house. I am bad guest and you are kind to me. And for this favor of marrying me. I hope I can repay you this some day.

I am sorry for being so bad guest. I can't help because my mind is dark. When I begin to think there is no good place to go in my mind. I think of my grandfather is dead, of those books he have to bury, of how I am disappoint to him now too. My mother and father and China, even my grandfather. If I consider to go back home I know I cannot do that. But also I can't stay in America without being hypocrite and coward.

I can think only how powerless I am. How I did nothing in the moment when it was important to do something. The more I think the worse I feel in my mind and the crazier in my body and finally I am so angry it make me want to kill someone. I have nothing now. Even nothing to give you to say thank you. I hope you will forgive me.

Da Ge

CHAPTER TEN

Junes

✳

SCHOOL IS OVER, AND THE CITY IS ON FIRE. WHEN THE TEMPER-
ature passes forty degrees Celsius in Beijing, the city is
legally allowed to close shop, so the government keeps the
thermometers perpetually at thirty-nine degrees. It feels
like fifty, and yet the flu's been contained so the streets are
alive again. Stores, trying to recoup losses, have strung
banners up—"Show you love our Beijing"—and held
marathon sales.

The touristy neighborhood of Wangfujing is like an elevator, so stuffed with people you can't walk in either direction. Everyone is still wearing masks, but no one can resist a
sale, so we're all back out on the streets, including Julia Too
and Phoebe and Sophie and Lili. They all have new, socialist
realist T-shirts that flaunt model workers "stamping out
sickness" with square fists. Buses with antiflu slogans zoom
by and we all feel united in a fight against this outside evil.
According to Beijing's new billboards, the people will be vic-
torious. The city feels blissfully awake again: its fountains
populated by chubby people in underpants and jelly sandals.
The ubiquitous Walls Popsicle carts have reoccupied street
corners and old people are back in the parks, birdsitting,
exercising, fanning themselves and chatting. Only the restau-
rants and dead businesses look tattered.

Julia Too and I went to Tiananmen Square today. We go every June 4, and it's usually the same scene: most of the other people there appear to be undercover cops with shiny shoes. I wonder why Da Ge always wore those black beetle shoes himself.

Julia Too wrote a history report this year about the Martyrs' Monument and lectured me proudly as we stood in front of it today, reminding me of Old Chen.

"It was built in 1952 to commemorate dead revolutionaries," she said.

"So I've heard." I smiled. I know the monument down to its tiniest detail.

"Mao's calligraphy," she said, pointing. "The People's Heroes Live On Forever."

"Right. I like that inscription," I said.

"Why?"

I shrugged. "It's open to interpretation. We get to decide who the heroes are."

"Did you know they used seventeen thousand pieces of marble and granite? That's a lot."

We stood for a moment. When she asked me what my favorite "picture" was, I said the simplest one, the May 4 movement panel. In it, a young Chinese man demands "national sovereignty as a defense against foreign powers" in front of a crowd at Tiananmen. He has square cheekbones, and a rock jaw set in absolute defiance.

"Why that one?" she asked.

"I like that hero," I told her, "he looks strong and brave to me."

"Does it remind you of my dad?"

I ran a hand through her bangs. "It reminds me of you."

 Twelve Junes ago the news was full of Tiananmen's first anniversary. Thousands of teachers and students gathered at Beijing University to mourn. They sang "The Internationale" and smashed bottles.

Da Ge left my Upper West Side apartment before I was awake on June 4, 1990. I tried madly to find him, left dozens of messages on his machine, alternately worried and cheery. It was a summer Tuesday, and I had nowhere to be, nothing to do. I asked Julia if I could borrow her car, and drove to New Jersey alone to sit outside of my father's house. I parked in their cul-de-sac and sat fretting about Da Ge, dying for my dad. I hoped to see two seconds of him, even if only walking by a window, but they were gone on vacation. The house was shady and silent. I stayed for two hours anyway, studying the garden she must have planted: blooming marigolds, roses, a bed of half-dead impatiens. I wondered who came to water her summer flowers when she was away. I saw her on a plane, probably resting her head in the crook of my father's neck. She had a magnificent magnolia tree next to the front door and giant bamboo stalks along the sides of the house.

When the sun began to set, I drove back over the bridge to my mom's. She was out with Jack, so I let myself in and read news on the blue couch until they came home.

"Hi baby," My mom said. "You hungry?" She disappeared into the kitchen before I could respond. I could hear her fixing dinner. Jack sat in an armchair across from me.

"What'cha reading?" he asked.

I shrugged. "Just news," I said.

"Marion Barry's drug trial started today," he said, his voice extra-animated.

I nodded, but could barely mask my lack of interest. Jack must have sensed it, because he turned to the Tonys, probably thinking I was artsy. I felt for him.

"I was reading about China, actually," I said.

"Oh. What about it?" he asked politely.

"It's the anniversary of the Tiananmen Square uprising."

"Oh right, of course," he said.

"Some guy tried to unfurl a banner, and was dragged away," I reported. "But he kept shouting 'Rise up!'"

Jack looked me over, trying to guess what I could possibly want in response.

I saved him. "I think it's brave of him," I said.

"I guess so," Jack said. He looked sad.

"They interviewed some parents whose kid got shot in the back while he was biking to work four miles from Tiananmen last summer."

"That's terrible," Jack agreed.

My mom walked into the room with a glass pitcher of gazpacho and three bowls. She began putting placemats on the table.

"The dad kept eighteen pigeons in a cage outside his living-room window," I was saying. "The mother is having fits of craziness."

"What are you two talking about?" My mom asked.

"Nothing," I said.

Then she and Jack and I ate soup, salad, and a baguette with brie. We talked about the weather.

I left later, desperate to find Da Ge. And then the day was emptied out and gone. That Tuesday night went blank, and then it was Wednesday. Unable to talk to Da Ge, I decided I would talk about him. For real. Julia and I were at her gym. She was in the hot tub, and I was on my way to join her, not realizing that you're not supposed to boil your unborn baby in 110-degree water. My stomach looked almost no different; it seemed impossible that a peanut-sized person was in there, growing a spine. I had decided not to tell anyone until I was twelve weeks pregnant—in August. I bought a copy of *What to Expect When You're Expecting* at the Columbia Bookstore, and discovered many things I should have been worried about, including eating two thousand kinds of yellow leafy vegetables I had never heard of—five times a day.

I walked the pink tile plank out to the whirlpool, where Julia was submerged in bubbles, leaning back on a jet with one arm stretched out of the water. I slipped in.

"I married Da Ge," I said.

Julia raised her hands to the surface of the water and looked at them as if she'd never seen them before. I thought I saw something fall behind her face, but she kept whatever it was out of her eyes and words.

"I thought maybe you had," she said, her voice staying even and warm. Her hair was slicked back, and the bones in her face were jutting out, wet from the steam and tight from chlorine. I loved her as wholly as I ever had. For protecting me from whatever she actually thought. For not bringing up the fact that I hadn't told her earlier, for not making it about her. For being so familiar and always agreeing to suffocate under the weight of whatever new weirdness I crushed her with.

I said, "I'm sorry I didn't tell you earlier. I couldn't really think of how to bring it up and then there was, you know, the Adam thing." As soon as it was out, I wished I hadn't punished her again, but it was also true. She winced.

"I was waiting for the right moment, I guess," I said.

"It's a citizenship thing? Or you're in love with him?" she asked me.

I couldn't help but wonder—if I answered about Da Ge, would she tell me that she and Adam were in love? I shrugged.

"Is he in love with you?" she asked hopefully.

I couldn't lie. "I'm not sure. I hope so." Hearing this embarrassed me, and Julia, knowing that, spoke right away.

"Have you told him about—?" she gestured toward my stomach.

"No."

"Why not?"

I sighed. "I don't know."

She waited.

"Because what if he has an opinion on whether to keep her?" I asked, "Or worse, what if he doesn't?"

"Right," she said. "Why her? Is it a girl?"

"I don't know. But I don't think it's a boy, somehow. And i-t-'s n-o-t-a-b-o-y fits on ten fingers." I watched my fingers pinwheel in front of us as I spelled. "M-y b-a-b-y i-s n-o-t a b-o-y is fifteen."

Used to this sort of tedium, Julia ignored it. "Are you going to tell him?"

"About the spelling?"

"No," she played along. "About the baby."

I smiled. "I guess eventually he'll notice."

"And you know for certain that it's his?"

Did she think it might be Adam's? And if so, would she be heartbroken?

"It's his," I said, and then, "Are you a good babysitter?"

She nodded.

"If I never see Da Ge again after I tell him, will you be the daddy?"

"I'll start right now," she said. "We should get a doctor appointment for you to make sure everything is going okay."

"Okay," I said. "Maybe I'll name the little muffin Julia."

She took my hand tentatively on the walk home and then increased her grip until I thought she might cut my circulation off. I knew, regardless of how many times it had been or whether it was still happening, how sorry she was about Adam. She called her doctor the next day, supplied prenatal vitamins, borrowed *What to Expect*, and began cooking leaves and weeds and bringing them to my apartment. She fussed over which fish had too much mercury, and bought me organic shampoo so no chemicals could seep into the baby via my hair. I was four and then five and then six weeks pregnant that June. The first time I saw Julia Too's heartbeat, a bright musical flutter in a sea of green ultrasound light, Julia One was with me in the room.

Da Ge came back to my apartment at the end of June, looking like a video game character. He appeared at my door, carrying nothing, not even a helmet or his backpack. He hadn't called or come by since the fourth. I pulled him into the apartment and hugged him and then held him out so I could look at his face. His skinniness had become a kind of horror. I did not ask where he had been. I didn't want to scare or crowd him, to "remove a fly from his forehead with a hatchet," as the Chinese saying goes. Maybe his problem was a manageable one, I pretended, something we could address gradually. As for avoiding the topic of our peanut-sized baby, I justified that with circular logic. Having told him nothing, I couldn't expect him to confide in me, either. And since he didn't confide in me, I couldn't very well tell him I was pregnant.

"It's hot," I said, "let me fix you some iced tea."

I cracked ice cubes out of trays and dumped them into a pitcher, poured cold tea over them, and squeezed lemons in. Then we sat on the futon together, drinking and watching light blast into the windows. Time was as slow as heat that summer, the pavement steaming with sun and pollution.

Tears were percolating under my eyes. "So," I tried. "What have you been up to?"

"Nothing," he said, "you?"

We were in an ESL skit. I was crying.

"I've been driving out to my dad's a lot."

"You have seen your father?"

"No," I said. I was too tired to form words that didn't crack. "Vacation."

"But you go to his house?"

"I sit outside his house."

He nodded, reached over, and saying nothing about it, wiped my cheek.

"They have a garden," I said. "She has a garden."

"Have you seen Xiao Wang?" Da Ge asked, surprising me.

"Her husband's here, visiting."

"I know."

I shrugged. "I haven't met him yet."

"I think she'll like to introduce you," he said.

"Have you? Met him?"

"No."

We sat silently for a moment while I tried to conjure up images of a baby's face with his scar across its fat cheek.

"Will you lie down with me?" I asked. He nodded, and we went into my bedroom where I took his clothes off first, slowly, and then my own. I pulled the covers over our heads. Underneath the blankets we were still and quiet, which I disliked. Feared. I climbed on top of him, propped myself up. If only I knew where he lived, I thought, next time he was lost I could go there and find him.

"Can you take me to your place downtown? I want to see your life," I said.

"Right now?" He looked at me searchingly, ran his hands up my sides.

"Afterwards," I said.

That night he took me to a Chinatown restaurant I would never have entered on my own. I wore my cream wedding dress. To my great displeasure, his wax-faced caramel apple of an uncle joined us. Zhen Ming ordered food for the whole table, which I found bizarrely rude, especially since it involved sea slugs, lobster, and beef tripe. It was a gesture of generous hosting, his way of wining and dining us. I wish I had been able to appreciate that at the time. Zhen Ming and Da Ge spoke in Chinese. Occasionally Da Ge turned to me to mumble a half translation.

"Zhen Ming is a businessman," he said. I took this to be an apology for not including me; maybe they were talking about business and Da Ge thought I'd be bored or couldn't understand. Zhen Ming didn't even try to mask what I took to be his utter lack of interest in me. I pretended to be engrossed in using my chopsticks to hide a shrimp under some fried noodles. Since growing a shrimp in my stomach, I had lost my appetite for the shiny, veiny things. They looked like little intestinal systems to me, science models of internal parts, ultrasound photos. Being pregnant was like being manic; every sensory experience was exaggerated. I kept myself busy for the duration of the dinner by sniffing the air and staring wide-eyed at food I once might have liked, unable to believe that anyone could eat anything but white bread, plain pasta, and marshmallows.

When Zhen Ming finally excused himself to go, Da Ge walked him to the front of the restaurant, shaking his hand the whole way. There was something about the way they walked together, shaking hands, that gave me a bad feeling.

When Da Ge came back to the table alone, I was sullen.

"For you," he said, "it's boring."

"Yes," I said. "It's boring."

We stared at each other.

"I think you want to see Chinatown," he said.

"If I wanted to see it alone, I would have come alone."

"Tonight," Da Ge said, looking at me, "you are pretty."

That was the moment I almost told him. And then the waiter showed up with cubes of cut watermelon, said Zhen

Ming, now long gone, had picked up the tab. And the moment was gone. Someone dropped a glass across the restaurant and it smashed.

"Once I break a bottle over someone's head," Da Ge said.

"You what?"

"I am angry, so I hit a bottle on someone's head."

"A girl?" I asked. I don't know why I asked him this. Perhaps I wanted to see where the line was. I found it right away; he was furious.

He put his hands on the table, hard, as if he were steadying himself. Some thick soup sloshed over the sides of its bowl. My stomach turned. "You think I hurt women?" he asked, through his teeth. "Why? Because American propaganda tell you this?"

"I just think you have a bad temper," I said.

"It wasn't woman," he said, "but you already knew that."

"Who then?" I asked. I cut a square of watermelon into two with a chopstick.

"Another student at Beida."

"Why?" I cut each of the two watermelon pieces into two more.

"He says this stupid thing about my mother."

"Did he know you?"

"Yes. We were in a meeting together."

"What kind of meeting?" The hot pink smell of watermelon bothered me, so I pushed my plate away.

"A political meeting," Da Ge said.

"What did he say about your mother?"

"A rude thing."

"Did he know your mother?"

Anger flashed across his face. "What, my mother? How is it possible for this?"

"If he doesn't know your mother, why do you give a shit what he says about her?"

"Nobody say this about my mother."

"Tell me what he said." I was punishing him. For bringing Zhen Ming, for ignoring me, for keeping secrets, for not knowing about the baby, not guessing, not asking. I wanted to provoke him out of himself.

"He say she is a whore. He say fuck her."

"That's all?"

"What if someone say these things about your mother?"

"I wouldn't break a bottle over anyone's head."

He looked down at the table. "Maybe people have been easy to you in your life."

"You're not easy to me."

He picked at two grains of rice with his chopsticks and refused to meet my eyes.

"You're not easy, either," he said.

"So maybe we're good for each other."

I reached across the table to touch his hand, and he set his chopsticks down, laced his fingers in mine. Electricity moved up through my arm to my neck. I flew the circle of my mind, looking for the right question to land on, the thing I could ask that would provide a real reveal. I wanted to peel Da Ge's skin and see underneath. I wanted to be inside him. I wanted to be him.

"Are you going to be okay?" I asked.

He glanced nervously around the restaurant and eventually looked at me and sighed. I remember feeling like he was looking down from the top of the restaurant, thinking I understood nothing. He was right.

"Sometime, I feel so bad I cannot leave the bed," he said.

"I know," I told him.

"For many weeks."

"I know. I'm sorry."

"Maybe I will be like it forever."

"No, you won't," I said. "Forever is—"

"Nobody can know this things about anybody else." His voice picked up. "Let's go to my apartment and watch movie and sleep."

He reached for my hand and led me out, past the fish tanks displayed against the restaurant's windows. Lobsters flicked the glass with their eyestalks, walking in a forward and backward trap. They were about to be boiled to firecracker effect, electrified red. Eating lobsters was so specific, two-handing them while their meat-packed shells clacked against white plates. What would it be like to be dead, staring out of a hot shell at a plastic bib and cartoon of your living self?

Da Ge and I walked along Mott Street. There were open-air stalls crammed together, selling replicas of purses, electronic toys, and watches. I wanted to ask Da Ge if it felt anything like China, but was afraid he'd be offended. Maybe if he were in China, I thought, he could be repairing damage he felt he'd done, rather than suffering from afar. In a window we passed, glazed ducks hung by their necks, and Da Ge noticed me flinch.

"Next time we have Beijing duck, okay? It's not like these Cantonese barbecue ducks. You have to order it the day before." He paused and looked over, as if remembering again that I was there.

"You are thin," he said, "sad girl."

But I was pregnant, fattening up to insulate his baby. I should have told him how much I hoped the baby would look like him.

"I'm happy to be with you, not sad," I said.

"It's here, this video store I like." He opened the door, and a bell rang. The owner waved to him and said something in Chinese. Da Ge walked over and leaned on the counter, forgetting or failing to introduce me. I studied the bindings of Chinese movies, the characters crawling up the spines like hieroglyphics.

Da Ge came over, holding up a tape. "I want for you to see this new movie, *Ju Dou*. It's a thing you don't know, Chinese peasants."

"It's good?" I asked.

"The peasant?"

"No, the movie."

"The end is stupid," he said, "but that's true."

"What's true? The stupid end?"

"No," he said, "every end is stupid." He walked with the movie over to the counter. The manager asked him something and he answered while looking down.

"What did he ask?" I asked.

"He asked why I want to show you this movie of backwards, peasant China."

"Why do you?"

"I think you would like this movie. It's not his business."

Da Ge lived a block from the store, less than a mile from Xiao Wang's Nai Nai. His apartment was a fifth-floor walk-up studio, and I trailed behind him, sniffing the air, which smelled of garlic and oil. Everywhere the clatter of pots, chairs, sizzling, laughter, foreign conversation. The windows in the stairwells were all open. It was hot.

"This building is mostly family from South China, you know, Guangzhou," Da Ge told me. "They speak Cantonese and eat everything with four leg except the table."

When we reached the door marked 5-I, he touched the brass number and letter. "Five is like 'wu' in Chinese," he said. "Sometimes this means none of something. So this means 'None of I.'"

"None of I?"

"The first time I call you, I am nervous," he said, opening the door.

"Why?" I asked, thinking he'd tell me he'd had a crush.

"Because your phone number," he said.

"What about it?"

"It's one-four-one-four at the end," he told me.

"And?" I have always liked the symmetry of those last four digits. I traced a finger up the back of his neck.

"It's bad news," he said. "This one and four, for Chinese, it mean bad things."

"Like what?"

"Number one means to want," he said.

"What's wrong with that?"

"But four mean death."

When he opened the door, cool air rushed into the hallway. He gestured for me to walk in first, then followed me. On the wall was an oil painting done in angry yellows, oranges, and reds. It was of four boxes, filled with a fish bone, a black bird, a distorted portrait of Marx, and a calendar. The calendar was made of more boxes, and in each of those was a small head with its eyes X'ed out.

Da Ge was watching me fall into the calendar boxes. "It's by my old friend Hong Yue," he said. "Red Moon. That's his artist name, not his real name."

"Are they supposed to be dead?" I asked.

"Who?"

"The people in the calendar."

"I don't know," Da Ge said.

"I like the painting."

Da Ge looked skeptical. He had taken his shoes off and set them carefully on a wicker rack that had several other pairs resting on it. He put plaid slippers on.

"Would you like me to take these off?" I asked.

"It's okay." I added my sandals to the collection, and he handed me some white cotton hotel slippers. "Come," he said. I followed him into an open room off the entrance. "This is it," he said, "It small to yours."

"It's nice," I said.

His bed was in the far corner, propped with two pillows and an army green sleeping bag. Facing that were a television and a shelf so full of books that half were stacked horizontally. A bare bulb hung from the middle of the room. He had a wooden table with one chair. I felt sick.

"Do you want to sit?" he asked.

"Can I look around first?"

"Nothing to look around, really."

I was hoping to find photographs, but there weren't any. Four scrolls hung in a row on the far wall next to the bed. Each had a different kind of flower growing up it, and a block of characters. I was relieved to see them hanging so neatly; the thought that he had measured before putting nails in place pleased me. H-e-'s u-n-h-a-p-p-y, I spelled out. He saw me looking at the scrolls. "Seasons," he said, "Tang poems for them."

"Tang poems?"

"Poems from the Tang dynasty."

"Will you read me one?" I asked.

He looked at the scrolls. "This one is a poem by poet named Wang Wei," he said. "He's quite famous in China. It says, 'I get off my horse, ask where you are going. You say you have trouble. And go to be alone in the hills of the South. Go then. I will ask you nothing else. White clouds forever.'"

"White clouds forever?"

"Eternal-ity, is this the right word?"

"Yes."

"China look like this," he said, pointing to an ink smudge behind one of the flowers. "There is more in the air and the ground there, even for the cities."

"More what?"

He thought. "Fog," he said. "That hide the buildings."

He slipped the movie out of its plastic case and into a VCR.

"Sit down with me," he said.

He turned the TV on and reclined backward onto the bed. I lay down next to him, and he put his arm under my neck. On the screen, rural China fanned out, dusty and expansive, and an old man kept a stunning woman from her true love. I turned toward Da Ge and rested my hand on his chest, felt his pulse. I turned to ask what town the movie was in, but he was asleep. I watched him for a long time—the way I now watch Julia Too.

My mother has arrived for the summer, equipped with gas masks, six best-selling books for me (even though I dislike bestsellers and can now get books easily in Beijing), and unacceptably fashionable clothes for Julia Too. Nothing about her ever changes, and neither does our chemistry. Her husband, Jack, loves her summer trips, although he doesn't come with her; he delights in what he considers her "international" lifestyle. Naomi still thinks of our lives here as hardship posts. Until Julia Too and I moved to Beijing, my mother was a quintessential New Yorker, worldly in the freakishly agoraphobic way you can be if you read the *Times* and the *New Yorker* and know every art gallery in New York but can't bear to leave the city. She could hardly tolerate traveling as far as Connecticut or New Jersey. But now she has all sorts of accessories and frequent-flier miles banked with every airline that flies to China. Jack travels on business, and she brags charmingly that she jets about with him, using her own miles to buy tickets.

Julia Too and I went to pick her up at Capital Airport, where she came down the ramp in a suit cut so precisely she looked like an origami version of herself. Her pearls weighed her collarbones down. She had almost no makeup on, and skin so thin her veins showed through. She smothered Julia Too with kisses, and then she did the same to me.

"Your hair is short."

"You love it, right?"

"It's cute," she said. "It's fine."

I had put lipstick on for the occasion, and was wearing a simple sundress and sandals. My mother held me out for a moment and continued to look at me. I tried to imagine what it will feel like when Julia Too isn't my little baby-faced girl anymore. How I'll feel about her neck once it loses the still recognizable creases I once plumbed for stray rice cereal, her silky feet that kicked my stomach while I nursed her. Julia Too is still little enough to belong to me, to live in my house. I still pack her pink lunch box with pretzels and sandwiches, and make her favorite dinners: hot pot, tacos, *yu xiang* spicy eggplant, and lasagna. Maybe looking at me that way made my mother want to see her baby. Or herself. What could she see and not see about me, who had I become to her once I wasn't hers anymore? She sighed. "You're really quite skinny," she concluded.

I smiled. "So are you, Mom."

Then we went home, where she and Julia Too sneaked off to gossip and try on whatever illegal outfits Naomi had brought.

For dinner, we met Shannon and Xiao Wang and their girls at *Yu Xiang Ren Jia*, Xiao Wang's favorite Sichuan restaurant. As soon as we arrived and she and Naomi had hugged their American hugs, Xiao Wang directed the waiter to bring a fish out because she wanted *shui zhuyu*, a giant cauldron of boiling oil with fish and bean sprouts and hot peppers bubbling to the surface. Julia Too and I love *shui zhuyu*, but I saw Naomi's eyes widen at the words. The first time she ever had it, also out with Xiao Wang, Xiao Wang took my mother into the kitchen to help pick the fish, and then they watched the waiter put it in a plastic bag and beat it to death with a bat. Maybe that's why *shui zhuyu* was the first Chinese expression Naomi ever effortlessly committed to memory. Now whenever we order it, Xiao Wang has the waiter bring the fish out to the table so we can judge that it's big enough and fresh with life, but the execution takes place in the kitchen.

"Naomi, you would also like some tofu dish?" Xiao Wang asked thoughtfully.

"Whatever you all are eating is fine," my mother said.

"Don't be a martyr, Mom," I said. I asked the waiter for some shriveled green beans, the dish Da Ge had prepared for me so long ago, his mom's favorite. And noodles and spicy eggplant. He nodded and rushed off toward the kitchen.

"And a bottle of fire liquor!" Shannon called out after him.

"Which kind?" he asked.

Shannon grinned at me. "*Erguotou*!" She called out, the cheapest, most throat-burning of the white fire liquors. Shannon loved my mother, and considered this a welcoming banquet, which meant she wanted Naomi drunk by the end of the night. And drunk on something "authentic," nothing too bourg-y. It worked. After the first thimble-full of *erguotou*, you can't feel it scalding you anymore, and I guess Naomi figured if she was going to have to eat eyeballs out of a pot of oil all night, she might as well Novocain her senses first. She was in a celebratory mood anyway, raucous about the men being absent—Jack in New York, Jin in Yunnan, and Zhang Sun at a meeting. She kept joking that it was a women's league dinner, finding it increasingly hilarious as she drank more fire—that we were all women, all had daughters.

Shannon's media consulting company had picked up a new client, so she was also boisterous, asking Xiao Wang boring questions about the insurance industry in China.

"You're representing an insurance company?" I asked.

"Liberty Mutual," she said, gleefully. "*Gan bei*!" Bottoms up!

"I think it will be strongly regulated for China, this industry," Xiao Wang warned. "China do not like to give up local business for foreign company like Liberty Manual."

"Liberty Mutual, Mom," Lili said, dropping out of the girls' conversation briefly.

"Their CEO is coming. I'm going to take them down the Yangtze," said Shannon.

Xiao Wang was laughing. "Maybe you can sing 'Unchained Melody' on karaoke night like Julia and Naomi did," she said to Shannon.

"You bet your ass I will!" Shannon said, and Xiao Wang shot her a look.

"You bet *your* ass!" Sophie parroted.

"Sophie!" Shannon said.

"What, Mom?"

Shannon laughed. "Good point. Nothing, I guess."

The girls' basi pineapple arrived, deep-fried fruit coated in a sugar sauce that's soft until dunked in ice water and then becomes a hard candy shell. They gobbled it up, trailing sugar silk across the table with their chopsticks. And once they were giddy with sweets, they began playing a Chinese drinking game, using *juhua* tea as reward and punishment. Xiao Wang and my mother made a long, involved plan to take a tai-chi class together at dawn on Friday, Shannon blabbed to my mother that I had a new boyfriend, and Xiao Wang scolded her for gossiping.

"Shannon is okay person," Xiao Wang reassured my mother (and herself). "She have mouth of a dagger, heart of tofu." I looked over, my heart skipping at the idiom.

Once we joined in the girls' drinking game, the level of chaos at our table rose until we were yelling so much that the loudest tables of men in the place looked over, dismayed. We spent an hour on drunken finger guessing, a complicated rock-paper-scissors game in which two people hold up their fingers at the same time while shouting out a random number. If your number ends up being equal to all the extended fingers, you win. If you don't win, which you almost never do, and Naomi literally never does, you drink. And since most cultures agree that words are more fun than numbers, instead of just shouting the number itself, the Chinese have "number phrases" like "two kind brothers," "three stars shining," and "making a fortune in four seasons." We were shrieking these, drinking everything in sight, and then, with the exception of my mother, faint with exhaustion by the time we left for home.

"Shannon and Xiao Wang seem so great," my mother chattered happily in the cab home. "I mean, everyone seems great—Sophie, and Lili, and—Julia! When do I get to meet the famous Phoebe!?"

"Soon, maybe tomorrow?" Julia Too looked at me, amazed to see Naomi in such a wild mood.

Late that night, after Julia Too was asleep, my mother came and sat on the edge of my bed, sober but lit with jet lag. I thought of the millions of times I'd sat on her bed. I was thumbing through a book of Chinese poems Yang Tao had given me. Eavan Boland's new book, *Against Love Poetry*, was on the nightstand. My mother picked it up.

"What are you reading, sweetie?"

"Some obscure Chinese poems a friend gave me. That book is for him."

"The friend Shannon mentioned? Is he—?"

I laughed. "He's my boyfriend, I guess." I gave in. In high

school, I would have stayed for as long as possible on the subject of the poems, knowing she wasn't interested. But I wanted to reward her for having waited all night to bring it up.

"Will I get to meet him?"

"First you have to memorize these," I said, handing her the book.

"It's worth it! I'll start right now. Um. By the way. I brought you something."

She set the book down and handed me a box, which I opened unceremoniously. I can't tolerate melodramatic moments with my mother. There were two rings in it, one simple band and one diamond, too large and overstated for my taste. "Are these yours?"

"Of course," she said. "I'm surprised you don't remember them."

"This was your engagement ring from Dad?"

"Right. I know it's got bad energy in some ways, but it's a diamond, and I thought I'd give it you. You can decide what to do with it—maybe you want to give it to Julia Too eventually. Or maybe you can have a necklace made out of it. Anyway, it's yours."

"Thank you," I said.

"He loved you tremendously, you know," she said. I sat electrocuted to the bed.

"You do know that, right?" she asked.

"Are you still drunk?"

She smiled. "No. But that was fun. I love your friends."

"I love them, too," I said. "And they love you," I added, feeling ridiculous.

"Anyway, your father loved you. That's all I wanted to say. He behaved terribly, but it wasn't because he didn't love you." She stood up. "Do you know what I mean?"

"I'm not sure, Mom," I said. I didn't want her to go. "What *do* you mean?"

She sat down again, and I was relieved.

"It's not that he couldn't forgive you. It's that he couldn't forgive himself, and didn't think you could ever forgive him."

"Are you an apologist for him now?"

"Absolutely not," she said, "But—"

"Did he tell you that? About thinking I couldn't forgive him?"

"Yes," she said. I thought this over.

"You can sleep in here with me if you want," I said.

She ran her hand through my hair. "Do you want me to?" she asked. I shrugged. "I will," she said. "I'll be right back. I'm going to get my book and put a nightgown on."

She went to change into something long and white while I put the rings in my jewelry box, next to the ones Da Ge and I had worn that day at City Hall.

July 1990, New York, NY

Dear Aysha,

In the morning when I am not still sleeping but also not awake, I thought how Beijing is cruel city. So many boys and girls were attracted by her and flooding in with their youth. On this exciting stage they perform and enjoy, splurge their success until time passed and their youth was used up. Then they woke up and realized that they want something human, maybe natural or simple. Then Beijing has not much to offer! The city cannot be your mother. At this point, Beijing finished playing her role. Like the love that go away suddenly.

Still I am envy those friends in China. The independent life, but also their family. I am float through the world like a bubble that will disappear any moment. No city. No family. No home.

I want to say to you how much I care you and the way your mind work and look. I hope you know what I mean. For me you are important and beautiful person in my American life.

Da Ge

CHAPTER ELEVEN

Julys

*

I WAS MARINATING CHICKEN THE LAST TIME DA GE CAME OVER.
I had never had chicken in the house until I met Da Ge. But
after we were married, I lived in fear that he would starve
while at my place and I would be excommunicated from the
Jewish faith. Jewish mothers are not supposed to let their
guests or their husbands wither from hunger.

I was almost a real Jewish mother by then, but no one
seemed to notice, including Da Ge. Of course I was barely
pregnant, but at the time his obliviousness surprised me,
made me think maybe it's true when guys say they can't tell
the difference between our skinniest and fattest selves. I felt
like a huge round bouncing fruit, broadcasting *baby!* Of
course, off drugs in honor of the baby, I was rocketing up a
bit. Now, when I look at pictures I can see how my pregnancy
would have been imperceptible to Da Ge. And if that, the
mania, and other certainties were invisible to Da Ge, then I
wonder what qualities in himself Da Ge considered obvious.
Perhaps the very fact of his ongoing internal meltdown
seemed to him to be embarrassingly public.

The bumpy bird on the counter turned my stomach, so I
returned to the hallway and sorted the day's unopened mail.
There was a letter from the city, and I tore it open. We had
passed our interview. A current went through me, one tough

to identify as fear or joy. Now, all he had to do was pass his American history test and he would be an American citizen. The dramatic part would end and—what? We would start our life together? Would he move in with me on 115th and be my husband? It seemed unlikely, even to me. Would he think it was okay to have a baby? Another ripple, definitely fear this time, moved outward from my body to my skin and lifted the hair in a stadium wave. Reluctant to return to the chicken, I shed my clothes and filled a bath.

I don't know how long I sat in the water before I heard him at the lock, keys to my apartment, his bike, 5-I in Chinatown, and whatever other places he unlocked knocking against each other like chimes.

"Da Ge," I said. In his name was an echo of the first time I'd said it.

He opened the bathroom door, and I could feel the blocks he'd walked, the outside on him. I turned the faucet with my right foot, added heat.

"Where've you been?" I asked, trying to sound casual.

"I had some business." His voice was blank, but he looked at me with interest.

"Do you want to get in with me? It's still hot."

"No, it's okay for me," he said. "Maybe you come to the living room?" His eyes had the bruised look I both liked and dreaded, one that suggested his life took place somewhere else, without me.

I walked down the hall in my towel and found him on the futon, flipping channels before he could see what was on any. The TV screen was a colorful mess.

"Are you okay?" I asked.

He shrugged.

"We passed our interview," I said.

"I know," he said.

"How did you know?"

"Zhen Ming already know. He find out last week and schedule my test."

"So, all you have to do is take the American history test, right?"

His eyes clouded over.

"Yes," he said, his voice low. "That's all. Then wait."

"That's good news, right?"

"Yes," he said, faking a smile. "Sometime I'll be American."

"When is the test?" I asked him.

It was Wednesday, he would take it in a large group, was lucky, usually there was a long wait, something about Zhen Ming.

"What does Zhen Ming do, exactly?" I asked him.

"He is businessman with connection."

"Like your father?"

"No," he said angrily, "not like my father."

I slipped away to make a dinner reservation on Wednesday night in the park. We would celebrate, I thought, and I would tell Da Ge about the baby. Wednesday. His citizenship exam would be done; I would be almost four months pregnant. Horse-drawn carriages would be pulling up, the city around us like a velvet curtain.

When I returned to the living room, Da Ge was sitting on the couch, watching local news, all the latest sordid deaths, tallied by plastic anchors. His eyes were spiraling.

"Maybe we should turn that off and study for Wednesday?" I asked him.

He shrugged again.

"Did you bring the test book?"

"No."

The phone rang, and I picked it up distractedly.

"Aysha!" shouted Ben Rosenbaum's voice, "I'm so glad to have reached you at home. Let's have dinner. I know it's a school night, but I know a great place."

Why had I picked up? "I'm so sorry," I said, "I can't go out right now."

"Oh, well, in that case, maybe I could stop by," he said. "I was just at a Columbia function, so I'm in your hood."

Hood? How did he know where I lived? "Maybe some other time," I said.

Da Ge was listening attentively, even though he continued to stare at the TV.

"Oh, come on. It'll be fun. I'll be there in a few minutes," Ben said.

"I'm afraid I'm busy, Ben," I said, wanting to soften the insult with his name but instantly regretting that I had used it, in case Da Ge made the connection. "I have company," I added.

He wouldn't let up. "I'm great in a group," he said.

"Shoot!" I called into the phone, "I'm burning something on the stove. Let me call you some other time. Thanks for the thought, though!" I hung up.

"You and Ben date?" Da Ge asked.

"Are you joking? I don't even know him, I—"

"Why does he call you the way he do?"

"What do you mean *the way he does*?" He caught this correction, even though I felt like it was a freebie since it wasn't my point. His jaw tightened.

"That's the first time he's ever called me, and it's not like I—" Why was I justifying myself?

"Ben has good English," Da Ge said.

"Spare me, Da Ge," I told him. "Xiao Wang has good Chinese."

"What does that mean?" He was sitting up now, straight.

"Forget it," I said. "Let's study."

"No," he said.

"What do you want me to say?"

"Say the truth," he said.

"Fuck you," I told him. "I'm supposed to 'say the truth' when I know nothing about you? Some loser colleague of mine calls me on the phone and you demand an explanation? There is no truth. Ben wants to go out to dinner with me and I don't want to go. Are you happy?"

"Tell him we get married," Da Ge proposed. The chill reclimbed my spine.

"No."

"Why not?" His voice was thin now.

Mine was pathetic, low, far away. "Because I don't know whether it's true."

At this, he backed off a bit.

"Are we?" I pressed, hearing the speed gather underneath my voice. "Married? Do you want to be my boyfriend? My husband? Should I tell Ben you love me? Do you? Do you want to have a baby with me?"

"Why do you ask me this things?" he shouted.

Because I wanted to know the answers. But before I could say that, he was off the couch, down the hall, and out the door. It was the kind of fight kids have the night before summer camp ends. You have to cut off your friends in anger, or you'll miss them too much to bear. It's better to be enemies when you have to leave each other the next day. I just wasn't in on the secret that Da Ge and I were parting ways.

At the end of my lesson with Teacher Hao today, he showed me his daughter's college application and essay. "Embarrassed to ask," he said. I waved my hand at him.

"No, no," I said, "Ask anything."

"Maybe you can look these over and also—" He paused.

"I'll be happy to look. What else? Is there anything else I can do to help?"

"Maybe take Sha Mei to the embassy?"

"Of course."

Sha Mei's essay was so penetratingly sweet and confused that I almost regretted having to comment on it. She said that her life had been shaped by books and newspapers because it was difficult for her to travel. But she had been on trains to Kaifeng, where her parents were from, and many times to Tianjin, a port city full of boats and swimmers. She believed that she could widen her perspective in America, and bring back whatever knowledge she gained to China—to help bring glory to her country. I gently fixed the most egregious grammatical glitches and then went to find my mom.

She was in Julia Too's room, decorating Julia Too, Phoebe, and Lili with makeup for a play they had written, a musical they apparently planned to perform after dinner. Phoebe is as in love with Naomi as Julia Too is, of course. Even Lili finds her irresistible.

When Xiao Wang and Yang Tao arrived, my mother was on her best behavior, delighted that I had agreed to introduce her and Yang Tao. She sized him up politely with questions about his pedigree and his parents. Xiao Wang watched their interaction as if it were a good sitcom, no doubt waiting to tell me later how blunt and nosy Americans are, forgetting that when I met her mother in Jinhong the first time I came to China, her mom asked me immediately why I had no husband, how much money I made in America, and whether she could please set me up with a "more suitable" man than the one I had mistakenly chosen myself.

Dinner took a long, luxurious time. My mom had prepared salmon and a mesclun salad with avocado and grapefruit and sesame seeds. She placed half a teaspoon of salmon on her fork, then set upon it several grains of rice. She was so focused it was if she were building a bridge that might collapse and kill people. Then she picked up her fork-with-gingered-salmon installation and slipped it into her mouth like an actress.

Yang Tao, after watching my mother's performance art, turned to Julia Too.

"How are rehearsals?" he asked.

Julia Too glanced at Phoebe, who was watching Lili. None of the girls answered.

"Are you still preparing to be professional actresses?" Xiao Wang asked. I was grateful to her for this question, which I took to be a kind of siding with Yang Tao.

"Maybe we'll go on *American Idol* when we move back to America," Phoebe said. They looked at each other, nodded.

"Why not stay here and do a CCTV show?" I asked, joking.

"What is CCTV?" my mother asked.

"CCTV sucks!" Phoebe said. "It's like the cheesy Chinese version of real TV." The thought crossed my mind that Yang Tao was the only Chinese guy I'd ever met who knew the word "cheesy." I wondered if Xiao Wang knew what it meant.

"It's China Central Television," Yang Tao told my mother, "and Phoebe's right. The programming is not so good."

Julia Too wasn't chiming in or ganging up, but didn't rise to his defense, either.

"China's been around a lot longer than the U.S., guys," I said, sounding like a TV program myself. "Maybe American things are just cheesy versions of Chinese ones. Like noodles and pizza!" I meant to lighten the tone and spark a fun debate, but Phoebe felt outclassed and attacked, and Julia Too was angry.

"Whatever, Mom," she said. "If China's been around so long, how come they don't even have their own coffee shops or movies or music?" She glanced at Yang Tao. "Maybe ancient culture was so great that China wants to stay back in it."

I was surprised. Phoebe laughed, but Lili's eyes widened. She looked nervously over at Xiao Wang, who was carefully watching the interaction but not involving herself. Lili was both enamored of Julia Too—the way Julia Too was of Phoebe—and a bit afraid of the scandalous things Julia Too was willing to say. Lili was a patriot like Xiao Wang, felt loyal, could lip-sync the pop song "I Love Beijing Tiananmen."

"Don't talk like that," Lili said to Julia Too, in Chinese.

Xiao Wang threw me a look of such pride that I had to smile and nod. Frankly I was relieved. Having Lili scold Julia Too was like being in a class in which one of the students gives another the comment you were hoping not to have to make. I guessed Julia Too hadn't meant the content of her attack any-way—she loves Chinese movies and music. She just wanted to fight. Coffee shops? Since when does Julia Too drink coffee?

"Who wants more salmon or salad?" my mother asked. Xiao Wang said no, thank you, but Yang Tao, winning my mother's love forever, took the platter and spooned another enormous portion onto his plate.

"Save room for dessert," she flirted. "I made a molten chocolate cake."

Maybe this was the straw that broke something, because Julia Too jumped up and left. Phoebe and Lili glanced around, awkward in their indecision about whether to follow her.

"Don't worry," I told them, "We'll be right back." I went after Julia Too.

"What's wrong?" I asked, in her room.

"Nothing," she said. "There's just too many people around all the time."

"I think Yang Tao would love to see your play," I said. "In fact I know he would. He really likes you. And I like him. Can we work on making this okay?"

"He's not my dad," she said, surprising me not with the sentiment but with the presentation. As soon as she'd said it, she added, "That sounds pretty stupid, right?"

"It's okay," I said. "I know what you mean."

I was interested that she could hear how much we sounded like a TV show or play. She was trying on roles, and even her attacks, although often articulate and well positioned to offend, had a childish affect. Julia Too had met other men, but she'd never protested so directly. I wondered if she perceived that there was something different about the way I liked Yang Tao. I wondered if there *was* something different about it.

"Anyway, of course he's not your dad. He's just a friend of mine. We can negotiate ways to make that friendship tolerable for you. This is your house. But just for tonight—can you please give him a chance?"

"I'm not sure I like him," she said.

"Okay," I said. "If that stays true, we'll revisit it. I won't have people over who make you unhappy."

She softened. "Can you go back to the table first, please?" she asked. I ruffled her hair and got up. She wanted to save face, to return to the table on her own time.

When she did, she was wearing red devil horns from some Halloween or another, and humming a Christina Aguilera song. Naomi immediately served her the piece of molten cake with the most insides, gazed at her lovingly. I thought of how Julia Too had reunited my mother and Benj, reignited Old Chen's heart, and saved me from myself. My mom wrapped her arms around Julia Too and kept them there; maybe she was feeling grateful, too.

After dessert we all sat on the couch, and the girls disappeared and then skipped out of the bedroom, stood side by side and began a synchronized dance that looked half like fly girl moves and half like Muppet seizures. Then Lili and

Phoebe froze in poses, and Julia Too popped to the front and sang an original Chinglish song that went like this:

> You can see that I'm *meili* (cute)
> *Ni kan bu dao de shi* (but you can't tell)
> I have girl *qiang li* (power).
> I'll tell you boy, I'll tell you boy
> There's some things you don't know.
> *Ni yikao wo* (you lean on me),
> *Ni xiang xin wo* (you trust me).
> *Ni yaole wo yi kou.* (You take a bite out of me)
> Let me tell you. *Wo gaosu ni.* Let me tell you, hey hey.
> So what you bite and *bu dong wo* (misunderstand me)?
> I love you anyway.
> Hey hey, *wo ai ni* anyway. Guess what?
> *Wo ai ni* anyway.

Yang Tao and my mother were stunned silent, and Xiao Wang occupied herself with creating an accurate translation for Naomi, showing off her fabulous English, although I had to supply the phrase "girl power." As soon as she'd heard the translation, my mother leapt off the couch in a standing ovation.

"Who wrote that?" she asked.

Lili and Phoebe rolled their eyes.

"Do you really have to ask?" said Xiao Wang. I was delighted that she felt comfortable enough to tease my mother. "It was your granddaughter, of course!"

"She's a real feminist," Yang Tao said.

"I'm not sure," I said, laughing, "I mean, she 'loves him anyway.'"

"You guys are losers!" said Julia Too joyfully. "It's a song, not an English paper!"

"Sing it one more time," my mom said.

"Yes. Encore, encore!" said Yang Tao. He leaned forward with real anticipation.

Julia Too threw me a grin.

Late in the summer of 1990, after Da Ge's and my fight, Xiao Wang finally called to invite me out with her and Jin. She was nervous and excited about introducing us. I asked if I could bring Da Ge, hoping we'd be made up by the time dinner took place. Xiao Wang did not like the idea, but agreed to it anyway. I called Da Ge and left messages about where we'd be and when. I didn't hear from him.

I arrived at Ocean Seafood five minutes early and saw that Xiao Wang and Jin were already seated. They looked as if they had been at the restaurant for weeks, waiting. I looked at my watch defensively, but Xiao Wang stood and put her hand on my arm, showing Jin how close we were. I was distraught that Da Ge wasn't there.

"Did you hear from Da Ge?" I asked.

"This is my teacher, Aysha," she said to Jin, who was standing.

"Aysha, This is my husband, Jin."

"Of course! Hi, Jin, how are you? I mean, welcome to New York."

He reached his hand out, and I shook it. He wore gray slacks, a white shirt with a label visible on its sleeve, and, to my surprise, a leather belt with a metal Playboy bunny buckle. He was significantly more handsome than I'd expected, thin and strong with a jaw so defined it made his face look like a TV set. His eyes were animated, suggested intelligence and wit. I felt pathologically nervous, as if he were about to interview me for a job.

"So, um," I said, "Da Ge didn't call you, huh?"

Xiao Wang shook her head no.

"Jin already orders for us—he gets nice food, I think you'll like."

I tried a polite nod in Jin's direction. Later, Xiao Wang let it slip that Jin had not approved, that he found me too *luan*, and *hutu*, chaotic and confused, to be a good influence. I can't blame him for that impression or for warning Xiao Wang. The fact is, I don't remember a single moment of our conversation that night, even though Nai Nai's health had begun falling apart and they must have told me, maybe even talked about it all night. Did I not respond? Did Xiao Wang guess what was happening? That I was pregnant? That Da Ge was gone? She told me months later that that wretched night was when Lili was conceived.

"Maybe because you are pregnant, it's easier for me to become!" she said.

"But you didn't even know I was pregnant yet."

"No matter," she said, "this is a situation of the body knowing."

All I knew that night was panic. What I remember is not my pregnancy, the news about Nai Nai, Xiao Wang's fertility, or Jin's disapproval. It's that Da Ge never showed up, and I was frantic because I knew something was terribly wrong.

He never called me about our fight or the dinner he missed. The next day, Wednesday, he was supposed to take his history test. When Xiao Wang called me, it was to say that Nai Nai was bedridden. I couldn't bring myself to ask her if she knew where Da Ge was. She was crying on the phone. I didn't know what to say.

I called Da Ge's and left messages on a machine whose outgoing words I couldn't understand. I tried apologizing, cajoling, begging, wishing him luck—anything. I said Xiao Wang's grandmother was sick, that she needed him. I said I needed him. Then I began walking. I walked block after block, uptown disappearing behind me. Exhausted at 42nd Street, I took the subway down to Chinatown. On the train was an ad featuring the Statue of Liberty. The photograph glistened, its water spinning out at me. I studied the city, perched vertically at the edge, while the Statue of Liberty raised her hand, flaming green-gray above the waves. I imagined calling on her in class. "Yes? Ms. Liberty? Do you have a question?"

On Mott Street, video shops were papered with posters of martial arts movies, the heroes' faces angling up toward cameras, violent and pretty. The planes of Da Ge's cheek flashed before me, his scar. I walked into a grocery store that reeked of roots and antlers. Vegetables I'd never seen were stacked, flanked by shelves of condiments so dark and sweet they looked solid. I touched as many things as I could: rice noodles in plastic packages, zip-locked bags of peppercorns, leafy cabbages. I walked the aisles, breathing in hot oil, peppers, fish, and blood. I wondered if babies can smell and then realized of course not, that there's no air for them yet. Reeling, I bought some Chinese sesame candy and then walked out as fast as I could.

The air outside was damp with heat that made the street lights sweat and glimmer. Fish vendors stood next to tables covered with melted ice and dead fish. The sidewalk was littered with shaved scales. Makeshift awnings hung from the roofs, flapping lazily every time a humid breeze oozed down Canal. I hailed the first cab I saw, pulled the door open, and climbed into the cold world of leather seat, air freshener, and car light that snapped off when I shut the door. "Where to, Miss?"

"Fifth Avenue and Eleventh, please," I said.

I cooled in the cab, safe. Chinatown, now out the window, was another world, one where I felt sure I'd never been. I unwrapped a piece of sesame candy and put it in my mouth. The rice paper melted on my tongue, the sugar dissolved and left the seeds, rough against the backs of my teeth. I watched the chaos of the city ride by outside, each frame gone as soon as I'd seen it. Then I closed my eyes, leaned my head back. The driver was listening to Latin music. I wondered whether he knew how to salsa and tried to imagine his hips, swaying back and forth.

At Fifth and 11th I paid him and jumped out, ran up the steps to Dr. Meyers. My mind was racing. As soon as I'd begun to have one thought, a new one chased it away. I thought of chasers. Chases, changes, chances. Words scrolled out in my mind, choices. I couldn't spell sentences because I couldn't finish them. Afraid, I told Dr. Meyers I might be in trouble.

"Would you consider getting back on lithium?" she asked gently. I hadn't told her that I'd stopped taking it. I was surprised she had figured it out.

"It's okay, Aysha," she said, reading my thought. "I'm not judging."

"Are you ready?" I asked Dr. Meyers.

"Aysha," she said, "look at me. Nothing you tell me can shock me. I will not be surprised, and I will not judge you. It will help you make it through whatever you're suffering if we iron it out."

I loved the expression "iron it out."

"I married one of my students, and I'm three months pregnant with his baby," I told her. When I said it, an image of a baby flashed through my mind, and I imagined I could feel our baby eating sesame candy.

"I see," Dr. Meyers said.

"I didn't tell him."

"You mean you haven't told the baby's father that he is the father?" she asked.

I said I hadn't told him anything, and when she asked what I meant by anything, I told her that I was in love with him.

"Or about the baby," she said, softly.

"Yes," I confessed, "or about the baby."

"Do you want to tell him?" she asked.

I felt stupid. "Actually," I said, "I was planning to tell him tonight."

She nodded, encouraging.

"He had his citizenship test and we have a dinner date, but I can't find him."

"Is citizenship why you two got married?" she asked me. She was careful with the words. I pictured how they lined up in her mouth first, auditioning for their parts in this sentence. They were well cast, too. Compassionate, nudging words.

"I don't know," I told her, honestly. "I think maybe it was the reason he wanted to marry me at first, but it's complicated. I mean, he knew me in the hospital, but I didn't realize it, and then he came to my house drunk and my mom was over and she knew him so I asked him and he said he'd been in a motorcycle accident—" I ran out of breath.

"Slow down," she said. "We can sort this out for a while together."

I wondered why shrink and laundry vocabulary overlapped so often. We will iron and sort, I thought. I imagined folding sheets with Da Ge again. This time, it would be the four of us: Da Ge, Dr. Meyers, Xiao Wang, and me. One on each corner of the futon, tucking a contour sheet underneath. At our sleepover, the roof would blow off my apartment building and the four of us would lie on our backs, looking up at the open sky.

"What are you thinking?" Dr. Meyers asked.

I did not hate her for this.

"I am thinking of folding sheets with you and Da Ge, and the roof blowing off my apartment and all of us sleeping in the living room."

"We're going to figure this out." Dr. Meyers promised. She smiled at me with such warmth and patience that I wondered for the first time who her children were.

"Your kids are lucky," I told her.

"Thank you," she said. I blinked. Instead of offering me a tissue, she lowered her eyes a bit, so that I would see where she was looking on the desk. I picked the tissue box up myself and put it on my lap.

"I don't know where he is," I said.

"He'll come back," she said.

"What should I do?"

"You should wait."

But he didn't come back.

I read "Cloud in Trousers" to Julia, who was watching TV from her bed. "You think malaria makes me delirious?" I read. "It happened. / In Odessa it happened. / 'I'll come at four,' Maria promised. / Eight. / Nine. / Ten."

"This is not a good time to read Russian poets," Julia said.

"I always think of this when I'm waiting for something. Eight, nine, ten. He was watching the clock, you realize, waiting for her."

"Maybe," she said. "But put that down and come watch mindless TV with me."

"I can't get back on lithium. The baby will have ten heads."

"I know," she said. "But you'll make it the next six months okay. Come watch."

She had turned to a talk show, the topic of which was "Married men who dress like women and sleep with other men." A hostess with breasts so enormous she looked like an inflatable parade float was interviewing a guest who had slept with his wife's gay brother. Julia changed the channels around and came back to the talk show. The man was going to confront his wife with this information on national TV and ask her to forgive him. Hope flooded me. I crossed my fingers that the baby got some, reached over Julia's bedside table, and called California information for my brother's number.

In the last five years, I had spoken with Benj only a couple of times. Once, when I was seventeen and still living at home, Benj came to New York and stayed with a girlfriend. He and I met for coffee that time, and he seemed to love me still. We did not talk about our father. Benj was grown-up, with a button-down shirt and clean fingernails.

I saw him a few times when I was at Columbia. And I know he came once when I was hospitalized, because Julia One told me. He wanted both to come to the hospital, and, if possible, to avoid my mom. So he and Julia coordinated. I do not remember that visit at all, but Julia told me later that he was "dignified." At her studio, I dialed the digits an operator had given me, and it seemed like magic when Benj picked up somewhere sunny on the other end.

"Hi, Benj?" I asked.

"Is this Aysha?"

"Yeah. Hi."

"Hi. You okay?"

"Yeah, I'm good. It's good to hear your voice."

"You, too. What's up, Aysh?"

"Could you come home, please?"

He paused. "To New York?"

"Yeah. I'm sorry, I know it's—"

"Is Mom okay?"

I was surprised to hear him ask this.

"She's fine, Benj. I just really want to see you."

"Oh. Okay. Um. Of course. Let me figure out a ticket."

Out of family habit or love, Benj spared me the embarrassment of further questions. I had never asked him for anything at all before, not even information on our parents. I wondered if now that the dam was broken and I'd begun begging favors, there would be no stopping me. I waited for him to respond. There was a shuffling on the phone, like newspapers.

"Would Friday work?" he asked me. "I have to work tomorrow, but I could come Friday night on a red-eye maybe and then—"

"That would be perfect, Benj—I can't tell you how glad I'd be to see you," I told him. "What should I cook?"

"Do you cook?"

"For you I can," I said.

Relieved that I had this happy news to hold on to, I repeated the conversation to Julia, word for word. She asked what we'd do while he was here.

"I'm going to tell him about Da Ge," I said.

"What about him?"

"That we're married and I'm having a baby. I think if he's here, he'll see that it's all okay, that I'm okay—and he can meet Da Ge, I guess. And maybe see my mom."

"I'd like to meet Da Ge too," she said. It was characteristically generous of her not to count the drunken encounter in my hallway or whatever glimpses she'd caught of him in the hospital as "meeting him," not even to mention those. I thought of my fight with him and wondered where he was right now, what he was doing. I hoped as hard as I could that he was okay, closed my eyes, and failed to conjure up his face.

My mother came into my bedroom last night while I was on the phone with Shannon, gossiping about my trip to the embassy with Teacher Hao's daughter. She got her visa. "Honestly," I was telling Shannon, "I don't know anyone—it was just luck."

"Did you cosign her financial papers?"

"Yeah, but that's not always enough. She's a brilliant student, and a huge patriot. She's definitely coming back."

"We'll see," Shannon said.

"Since when are you so cynical?" I asked. "And besides, life in the States isn't better than life here anymore. Why would she want to stay?"

"She'll marry an American," Shannon said. My mom was tapping her foot.

"I gotta run," I said. "My mom. I'll see you Friday night for majhong?"

"Bring Yang Tao," she said, "and your mom. And Julia Too can sleep over."

I blew her a kiss through the phone, and hung up. My mom pounced on the bed like she'd been stalking me for hours.

"Who was that?"

"Shannon. She says hi."

"Oh! Tell her I say hi."

"I've already hung up the phone, Mom."

"I *really* like him," my mother said, ignoring me.

I squinted at her. "Yeah?"

"He reminds me a little of Da Ge."

This made me quiet.

"I don't mean in you know, that sense. I just mean he's kind."

"I don't know if Da Ge was kind, exactly," I said, surprised she would even bring him up. We almost never mention him.

"Do you ever talk about him with Julia Too?"

"Yang Tao? We had a scalding conversation about him last night during dinner."

"I meant Da Ge, but what do you mean, *scalding*?"

"She doesn't like him as much as I do." I smiled.

"Does she get a vote?"

"She gets the most votes. If she doesn't come to like him, I'll leave him."

"I'm not sure that's the right—"

"I know. But this is her house, and she and I have been on our own together a long time. If she's unhappy it's not worth it to me."

"What about you? What about you being happy?"

"Right," I said. "There is that, I guess." I shrugged. "But my happiness depends less on Yang Tao than it does on Julia Too."

"Did you tell her that?"

"In so many words."

"Maybe that's all she needed to know. Maybe she'll like him now."

"I hope so."

"Do you ever talk to her about Da Ge?"

I felt exhausted by my mother. "I try to."

"Do you and Old Chen talk about him?"

"Never."

Now there was a long, awkward pause.

"I tried to talk to you about your father sometimes, darling."

"I know you did. Don't worry about that."

"Is there anything you want to ask me now?" She looked at me fretfully.

"No," I said. I did not add that it was late, or that I wouldn't know where to begin. Instead, I turned mild. It was what my mother would have done.

"I appreciate all your help with Julia Too this summer," I said.

She sighed with relief. "I want to help give you time to yourself. I think it's wonderful that you're writing a story for her. I can't wait to read the story myself."

"I hope you like it," I said, knowing she wouldn't.

"I will," she promised. "I wish I'd written something for you."

I looked at her. "There's still time."

My mother and Old Chen showered each other with bizarre presents this morning at dumplings, as is the custom and their habit. My mom brought the old man Cuban cigars, which he loved even though he doesn't smoke, a Gucci tie, and a Mont Blanc pen set. He had outdone himself with his present for her, a sculpture of a plump ballerina in a rough, textured dress. Spinning, with her arms out and palms up. It reminded me of the giant stone statue in Red

Moon's courtyard. My mother shrieked with delight when she saw it, and then spent such a long time kvelling and asking questions that Old Chen was finally too embarrassed to continue and had to wave his hands in the air to shush her.

"It's nothing! It's nothing!" he said, "just a little gift from China for you to have in New York. Maybe your dance students will like to see this Chinese art."

"Well," my mother said, "they'll have to come to my house to see it, because this is going right in the center of my living room. It's the most incredible thing I own."

"Um, can we eat, please?" Julia Too asked.

"It's like a Chinese Degas in 3-D," my mother said. "I mean, the delicacy of her body under that rough dress—it's a statement about human frailty, don't you think?"

I was worried about how Old Chen might take this, but he smiled. "That's something common to us all. This piece is called *I don't know don't know do you know.*"

"What does that mean?"

"I don't know," said Old Chen. "That's why I like it."

His maid came out with a tray of dumplings, and Julia Too began eating as if we'd been starving her for years. My mother held her chopsticks all the way at the top and lifted a dumpling off the plate as if it were a rare gem she was holding up to the light. She took a tiny nibble and none of the filling dribbled out. I watched, mesmerized.

"What do you mean that's why you like it—because you don't know what it means?" Julia Too was asking Old Chen in Chinese.

Old Chen answered her in English, rare for him. "A bird doesn't sing because it has an answer," he said, "but because it has a song."

"Or some ancient Chinese wisdom it wants to tell me," said Julia Too.

CHAPTER TWELVE
Augusts
✳

A PHONE CALL WOKE ME ON THE FRIDAY MORNING MY brother was scheduled to come to see me in New York. It was August 10, 1990. Bolts of light jutted through my windows, and I jolted awake at the sound of Bonita Verna's hello. She was the administrator from Embassy, on the phone. But school didn't start for three more weeks. Her voice made no sense. Before the words were even out of her mouth, my blood had become something other than blood. It was soda, bubbling through my veins.

"There's been an accident," she said, apologetically. "I'm calling the staff."

I was instantly so cold I thought the baby might be born a Popsicle. I heard my voice as if it were on a tape. "What happened?"

"It's Ben Rosenbaum. He was assaulted last night outside his apartment. Um. He's at Mount Sinai." My lungs clamped shut. "Aysha," said Bonita, "you still there?"

"Yes," I said. "I'm here. I'm here." I took some breaths. "Will he be okay?" As soon as I had asked, I already didn't want to hear.

She said, "They don't really know yet." She paused. "Something about his jaw, maybe, or his mouth. It's wired shut? And something about his eyes, maybe. We're all sending a gift together. Should I sign your name?"

Twenty minutes later, I sat facing Julia on my couch and repeating compulsively, "He spoke such complicated English!" She had come over, and we were waiting. "What are we waiting for? What are we waiting for?" I kept asking.

"Try to breathe deeply," she said. I felt for her. I stood up. I sat down. I stood again.

"Should I call your mom?" she asked. I didn't think so. How could I explain everything I hadn't explained? I didn't think my mother could manage the avalanche of all of it at once. I know, I thought, we would go to Da Ge's apartment in Chinatown. That would be a way to show him I was worried, to take initiative.

"That sounds fine," Julia said when I asked her to come. She was scared.

We took the subway to Canal Street in a blur. I wasn't sure where Da Ge's apartment had been. We wound through tight streets, purses, fish and fake name-brand watches everywhere. I was frantic to see Da Ge, even to show him off to Julia. We passed a brick wall painted with the words "dim sum." They seemed nonsensical, the way words get when contorted by repetition. It wasn't until we accidentally saw the video store where he had rented *Ju Dou* that I recognized his apartment building and pointed at it.

"It's right over there," I told Julia. She looked skeptical.

"Are you sure?" she asked. She could not imagine that I knew anyone who lived in Chinatown, or that any of the apartments we were walking toward was familiar to me.

We trekked through the rush of garlic and oil up five flights of stairs, and knocked on 5-I. There was no answer. We waited in the hallway, looking at each other anxiously. The more we knocked, the more agitated I began to feel. A cool, sinking feeling rose through my bones. There was a sickening energy in the building.

"Maybe he's out. Or doing laundry or something," Julia said.

"Should we go downstairs?" I asked.

She said sure, relieved to have even a pointless Plan B. But down the stairs in the basement there were no washing machines. I guess Da Ge must have taken his laundry to a laundromat. As we moved from the dingy trash room into a corridor, I saw a shadow against the concrete wall. I stood looking at the shadow. "What's that?" I asked Julia.

"What?" she said. And then she was screaming for me not to move, not to look, but it was too late. I had already stepped into the hallway and seen him. He was completely still, but had the after-look of hanging, a look I had never seen but recognized instantly, knew in some animal way that involved no words. He hung from a cord strung up over an exposed pipe. His neck was sideways. I couldn't manage that part somehow, couldn't take it in. I kept looking at his neck. Why was it sideways like that? Crooked, broken, wrong, the wrong angle, color, shape. There were his clothes: his collar, a button-down shirt I'd never seen, his chest and stomach still underneath. I knew the cargo pants, his thighs, knees, calves. His feet. I looked again, he was whole. But his neck. Why was it sideways like that? He could be rescued, I thought. My eyes fell back to his feet, saw the shiny shoes once maybe or a thousand times, flashing and motionless after what must have been the force of the swinging, and back up his ankles, waist, chest, shoulders, face, his cheek, the scar, everything, suspended, dead. He was dead. The word itself took shape in my mind. He faced down, was looking at the floor. I couldn't see his eyes, didn't know if they were open or closed. Underneath him was the metal bucket he had kicked savagely onto its side. I could hear it clattering, feel the cord scraping against the pipes and the delicate skin on his neck. His shoes were untied.

My mother tried to give me a pill, and I told her I was pregnant. There were some policemen in her apartment. Jack was there, in the background. "You're what?" she said.

I lifted my shirt up and showed my stomach. She put her hand on the baby.

"Oh, Aysha!" she cried, "why didn't you tell me?"

"I was going to, Mom," I said. "I was waiting for the right moment."

Maybe we were both thinking about that moment and how it wasn't the right one. Julia was balled up on the floor, with her knees pulled up to her chest. I had two notes we had found, both in Chinese. I didn't know what they said. Where was Zhen Ming?

Maybe we should go back to Chinatown, I said. I didn't remember how we had gotten uptown. My head was on my mom's shoulder. She combed my static hair with her fingers. The police were peering around. For what? Da Ge? The murder weapon? I thought of Clue. Mr. Tigerfood, on the pipes with the bucket. I didn't cry. My head was dried up. I thought of the only word left: finished.

It is Friday, I thought, Friday. It's August. The police were asking me could they ask me. My mother was shouting at someone. My mother, who never shouted. I couldn't speak at all. Then it was Saturday, early morning. We were at my apartment.

My mother and I were in my bed. Life was a photo album: there were only several moments, and in each of them, we found ourselves in specific poses. I looked at us from the outside, as if flipping pages with plastic sheets over them. I suddenly wanted to have a baby. Of course the fact that I was actually having one was a coincidence. Julia was on the couch in the living room. Adam called. My mother took the call. I didn't want to talk. My mother fed me some kind of breakfast that involved milk. "For your baby," she said, tipping the cup. I didn't know if she was talking to me or to herself. All of a sudden, I remembered my brother.

"Benj!" I said, "What time is it?"

"Your friend? We can visit him in the hospital," my mother said, her face lighting up because I had spoken. "He's going to be fine, Aysh. They say he's going to be okay."

I didn't mean Ben Rosenbaum, but I said nothing. It was too much work. I figured Benj would find his way to my place, realize what a mess I'd created, and leave. I felt for Da Ge's notes in my pockets, but they were gone. I no longer had the same jeans on. I rummaged through the laundry, but there was nothing in the pockets. My mother is not the type who accidentally washes coins and notes.

"They're in your jewelry box, sweetie," she said, quietly, when I asked.

Some people from Embassy appeared at my house. I was confused. I wasn't sure who they were, or why Bonita had brought flowers. My mother organized them into a vase on my glass table in front of the dragons.

"I didn't realize," she said, and then, "you were very discreet." She was crying.

I didn't know what she was talking about. I began to wonder where Da Ge was.

When Xiao Wang showed up, I led her into the bedroom and opened my jewelry box. I took the two notes out and handed them to her. Her eyes moved over the paper.

"It says, '*erzi tingzhe mama*,'" she said. I looked at her. "This means something about the son listens to his mother."

I was holding my breath. She looked at the other note, shook her head.

"Please tell me what it says," I said.

"This one say, '*dou shi gei laoshi de*.'" I waited. "It means 'everything for my teacher,'" she said. We stood looking at each other, blank. Then she hugged me.

Julia must have explained something to Benj. When I woke up, he was sitting on the edge of my bed, holding my hand. I thought he might believe that I had set him up, knowing my mother would be over at my place, and I wanted to explain to him that it wasn't the case, but I couldn't. I was afraid he would leave and not come back. He saw me watching him and said, "I am so sorry about your boyfriend."

Who did he mean? I thought something bad had happened, but I wasn't sure what.

Finally, I spoke. "What's wrong with everyone?"

"Oh, Aysha," my mom said.

I looked down at myself. The baby, I thought, and relief surged through me. She was still there. I put Benj's hand on my stomach. "I'm pregnant," I said.

"I know. Congratulations, Aysh."

Benj was handsome. I knew he would be. His hair was dark and neatly cut, but still curling up a bit at the sides. He had long eyelashes and sharp face bones. I thought we looked alike, both like our mom, and was glad. I closed my eyes.

I woke up again and again. The next time it happened, it was night and I was alone in my room, crying. I wondered how a body cries before it wakes up. I saw my body sometimes then, as if it belonged to someone else, the quick dip of my hips, bones still visible even as my belly rounded out with Julia Too. I checked in with myself occasionally, running my hands down my sides, or over my stomach, wondering if I could bring Da Ge back by touching what he had touched. By living places where he'd lived. China. I thought of China. But I couldn't even make it into the living room, couldn't find it. I couldn't remember my name. I was asleep again.

I was awake, trapped between tight white sheets. My mother must have tucked me in like that; I prefer to let a foot stick out. She was sitting on the bed now, talking to

Benj. They were on either side of me. I wanted to shout. To jump on the bed, to be manic again. Anything other than this, this slogging through air so thick it was chewable. I thought of the Goo Goose in Dr. Seuss. *If sir, you sir, choose to chew sir, with the goo goose, chew sir, do sir*! I was breathing, filling my lungs with gum. I wanted to ask my mom and Benj how it was after so much time, if they forgave each other. But I couldn't put consonants together what with my mouth stuck shut.

I heard Julia's voice. I was in the living room, propped up on some pillows and sipping from a glass. Milk? Da Ge was hanging from his basement pipes, his lovely neck twisted, the collar of his shirt ripped open. There was blood on his throat. Rope burn.

"She tried to tie his shoes," Julia was saying. "And take him down. She wanted to take him down." She must have disliked talking about this, and I felt grateful to her for the sacrifice. I wondered whether Adam was relieved that we were not friends anymore, now that something was wrong all around me. Where was Adam?

"A few months ago, I guess," Julia was saying. She meant Da Ge and me, when we had gotten married. I twisted my wedding ring. I was thinking about how once I'd been swimming naked at night. I couldn't remember where or with whom. Maybe Adam, upstate somewhere. Or was it high school? That night had been blue black and smooth. Maybe something like being dead. Maybe being dead was okay, like swimming naked in dark water. Cool and full. The police had come back and were asking why Julia didn't know some date. She said she hadn't been there.

"Didn't she tell you right away?" someone asked Julia.

"No."

"Why?"

"She likes to wait for special moments—it's a kind of habit for her."

"Did she ever mention Da Ge's family?"

"Not really," Julia said. I could hear her voice flattening. You're doing a good job, Julia, I thought, keep it up.

"What about a man named Zhen?"

"No."

"What about Ming?"

"No, I don't think so."

"Did she ever mention a man named Ben Rosenbaum?"

"Maybe. The name rings a bell."

"Were they *involved*?"

"No."

"Would you definitely know?"

"Yes."

"But you didn't know that her and the Chinese kid got married."

"I *did* know that."

"Do you think the kid killed himself because of what he did to the other guy?" one of them asked, more to the other than to Julia, I think.

But Julia started crying. "I don't know," she said. "I don't think so. I mean, I think he was just depressed. I don't think the two things were—I don't know, connected."

"So," one of them said gently, "after she took the body down, what happened?"

"What do you mean 'what happened?'" Julia snapped.

"I mean," he said, "what transpired then?"

"Well," Julia said, "let's see. She collapsed under the weight of the body and I tried to pull it off her but it was really heavy and I couldn't move them and I called 911. Is that what you meant? Is that what you meant by 'transpired'?"

My mother and Benj looked at each other, and he walked the cops out.

Xiao Wang and I met that week at Grand Sichuan, where she ordered noodles so hot they numbed my mouth. We bent over our bowls, unable to look at each other.

"I'm really sorry," I finally said.

"Yes, I'm sorry too. I—" She was flushed, her eyes red and swollen.

"You can say anything you want, Xiao Wang. I know this is a nightmare."

"It's not polite question," she said.

"I don't care." I thought of Da Ge's "It's not polite talk."

"Do you love Da Ge?"

I folded my mouth into an expression I didn't recognize from the inside of it.

"Yes," I said, "I love him."

"I loved him, too." She put extra emphasis on the past-tense "d," something she usually missed. I wondered whether this was because she was making a grammatical point or because he was dead. Was it possible to love him now?

"I'm glad," I said. "I'm glad we both loved him." Neither of us was crying. It was too late for that.

"Da Ge met my mother in the hospital," I said.

"Yes, he said it to me."

Of course he had told her. "Did you know he wanted to marry an American?"

Her eyes flickered over me. "Actually, he wants to marry with you, I think," she said. Her voice had no inflection. "He also want to be American, but he choose you for his private reason of love, too. You should not feel only sorrow for this."

"Did you two talk about it? Did he tell you that?"

"We don't have to talk that," she said. "For you, Da Ge is like going abroad. For me, he is coming home, familiar, like so many Chinese guys I have known."

I rested my chin on my hands and remembered him for less than a second, the way it's possible sometimes to understand *forever*. As a little kid, late at night, I used to get death so clearly that the getting made me gasp with fear. And then it was gone, my grasp slipped, and I could live again with the fact that I would someday die and be gone forever. Death was back to abstract, the way it has to be.

"When you said you want to have dinner to ask me some things, I do not think it is this," Xiao Wang was saying. "I think it must be what kind of friendship Da Ge and I have. Or what he say in class." His name sounded so good in her accent that I wanted to wrap her up and keep her close by forever, suffering with me. I hated myself, hated him.

"You don't have to tell me either of those things," I said.

Xiao Wang exhaled. "In your class, Da Ge is always furious to me. He think I am ruin his chance to be American."

"Why?"

"Because I make him feel Chinese. Because I am asking why he want to be American. He say, he is not Chinese. So I ask is your father Chinese? And he say, 'Fuck my father.' So I say, in Chinese, 'You don't love your own father? This is wrong,' I say, 'You should be proud to be Chinese,' and he say to me, 'Fuck China and fuck you.'" She took a sip of tea. The leaves had been steeping for so long that the tea was black. She chewed a leaf. "Do you want to know the other time?" she asked me. "The time it's so bad word it's not in the dictionary?"

"No," I said, "forget it."

"I have something for you," she said. She handed me a wrapped gift. I took the pieces of tape off as if I were operating on a patient, unfolded the wrapping paper, and pulled out an unopened VHS tape of *The Sound of Music*.

"It's my favorite American movie," Xiao Wang said, her face lighting up with hope, "but we never watch it together. Did you see it before?"

"No," I lied. "let's watch it tonight."

She brought vanilla Haagen-Dazs, and we watched *The Sound of Music* from beginning to end, twice. It took like six hours. When the movie ended the first time, she turned to me and said, "Maybe we watch it again," and I rewound the tape without speaking and pushed play again. I was grateful for Xiao Wang, for Julie Andrews, for the nuns. Neither of us mentioned the possibility of sleep. We sat up until it was light outside. Then she left to check on Nai Nai, and I began a habit that would organize the two weeks between Da Ge's death and Embassy starting up again. I rode the subway for entire days, listening to names, watching the map, groping for a correspondence between what was written and what I heard. *This is a Wakefield bound 2 express train; the next stop is Intervale Avenue. Intervale, Stimpson, Freeman.* Sometimes I tuned out and came to dozens of stops later: *Burke Ave, Gun Hill. Nereid. Wakefield.* Then I'd turn around and ride backwards from the tip of the Bronx to Wall Street, watching people move and stop and move and stop. Their urgency was my movie, a documentary about some species I'd once belonged to. Sometimes people talked to me, mostly I just rode quietly, comforted by the infinite places I'd never have to stop. It made no difference where I was, what neighborhoods I skimmed over, rode under, passed through. I never wondered what was happening in any of them. I didn't even have to be me those days, could just blow by, watching worlds melt in the instant I passed. *Stand clear of the closing doors.*

Shannon, Xiao Wang, Anne, and I took the girls camping on the Great Wall Friday night. My mother stayed home; she hates nature. Yang Tao offered to drive us out there, leave, and then drive back the next day to pick us up. When I protested that it was way too much *mafan* for him to go to, that we'd just rent a minivan, he insisted.

"I'd like the time with you and Julia Too in the car," he said. He hadn't been over in a while, hadn't pressed it. I said he could take us there, but we'd go back with Anne.

So Yang Tao picked us up and we drove three hours to the "wild wall," a lesser-known access site, listening to a painful CD Julia Too had burned of Beyoncé, Ludacris, Avril Lavigne, and Nelly. Yang Tao asked polite questions about the MTV music awards, and she lectured him Old Chen–style, happily. When we arrived at the wall, he unloaded sleeping bags, then kissed Julia Too once on each cheek before kissing me. She smiled, kissed his cheeks back, and ran to greet Phoebe and Lili.

"Thank you for schlepping us out here," I said, looking up at Yang Tao.

"It was nice for me," he said. "I'm glad she's giving me another chance."

He got into the car, rolled the window down. "Have a good night on the wall."

"Will I see you tomorrow when we get back?" I asked.

"Do you want to?"

"Terribly," I said.

He smiled, turned the key in the ignition.

"Mom!" Julia Too called. "Look at this!"

I walked over to where Julia Too, Lili, and Phoebe were crouched over a dead snake.

"That's odd," Anne was saying. "It's a water snake." She flipped it over with her hand, shocking me with her un-squeamishness. "A tiger-striped neck groove snake."

"A what?!" I asked.

"A tiger-striped neck groove snake. They're common in Beijing," she said.

"You're a freak," I told her. "How do you know esoteric snake names?"

She smiled, pleased. "It's not esoteric. We had one in our garden once."

Weeds as tall as the girls rose up, and we swashbuckled our ways through them. Unlike at Simatai or Mutianyu, the tourist sites on the wall, there was no cable car, no slide, and nobody following us up the wall. I somewhat missed the chatter of the old women who climbed the wall with us when we went to Simatai, hoping to sell water or postcards at the top. We stopped in a fortress for lunch, ate mozzarella and basil sandwiches from the Kerry Center deli, and looked at the dozens of miles of sky visible in every direction. It was so hot that the air felt thick and supportive, as if we could collapse and still be held up by humidity. There was the slow drone of insects so utterly absent in the city, and after I finished my lunch, I leaned back against a stone wall and listened. Julia Too and the girls were talking about seventh grade, who had moved, whether Kevin and Phoebe would continue to be in love, whether they'd be allowed to go to the Glay concert in October, since we moms had waffled and agreed to let them go unchaperoned to the Beijing jazz festival the last week of August. Xiao Wang was sitting next to me, fanning herself.

"I am reading this book called *Kitchen*," she said, "a Japanese book."

"In Chinese?"

"Yes. They have it in English. Maybe you can read it so we can discuss."

"Okay. Is it good?"

"I think it's good, yes. The story has some nice feeling, but it's a little bit soft, maybe inexperienced."

"Inexperienced?"

"Young, I mean. The author was young when she wrote it."

"How old?"

"Maybe in her middle thirties."

"Our age, you mean."

"Yeah. Maybe there are experiences you must have before you can be maturity or perspective. Especially to write a story or book about life experiences like love or death."

"I agree." I smiled, accepted with salt her warning that I should wait to write.

We hiked the rest of the afternoon until it began to get dark. Then Anne flaunted her Girl Scout résumé by making a voluptuous illegal fire. We sat around it, ate our second batch of Kerry Center sandwiches and roasted marshmallows before unrolling sleeping bags and staring up at a billion stars invisible in the city. When everyone else was asleep, Julia Too rolled her little burritoed self over to me. "See those stars?" she whispered.

I woke myself up enough to say, "Of course. They're beautiful."

"You can see the same ones from New York and China," she said, so quietly I wasn't sure I'd heard her right. "Don't you think that's weird?"

"Weird how?"

"How they're everywhere and nowhere."

"They're not nowhere, exactly. Just far away."

When the sun poured heat over us in the morning, we awoke, drank Cokes for breakfast, brushed our teeth over the edge of the Great Wall, and climbed down.

Then Julia Too and I picked up my mother and went straight to Old Chen's. He was sitting under a tree in his courtyard, with a thermos of tea and a book. Dressed in khakis and a button-down shirt, he looked oddly Western to me. Maybe my father looks like Old Chen now, now that he's old. I looked over at my mom, to see what she was thinking. But I couldn't tell. Her eyes were on Julia Too, hugging Old Chen.

"Sit, sit," he said to us. He stood and got a chair ready for Naomi. She thanked him and the maid went to get more tea.

"Thank you for doing today instead of yesterday," I said.

"No problem. How was the Great Wall?" He used English for Naomi's benefit.

"Fun," Julia Too said. "I brought you this." She held out a rock she'd found, perhaps part of the wall, but ground down enough to have a glassy affect.

Old Chen turned it over in his palm. "You know," he said to Julia Too, "your father loved to sleep outside. It's not common. Maybe you get this hobby from him."

Naomi and I looked at each other, surprised.

"He was a lively person, like you. When he was little," Old Chen continued in English, glancing over at Naomi, who had folded her hands in her lap. Old Chen turned back to Julia Too. "Maybe there are things you'd like to know about what happened? If there are, of course you may ask me."

"What *did* happen?" Julia Too asked.

I think she asked it faster than Old Chen was expecting, and that it was a bigger question than he had anticipated. Julia Too was usually so specific.

But maybe he'd been practicing, because he only paused for a breath before responding in Chinese: "Your *baba* died from heartbreak, a real illness. First it infects your heart and organs, and then your mind. In your mind, it can kill you. Just like his mother, your grandmother."

He continued in Chinese. "This kind of disease can be inherited. But you don't have this kind of constitution."

Julia Too was looking at Old Chen as if she'd always known they'd eventually get to this point.

"I know," she said, in Chinese. "I know I don't."

"This is the anniversary month of his death," Old Chen said.

"I know," said Julia Too again.

Old Chen took a rumbling breath and looked over at Naomi. He switched back to English. "Maybe he would like if we talk about him. Maybe we can remember some things about him now that you're older. It's okay for you?"

"Of course," Julia Too said. "It would be great."

"Once," Old Chen said, smiling, "he burned our house with a cigarette." He stopped smiling and looked at Julia Too seriously. "You should never smoke cigarettes. They're bad for you. In spite of what everyone says."

"Don't worry," she said. "I won't."

"Or once, when he was small, he tried to cook dinner for his mother and me. He made rice, but he added so much water, we called it congee. We said it was the best thing we had ever eaten. He was so little, maybe only seven years old, and proud when we joked that it was breakfast for dinner. His mother loved congee."

"Why did he go to New York?" Julia Too asked.

I stared at the tree in Old Chen's courtyard, wondered how old it was. It looked thousands of years old, petrified. I thought how small we all are anyway, how short-lived. I braced myself.

"Da Ge moved to New York when Beijing was dangerous," Old Chen said, this time both to me and Julia Too, in Chinese. I took my eyes off the tree, tried looking back at him. "I thought it would be better for him with Zhen Ming in America. Now of course I . . . Well, I thought it would be safer. I didn't realize—" Here, he faltered. "I was busy; perhaps I didn't pay enough attention. Perhaps he even thought it was for convenience—"

Julia Too scratched at an imaginary fleck on her chair.

"No," I said in Chinese, "he knew you sent him to be safe. He told me that once."

Old Chen's face lifted. "*Zhende ma*?" Really?

I nodded, looked toward my mom to see if she wanted a translation, but she waved me quiet.

"Maybe I should have let him stay here, be in the square that week, even that day," Old Chen continued. "But you know, he might have died there. He could have died there, too."

"Of course," I said in English, honoring my mom. "It could have happened here, too." Old Chen looked ancient in the harsh sunlight, shadows of leaves over his skin. "You made the right decision—it's what any parent with the resources would have done."

Naomi nodded. Old Chen shaded his eyes with his hand as the sun shifted. "He tried to contact me before he—"

He stopped. Julia Too was watching Old Chen. Naomi was watching her.

"He tried to call me that week, you know, but I—he tried to call me, but I wasn't—"

Now Julia Too stood quietly from her chair and walked over to Old Chen's. She put her right hand on his arm. He sighed.

"I was traveling. I didn't hear the message until, well—"

"Until it was too late," Julia Too said. She said it gently, as if it were a shared regret, one for which she was also in some way responsible. She rested her head on Old Chen's shoulder.

"Maybe next week, on our way to Beidaihe, we should stop by the cemetery and leave some dumplings," Old Chen said. "I like to do that on Saturdays, after I see you two. I like to feed him some dumplings. Maybe—" He made no move to wipe his eyes. My mother stood up in a graceful sweep and handed him a handkerchief from her purse.

"Thank you," he said in English.

"*Bu keqi*," said my mom.

I have been to Da Ge's grave, always alone. Julia Too has never been, because when I've asked, annually, whether she wants to see it, she has always said no. She says she prefers the monument in Tiananmen. Now, with her skinny arm still slung over the old man's neck, she bravely said, "*Wo gen ni qu.*" I'll go with you.

CHAPTER THIRTEEN
Septembers

✳

SO THIS WAS IT. THE LIFE THAT CIRCLED BACK AROUND INTO itself. And, amazingly, produced other lives. I was impressed even before she was born by what I sensed was Julia Too's resilience. I asked my doctor once whether my baby would be hurt by the tragedy of her dad. "Not until later," she answered, honestly. I couldn't bring myself to look at my mother, who had insisted on coming into the exam room.

"Fine and healthy," the doctor said, measuring images of the baby's miniature arms and legs. She looked like an unlikely revolutionary, my green ultrasound baby, with a strand of pearls holding up her face and one fist pumping angrily.

"A little girl," the doctor added.

"A little girl!" my mother said, genuine bliss in her voice. My mom is a bright light, the only person I can imagine who could have beamed at that monitor, given the circumstances. I moved my eyes from my mom's face to the monitor. I wanted to tell Da Ge about the experience of simultaneously watching something on a screen and feeling it in your stomach. He would have liked that idea: the movie of a life and that life, happening and experienced simultaneously. Maybe he would have loved our baby. This was just what Romeo and Juliet would have been like, except I wasn't dead.

If Da Ge had been convicted for hurting Ben Rosenbaum,

he might have been deported or imprisoned, depending on what charges Ben had decided to press. For years I longed to rewind, end up with either of those endings. Ben recovered okay; maybe he would have been generous. I can't know for sure, since I never spoke to him again. I always thought if Da Ge had just been in jail, I could at least have visited, brought cookies or tiger food. Waited for him to get out. I always thought I would have.

His death was confirmed a suicide. My brother, Benj, offered to help if I needed a lawyer, said Da Ge's estate had to be turned over to someone and that there was usually tension over such matters.

"His estate?" I asked. "He was twenty-three. And aren't you a copyright lawyer?"

He smiled. "If there's any paperwork, I'll be happy to help with you with it."

"Paperwork?"

"There's a will, apparently. And he left you something. Something of his grandfather's, maybe? Papers, maybe? Or books?"

Books his Yeye had buried and dug up. He had hoped Da Ge would marry a nice girl, have a baby. Now I was the nice girl having a baby and the books were mine. It struck me as grotesque. Benj put a hand on my shoulder. "How's your Chinese?"

I shrugged miserably. "Not good."

"Well, maybe he wanted you to learn Chinese?"

"I have a textbook for that."

"Maybe they had some specific meaning for his family?"

"His grandfather buried them during the Cultural Revolution. Da Ge's father probably wants them. He's punishing his father by giving them to me."

"Did you guys ever talk about it?" He sounded hopeful that we had.

"Not really," I admitted. "I don't know if we ever talked

about anything, really." No one better understands the decision not to talk about things than the members of my family. But I apologized for it anyway.

"I should have asked him more, Benj. I should have—"

He cut me off. "That's not what I meant."

"I know, but it's true nonetheless."

"But you didn't really have access to each other, right?"

"What does that mean?"

"It's hard to know much about someone whose language you don't speak."

I didn't argue. Maybe Da Ge believed that even pale ink trumps memory. He robbed me of himself and left some illegible books as a way to spend time with his ghost. I hated him. Repeat after me, I used to think: My name is Da Ge. I am a newly made and dead American, my family is crippled with loss, and my fake wife rich with pages she can't read. I am a tragic, hideous waste.

And then there was my dictation, composed by and for the crazy teacher-wife: *what am I?* I am your English teacher, Chinese student, lucky benefactress of access, martyr status, and your father's treasure, heartbreak. The one you took because you knew I'd do it.

I asked Benj whether Da Ge would have been able to become a citizen without marrying me.

"No." He sounded sorry to say so. "And as you know, he wasn't a citizen yet anyway, when he—It would have taken—"

"I knew that." I shrugged, but a sharp feeling in my chest had taken over my voice. "It was just a point he was making. A statement." I thought of China again, of becoming Chinese. Replacing him. Or trading places.

"Maybe you could talk about some of this with Da Ge's father," Benj said.

"Da Ge's father? What are you talking about?"

"It might make you feel better."

"Da Ge hated his father. They were estranged. And any-way, I'd have no idea how to find him even if I wanted to, which I don't."

"He's here," Benj said. "Maybe it wasn't mutual, because he came to get his son."

Old Chen and I met for the first time at my apartment on 115th. I opened the door and saw him see the scroll, saw his face collapse and regroup before he spoke. I had agreed to see him half because I was livid and wanted to betray Da Ge, and half because I wanted to keep the case open, wanted anything left of him.

"You are my son's friend?" Old Chen asked, and we shook hands.

"Yes," I said, "please come in." I blinked up at him, unable to believe that Da Ge could have been that angry. His father just looked like a person, stunned and ruined, not powerful or big the way Da Ge had described him.

It's sometimes still that first meeting, when I'm at dumplings on a Saturday morning with Julia Too and Old Chen, when I'm teaching, when I'm sleeping or watching Julia Too sleep, when I'm wishing things had gone a differ-ent way. It's not, in my memories or dreams, usually the day I found Da Ge. It's always the day Old Chen walked into my house, looking like a scrubbed, taut version of his son.

"I mean you are his wife," he said, as if testing that new word *wife*, or maybe just worried that I wouldn't like to be described as Da Ge's friend. His eyes moved to my stomach, and back up, but didn't meet mine. He cleared his throat and there was a swinging noise in the background of my mind, rope on pipes. I squeezed my eyes shut.

"I made tea," I said, turning.

In my living room, I gestured to the futon. Benj had asked if I wanted him present for this meeting, and I'd said no. I didn't want a lawyer or even a brother, just to be reminded of Da Ge. To be alone with his father. It didn't occur to me then that Da Ge had left me his father on purpose. Because I needed one. But maybe he had. Maybe Old Chen in my life was Da Ge's thank-you. For the citizenship, the language lessons, or for having loved him.

I poured two cups of jasmine tea De Ge had bought me in Chinatown and sat at my table. Old Chen looked at me from the futon. I could think of nothing to say.

"You are the wife of my son, Chen Da Xing," he said again, this time without clearing his throat. I looked up.

"Da Ge," I said, baffled, waiting for whatever unbearable realization awaited me. Old Chen's mouth was a straight line across his face. I thought of Da Ge's scar. He set the tea down and crossed his arms across his chest. He looked stern, but I thought if he moved, each working, breathing part of him might be in discord, that they'd revolt against each other and turn him into a broken puppet. My arms ached. Da Ge's neck flashed through my mind, snapped by the weight of the cord. I couldn't swallow. I wondered if Da Ge's dad would ask me what had happened. I didn't know what I would say if he did: I tried to take him down, put him back together again?

"Da Ge is a nickname," Old Chen said. "It means big brother in Chinese. His real name is Chen Da Xing. Big Star."

"Dah Shing," I repeated. I hadn't even known his name. What would his father make of this? I thought of the days ahead of me, weeks, months, years. How long would it take to recover from each new secret grief that revealed itself?

"Da Xing is dead," his father said, incredulous, no doubt imagining his own relentless future. "My father dies just—my wife, my father—my son." He waited for a minute. "My son," he said again. He sat back, seemed to swoon against the futon.

My limbs were so heavy now that I could barely lift myself up. But I did. And once I'd stood, I walked over to the futon and sat next to Da Ge's father. Up close, his face was dark; its lines looked like they had been carved with a chisel only several hours earlier. I half expected him to bleed from his wrinkles. He lit a cigarette, and the fire smelled sharp and lively. I wanted to press the burning end into my hand, to feel anything other than what I felt.

"I didn't even know his name," I confessed, my voice so low I thought maybe the old man hadn't heard me. I said it again. Old Chen closed his eyes, and I reached out to touch his face. I couldn't guess which of us this surprised more. But he didn't move. I dragged my fingers down his cheek, stunned that he was warm and human. Unable to resist, I moved toward him and rested against his side. My face was somewhere between his shoulder and chest; my hair was matted against the fabric, fresh with pinstripes and dry cleaning. He patted me awkwardly.

"Um," he said, "you are pregnant, yes?"

"Yes." I did not ask who had told him. Instead, I sat up and tried to visualize us from above: an old, handsome Chinese man and a pregnant twenty-something girl, in my living room. For some reason, I was glad to be wearing earrings. I reached up and touched them.

"He was nice to you?"

"He cooked a lot."

His father's eyes brightened. "Really?"

"Yes, he made tiger food."

"*Lao hu cai,*" he said.

"Right. And fish, chicken, eggplant, noodles. We went to the zoo."

"I live in Beijing," he said, more to himself than to me. He was looking at me, with a question. "But if—" he stopped. "If—" he said again.

"Do you want to ask me something?" I asked.

"If I can know this baby," he said, "your baby. If I can see the baby and tell him some things about China, will that be okay? If I know this baby, is it okay?"

Old Chen glanced at my stomach longingly. I was wearing cotton overalls Julia had bought me, hoping to look more than four months pregnant. Tears followed one another down his cheeks. One dripped from his chin.

"Of course you can know her," I said. "And be her *Yeye*." He looked up at me, and I smiled, proud that I had been able to remember this word in Chinese. Grandpa. Then, as an afterthought, I added, "For us, it's okay."

I returned to Old Chen all but three of his father's books. Those three, which I selected randomly, I kept for Julia Too in a trunk at the foot of my bed, with Da Ge's and my citizenship album and all of his Embassy "Dear Teacher" essays. I don't think she's ever looked at the books. When she asks for them, I'll show her. Now that she's worked Old Chen into a frenzy of grandfatherly love, I imagine the rest will be hers someday as well. I have never wanted them myself, never planned to read them. If Julia Too ends up with that library, I'm glad it will have come directly from Old Chen. I consider it his legacy and property. Not to mention it's as close as we'll ever come to the presents Julia Too wishes her father would give her.

Nai Nai died in her sleep in New York City in the late fall of 1990. When Xiao Wang told me she would take Nai Nai's ashes back to China, I asked if I could go with her. Maybe we could wait until the Embassy term was over and go together. We were in Central Park walking through red leaves, and she stopped when I asked, sat down on a bench and put her head in her hands.

"I cannot make this sacrifice of my Nai Nai," she said, and started weeping.

I was horrified. "I didn't mean to intrude. I'm sorry. Of course you shouldn't wait, and I don't have to come. I just thought since you mentioned—I just thought—" I debated whether to put my arm around her.

"No, no, Aysha. This is not if you come or don't come. I just cannot stay here anymore. I think I will not be back to New York after that trip."

"But what would be wrong with that? I mean, other than my missing you."

She looked up at me. "Maybe my family, even Nai Nai, would be disappoint."

"I don't think so," I said. "They're going to want that baby around desperately."

I remember the way we were then: young, shocked, freshly finished teaching and studying, six and three months pregnant. We waddled onto a plane east with our prenatal vitamins and Nai Nai's ashes in an urn in the overheard compartment. It was almost comical, even then. Xiao Wang clucked about, feeding and bossing me endlessly about her theory that once we delivered our babies, we had to do something called "*zuo yuezi*," which meant we weren't to leave the house for a month.

"I will be home in Jinhong so for me this *zuo yuezi* will be convenient. Maybe you will have to find some friend to help you in New York. I know a Chinese girl who—"

"*Zuo yue*—what? Not leaving the house for a month sounds like clinical depression to me."

"This why American women have so many wrinkle. You don't rest after baby, so skin—how do you say?" She spread her hands as if she were making Jacob's cradle out of lanyard.

"Stretch?"

"How do you spell?"

"S-t-r-e-t-c-h." Seven fingers.

"Okay. You also get disease of this." She pointed to her elbow.

"You're telling me that to prevent arthritis and wrinkles, women should stay home for a month after their babies are born."

"Yes. And no water into the body." She opened a bag of dried cuttlefish and offered me some. It smelled so strong I thought I might go blind.

"No thanks," I said. "What do you mean, no water into the body?"

"No shower."

"No showering for a month after you have a baby?"

"Shower makes cold and easy to get sick."

"Maybe this is a cultural thing, but I think I have to shower after I give birth."

I should add here that Xiao Wang still looks identical to how she looked that day, and I, somehow, am twelve years older. I'm not saying I'm crippled with arthritis, but she could absolutely pass for twenty-five. So maybe I should have *zuo*'ed *yue zi*.

When we arrived at the old Capital Airport with our dusty throats and eyes, we rode a moving floor past shops empty of customers and full of bored women in blue pinafores. I had the sensation of riding in a barrel over a waterfall, surrounded by the pouring sounds of a language I could not understand. I had expected China to be either as rural as a movie or as dark as in American accounts, so I was surprised to find Beijing neon even then, its streets a scatter of brilliant billboards and rainbow light displays on highway overpasses. The roads rippled out in rings around the city, as if a stone had been thrown into its center: second-ring, third-ring, fourth-ring roads. New decades will mean fifth, sixth, seventh, eighth. Beijing loves to count. Just like me.

Xiao Wang took me to dinners with her cousins, her classmates, her husband's colleagues, her mother's old friends, and what seemed to me to be thousands of people. They all exchanged gifts with her, and to my chagrin, with me, even though I hadn't brought any. Xiao Wang's presents for them included Levi's jeans, "I love NYC" T-shirts, and ceramic miniatures of the Statue of Liberty, the Empire State Building, and hilariously, the Eiffel Tower. Her friends presented me with oranges, cooking oil, a rubber moose, a poster of Whitney Houston from her *Body Guard* days, and a plate with a furry, marble-eyed cat between two layers of glass.

"It's for decorate the house with," Xiao Wang explained later. I scolded her for not having warned me to bring gifts. She dug in her suitcase and came out with a stuffed penguin in a Central Park Zoo T-shirt.

"What's this?" I asked.

"You can give to my mother when we arrive to Jinhong."

"Perfect."

On rides out to the Great Wall and Ming Tombs, I pressed my face to bus windows. Cotton-padded people filled the wide streets. Laundry waved out windows, surrendering to coal smoke. Traffic was flanked by a rush of bicycles, and everything seemed to me to be taking place on a screen, rather than in real time, just like Da Ge had described life in the United States. Grief is similar to being abroad. Everything's changed, awkward, off, and unfamiliar. Of course the same thing can be said of falling in love.

We went to Tiananmen on our last day in Beijing. Maybe we had waited out of fear—that his ghost would be there. Or that it wouldn't. Xiao Wang stopped talking when the cement square came into view from the cab. My throat went tight, as if sealed off by pollution. I studied the guards in green before we got out and walked from corner to corner, saw the history museum, Mao's mausoleum, the Martyrs' Monument, the Great Hall of the People. I fought my feeling of surprise and disappointment. It was a place, not a person, not a time. I could sit there forever and he'd never show up again. Xiao Wang read Mao's calligraphy from the Martyrs' Monument, identified uprisings for me.

"Maybe you even feel now you have Chinese history, too," she said, kindly.

I laughed. "My own Chinese history."

"Maybe Da Ge was teacher for you, too."

On the way back to the hotel, we walked by a market. Fish eyed me, and Julia Too kicked in my stomach like a many-legged sea monster herself. A vendor arrived pulling a rollerbag. When he opened it, six ducks came quacking out in a mad parade. I had an out-of-body experience, thought maybe we were in a *Sesame Street* episode.

I needed grounding, told Xiao Wang I wanted to buy some vegetables.

She disapproved. "We can't eat it," she said. "Must be cooked."

But I paid for some cilantro, only to put it on the nightstand back at the hotel. "I didn't want to eat it," I tried explaining. "I just wanted to buy it."

She clucked her tongue. "Wasting that!"

"I wanted to buy the things Da Ge and his mother bought before she died," I said. *Before he died* I did not say. Xiao Wang went into the bathroom and turned the water on.

The next morning when Xiao Wang and I packed up to head to the airport for Jinhong, I put my cilantro, still reasonably fresh, in my purse.

"Maybe I must teach your baby to be reasonable person," she said, tucking Nai Nai's urn under her arm.

"Or maybe I'll teach yours to be impulsive and unreasonable," I said.

She looked me over. "I like it if my baby learn from you. Even if she become like you, it's okay for me."

"Thanks." I pulled my roller bag out in the hotel hallway, crumpling our complimentary *China Daily*. Xiao Wang held up Nai Nai.

"Time to go home," she said. In English.

Jinhong was the first Chinese city that had ever existed in the landscape of my imagination, before Beijing, even. It was the place Xiao Wang described at Embassy, and at dinner at her grandmother's Chinatown place, home of the swimming Mekong, of palm trees and fruit trucks that spray papaya juice as they wind around mountain roads.

"Usually we have the whole person. This ashes is unusual," Xiao Wang told me on the drive to Nai Nai's memorial. Her parents and husband Jin were silent.

I was disoriented when we arrived, stumbled from the car into sunlight and a crowd of mourners. In a big, open room, shafts of white light divided the floor into rectangles and Nai Nai's urn sat on a raised bed draped with red cloth, lilies, fruit, and three framed photographs of her: one young, one old, and one somewhere between, standing with her son, Xiao Wang's father. He looked young and earnest in the photo, old and sad now, standing with his family. We mourners moved in a line, starting at the entrance, passing first the urn and then Xiao Wang's family, exiting after having completed a full circle. Two old women were screaming with grief. Xiao Wang, her father, mother, and Jin shook each mourner's hand and accepted red envelopes I guessed immediately must contain cash. Bewildered and nervous, I moved through the line, too.

When I reached Xiao Wang, I whispered, "I don't have a red envelope—I didn't realize. I'm so sorry about Nai Nai. I should have brought—I can still—"

"Calm down," she said. She pulled me from the line. "Stand here. Be my family."

Xiao Wang's mother was my mother reinterpreted, a burst of energy and chatter, force feeder, happy family-running hen. If she was grief-stricken over her mother-in-law's American death, she nursed herself back to emotional health by taking care of Xiao Wang and me while Xiao Wang's father watched her with a combination of amusement and sorrow. I wondered whether she reminded him of his mother. He was a quietly busy person, moving about the house in a precise and committed way, feeding the two birds they called Po and Bo, weeding in the garden, fixing the table a neighbor's child had sat upon and broken. He wore glasses and drank tea from a jar. Her mother was noisily busy and clucked an endless list of questions about America, including what Xiao Wang had worn every day to my class, whether she'd eaten porridge for breakfast, why I'd allowed her to get so skinny, even pregnant, and why I wasn't married. I said I was married, that my husband had been killed in a tragic accident, and Xiao Wang's mother suggested I marry a new man; perhaps she could introduce a local one I might like. She asked how much money I made, only to exclaim over how little it was. She asked after my classes, my books, my haircut, my eyebrows, whether I wore long underwear, why not, why I whistled, how my skin stayed so white. She kept the conversation alive every minute of every day I spent there, bustling around, shoving bowls of "crossing the bridge" noodles into our hands every twenty minutes, stuffing moon dumplings with sesame paste, seeping tea, feeding us marrow soup, tucking us in. When I presented her with the stuffed penguin, she said she would call it Aysha. Xiao Wang barely stopped translating long enough to take breaths.

In the late afternoon of my last day there, Xiao Wang and I took a walk alone and watched women with babies wrapped to their backs in brightly colored cloths.

"Will you carry your baby like that?" I asked.

"Of course I do!" she said, and then, as if sensing my desolation, she said, "I'll send you some this cloth for New York. You can be like Chinese peasant woman at the Upper West Side." Then she threw her head back and laughed. I've never seen her cover her mouth when she laughs in China; here she's free.

We sat on the bank of the Mekong, its water so dark brown it looked almost black, and Xiao Wang chattered uncharacteristically about how she was going to find a job as an environmental specialist and help China.

We walked out onto a handmade bamboo bridge over the water. The planks shivered enough to make us catch our breath.

"Tomorrow you will go home," Xiao Wang pointed out. "That make me miss New York." I thought of my new students at Embassy, who had only known me pregnant, who, if they knew anything of the year before, had said nothing. I thought of the courses I had signed up to finish that spring at Columbia. I reached my hand out and felt the breeze while my mind zoomed back to the city, which seemed now like a board game: Broadway, Amsterdam, campus, downtown, uptown. Plastic hotels and miniature skyscrapers. Students and classmates. I wondered what it would feel like to be pregnant at Columbia, whether I would mind. I wasn't looking forward to anything.

"I don't miss New York," I said. "I want to stay here, far away from everything."

"No, no," she said. "You have your baby in America where your mama live and finish your teaching and your study. That's the business you must do. I will stay here, and sometime we will see each other again."

The light changed, turning the fields and river from green and gray to black. Then the sun set and everything began to disappear. Xiao Wang and I walked back out ragged paths, chickens clucking and scattering as we went.

The night Julia Too was born, there was a sliver of white moon over New York. I saw it above buildings on the way to St. Luke's, and again from the window of a twelfth-floor labor and delivery room. It was the same moon Xiao Wang would see when Lili was born at midnight in China three months later. My mother, Julia One, and I breathed, sang, jumped, stretched, shouted and chewed ice chips. Long after the sun had taken over, we had our baby.

My mother was bionic with excitement, taking pictures so graphic I almost can't look at them myself, running through the hospital halls telling everyone *7 lbs 10 ounces, 21 inches*, even though they were all having babies, too. When the nurses handed Julia Too to me, I realized immediately that she was a whole person—with eyelashes and toes and a personality. I had been expecting a vaguely defined cartoon character of some sort. But she was crisp and detailed. They waited before slicking her eyes with gelatinous antibiotic so we could see each other. We looked for eleven seconds, and I recognized her in a way so wordless it was as if I had fallen asleep and was dreaming. I wondered what she saw. I thought of my grandmother, her mother, and hers, our entire line having this identical experience, each unable to believe it wasn't singular.

"She's fantastic," said Julia One.

"She looks just like him," I said.

"No. To me, she looks like you," Julia One said.

My mother had come back in. "She looks just like herself," she said. "Give her here."

Once, when she was three, Julia Too described death to me.

"Today I pretended you were dead!" she said when I picked her up at day care. "Because I was such a big, big girl that I didn't need a mommy anymore. And Emma played that her daddy was dead, because she was such a big, big girl that she didn't need a daddy." She laughed.

"No kidding," I said, my voice impressively even. "But everyone needs mommies and daddies, even when they're grown-ups. Do you remember who my mommy is?"

She grinned, triumphant. "Nomi!" she said.

"Yes!" I waited for what I thought was a calm interval. "So, Julia, what does it mean to be dead?"

She said, "You just fall over. You fall right over!"

"That sounds about right. What else?"

She scrunched up her face. "You have no eyes and no mouth and no head," she said. She began pointing at her limbs. "No arms and no legs, your body just goes away! And you stop having days." She brushed her hands against each other as if she had just finished the task of putting away some blocks.

"Where did you hear all those things about being dead?" I asked.

"I learned them up in my mind."

"You know what, though? Even though you stop having days when you're dead, all the people who love you still remember you."

She looked up at me. "Mommy?"

I collected myself. "Yes?"

"Did you bring me a purple Fruit Roll-up?"

Sometimes I take inventory of the memories Da Ge didn't get to have: Julia Too riding my restored yellow wooden giraffe through Riverside Park, toddling up to leaves, twigs, dogs, and strangers. He never saw the stretch of mornings that made up her babyhood, or lazed away New York afternoons in the sandbox when she was two. He never pulled on or off her plastic rain boots, the ones with butterflies on the toes, wiggly antennae preceding her into puddles. Those boots are in Da Ge's backpack, but he never held her, never slipped off the leather crib slippers with "dad" tattoos on them, an unfortunate gift from my mother's daft second cousin. He never smelled her bald head, washed the scrumptious creases in her neck, or cut grapes into eighths. He never counted her new, mini-teeth. I collected her and her things alone or with my mother at the ends of those days: diapers, bibs, spoons, rattles, pacifiers, balls, bears, ducks, dolls, and all the nouns in a baby's collection. Later, sparkling wands, the black stuffed cat she mysteriously named "Binderlutie," plastic beads, water colors, ballet slippers, alphabet letters, cardboard books, rubber animals, little people, bright buses. He missed every texture, stopped having days just as Julia Too and I learned to make them.

I pined for China. That gave me a measure of cool control; China was still possible even if he was not. I could always fly back to Xiao Wang and live the movie *Ju Dou*. Even though Xiao Wang had long since moved to Beijing, in my dreams were dusty village houses, bolts of silk unraveling from rafters. And Da Ge; we would find him and be three people. He and Julia Too would fly kites, ride bikes, scratch characters in the sand. She and I would come in from sunlight outside to find him cooking dinner.

Two months before I graduated, I called Xiao Wang. "My business in America is finished," I said in Chinese. I had been practicing that phrase like an Olympic athlete.

She laughed, asked in English, "You like to visit me and Jin and Lili in Beijing?"

"Can we please?"

"Of course! For as long as you like. You are welcome forever, if you still like it."

It was Old Chen who picked us up at Capital Airport. He was so polished he shone like a lamp, nervous and sad and ecstatic, clutching a sign that read "Ai-sha and Zhu Lia!! Warmly Welcome Home to Beijing."

It was the second time I had ever seen him, three years after our encounter in New York. Julia Too was asleep when we came down the ramp, and Old Chen insisted on carrying her out to the car, leaving the luggage to his driver and me. On the way to the hotel he had arranged in case his courtyard house was too old-fashioned or uncomfortable, Old Chen told me shyly that he hoped even if we didn't decide to live with him, that we'd come "home" for dumplings every Saturday.

 Sometimes in the early fall, when I'm walking though an outdoor market, I can hear Da Ge's voice in the collected chatter. Sometimes I see teenagers on the street, nerdy with backpacks or rebellious with tattoos and earrings, and I smile. My Global Beijing students, with their often broken speaking and the earth's most earnest essays, give him back to me, and so does the city.

Beijing wakes up in the mornings, pavement alive with the smell of sun. Vendors call out their offerings: fried dough, soy milk, steamed buns, fresh fruit. The vowels float up, wake Julia Too and me and we shower, eat pancakes or *mantou*, steamed buns, take our places in the spaces we call days. I imitate the voices from the street, try to turn my Chinese fluent, pack lunches, take my girl to school, read, teach, eat, sleep. Buy bean sprouts, fish with cheeks and eyes. Write this for her. Make tiger food. These are the patterns, and they somehow need less counting, stepping over cracks, or spelling out than they once did. There's comfort in forever unfamiliar things: split pigs on the backs of bikes, Chinese TV, my life between two languages. I couldn't have known when I lost Da Ge what he would give me. Permanence.

I arrived home Monday night from the first parent-teacher conferences of the fall, found our apartment warm. My mother was back in New York, but a mist of her perfume remained. I set my book bag down, the delicious list of my new students' names inside, and walked in my socks to Julia Too's room. Something made me quiet. I peered in, saw her and Yang Tao under the light of a reading lamp. They sat cross-legged on her bed, hunched over an old Chinese book. He traced his fingers vertically down a row of characters, perhaps right where Da Ge's grandfather had once moved his. Yang Tao watched Julia Too and the words alternately, listened to her translations. The words she didn't know yet, he filled in. He looked up, saw me in the doorway, smiled. Julia Too had her head bent down over the page. Before she could see me, I tiptoed back to the kitchen to make them dinner.

ACKNOWLEDGMENTS

THANK YOU TO ROBERT PINSKY FOR YOUR BRILLIANCE AND FOR a decade of feedback, support and generosity. To Derek Walcott for reading and commenting thoughtfully so many times on this book and my poems, and for all the geography, landscape and meter. Thank you to Anne Carson for improving my own and my students' lines and imaginations, and for letting me use your beautiful stanzas to begin this book. To my agent Jill Grinberg—I so appreciate your wisdom, extraordinary level of engagement, and friendship. To Juliet Grames for the detail with which you read and edit, and for our conversations about writing, China, women, and the world. Thank you to Lesley Thorne for your time and energy and enthusiasm, and to Deborah Landau for making me part of your fabulous writing community at NYU.

To my readers: Julia Hollinger, for multiple reads, sharp eyes, and 30 years. Lara Phillips, for unflappable encouragement and a life I love to live vicariously. Donna Eis for dozens of pages of red-ink. How did you possibly find the time? Heidi Schumacher, for shrink knowledge that served both this book and me. Bear Korngold and Willow Schrager for teaching me something important about how to listen. Greg Lalas, for all the early reads and stark rejections of worse titles. Molly Smith Metzler for reading a 500-page draft of this and still being my friend. Harry Kellerman and Thai Jones, for your straight-to-the-point-of-what insights.

Kirun Kapur and Fred Speers, thank you for my poetry life; you are its center. Erika Helms for *pinyin*, for living Beijing with me and then forever, and for being *the* demographic for everything I write. Chen Shanying, for your perspective on China, America, politics and parenting, and your beautiful English. Chen Daming for your movies and memories and inimitable ways of talking and thinking about art and the world. Thank you Alex Xie, Cui Jian and Hei Yang —for so many chats about this book, and for continuing to share drafts of your work with me. Martina Dapra for the story of your marriage and citizenship interview; and Susanna Rosenstock and Philipp Angermeyer for yours. To Christine Jones for your genius art and friendship; I cherish you. Thank you to the Basic Trust community for caring about this book and my family. To my writing students at NYU; and to Teachers & Writers and the 9th and 10th grade ESL students at ASE in the Bronx. Thank you so much, Bess Miller.

Kathy, thank you for covering hundreds of hours that let me write and think, and for so much love and engagement with our girls. Bill Ayers and Bernardine Dohrn, thank you for years of full-tilt feedback, for your uniquely wide perspectives, for caring genuinely and passionately about the world, and for providing a model of how to live graciously and fully as artists, activists, parents and grandparents. Malik Dohrn and Chesa Boudin, my monkeys' uncles: thank you for taking us to see revolutions, translating in mission hospitals, visiting and loving Beijing, and reading my books and so many books to my babies.

Thank you to the amazing Naomi and Saul Silvermintz, for your genes, names, inspiration, and 65-year marriage. To my Aunt Gail, for everything from Avanglavish to lip liner and dance lessons. Thank you to the beautiful, inspirational Lee and Bob Greenberg. To my mom and dad, Judith and Kenneth, who together read no fewer than ten drafts of this, who flew thousands of miles, revised, babysat, helped translate poems, organized flights, meals, and an entire working life for me in Beijing so I could research and write. Who came up with hundreds of titles, including the one I used. Who are brilliant, giving, ever-present, and tremendously fun. To my hilarious, loving brothers Jacob and Aaron, for thanklessly providing encouragement, humor, stories, and a sister for me—Melissa. Thank you for Adam and McKenna. Absolute sunshine.

To my brave and lovely girls Dalin Alexi and Light Ayli, for your singular, beautiful Dalin and Lightness, for teaching me the present tense, and for saying and doing things that crack the world open freshly again and again, often hourly.

Finally, thank you, Zayd. You're the intro, body and conclusion, my first and final reader, one love. I'll forever take your every edit.